THE GHOST THAT ATE US

DANIEL KRAUS

RAW DOG
SCREAMING
PRESS

The Ghost That Ate Us © 2022
by Daniel Kraus

Published by Raw Dog Screaming Press
Bowie, MD

First Edition

Cover Design: Tim Daniel/Second Rocket Creative
Book Design: Jennifer Barnes

Printed in the United States of America
This book is for Bug.

ISBN: 978-1-947879-55-3

RawDogScreaming.com

THE GHOST THAT ATE US

THE TRAGIC TRUE STORY OF
THE BURGER CITY POLTERGEIST

DANIEL KRAUS

In Memory of Those Who Died on June 1, 2017:
Quindlen Arthur
Tamra Longmoor *(presumed)*
James "Mickey" McCormick
Cheri Orritt
Yesenia Ruiz
Zane Shakespeare
Javier Villareal

Poltergeists are difficult to prove for a number of reasons. Reportedly, the phenomenon often involves adolescents or teenagers, who may be prone to trickery or at least to manufacturing attention for themselves.

Michael Clarkson, The Poltergeist Phenomenon

I entered the game of pricks
With knives in the back of me
Can't call you or on you no more
When they're attacking me

Guided by Voices, "Game of Pricks"

AUTHOR'S NOTE

It sounds funny, doesn't it?

Published in the Spring 2019 *Journal of Neuropsychiatry and Clinal Neurosciences,* "Disintegration: Ethos and Intolerance at Burger City"[1] is the central text of the still-new field of Burger City Poltergeist scholarship. The author, Rachel Heinzman, M.D., Ph.D., posits that humor is the highest hurdle to clear for any probe into the Burger City disturbance. She and I agree that all previous attempts have failed, from the earliest published mention of the "ghost" in the December 1, 2016, *Muscatine Journal Newspaper,*[2] to the Starz documentary *Blood at Burger City,*[3] first broadcast on February 5, 2019.

The failure is easy to understand. All of us are steeped in solemn, gothic imagery popularized by famous hauntings. The Trans-Allegheny Lunatic Asylum. The Gettysburg battlefield. The Winchester Mystery House. The Lizzie Borden Bed and Breakfast. The Stanley Hotel.

Burger City, on the other hand, *was a fast-food joint.*

Belief in the supernatural isn't required to appreciate what unfolded at Burger City Franchise Location #8 near Jonny, Iowa (population 33), from October 2, 2016, to June 1, 2017. It is the most exhaustively documented alleged haunting in history. The famous Enfield Poltergeist (witnessed by over thirty people near London in 1977) and the Columbus, Ohio, poltergeist of 1984 (in which 14-year-old Tina Resch was photographed as a telephone flung itself across her lap), are tepid rumors in comparison. Yet people laugh at the Burger City Poltergeist. You may recall the February 17, 2019, *Saturday Night Live* sketch in which Kenan Thompson played a ghost trying to tell Burger City diners it was the greasy food that killed him. It's funny, right?

---

1   Rachel Heinzman, "Disintegration: Ethos and Intolerance at Burger City," *Journal of Neuropsychiatry and Clinal Neurosciences* 31 (2019): 140-157.

2   Gabrielle Carver, "I-80 Burger Joint Gets Spooky," *The Muscatine Journal Newspaper,* December 1, 2016.

3   As of this writing, the film, directed by Maureen Frodsham and Patrice Tellis, sits at a more-than-deserving 29 percent approval rating on Rotten Tomatoes.

There is nothing funny about six dead people.

Or seven, eight, nine, or ten, depending how one does the macabre math.

Hanford Pendergast, a retired conservationist who lives a quarter-mile from the Burger City ruins, reports seeing two to three groups of visitors per week. If you wish to be one of them, and are coming from the east, you'll pass through the Quad Cities, a conglomeration of four towns that hug a forty-five-degree crook of the Mississippi River—Rock Island and Moline on the Illinois side, Davenport and Bettendorf on the Iowa side. You can loop around the whole mess via Interstate 280, but not if you want to learn anything about the people who live here.

Pulling off into Davenport or Bettendorf proper, one can't deny the Norman Rockwell charm of the riverwalks, Mel's Diner-style cafés, and Art Deco movie theaters. But most of these cafés are chilly, fly-spotted, and sparsely populated, and the marquees are empty promises—only rats scuttle amid the dust-softened seats.

The sound of commerce, rather symbolically, is drowned out by the rushing river, untroubled by civilization's slide. There are floods in these towns, lots of them. In spring 2019, the worst catastrophe since the Great Flood of 1927 devastated the Quad Cities as the Mississippi crested nearly twenty-three feet, putting several towns underwater.[4] The people here are stoic, the only option in defeat. The busiest spots are liquor stores and strip clubs. This is the fertile land bloodily wrested from Sac, Fox, and Ho-Chunk Indians. This is where the Rock Island Railroad built the first railroad bridge across the Ole Miss. These are the towns that boomed with railway jobs, steamboat ships, and heavy-industry plants. Today, the dominant color of these towns is rust-red.

Even without a poltergeist, these places are haunted.

A casual study of towns like these highlights the root of so many rural problems: boredom. Daily monotony makes you crave something, *anything*, to break the patterns, no matter how dangerous that thing might be. Frequently it takes the form of sexual affairs. Today in Iowa, it is just as often opioid or methamphetamine abuse.

"Getting fucked up is the only way not to *feel* fucked up," said Kit Bryant, the notorious teen at the center of the Burger City Tragedy.[5]

Now imagine the thing to clear your fog of boredom wasn't sex or

4 Tyra Stockwell, "Quad Cities Flood One for the Record Books," *Quad-City Times*, May 30, 2019.

5 This quote comes second-hand, via Amber Smyrna.

drugs, but something so fresh and invigorating it sparked passion and creativity you never knew you had. Imagine it made you feel wholly alive for the first time, a star in the greatest show on Earth. You might be unequipped to handle it. It shouldn't surprise gawkers like us that the employees of Burger City, residents of minuscule towns, fell apart the way they did, so hard and so quickly.

"I don't think I was ever happier," Burger City manager Bob Nutting says in *Blood at Burger City*. Nutting isn't an articulate man, but his statements are threaded with phrases of accidental grace. "Happiness—it made me see things that weren't there and not see things that were."

Let's carry on with our terrible tour. From the Quad Cities, occult fanatics should head due west on Interstate 80. Christened in 1956 as one of the original arms of President Eisenhower's Interstate Highway System, I-80 follows the route of the 1913 Lincoln Highway, and today is the second-longest highway in America, running 2,899 miles from Teaneck, New Jersey, to San Francisco, California. It saws through the Pennsylvania-Ohio rust belt before scything across Indiana, Illinois, and Iowa farmland.

The only landmark between the Quad Cities and the University of Iowa is at Exit 284, the Iowa 80 Truckstop—aka the World's Largest Truckstop—where Kit Bryant, Amber Smyrna, Quindlen Arthur, Clemens Dumay, Amy Mold, and Yesenia Ruiz wiled away so many hours, guzzling caffeine and mapping their next foolhardy steps. If you stop there, you'll want to grab a bite at the food court, or you might end up hungry later. The Burger City off Exit 269, as you might have heard, is closed.

You used to be able to see Burger City's sign atop a seventy-foot pole. The restaurant was 80 feet from the interstate. Such off-ramp tracts are America's ugliest areas. Garbage-strewn ditches, peeled tire rubber, seared roadkill, sun-roasted grasses, woody bramble. These places stink of hot oil. The thump of vehicles along the interstate is an aggravated heartbeat. Behind a visible swelter, the foul horizon offers no respite.

This raw netherworld is where our story takes place.

There's no jump-scare reveal to what's left of Burger City #8. A rectangle of gravel and ash marks where it burned to the ground on the night of November 14, 2017. The Cedar County Sheriff's Office declared it an act of arson, but might as well have declared it a local holiday too. No evidence exists that anyone was questioned about the fire. Cedar County law enforcement, as well as the residents of the county's biggest metropolises—from Tipton (population 3,221) to Mechanicsville (population 1,146)—probably raised their drinks to the unknown firebug that night.

Aftermath of the Burger City fire (courtesy of the Tipton Conservative).

Post-arson photographs depict yellow police tape rippling before jagged piles of charred wood. Today there is nothing to keep "dark tourists" from pacing the grounds. In my trips to the site, I've seen visitors call up photos on their gadgets to triangulate the locations of the six alleged phenomena: the Coldest Cold Spot, the Men's Room Bully, the Drive-thru Phantom, the Living Grill, the Biting Room, and, of course, on a patch of dirt so popular it's packed tight as concrete, the precise location of the Lil' Beefy Anomaly—the moving mascot that started it all.

The wail of the Trapped Woman, considered by some to be the seventh phenomenon, is the only disturbance reported by modern visitors. I understand why they might think they hear it. Out here, spooky sounds abound: wind howling through branches, crows growling, the squeals of tires down interstate pavement.

Some dark tourists pick up fast-food en route so they can take selfies gobbling a burger at the Burger City ruins. This is in poor taste, but I throw no stones. How is mugging in front of the place where multiple people were killed any better than how I spent much of 2017 forwarding bizarre (and *funny*, let us not forget how *funny* it all was) links about the Burger City story to friends. I am not proud of it. Neither am I proud to admit I've walked over the site's cold embers, eyes shut, hoping to hear the Trapped Woman or feel interference from a spectral plane.

I never have.

Yet I felt the touch of the Burger City Poltergeist long before I took on this project. As of this writing, I've published twelve novels, most of which you'll find filed under Horror. Not a single one centers upon paranormal activity. So why did I choose such an event for my first nonfiction book?

The reasons are personal. Today I live in Chicago with my wife. But I grew up in Fairfield, Iowa (population 9,464), a one-hour-forty-minute drive from Jonny, and received my undergrad degree in Iowa City, thirty minutes west of Jonny. I feel little nostalgia for my former home. I suppose I've set several novels in Iowa to process my feelings about it, a spectrum ranging from ambivalence to resentment.

Let me cut to the chase. I did not believe in the Burger City Poltergeist when I began this project. Here, at project's end, in spite of scenarios that evade obvious debunking, I still do not believe in the Burger City Poltergeist. Each of us brings beliefs and biases to any situation. Mine happen to include the certainty that *ghosts do not exist.* I think the Burger City survivors know this too, deep down. They simply won't admit it, and for good reason.

Words artfully dodged in most Burger City discourse include *hicks, rubes,* and *white trash.* I don't buy it. Yes, much of Iowa is rural, and only 28 percent of Iowans have a bachelor's degree or higher.[6] But the high-caliber colleges dotting the state (Grinnell, Coe, Drake, Cornell, Luther, and Simpson, as well as the Universities of Iowa, Iowa State, and Northern Iowa) foster pockets of sophistication. Try to find savvier hicks, rubes, and white trash, I dare you.

So why do the Burger City survivors categorically believe in this supernatural event? For a good four months, it was a fun, even inspiring, thing to believe in. Like me, the Burger City staff had been raised on torpid inspirational posters tacked to church and classroom walls. *Bloom Where You Are Planted. Let Your Failures Inspire You.* In accelerating their own downfall, the staff was only doing what they'd been taught.

Later, post-tragedy, it was dangerous *not* to believe in the poltergeist, as that would leave only themselves to blame.

What kept me up at night while working on this project was not the

---

6 Vanessa Miller, "More Americans Earning Degrees, Iowa Aiming to Keep Up," *The Gazette*, March 30, 2017.

notion of some paranormal entity but the reverberating sadness of these people. Despite having lived in Iowa from age 5 to 22, I'd never heard of Jonny (Burger City #8 opened in September 1989, when I was a high-school freshman), yet intrinsically understood the employees as well as the patrons—their frayed coveralls and dirty fingers, the contrite way they mumbled their orders. I knew Burger City itself, the lobby air as thick and salty as deer blood, infused with odors of engine oil and manure. I knew how it felt to live on America's edge, paradoxically by being smack in the middle of the country.

When I drove from Chicago to Iowa in February 2020 to interview the lead detective in the Burger City case, I predicted it would satisfy my interest. Instead, nearly thirty more interviews followed as the two-day trip ballooned into eight months.

Thanks to a suite of expiring statutes of limitations, I was the first researcher granted access to five boxes of court materials unavailable to Heinzman, Starz, et al—shift schedules, time-off requests, corporate memos, employee evaluations, police reports, and, most crucially, Kit Bryant's infamous *IDEAS* notebook. Also included were hundreds of hours of video: Cedar County Sheriff crime-scene footage, WNOG-TV9's raw news tapes, Burger City security-camera backups, over 200 amateur Lil' Beefy videos uploaded to the web, and, of course, the pseudoscientific "Game of Pricks" archive.

On top of this are seven hours of footage no one but I has ever seen, shot in secrecy during the final two weeks before the tragedy.

Finally, I am the first person to interview every survivor. Aside from Bob Nutting, always restless to clear his name, and Dez Mozley, who raved conspiracy theories to media for months before abruptly dropping from view, the Burger City survivors have avoided much talking. One way to interpret my success with them is that I grew up not in Starz's New York or *Spectral Journeys*'s L.A., but in a town like theirs. Or simply that books have so much more space than film or TV, surely enough to tell the truth.

Here I must address the controversy this book has generated prior to publication. The gist of the allegations is that I hoodwinked the survivors, fraudulently "befriending" them to bolster my sordid account. If you follow the Burger City story, you know about the October 2020 suicide of one of the survivors. I was the sole witness.

I cooperated with police and medical officials, and days later attended the outdoor funeral, where I was coldly received. A friend of the deceased told me that I should leave, and I did. If you wish to blame the suicide on my interview, or more broadly on the true-crime industry to which I temporarily belong, you'll find plenty of support on social networks. By dredging up memories of awful events, the argument goes, I helped drive this person to take their life.

In my darkest hours, I know this is possible. It is also possible that I, like the alleged poltergeist, only hastened the inevitable. In ways beyond my control, this book has become a redemptive bid for both the survivors and myself. I can't help it, I want to prove that this book, and others that deal in real-life tragedy, have value beyond the salacious. Not the value of a human life, surely, but something.

Off a shrieking highway, along a stretch of America no one cared about, the employees of Burger City #8 were a tight-knit group before the violent opening salvo of September 4, 2016. What unfolded over the subsequent year would bind the staff as closely as any family—often for the inspirational best, ultimately for the catastrophic worst. This is why I will refer to Burger City employees by their first names (except for Bob Nutting, who stands apart). This is in keeping with my aim to portray my subjects and their relationships sensitively but realistically. The staff loved one another, at least at the beginning, and love can make you do stupid things.

Except when noted, quotes are drawn from personal interviews I conducted between February 2, 2020, and October 30, 2020. When not drawn from recordings, dialogue has been reconstructed and approved by those involved. All names are real except for Bob Nutting's Regional Manager, whom I have given the pseudonym of Beauregard Waterhouse. This has no effect on factual events and was done to avoid the legal hassles of a company that has proved litigious.

I wish to convey gratitude to the following people who helped me navigate worlds both normal and paranormal: Richard Abate, Tara Altebrando, Jennifer Barnes, Kate Bassett, Mark Bilsky, Bryan Bliss, Nora Bliss, Steve Brezenoff, Daniel Castanho, John Cunningham, Benjamin Dreyer, Adrian Durand, Joshua Ferris, Mike Ford, Pete Hautman, Corey Ann Haydu, Grady Hendrix, Brian Keene, Amanda Kraus, Dale Kraus, Shad Kunkle, John Edward Lawson, Simone Lueck, Ellen Major, Judy Melinek, Carrie Mesrobian, Noel Murray, David Newgarden, Adele Nicholas, Craig Ouellette, Cynthia Pelayo, Dan Poblocki, Emily Poblocki, Robert Pollard, Javier Ramirez, Mary Roach, Adam Sandler, Julia Smith,

Becky Spratford, Martha Stevens, Scout Tafoya, Eugenia Williamson, and Sara Zarr. A handful of the above asked me to abandon this project along the way, fearing that I'd put myself in danger. I apologize for the distress I caused. It is my hope that all reasons for worry are behind me, although in matters like this, one can never tell.

SEPTEMBER 2016

KILL ME NOW

The Mead Drive 8 Stiletto Automatic Knife is an overwrought name for a pretty standard switchblade. Its carbon fiber build makes it a mere two-point-four ounces of weight. Depress the button and the stonewash-finished, three-and-half-inch blade leaps from the black, eight-inch handle. I can report that it has a satisfying snap.

The most startling fact about the Drive 8 is its retail price of $159.99, putting it well outside the means of Scotty Flossen, who, on September 4, 2016, was unemployed, squatting in his cousin Ian Flossen's basement, and a regular at pawn shops that didn't question his latest cache of bicycles, car stereo devices, or wiped laptops. Flossen would later tell arresting officers, detectives, his court-appointed lawyer, and the judge that he'd found the Drive 8 at Jane Galveston Park, at the east end of Jonny. He was lying.

Flossen had stolen the knife, same as he'd stolen everything else.

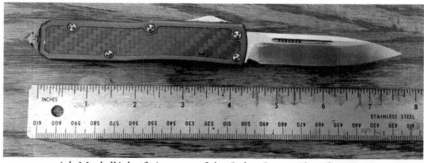

Ash Muckells's knife (courtesy of the Cedar County Sheriff's Office).

Scotty Flossen, 28 years old at the time of the crime, had been addicted to crystal meth since age 18, and his September 4 mugshot is an archetypal study. Dilated pupils out of focus from twitching. Scab-speckled skin carved with chapped arroyos. Lip sores gleaming beneath jailhouse fluorescents. A neck as skinny as the Drive 8's handle.

For most of his decade of addiction, Flossen bought meth by the dose from a shifting network of at-home batchers whose labs burned down only to rise back up with Hydra-like vigor. At an average price of twenty bucks a pop, that didn't leave much for grub. Flossen knocked over his first gas station at 19. He snatched so many purses outside of rest homes and bingo halls it led to a spike in area security-cam sales.[7] He took to carrying a rug in his backpack so he could punch out car windows without cutting himself.

Flossen stole the Drive 8 from Ash Muckells, a man with whom he shared a lot. Flossen and Muckells had been buddies at Rose Community High School (south of Tipton, 14 miles from Jonny). Since graduating Class of 2006, both had seesawed between being sheltered and homeless. Both were addicts. And both had been at each other's throats for five years. The origins of the animosity remain obscure. Something about a woman, maybe several? Some kerfuffle over the plot of the Star Wars prequels?

What matters is they engaged in a series of back-and-forth thefts (or perceived thefts) that culminated in Flossen stealing Muckells's beloved Mead Drive 8 Stiletto Automatic Knife—his father's knife before his passing. Reports suggest the Ash Muckells of 2016 valued little, which may have magnified the knife's significance into a reminder of the literal Boy Scout he'd once been (Troop 124 out of Bennett, Iowa).

In retaliation, Muckells pissed over Flossen's belongings. At least that's Flossen's contention. Ash Muckells would never have a chance to confirm or deny it.

Police records place Muckells entering the south end of the Burger City parking lot at approximately 8:40 a.m. on September 4, 2016. This suggests he was heading from the direction of I-80, which itself suggests he'd spent the night under the Exit 269 overpass. Physical evidence supports this: a moldy blanket, an empty can of corn, the scorch marks of a small fire, the crystalline traces of meth. Where Muckells obtained cash we'll never know, but that morning he was set on spending it.

To enter the building, he needed to circle around to the restaurant's northern side. Burger City #8 had only a southern entrance/exit, a cost-saving flaw shared by all Burger City locations built prior to 1990. Limited points of egress were rare in the fast-food biz following the 1984 McDonald's Massacre in San Ysidro, California, in which James Huberty killed twenty-one people and injured nineteen.[8] The San Ysidro McDonald's had three

---

7 Christie Frith of Frith Security in Tipton, Iowa, put it to me this way: "One gray-hair asked if I sold handcuffs too, so she could handcuff her purse to her body when she went out."

8 In just two days, the San Ysidro McDonald's was entirely refurbished and ready to open again. Eventually, though, community pressure led to the building's demolition less than two months after the incident.

public exits, and even that hadn't been enough; Burger City #8 had just one, plus an employee access point by the dumpster.

The drive-thru was on the south side of the building. Unlike the two-window system of modern fast-food outlets, Burger City had a single window. That Sunday, the drive-thru was being handled by 18-year-old Amber Louise Smyrna, the epitome of the all-American Prom Queen.

While not the drive-thru virtuoso of her mother, Darcy Smyrna, or her classmate Amy Mold, Amber had been working at Burger City since 2013, and could make change and dole out Egg-a-Beefys and Hog Heavens while keeping an eye on Ash Muckells as he meandered to the rear of the building. She recognized him, though they had no relationship. Muckells was a grim decade beyond the kind of struggles she, a newly minted high-school senior, knew anything about.

"He looked screwed up," Amber told police later. "He was walking crooked, right where the drive-thru lane turns. It looked like he might wander into it. So I yelled back to Javi and Mickey to look out the back door and make sure he was okay."[9]

Probably because they couldn't hear Amber over the sizzling grills and the "Soft Rock Hitz" of Bob Nutting's beloved 95.6 WKES, neither batch cook Javier Villareal nor finish cook Mickey McCormick did as Amber asked. She didn't think about it; she had a new order crackling through her headset, a new car pulling up to her window.

In five minutes, Ash Muckells would enter Amber Smyrna's mind again, and thereafter never fully leave it.

The man who took the testimony of Amber and other eyewitnesses was Detective Curt Laurent "C.L." Bank of the Cedar County Sheriff's Office. Detective Bank knew Scotty Flossen as much as anyone could in 2016. From 2007–2016, Bank contributed testimony to nine misdemeanor charges against Flossen, including Assault, Disorderly Conduct, Trespassing, Possession of Drug Paraphernalia, and Theft.

But on February 2, 2020, when I interview him, Bank feels no derision for Flossen. Kicked back on his office chair's back legs, meaty fingers laced behind his shaved head and steel-toe boots planted beside his inbox, Bank claims he feels the opposite.

"The first time you pick up a kid like Flossen, that's when you get angry. 'Here's another meth-head popped up like a pimple. More crapola I got to do.' But the second time, the third time? You got two

---

9   Per Detective C.L. Bank's report of September 5, 2016.

choices. Choice one, you get angrier and angrier. I've seen officers eaten alive by it. You may think meth is an epidemic, but I'll tell you what else is. Police giving up, losing their humanity. Carrying it home, beating their wives and kids. Or taking their piece and blowing their own brains out. I don't want to sound tooty-fruity, but you give in to anger like that, in a job like this? You're finito."

Bank shares his stuffy second-story office with two other detectives. The room, which smells strongly of cologne, barely contains their desks, much less their file cabinets, which makes the place feel like a storage room. Only the slenderest path exists toward Bank's desk; I wonder if he entered through the window via cherry-picker. By his own proud declaration, the Oakland, California, native is 6'3", 260 pounds.

"Choice two is you recognize they're human beings, same as the folks you hold dear."

He picks up a framed photo depicting a wife, six kids, four dogs, some scenic gorge.

"These folks on meth are possessed. That's the way I tell deputies to think of it. There's a devil in their brains and all a meth-head wants is to feed it. Doesn't do a lick of good if you put Scotty Flossen in jail for thirty days. Or sixty days, or ninety days. Meth hibernates like a bedbug. Whole time a meth-head's in the clink, he's thinking, where will I find a rock the second I'm out?"

Bank describes the penultimate time he collared Flossen. It was on Highway 44 near Sunbury (population 50). Flossen was sprawled in the middle of the road. Bank says Flossen didn't resist as he dragged him to the shoulder. Flossen handed over an Aldi bag filled with stolen pharmaceuticals. A plunged needle waggled from an ulcerated abscess in his biceps. He was out of his mind, babbling about cemeteries and blood. Bank could feel the wetness of Flossen's suppurating sores, but he didn't let go. When I ask the detective what he said to Flossen during all this, he shrugs.

"I kept saying, 'We love you, we love you.' I don't know what I meant. The sheriff's office didn't, that's for sure. The community neither. Most folks would just as soon run meth-heads off a cliff like lemmings. Just seemed like the right thing to say. Even Scotty Flossen has to have people somewhere who give a crapola."

The hot office grows hotter when I steer the conversation to the Burger City Poltergeist. Detective Bank was the major local law-enforcement official handling the June 1, 2017, tragedy, and unlike Sheriff Hutton Weltch, he's made himself accessible to the press for three years, if only to squash stupid rumors like bugs. When I ask how Scotty Flossen's attack on Ash Muckells drove the future events at Burger City, Bank gives me the longest, slowest blink I've ever seen.

"Murders don't affect ghosts," he says with icy derision. "Because ghosts aren't real."

Camera 2 footage shows Muckells entering Burger City at 8:44 a.m. He's wearing a Cedar Rapids Kernels baseball cap and has what witnesses report are three dollars in his left fist. Burger City's quartet of security cameras aren't infamously terrible yet; in 2016, they are merely terrible. Bright spots, such as the Chillee Shake Machine's chrome, are overexposed enough to look ablaze, while darker areas ferment with static.

The Sunday morning rush. Both tills going strong. Customers three deep. Men yawning like old dogs, women hypnotized by gadgets, the underwater sway of the queued. Muckells stands out for the obsessive way he studies the menu. How far can three bucks go at Burger City? He could get two Beefyburgers and an order of Spuddy Buddies for $2.75, and if tax brings him a bit short, that's okay. Cheri Orritt and Kit Bryant are working the registers, and neither are the sort to let a few cents stand between a hungry man and his sack of grease.

At 8:46, Ash Muckells steps before Till 2, operated by Kit Bryant. Camera 2 is mounted over Kit's left shoulder, but he's recognizable by the black ponytail sprouting above the strap of his Burger City cap. Concurrent with Muckells's move toward the counter, Scotty Flossen explodes into the restaurant. The door rockets open, only the hydraulic hinge stopping it short of striking the tray return.

Camera 3, opposite the counter, picks up the action. Flossen moves at such speed that napkins on the floor come alive with square-dance swirls. He takes five long steps from the door to Till 2; it lasts one second, or an eternity frame by frame. The Mead Drive 8 Stiletto Automatic Knife, first owned by Patrick Muckells, then Ash Muckells, now wielded by Scotty Flossen, is more than visible. It's white-hot under the floods, a spectral vision in tune with the ghostly disturbances to come.

Under Iowa Codes §727.8, 808B.1, 808B.2, and 808B.8, security footage mustn't record audio. When Flossen plunges the switchblade into the back of Muckells's neck, it feels as gentle as a finger-tap. The yawning, thumbing crowd is unruffled; most Iowans wouldn't jump out of the way of a careening vehicle so as not to offend the driver. The sole reaction comes from a woman in Till 1's line, later identified as Ridgeley Maddison, a financial analyst from New York on a soul-searching cross-country trek. She behaves like a New Yorker—in other words, *fuck this shit*. Like a cat dropped into a cattle pen, she darts for the door.

The impact bends Muckells's neck 90 degrees down, the squatchee button of his cap pointing straight at Kit Bryant's chest. As Flossen backs off and raises his arms in a curious I-didn't-do-it gesture, Muckells's chin drops to the top of the register. His left hand flops onto the change carousel and his precious three dollars drop.

There are good reasons even the Starz doc didn't air the following 30 seconds of footage.

Never have I seen so much blood.

"The 30 Seconds," as I call them, give us a thorough look at who was working the morning shift on September 4 and their moment-by-moment reactions to the unfolding incident. Awareness of the stabbing rolls out in three echelons: the front of the house (FOH), back of the house (BOH), and finally the arrival of Manager Bob Nutting.

To visualize this and future events, it will help to understand the layout of Burger City #8.

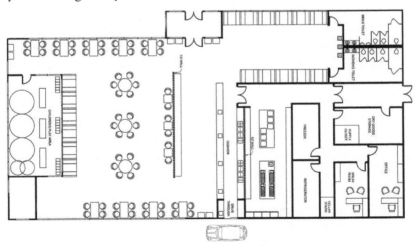

Burger City Franchise Location #8 blueprints.

The interior is 10,429 square feet. We can divide the building into five spaces of roughly equal size, progressing west to east. First is an enclosed children's play area called the Puppy Pen, floored with rubber tiles and equipped with a slide, seesaw, and three two-top tables. When asked about the Puppy Pen, nearly every survivor I interviewed renounced the zone as a hotbed of kiddie boogers, secret urine, forlorn Band-Aids, and swirling pestilence.

Regrettably adjacent to this noxious cage is the main dining area, which Nutting, per the Burger City Manager's Handbook, called "the Grand Room." It goes without saying there is nothing grand about it. Consisting of nine four-top booths (B1–B9), three two-top tables (T1–T3), and three six-top tables (T4–T6), it is like every fast-food joint you've seen, only grungier. Burger City's regional rise peaked around 1994; no major remodels followed. Burger City #8's plastic booths have the worn, fuzzy seats of commuter buses. They'd looked okay when the Burger City colors of yam orange and royal blue were bright. By 2016, the booths look rubbed to the bone.

Progressing eastward, we come to Burger City's transactional area. To your left upon entering is a short hallway to the restrooms. Ten feet ahead, the cashier counter. Behind it, the tray where wrapped Beefyburgers, Puppy Packs, and more are slotted for cashiers to bag. Also back there is the Chillee Shake Machine, BC Deluxe Select Brew coffee maker, and the soft drink dispenser. At the southern end of the counter, past Kit Bryant at Till 2, is Amber Smyrna's drive-thru alcove.

Now we're in the BOH. Usually, here's where the danger's at. Sweltering ovens, fritzing microwaves, boiling fryers, knives clopping against prep stations, water from leaky sinks creeping across the tile. The grease hangs as heavily as a jungle mist. Around a corner are the walk-in refrigerator and walk-in freezer, the latter of which is going to cause a lot of trouble in exactly 82 days.

The easternmost fifth of the building contains the dry goods storage room, the staff break room, Dez Mozley's janitorial closet, and Bob Nutting's office. More about these spaces later. But let's linger upon what too many treatments of the Burger City Poltergeist brush past: the small cellar door, wedged between break room and walk-in fridge, leading to what Amber Smyrna called "the Biting Room." The cellar has remained a place of mystery until now: the seven new hours of footage I have seen changes that.

So the knife sinks into the neck. Ash Muckells crumples against the register. There goes the Cedar Rapids Kernels cap. Kit Bryant reacts first. He takes Muckells's scabby face in his hands with the firmness of a doctor checking lymph nodes. In other words, Kit's instinct is to offer immediate, selfless care to a possibly tweaking meth addict. I don't believe anyone else in Burger City that day would have reacted so readily.

Remember this about Kit Bryant as his story darkens.

Camera 3 catches the first spray of blood. Because of Muckells's bowed neck, the blood fountains straight up before splattering red blotches across his ratty white T-shirt. *Now* the customers care. Heads turn. They don't comprehend what they're seeing. We're at Second 3.

A liter of blood belches from Muckells's mouth, dousing both the register and Kit's chest. Dulled by years of mild Iowa hues, Camera 2 can't handle so much red. The pixels panic. Kit recoils. He knows the same facts Detective C.L. Bank rattles off to me four years later. Meth users share needles, have heightened sex drives, have more partners, and use less protection, magnifying their rates of gonorrhea, chlamydia, syphilis, and HIV.

Of course Kit recoils—but he doesn't let go. Even dripping with hot blood, he drags Muckells by the arms in the direction of the drive-thru to clear the register between them. The effort fails. Whatever stage of meth Muckells is at—rush, high, shoulder, tweak, or withdrawal[10]—pain pierces it. He rips his left arm free to slap at the knife. Kit can't hold that much weight. At Second 7, Muckells falls to the floor, knocking the Driver 8 from his neck. How can I explain what follows? You have a champagne bottle. You pop the cork.

Dr. Marilyn Jagodowski performed the autopsy of Ash Muckells on Monday, September 5, 2016, at the Des Moines Medical Examiner's lab, beating the best-practice 24-hour protocol by two hours. The near-lateness wasn't Jagodowski's fault. The Burger City crime scene was the ugliest thing Jonny, Iowa, had seen. Local law, led by Sheriff Weltch, were skittish, cautious, and slow.

Jagodowski received Muckells's body via Cedar County Medical Examiner Jules Kennett, who had done fine work at the crime scene but, for this homicide case, deferred to a higher authority. By Jagodowski's account, the autopsy was strenuous but familiar.

"Crystal meth does wild things to bodies," Jagodowski tells me on February 18, 2020, from a chilly Des Moines office warmed by about 50 photos of her dogs. "Remember that thing from the nineties? *Alien Autopsy*? It's like meth users are humanoid, but not quite human anymore. Their hearts are too big. Their digestive organs are shriveled up. Forget about their brains. Dopamine transporters in the orbitofrontal and dorsolateral prefrontal cortex are gonesville. The neurological damage—I

---

10 Nick Reding, *Methland: The Death and Life of an American Small Town* (Bloomsbury, 2009), 51.

don't even think we've *begun* to appreciate it. There's loss of gray matter, shrinkage of the hippocampi. I'd know a meth addict's brain blindfolded. The surface is, like, reptilian. Maybe that's an insensitive word. It's been a shitty morning."

Coming straight from an early autopsy, Jagodowski unleashes a bun the size of a second head into a cascade of curly brown hair. She collapses into a chair perfectly positioned to roll backward toward her tea kettle. As we talk, the 48-year-old heats water, loads a tea infuser, and adds an inch of honey to her mug.

"Someone ingests a sizable enough dose, there's a whole menu of potential CODs. Stroke, heart attack, arrhythmia, cerebrovascular hemorrhage, liver failure. Now consider that half of fatal meth cases involve a second or third substance. Alcohol, cocaine, heroin. Now we're really having fun. Did Drug A amplify the mortality of Drug B? Did Drugs A and B weaken the cardiovascular system, paving the way for Drug C?"

Jagodowski's hands spider around her tea mug. It's easy to visualize those hands shearing ribs, scalpeling pleural adhesions, nestling fatty livers into weighing trays.

"I've heard, and I have no idea if this is true, but I've heard that scavengers won't feed off bodies of meth users. That right there is a wake-up call. Sure, we need to save the environment, but there's an *inner* environment too, and if we don't rescue it here, in places like Iowa, Illinois, Indiana, that devastation is going to spread."

If you feel like all you hear about is the opioid crisis, you're right. Opioid overdoses, which now exceed car crashes in preventable fatalities,[11] can be *like* car crashes: swift and dramatic. Meth deaths, by contrast, are slinking, insidious, putrefying. Often meth isn't even identified as the cause of death, unless someone like Marilyn Jagodowski gets her mitts on the corpse. With a degree of professional enthusiasm, she clicks open a folder of Burger City crime-scene shots. Tea steam fails to soften her words.

"The neck has some wonderful vascular structures. Mr. Flossen's knife hit about an inch left of Mr. Muckells's midline." Jagodowski touches her own neck with a pinkie daubed with tea. "Here's the carotid. Here's the jugular. Mr. Flossen's knife incised both. The arterial patterns are classic. Look at that arc across the floor. That's beautiful. Look, way up the wall. Hang on, there's a photo that shows blood on the ceiling."

---

11   Shanley Pierce, "Odds of Dying: For the First Time, Opioid Overdoses Exceed Car Crashes," *Texas Medical Center,* January 17, 2019.

I've seen the photo and don't need to see it again. I return to what she said about addiction spreading like disease. I ask her if she think we'll all be addicts someday.

"How about already are? We're just addicted to different things. Why are you addicted to this story? Why am I addicted to my phone? Picture the whole bunch of us floating around, wanting nothing but the next fix. When that's all that matters, we're not going to be fixated on one ghost. We're going to have a whole *country* of ghosts—us."

At Second 8, Cheri Orritt springs into action. If there's anyone at Burger City you want around in a crisis, it's not Manager Bob Nutting. It's not the physically imposing Zane Shakespeare (who's off that day) or Tamra Longmoor (who's working the fryer). It's Cheri Orritt, who at age 53 isn't only the longest-term employee at Burger City #8, but the longest-term employee in Burger City *history* following the 2013 death of founder Aldo Hucklebridge. That's twenty-eight years—and Cheri had the plaque to prove it. More accurately, she was *sent* a plaque.

The plaque hangs in the employee break room, the one space Nutting has decided not to police. This windowless nine-by-seven box, redolent of the cigarettes smoked there until the Iowa Smokefree Air Act of 2008, boasts a chipboard table carved with the initials of every employee since 1989, four decrepit plastic folding chairs, an asthmatic mini-fridge, sloppy heaps of personal belongings, and walls enlivened by defaced posters from past promotions. Glimpseable in one Game of Pricks video is a 1991 poster of a cowboy with the tagline *The Big Beefy—That's For Me.* The cowboy's eyes and teeth are blacked out.

Cheri's plaque hangs crookedly above the table. Adhered to it is a Post-It note scrawled in Cheri's own hand. In hindsight, the sentiment is unsettling:

KILL ME NOW

In twenty-eight years on that off-ramp, Cheri Orritt had seen everything *except* murder. From what Camera 3 depicts, all of it—the epileptic seizures, the bathroom fires, the belligerent customers, the pick-up truck that wiped out the Puppy Pen in winter 2001—was training for September 4, 2016, when Cheri displayed behavior deserving of a second plaque, if not a second life and a second chance.

With her left elbow, she slams her register shut; Nutting will praise her for that later. The north end of the counter has a flip-top like the end of a bar, and she flings it up. The French fries waiting there fly, a quiver of potato arrows. Cheri's back is bowed by three decades on her feet. Her fat looks burdensome. She has the frizzled hair and wrinkled skin endemic to those who work over hot stoves, though the tinted glasses she wears for photosensitivity give her a leathery rock-star look.

By Second 10, Cheri is a riot cop, arms outstretched, corralling people in the Till 1 line into the Grand Room. In a flash, half the customers are safe.

On Second 13, Cheri whirls around, Burger City cap askew, and fixes her eyes on Scotty Flossen. She's the first to pinpoint the assailant. Because there is no second exit, no one in the Till 2 queue can escape without passing Flossen. They retreat from the gouting blood with the exception of Elisha Levesley, 44, a UPS driver on his way to a West Branch loading center. Levesley is on his knees, his brown uniform going purple with blood. He's trying to staunch Muckells's neck wound but the man's spasms stymie him.

At Second 14, Scotty Flossen looks directly at Cheri Orritt. It's like the cowboy in the 1991 Big Beefy promo has stepped off the poster and doubled: here are two gunfighters ready to draw.

Interviews confirm Bob Nutting's tendency to go soft on pretty girls. No one was ever to be without a Burger City cap; Amber Smyrna liked to forget hers at home when her hair was looking good. Fingernail polish was prohibited; Amber applied fresh coats on break. One ring per hand and three rings per ear were the handbook limits; Amber, when the muse struck her, would sport up five on the fingers, eight on the ears. Facial piercings were forbidden; Amber's colored nostril studs were her trademark.

None of this hindered Amber's popularity among Burger City coworkers. Even Amy Mold, greatly feared for her "zero fucking tolerance"[12] of gender bias, viewed Amber's rule-flaunting as a feminist flex. At least someone was sticking it to the Man.

No rule was enforced more stringently than cell phone use. Nutting allowed phones to be kept in pants pockets until 2014, when "he went DEFCON 1," according to Clemens Dumay, striding up to each employee, demanding their phone, and dumping them in a pail he slammed to the break-room table and labeled in black marker, *FOR USE ON BREAK ONLY!!!* A day later, a photocopied segment of the Burger City Team

---

12 This exact three-word phrase seemed to be an Amy Mold trademark; three different people I interviewed quoted it verbatim.

Member Handbook was taped to the break-room door:

> 7.1. Cellular phones cannot be used, seen, or heard while a Team Member is clocked in, including via 'ear buds' or 'blue tooth' devices. Lack of strict adherence to this rule will result in disciplinary action, which may include suspension or termination. Emergency calls must not exceed two minutes in duration.[13]

None of this applied to Amber Smyrna. On September 4, her iPhone isn't in the so-called Break Room Bucket. It's on the drive-thru register, opened to YouTube, playing Tegan and Sara at a volume that won't register through the customer speaker. The drive-thru alcove is an obstacle course of cups, cup holders, cup lids, coffee lids, creamers, stir sticks, sugar packets, fake-sugar packets, straws, napkins, plastic utensils, condiment packs, and Puppy Pack toys, yet Amber wiggles through it, and with the grace of millions of teens like her, swipes up her phone.

The back of Amber's head (sans hat) appears next to Kit in the Camera 2 footage at Second 10. It's hard to beat Kit and Cheri, but Amber's reaction is nevertheless impressive: all that chaos, all that blood, and by Second 13, she's dialing her phone.

The Cedar County Sheriff's Department received the 911 relay at 8:50 a.m. Detective Bank confirms the call was made by Amber Smyrna, three minutes before Bob Nutting called, five minutes before any customer did the same. By then, the closest officers, Bradshaw Simon and Matt O'Doherty, were hurtling down Old Muscatine Road with lights and sirens employed. Bank wouldn't be far behind, and neither would Sheriff Weltch.

Bank is less impressed than I about the staff's response.

"Ms. Smyrna might have been the *only* one to act appropriately that day. Mr. Bryant put himself and others at risk dealing with the injured individual before assessing the threat. Mrs. Orritt's"—[sic]; Cheri Orritt never married— "involvement could have gotten more people killed. Señor Villareal was the worst of the lot. The first rule is don't escalate the situation. What if Mr. Flossen had a gun? We'd have bodies stacked all the way to I-80."

This doesn't sound like the same man who whispered *We love you, we love you* to Scotty Flossen on Highway 44. When I make this point, Bank's boots swing from desk, crashing to the floor like anvils. His chair makes a

---

13 *Burger City Team Member Handbook*, 2015, 7.

shogun-loading *ka-chung-chung* noise as he leans his goliath torso so hard against the desk that its edge begins to bisect him.

"That's the trouble with you people. It's easy doubting law enforcement when you're writing about maybes. There's no maybes when your butt's on the line. I liked Scotty Flossen as much as I could afford to, but this was his meth-head butt versus the butts of law-abiding individuals. I don't even understand why we're talking about Scotty Flossen. No one said we'd be spending all this time on Scotty Flossen."

I suggest that Muckells's murder, coming twenty-eight days before the first supposed paranormal event, shell-shocked the Burger City staff, making them vulnerable to illogical ideas. Bank's not biting. He rolls his chair back and hooks a thumb at the window.

"You want to see ghosts? We can hop in a cruiser and do a whole Eastern Iowa ghost tour. Haunted houses around here are real easy to spot. Because they're burned rubble. Pseudoephedrine, acetone—that stuff is real flammable. Red phosphorus, they put that junk in fireworks. The methods some of these batchers used, even *air* becomes combustible. Burger City, bad as it was? It doesn't even rate."

During the Cheri Orritt and Scotty Flossen standoff, Seconds 14 through 18, customers from the Till 2 queue shift into the Grand Room. They shuffle past B9, the home base of the self-styled "Geezers," a group of five retired locals who meet for breakfast at Burger City for upward of three hours each morning. So emphatic was their gathering that Bob Nutting, in a rare breach of corporate code, made a laminated *RESERVED 6:30-10am* sign to protect unwitting motorists from the surly codgers. On September 4, the Geezers enjoy a full house: Stu Blick, Zadie Budden, Vandyke Elbutt, Silas Ireland, and Maxine Pinto, all in their usual spots.

The chair they use to accommodate a fifth Geezer impedes the thoroughfare. Customers plow into it, sending 77-year-old Vandyke Elbutt to the floor. He breaks his left elbow, a lateral condyle fracture that will keep Vandyke in a cast for most of the poltergeist's duration. "Elbutt's Elbow," the Geezers will call it.

During these same five seconds, the BOH personnel emerge. First is today's shift manager, Tamra Longmoor, the restaurant's only Black employee. Her Burger City uniform is a size small so as to detail her muscles. Of all the people in this situation, Tamra is the only one who looks like she belongs, lean and shining with kitchen sweat, hair buzzed to military length. She wields the last tool she touched, the French fry funnel scoop. It gleams like a hatchet.

Second is Mickey McCormick, scuttling from behind the prep station in a low crouch. He sports all the modifications that make him feel like the Springsteen he once dreamed of being: polo sleeves folded back, buttons opened to display chest curls, hair dyed of grayness, his goatee (also dyed) so key to his self-image that he submits to the Burger City-mandated beard net. Mickey is bearing a cleaver.

Third is Javier Villareal—*Señor* Villareal per the contemptuous Detective Bank—unarmed but pushing past Tamra and Mickey. Before he does, let's take the temperature of Cheri and Flossen. By Second 18, Flossen's sinewy, crystal-powered strength is gone; he's a knotted shoelace pulled loose. You can see why Bank told him we love him. Flossen, it turns out, has big, pretty, soulful eyes that read even on low-res security cams. Partly due to the meth, but still.

Cheri Orritt's outstretched arms are no longer riot-cop batons. They offer an embrace. During these five seconds, she performs a single action: she takes off her tinted glasses and takes a step toward Flossen. Can't see worth a damn now. Won't be able to dodge if Flossen whips out a backup blade. *KILL ME NOW* might have just become prophecy.

Javi's entrance into the Camera 2 footage is big. He isn't a large man—5'6", 180, regular build—but he might be a Ferrari for all we can tell from his blur. One second, Flossen stands there. Next second, Flossen's gone, slammed by an open-field tackle into one of the building's abundant security-camera blind spots. Burger City #8 has four cameras, three less than the franchise average of seven,[14] and among Bob Nutting's managerial shortcomings following the murder will be his failure to bolster that number, even after things get weird.

From Second 19 to Second 24, Javi struggles alone with Flossen—we can tell by the condiment-station scree. Meth users often report super strength, but it is imagined. Anyway, it's a moot point. Anyone who saw how Flossen looked at Cheri knows the 28 year-old addict has no fight left in him.

On Second 25, three male customers join Javi off camera, led by none other than our blood-soaked UPS hero Elisha Levesley. You can't quite see Norville Patton, 35, a gas station owner from Stockton (population 195), but you can see the thrashing legs of Sven Naysmith, 30, a food bank organizer from Lowden (population 789). By Second 30, Sven's legs go still. The threat is neutralized. The footage has no audio, but one minute

---

14 Per the opening statement of Kit's lawyer, Lewis Kaul, delivered at the July 24, 2017, plea hearing.

later, the heads of all visible FOH and BOH personnel turn north as they hear sirens: Officers Bradshaw Simon and Matt O'Doherty closing in.

Dicing crime footage into individual frames has a deleterious psychological effect well-known to high-paid legal defense teams. It seeds doubts about the purpose of this punch or the forcefulness of that kick, until a jury loses sight of a bigger picture only graspable when the footage is viewed at regular speed. This is partly how eighty-one seconds of Rodney King being clubbed fifty-six times can result in exoneration.

So let's take a step back. In the outbreak of rage, tumult, gore, and pugilism, it's easy to be distracted from the most important thing of all, present in every one of the 30 Seconds.

Ash Muckells is dying.

Meth-related deaths, frequent as they are in Iowa, don't often look like this. Every joy, grief, hope, and shame of Ash Muckells's life is reduced to raspberry liquid spraying across a dirty floor. At Second 9, blood is jetting ten feet. By Second 25, the action could better be described as *spurts*. His blood begins to pool in a slight concavity near the southern wall. It happens to be the location of Burger City's cardboard mascot.

Bob Nutting finally appears at Second 30. His office is in the building's southeastern corner, and his door was closed. Nutting's police statement says he was on the phone with his estranged wife, Lisa Nutting, at the time of the murder, and it was only via irritated browser tabbing that he landed on the security-cam portal and saw Kit Bryant climbing over the front counter. Nutting hung up on Lisa and bolted through the kitchen, anticipating a final confrontation with his 19-year-old nemesis.

Kit is kneeling in blood. Replacement Burger City uniforms cost $40 (optionally deducted from the next paycheck),[15] a bill even Bob Nutting won't make the kid foot. Kit shouts and shakes his left arm impatiently, spattering blood across the counter. Nutting deserves credit for responding. He knows right where the First Aid Kit is. He ought to; he drives his staff bonkers with a daily curriculum of checklists even the regional office has deemed "excessive."[16] The kit is beneath Till 2, flanked by two of the many safety notices Nutting bought with his own money: the infographic *First Aid for Choking* and the horrifying *Burns & Scalds*, featuring an unlucky fellow caught in a variety of blazes.

15 *Burger City Team Member Handbook*, 5.

16 Per the entered evidence of an email from Beauregard Waterhouse, dated August 31, 2014.

The dazed Amber Smyrna removes the kit and tries to hand it to her boss. They sort of tussle over it. It topples over the counter.

The final insult of Ash Muckells's life is a Rapid Care ANSI/OSHA Compliant Emergency First Aid Kit dropped on his head. The plastic latch breaks, releasing all 334 pieces. Adhesive bandages, tape rolls, trauma pads, plastic gloves, cold compresses, antiseptic towelettes. All those scientifically crafted health products soaked by primal fluid: we won't find a better metaphor for the Burger City Poltergeist than that.

As Marilyn Jagodowski escorts me out of the Des Moines Medical Examiner Lab, she asks where I live, where I grew up, what kind of books I write. When we get to the parking lot, she asks if I have a strong stomach. Horror writers get this question a lot. I tell her the truth: I don't. She nods as if suspecting as much. I ask her if a weak stomach is such a terrible thing.

"I wonder about that. On the one hand, it probably means you're not a crusty old misanthrope. On the other, it's probably healthy to be able to look at the world's worst things if you're going to try to understand them."

Before I can think of how to reply, she asks another question.

"Did you know hunters growing up?"

Yes, my father, in fact, whose passion is evidenced by basement walls lined with taxidermied deer, antelope, moose, bear, and more. Jagodowski and I discuss how my dad butchered and ate what he killed.

"That's what I'm talking about," Jagodowski says. "If you're going to kill something, it's best to know how it bleeds, what it looks like when it dies. Keeps you honest—a good thing if you're trying to write a true story."

I tell myself it's more caution than criticism. But I push back a little. Does she, I ask, personally shake the paw of every animal she eats? Jagodowski laughs and wags a finger at me.

"Not my problem," she says. "I'm vegetarian."

Kit snatches up a four-inch-square gauze pad, rips open the packaging with his teeth, and presses the pad against Muckells's neck with both hands. Tamra Longmoor joins him in the lake of blood, grabbing a medical tape dispenser. Together she and Kit get the gauze to stick, but it's too late. When Officers Simon and O'Doherty enter, guns drawn only to find Scotty Flossen entirely subdued, Ash Muckells is dead.

And the Burger City Poltergeist—so say the survivors—begins to live.

OCTOBER 2016

SICK, GHOULISH DEGENERATE

Decorah, Iowa (population 7,701) lies three hours north of Jonny, right at the Iowa-Minnesota-Wisconsin junction, on the western edge of what geologists call the "Driftless Area," a region marked by plunging river valleys, sixteen miles of underground caves, and steep hills.

Bruce P. Chernow Medical Health Institute sits atop one of the highest. Chernow, as it is called locally, is attractive in the morning, with bald eagles circling as the red dawn brings jewel tones to its four stories of windows. Later in the day, however, it looks like a standardized, suburbanized, big-box institution, with the same reddish concrete walls and sky-blue plastic windows as most of the schools, hospitals, and office buildings built in the 1990s. It isn't until I visit Chernow that I internalize the goal of this architecture: to lull you into compliance.

Bruce P. Chernow Medical Health Institute (via Winneshiek County website).

My interview request sparks counseling events with the patient, sheaves of consent forms, and deep discussions between the patient's family and lawyer. To my surprise, the request is accepted twenty-six days later. In a tense phone call, Facility Superintendent Stacy Anstee informs me that leeway is being granted due to the patient's unexpected enthusiasm to speak to me. Chernow psychiatrists see his interest as a positive sign.

Anstee lays out a lot of rules, most of them *Nos*. No scarves, belts, shoe laces, bandanas, nylons, tights, leggings, hoodies with cords, lighters, matches, aerosols, alcohol, bags, cans, glass bottles, ceramics, mirrors, makeup, medications, scissors, jewelry, spiral-bound notebooks, staples, paper clips, pencils, or loofahs (don't ask me). I can't bring liquids or food; instead I can bring 20 dollars to stuff into vending machines. D-Wing visiting hours are limited to 1:00–6:00 p.m. on Saturdays and 1:00–4:00 p.m. on Sundays. By specific, adamant request of the patient, I am to come alone.

More than anything, Anstee stresses that no videos be recorded. My audio device mustn't have video capabilities. For reasons that make sense to anyone conversant in the Burger City Tragedy, the patient is triggered by video devices. He is kept out of common areas containing screens, and, as much as possible, rerouted through Chernow so as to avoid the sight of security cameras. How his reaction manifests Anstee won't say, though she repeats, in a way she probably thinks is comforting, that security personnel will be present for my two-day interview of March 7–8, 2020.

No one knows it yet, but one day later, March 9, Iowa will confirm eight cases of the Covid-19 pandemic, prompting Governor Kim Reynolds to sign a Proclamation of Disaster Emergency.[17] The day after I leave Chernow, it closes to visitors for the rest of the year.

On March 7, an afternoon stormy enough to provoke maximum dread, I steer my rental car up the hill to Chernow. The check-in desk prints a photo ID and slips it into a color-coded plastic badge. The elevator is clean and equipped with good signage. But I don't need signs to tell me which way to turn at the second floor. The hallway to the right is filled with framed pictures, plastic plants, and benefactor appreciations. The hallway to the left is white and empty, with nothing but a locked door and an intercom.

I announce my credentials and am buzzed in. A worker in light-blue scrubs assigns me a locker inside which I stow my wallet, keys, and jacket. My recording device is examined and I'm patted down. Anstee makes no appearance. I'm escorted by another worker in blue scrubs who doesn't like to talk and doesn't introduce himself, though a name tag (plastic, no pin) identifies him as "Nuncio." Nuncio leads me through another set of locked doors printed with the words *HIGH ELOPEMENT RISK*. I ask what it means.

"We got wanderers," Nuncio says.

---

17 Polly Carver-Kimm, "Proclamation Following Additional COVID-19 Cases in Iowa," *Iowa Department of Public Health*, March 9, 2020.

We continue through several locked doors toward what looks like an open hospital room. Nuncio halts before we enter and looks me in the eye.

"Trust me. Don't listen to anything he says."

He gestures his head at the door. I carefully enter a small room painted a restful mint green. I'm hit by the warm musk of a young man. Along the left wall is a bed. Flush against it is a small dresser, atop which are piled journals and books. The chair belonging at the desk has been moved to rest against the opposite wall. The seat literally has my name on it, a piece of paper markered *MR. KRAUS.*

Standing perfectly still in the center of the room is Kit Bryant.

For someone who has studied the same few photographs for years, meeting Kit is like seeing a celebrity in the flesh. More specifically, a celebrity who has gone through aggressive Photoshopping. Can this really be Kit? After only three years?

He's large. Really large.

The last time the world glimpsed Kit was December 12, 2017, the day he was transferred to Chernow. The intake process included the careful logging of his 5'11" height and 131-pound weight. As I will later confirm, the Kit Bryant of March 7, 2020, is *355 pounds.* That's a gain of 224 pounds.

Survivors of the Burger City Tragedy have been through trauma, and weight loss is a common side-effect. Kit's packing on of pounds feels more mysterious. It has to be the pharmaceuticals.

There is no way to conceal my shock. But those blue eyes. The nose crooked slightly to the left. The bright teeth cresting from his trademark grin, also crooked.

And, of course, the scars. His shirt hides the one that supposedly circles his left shoulder, but the three-inch scar down the underside of his left forearm is in full view, slick and puffy.

It's him, all right. Kit Bryant, the "diabolic mastermind"[18] behind the Burger City Poltergeist. Kit Bryant, the so-called "Jonny, Iowa, Sadist."[19] Kit Bryant, "[The] sick, ghoulish degenerate [who] led his coworkers to slaughter."[20]

---

18   Janie Tewkesbury, "Burger City Murder Case Moves Forward," *Des Moines Register,* July 11, 2017.

19   Sophie Best, "Burger City Teen Should be Thrown the Book," *Sioux City Journal,* August 1, 2017.

20   Rocio Landymore, "The Burger City Murders," Episode 60, *Murders in the Midwest,* podcast audio, September 3, 2017.

After he was judged incompetent to stand trial in August 2017, Kit spent fifteen months under observation at the Iowa Medical and Classification Center in Coralville, Iowa, where the center's chief medical officer, followed by a state psychiatrist, identified him as having "schizophrenia demonstrating as hallucinations, delusions, and thought disorder."[21] Under Iowa Code §701.4, this precluded Kit from a jury trial. Instead, on December 12, 2018, the state committed Kit to long-term treatment at the Iowa Department of Human Services' Bruce P. Chernow Medical Health Institute. The decision angered plenty, but it's hardly a get-out-of-jail-free card. Under orders of Judge Faisal Mousley, Kit can't leave Chernow without submitting to a new hearing.

Just as unexpected as Kit's physical condition is his verbosity. I'd anticipated a slouching young man muzzled by the indignities of facility life. But this much larger 23-year-old version of Kit sticks out his hand. I glance behind me. Nuncio sits by the door, not even looking at us. That must mean I'm safe, right? I shake Kit Bryant's hand. Kit Bryant, murderer. Kit Bryant, who, unlike the Burger City Poltergeist, has always been real.

"Super-cool to meet you. So you want to do the Burger City thing, huh? Yeah, man, we can do that. We can totally do that. I've got a lot to say too, so I hope you have a lot of questions! I've been psyched ever since I heard. Nothing cool ever happens here. Isn't that right, Nuncio?"

Nuncio does not reply. Kit laughs, like this is a game the two of them play. He puts his hands on his hips, looks me over, and shakes his head like he can't believe I've actually come. He flings himself onto his bed. I give him a heads-up that I've started my recorder. Because only empty tile separates us, I place the recorder in the middle of the floor. Kit looks down at it and laughs. I do too. It looks funny there, a jack-in-the-box ready to pop.

"Where do you want to start? Game of Pricks? *Spectral Journeys*? Or even earlier? Like how many times I peed my pants in kindergarten?"

He laughs again. I do too. Suddenly a lot about what happened at Burger City #8 makes better sense. Kit's enthusiasm is catchy; you can't help but want to encourage that crooked smile. But Nuncio's warning still rings: *Don't listen to anything he says.* I suggest to Kit we begin with the October 2, 2016, paranormal event that kicked off the whole thing. I don't qualify it as a "so-called" paranormal event, not out loud.

"Wow, right, sure. Yeah, man. I remember it like it was two seconds ago."

---

21 Per the court transcript of September 1, 2017.

He plants his elbows on his kneecaps, frowns soberly, and nods like I'm a casting director about to critique his audition. It's a caricature of an eager scholar. On instinct, I table my first question and instead ask why he's so interested in talking to me.

Kit's reply is the most unanticipated thing yet, beating his astonishing physical appearance and chatterbox tongue. He reaches for the stack of books on his desk. It has surprised me since I entered; Kit Bryant was a lousy student with no interest in reading.

"I got really into these strange rectangular objects after I came here," he jokes. "And this one's my favorite."

He swipes the top book and holds it up. It has a blue-black cover and yellow-orange lettering. I recognize it. I ought to. I wrote it.

It is a battered library copy of my 2011 novel *Rotters*.

"Dude," he explains. "I'm your biggest fan."

LIL' BEEFY

Lil' Beefy took her first step on October 2, 2016, at 4:24 p.m.

There is debate over who saw it first. Kit Bryant is usually credited. This is no surprise, seeing how he was the story's chief instigator. But my interviews indicate it was Tamra Longmoor who first noted it. Tamra had 20/20 vision at age 38, and her hawklike vigilance explained her swift rise to shift manager, despite clashes with Bob Nutting over scheduling around her avid churchgoing.

"Lil' Beefy moved," she grunted over a basket of sizzling fries.

As with the murder of Ash Muckells one month earlier, it was a Sunday, but Nutting didn't let anyone log over thirty hours a week. This meant the personnel for the 4:30-11:00 p.m. shift largely differed from than that of the 5:30-11:00 a.m. shift.

Tamra and Kit, however, were doing doubles, and her mutter caught his attention. As Kit made change for a ten at Till 2 (veteran cashiers lay customer bills horizontally across the drawer to avoid claims of having been handed a bigger bill), he gave Lil' Beefy a glance, and at that precise second, he saw it move too. Kit would later describe it as "a little hop."

The Lil' Beefy Anomaly had begun.

Burger City #1 opened in the Swiss-German town of Highland, Illinois (population 7,122), in 1981. Founder Aldo Hucklebridge was familiar with McDonald's, but it was Wendy's, established in in 1969, that inspired him to start his own burger joint. Why Wendy's? Because their burgers were *square*. This trivial detail inspired Hucklebridge. Sure, most fast-food burgers tasted similar (aside from White Castle, an aberration since 1921), but if Wendy's could pull off a square, what other shapes might be possible?

Hucklebridge's innovation was "the paw," a patty with four rounded "toes." After a good grilling, the paw looked more like a botched oval, but the walls of Burger City #1 were filled with illustrations of what it was *supposed* to look like, and that was enough for kids. In 1984, Aldo Hucklebridge opened a second location. In 1985, a third. By 1989,

Burger City had seven spots, and had broken ground on an eighth, off Interstate 80 near Jonny, Iowa.

Burger City Franchise Location #1 (official Burger City press photo).

Aldo Hucklebridge grew up as one of five sons on a family farm between Highland and Pocahontas, and every daylit minute he wasn't at school, he was tending crops or shepherding, from cradle to grave, the Hucklebridge farm's most valuable commodity: two-hundred heads of cattle (roughly thirty-five milk cows, thirty-five replacement heifers, thirty steers, and an equal amount of calves being raised to fulfill equivalent roles).

In both its visceral reality and existential weight, beef was the whole world to little Aldo. When beef or milk prices soared, Grale Hucklebridge, Aldo's father, belted German songs and strutted with enough brio to lift clouds of dust. When the market dipped, or cattle became afflicted with blackleg or yellow fever, Grale belted in a different way, making sure the backsides, and sometimes the frontsides, of his wife and kids suffered.

Hucklebridge cattle were slaughtered elsewhere, except for the meat eaten by the family. These choicest beeves were led, often by Aldo, into the confines of a small wire fence that had the feel of a sacrificial circle. The dirt there was black with blood.

Grale did the killing. He slit the throat, skinned, and quartered. Mere hours would pass before a pink side of beef was placed upon the dinner table hissing in its own juices. For these meals, Grale poached prayer duty from his wife, and Aldo noticed how the word "cow" at the start of the prayer turned into "beef" by the end[22]—a convenient transubstantiation.

---

22   Aldo Hucklebridge, *Hail to the Beef: Life Lessons from the Founder of Burger City* (CreateSpace, 2005), 49.

Aldo Hucklebridge grew up believing beef (not cows) to be a holy offering similar to Aztec priests proffering human hearts to the glory of Huitzilopochtli. One had to consume beef to release its magic. Fast-forward to 1981, when the 39-year-old Hucklebridge was devising the menu for Burger City #1. He had no interest in Ray Kroc's innovations at McDonald's: the Filet-o-Fish, the Hot Apple Pie, the Shamrock Shake, the Egg McMuffin. With the solipsism of countless entrepreneurs before him, he wanted All-American beef on his plastic tray, that's it, and assumed that's what the public wanted too.

His timing was perfect. Due to a late-1970s chicken shortage,[23] beef got a national advertising push that lifted all fast-food ships. His paw-shaped hamburger was the Beefyburger™. His response to McDonald's Quarter Pounder was the Big Beefy™. His response to the Big Mac was the Grampa Beefy™. Until Hardee's put out their Monster Thickburger in 2004, nothing in the fast-food biz could lay a hand on Burger City's BeefBomb™ in terms of pure caloric insult: three quarters of a pound of beef, twelve-hundred calories, eight grams of fat, two-thousand milligrams of sodium, fifty carbs, seventy-five grams of protein, and all of it cooked as rare as local law would allow. Aldo Hucklebridge liked his meat bloody.

Hucklebridge allowed a few non-beef items to trickle onto the menu as times changed, though he always counterweighted these offensive options with more beef.[24] The McNuggets clone Chik-a-Chunkz™ debuted alongside the chalupa-like BeefBoat™, and the Healthy Cowboy Salad™ (buried in bacon, slathered in ranch, and in no way healthy) entered beside the BeefBowl™, a salt-drenched loose-beef dish that forwent buns altogether.

Hucklebridge had a knack for branding. He'd chosen the paw shape to honor his beloved cocker spaniel Bessie, a puppy he'd spoiled into such chubbiness her name morphed to "Beefy." By 1983, Ronald McDonald was on his way to becoming the world's second-most recognizable figure after Santa Claus,[25] showcasing the potential of a business mascot. Beefy was catapulted into regional stardom, or at least her cartoon counterpart was.

In Burger City's mid-1980s boom, Lil' Beefy—a blond, tail-wagging puppy in a fringed vest labeled "BC"—starred in print and TV ads

23 Lauren Cahn, "Here's What the McDonald's Menu Looked Like the Year You Were Born," *Reader's Digest*, April 10, 2020.

24 After Burger City's bankruptcy filing of March 22, 2018, an anonymous Burger City executive posted dozens of internal memos, including ones that bolster this claim, via a short-lived Twitter account called @BurgerCityTruth.

25 "Dated Ronald McDonald Faces the Chop," *Campaign*, September 9, 2002.

begging for burgers with a pink, salivating tongue. In a squeaky voice, she led children in barking for food, especially the Happy Meal rip-off Puppy Packs™, which debuted in 1985.

The 2000s were unkind to fast-food mascots, and to Burger City in general. Still, you didn't run a Burger City franchise without a couple pieces of puppy signage, and when Bob Nutting took over the Jonny franchise in 2006 and set about refreshing the decor, he left in place the five-foot-tall, two-foot-wide, heavy-gloss, half-inch-thick cardboard standee of Lil' Beefy posing above the words *CHASE ME DOWN TO BURGER CITY!*

To Kit Bryant, what he witnessed on October 2, 2016, was instantly and absolutely unexplainable. If something heavy, say a high chair, had fallen nearby, it was conceivable Lil' Beefy might have trembled. If air from a floor vent had shot out, it was possible Lil' Beefy might have shifted. But this was a *hop*. The standee's base left the floor entirely, like it had been jerked upward by a string.

It wasn't the kind of thing to make you shriek in fright. But it was weird. Tamra had other things to do. With customer flow tepid, she locked Till 1, checked on Amy Mold at the drive-thru, and circled back to the kitchen to assist Zane Shakespeare. This left Kit alone at the counter. He could operate the POS system blindfolded, and logged orders for a Grampa Beefy with fries, a Roast Beefy Meal, and an eight-piece Chik-a-Chunkz, all while keeping an eye on Lil' Beefy.

During the time it took to cycle through the waiting customers—the soon-to-be-famous six minutes spanning 4:24 to 4:30 p.m.—Kit Bryant witnessed Lil' Beefy make three more hops. At approximately 4:32 p.m., with the queue cleared, Kit vaulted the counter and squatted next to the standee.

He checked for a baseboard vent. Nothing. He looked up for a ceiling vent. Nothing. He looked to the right into the Grand Room. Nothing was out of order. He lowered his face to within an inch of the ground. The floors were clean, but Dez Mozley was a minimum-wage janitor, which is to say, she didn't keep hospital standards. In the eight inches between standee and wall, Kit found what he'd hoped to find.

Five distinct marks disrupted the unmopped dust—to Kit, hard proof of Lil' Beefy's hops.

Kit pounded the wall separating him from the drive-thru alcove.

"Amy Mold! Get out here!"

"Tamra sees it first, but oh no, let's not give any credit to the strong, mature Black woman. Let's give all the credit to the teenage white guy. It's so classic."

Amy Mold (who has the kind of name people always use both halves of), tells me this outside Astral Adventures, a gift shop located in my own hometown of Fairfield, Iowa. It's June 2020 and Iowa has reacted hastily to declining Covid-19 rates, allowing stores to reopen at reduced capacities. This seems unrelated to Amy Mold's skittishness—quite a contrast to the Amy Mold of 2016. Classmate signatures in her Rose Community High School 2015–16 Yearbook call her "world-weary" and "the oldest young person I know." Back then, she was wise beyond her years, staring through cat's-eye glasses at a horizon glowing bright above the corn.

Amy Mold was supposed to bloom in college. Everyone knew it, including her.

But she's not at college. She's in Fairfield, the home of the Maharishi University of Management, the world's largest Transcendental Meditation training center. Instead of majoring in International Relations and minoring in Sustainability and Resilience, Amy is selling homeopathic adrenal correctives, chakra-energy empowerment candles, diatomaceous earth dietary supplements, and DVDs on the Vedic wisdom of His Holiness Maharishi Mahesh Yogi.

She'll try anything to counteract what she believes is a curse. Exhibit A: her weight. Amy Mold weighed 180 in 2016. Today, she tells me she's down to 126 with no end in sight. When pounds began dropping following the Burger City Tragedy, she'd attributed it to stress, grief, shock. She no longer believes that. Her clothing billows like sheets on a backyard clothesline. Every freckle on her face seems large as a penny. Even her glasses, the same cat's-eye set, look too large for her face.

She holds up her left hand so I can see the burn scars without having to ask. Though it has healed over three years, there is no hiding the damage. Indentations like seams pinch the too-glossy skin. The flesh is multicolored swirls: pink, ivory, sand, butter, tangerine. I give her a nod and Amy slides it out of view.

Seconds after making the Tamra comment, she retracts it.

"What am I saying? There's no credit. Only blame. Loads and loads of it. Do you want some tea? I've got Vata tea in the store. You feel like a Vata to me."

I let Amy remind me of the Ayurvedic pseudo-science. The recitation appears to calm her. Three biologic energies called doshas purportedly govern all physical and mental processes, and by taking a quiz ranging from the quality of your sleep to the quality of your stool, you can identify yourself as predominately Kapha, Pitta, or Vata.

"My doshas keep changing. My teacher has never seen anything like it. She wants to write a paper. God, no. No more papers. No more TV shows. You're the last one. Everyone here knows you're from Fairfield." She laughs, but mirthlessly. "We're counting on you to get it right."

Long story short, five minutes later I've got my pandemic mask down to sip a mug of Vata tea, which I must admit is tasty. Maintaining social distance, we re-situate on a bench across from a store apparently called "Computer." Amy tells me how she ended up here, an abridged version, as I think it hurts her to describe. Fairfield attracts those looking to cleanse themselves, and polluted by guilt for her part in the Burger City drama, she badly wants to be cleansed.

"The girl who did those things wasn't me. The whole crazy Bible thing. What I did to Mickey. God, I *hope* that wasn't me. I hope that was the ghost. It got inside all of us, I'm telling you. It's like, while most of us ate Burger City's greasy food, the ghost ate *us*. Do you believe any of this?"

I tell her the truth, an old chestnut: I believe she believes.

Amy quirks her lips, a big-sister expression.

"Give it time. You will."

I ask her if *she* believed Kit Bryant when he told her Lil' Beefy had moved.

"Hell no. Kit was only reliable when he was taking orders or building burgers. The second he stopped having stuff to do, watch out. He'd get stoned out of his mind. One time he chopped down a big tree in front of the school? I don't even know why. He had a total Jekyll and Hyde deal. Drink your tea."

There is a glow of admiration in Amy Mold's eyes, and I pursue it. I'm no love doctor; plenty of writers before me have noted Amy's old crush on Kit Bryant. She's never denied it.

"Oh, I'm the worst. The absolute worst. Every stupid girl I knew in high school had a bad-boy thing. I was like the one girl who knew better—and I had it too! I know there's people online who think I'm some feminist hero for what I did to Mickey. But I was as dumb as the rest of them. They must teach us to be that way. It's part of the patriarchy. They plant the seeds of our own ruin right inside us."

Had Kit Bryant ended up at Bluefeather Prison instead of Bruce P. Chernow Medical Health Institute, he might be the kind of inmate to inspire adoring letters from "prison groupies" who suffer from hybristophilia (aka

Bonnie and Clyde Syndrome). Kit didn't have a square jaw or chiseled abs. One year out of high school, he looked like wire clothes hangers wrapped in skin. But he wore it well; his gangly, twitchy body was well-matched by his patchy black scruff, tangled hair, and sleep-deprived eyes. Game of Pricks videos, as well as photos provided by Amber Smyrna, depict Kit as a whip of nervous energy, twirling his hair, biting his nails, or doing one of the other things that made him, in the parlance of the time, eminently fuckable: lighting a cigarette with practiced fingers; spinning a vinyl record between his palms; letting strange dogs on the street lick his grinning face without a trace of fear.

Kit Bryant, circa 2015 (photo by Amber Smyrna).

In 2016, Kit lived where he'd always lived: in the basement of his dad's house at 3389 Ocean Avenue in Wilton, Iowa (population 2,839). Today the house is no more, having been torched to its foundations on January 5, 2019, shortly after Kit was sent to Chernow instead of trial. As with the Burger City arson, there were no suspects—or, if you prefer, there were too many suspects. Though the Bryant house's postal address was Wilton, no Burger City employee lived closer to the restaurant as the crow flies. But Kit could hardly traipse through barbed-wired neighboring properties and sprint across I-80's four lanes. He had to go the long way around.

The two known photos of Kit's room typifies it as that of a boy one year out of high school and going nowhere fast: dank, underlit, and with clothes not so much strewn as herded into corners. Empty bags of chips were placed like scented candles. There was a TV, a slag heap of DVDs, a laptop, and a printer—all of them on the floor. Posters taped to the walls spread fungally from a point over a futon and featured subject matter emphasizing Kit's fondness for 1990s culture: Kurt Cobain, Tony Hawk, *Reservoir Dogs*. There are no books.

The neck of a guitar is visible in one of the photos. Kit acquired it in 2014 in order to play Amber two pretty songs by his favorite band, Guided by Voices: "When She Turns 50" and "Drinker's Peace" (both released in 1990, natch). He'd never held a guitar before, yet taught himself both songs in a single day. It worked; Amber swooned; and he never picked up the guitar again. It was classic Kit—capable of fleet, virtuosic skill, incapable of sticking with anything.

Casper Bryant, Kit's father, worked eleven miles southwest in Atalissa (population 311) at Newman Agricultural Services, a provider of crop-yield solutions. Like most of his male contemporaries, Casper was an able provider but emotionally stunted, qualities a more demonstrative spouse might have ameliorated. Unfortunately, Kit's mother, Melinda, had a nervous breakdown in 2003, when Kit was five, and took off for Alaska, where she lives as of this writing, ignoring all requests for comment. Both Amy Mold and Clemens Dumay told me that Kit said his mother was dead.

Kit molded himself in contrast to his parents. He didn't want to be Casper Bryant's inexpressive boulder, nor did he want to be Melinda Bryant's self-obsessed train wreck. His goals were articulated through altruism—by all accounts, his finest quality. For two weeks in 2013, he loaned his 2007 Chevy Impala to Darcy Smyrna, Amber's mom, never mentioning he'd have to go back and forth to Burger City on foot, one hour each way. In 2015, Kit stole the equivalent of two bags of groceries for Clemens Dumay after Clem's mom, as she was wont to do, disappeared for three weeks. In early 2016, Kit emptied his bank account to pay for a mammary tumor operation for Yesenia Ruiz's cat; he'd known Yesenia for only ten weeks and certainly had no opinion of the cat.

Yesenia's cat proved the maxim: Kit Bryant would give you his last dollar. By his own accounting, he owed you. Either he'd failed you in the past or would fail you soon.

"Hot," Amy sums up. "Kit was hot, hot, hot. But he and Amber always had their on-and-off thing going. The only effect my hots had is I probably gave him more credit than I should have. If [assistant manger] Dion [Skerry] had said Lil' Beefy was moving, I would have rolled my eyes. No, don't take the bag out. The longer you keep the bag in, the better Vata tastes."

I let the bag plop back down and ask her to describe what happened next.

"I asked Tamra for a bathroom break and I got down on the floor with Kit. He was pointing at—I guess it was dust? He was worried Dez was going to mop over it later. He wanted to take a picture but of course we weren't allowed to have our phones. Tamra wasn't *Nutting* bad, but if she saw Kit rooting through the Break Room Bucket, she'd write him up." She pouts at my mug. "We have Vata spices for food, if tea's not your thing."

The tea's sweetness is, in fact, starting to go foul. But this is no mere cup of tea. Approval of this tea is approval of the homeopathic remedies Amy Mold has entrusted to fix her broken life. She is dying—perhaps literally, judging by her rapid weight loss—to find a place where all her doshas can coexist. She gazes at the patchwork mess of her scarred left hand.

"I work in a wellness store," she says miserably. "But I am not well."

Sunday afternoon shifts had the lightest dinner crowds of the week, but from 5:00 to 7:00 p.m., the Burger City crew still had to look alive. Kit returned to Till 2 and Amy Mold strapped on one of the two 3M B1099 headsets. Purchased new by Bob Nutting back in 2005, the headsets were uncomfortable, glitchy, and gummed with eleven years of grease and grime. But they functioned—and the Drive-thru Phantom was still three months from clearing its throat.

Kit waited for Lil' Beefy to move again. Amy felt his frustration. Between customers, he suggested, sotto voce, a variety of bad ideas.

"Should I call Clem? Or Javi? Get Clem and Javi out here?"

"Welcome to Burger City, home of the Big Beefy, may I take your order?" Amy switched off her mic. "Don't you think they have better things to do than stare at a cardboard dog?"

"Maybe we should call the cops," Kit said.

"So that's a Healthy Cowboy Salad with double bacon ranch, onion rings, and a Dr. Pepper." Amy disarmed the mic. "No way. I don't want to see that skinhead detective ever again."

"We should at least call Nutting."

"Thank you, pull up." Amy wiggled out of the drive-thru alcove and joined Kit at Till 2. "He'd just assume you're high. Wait. Are you? High?"

Kit pointed at Lil' Beefy's base. A mother and two kids walked in, and Amy heard a car approach her window. But she indulged Kit an extra few seconds. As you recall, he was hot.

"The stain on the bottom of Lil' Beefy. See it?"

Amy Mold hadn't been present for the September 4 stabbing. She regretted it. A gumptious young woman bound for a life of globe-trotting adventure should get used to witnessing the occasional murder. It drove her nuts thinking of the mileage she could have gotten from the story in dorm lounges, cocktail parties, and beyond. Soon she would discard that fantasy in favor of the better reality: she was one of four people present at the start of the Lil' Beefy Anomaly.

"Blood," Amy replied. "Ash Muckells's blood."

"I'm calling Nutting," Kit said.

GHOST TOWNS

Bob Nutting will sell you a used car at a fair price. By the time I interview him on July 12, 2020, amid the pandemic's global car-sales slump, he's been named Salesperson of the Month three of the first six months of the year, an accomplishment the other salespeople at Hawkeye Hank's Pre-Approved Used Auto in Burlington, Iowa (population 25,663), take with grumbly good grace.

"Bob will sit you down and just have a conversation," compliments coworker Charity Bishton. "Where are you at in life, where do you see yourself in ten years, your hopes and dreams. Sales grow out of that organically."

"We had a 2005 Altima the previous owner painted puke-green," praises coworker Timothy Llewellyn. "Butt-ugly thing sat on the lot for three years. Second week on the job, Bob tells a couple, 'Life is best lived colorblind,' and they drive it off the lot that day. I don't even know what that means, but it sounds good, don't it?"

"He's especially good with first-time buyers," flatters owner Hawkeye Hank Ainsley. "I figure it comes from being able to talk to the young folk that worked at his burger place. Bob always gives 180 percent, as he likes to say."

Hawkeye Hank invites me to watch Nutting finish his shift. Nutting gives 180 percent all right, but as if from a pirate-ship plank. He improvises, extemporizes, free-associates, waxes poetic. Nutting sells like his life depends on it.

It might. The man was a chubby 280 pounds in 2016. Today, as he lurches around the lot, his dress shirt, slacks, and tie ripple from a 150-pound frame.

No one had a rougher time following the Burger City Tragedy than Bob Nutting. He was savaged by salivating prosecutors ("Bob Nutting is a negligent fool")[26] and scornful reporters ("It's difficult not to pin the tragedy

---

26 Per an unusually vitriolic July 30, 2017, court filing from state prosecutors.

on the blinkered Bob Nutting").[27] Burger City Inc.'s first official reaction to the tragedy wasn't their toothless thoughts-and-prayers June 2 press release but rather their 4:30 a.m. firing of Bob Nutting. This laid bare their legal plan: the deaths were the fault of a franchise rogue, not Burger City culture at large.

Nutting had, in fact, gone rogue in a number of egregious ways, beginning with his penny-pinching failure to install additional security cameras after the Ash Muckells murder. Even that feels negligible next to what he did inside his locked office from April to June 2017. It's difficult to see the photos of that and understand how it's Kit Bryant inside Bruce P. Chernow Medical Health Institute and not Bob Nutting.

Yet it's easy to feel sympathy for the man. You don't end up the manager of a middle-of-nowhere Burger City unless things haven't gone according to plan. By age 33, Nutting was unemployed and married to high-school girlfriend Lisa, father to 9-year-old Kristina and 4-year-old Brandine, and flat broke. While dining with his family at Burger City #6 in Ames, the idea settled over him like the film that settles atop scorched cups of BC Deluxe Select Brew. He'd never had a Beefyburger go down harder.

Nutting spent 2005 trudging through BCU (Burger City University) managerial training and serving as an observed assistant manager at Burger City #14 in Sioux Falls. In 2006, Nutting was assigned Burger City Franchise Location #8 in the town of—well, technically it wasn't in a town at all, just an off-ramp in the postal delivery zone of Jonny, Iowa. Laying eyes on Burger City #8 for the first time, both Kristina and Brandine started crying, while Lisa stared at I-80, perhaps wondering if she ran over there and stuck out her thumb, where else life might take her.

Did Nutting enjoy the job at first? He doesn't think so. But the relief was instant. You say "Burger City" in Iowa and people know what you're talking about. Nutting liked being known. He liked ordering an employee to wipe up a spill and hearing "Atta boy, Bob" from a regular. He liked demanding that good old 180 percent from a worker and being rewarded with a local's approving wink. He liked the Geezers huzzahing him like a friend, even if they never did invite him to sit, not once in ten years.

The timing of the Burger City Poltergeist was particularly poor for Bob Nutting. Nineteen months earlier, the night of April 5, 2015, at the Burger City Manager's Conference at the GrandStay Residential Suites Hotel in St. Cloud, Minnesota, Bob Nutting kissed Deirdre Benji, a vendor with Superior

---

27 Randolph Tomas, "The Burger City Murders: What Happens Next?", *Telegraph Herald*, October 15, 2017.

Food Service Supply out of Buffalo. This was no protracted dalliance. There were no sexual events. You couldn't even call what they did "making out."

"It was a kiss?" I can hear Benji's shrug over the phone. "As I recall, it was cocktail hour. We were tipsy. He sort of planted one on me, and I don't know, I kissed back, and that was it. I had to pee so I left, then just decided to go to my room and watch *Shark Tank*. I basically didn't think about it again until I saw Bob's name in the news. Even then, I wasn't sure it was the same guy. The pictures in the news—I mean, he isn't my type. This sounds mean, but I doubt he's *anybody's* type."

Exit Deirdre Benji from this story. Not her influence, though. In Nutting's mind, the food-service sales associate from Buffalo ballooned in significance. The awkward fact to insert here is that Bob Nutting is an unattractive guy. He has that Paul Giamatti thing going on: pear shape, recessed chin, hyperthyroid eyes, clownish grin, helium voice. His romantic experience began and ended with Lisa.

If you know people who wed their teenage sweethearts, you know the chaos that can sprout from the slightest extramarital attention. What Deirdre Benji unearthed in Bob Nutting was the wistful ache of wild oats left unsowed. He wrestled for weeks with operatic emotions. One night, Nutting sent the girls to their rooms and confessed to Lisa the whole torrid, tempestuous, thirty-second affair, concluding with the dramatic declaration that they should have an open marriage. Bob Nutting, he said, had never gotten to know Bob Nutting.

It was a declaration he'd regret. Lisa didn't cry. She only shuddered, as if shedding a skin. After a single-day confab with her sister in Columbus Junction (population 1,855), a flinty Lisa returned home to take her husband up on his offer. Right away, Nutting sensed his blunder. The realities of looking for sex as a short, balding 44-year-old Burger City manager were harsh. Even on a dating app profile, there was no good way to spin it.

Instead, it was Lisa Nutting who got to know Lisa Nutting. With a confidence that rattled her husband, Lisa began dating once or twice a week. Nutting was forced to shake hands with a parade of younger, prettier men (and occasionally women) before they and his wife headed out to do God knows what. Most days, Nutting went to work sick. He couldn't eat. He puked bile in the men's room. If some got on the tile, who cared? He'd get Dez to clean it.

"Cuckolded is what they call it. And I couldn't do a goddamn thing. The whole arrangement had been my idea!"

Bob Nutting offers to drive me from Hawkeye Hank's Pre-Approved Used Auto to Jonny so I can get the lay of the land. I ask him if he feels up to revisiting sites haunted in multiple ways. "I give not one shit," he says, with the showy crudeness of a teenager still new to swearing. Maybe after all this time, the uptight Bob Nutting is indeed getting to know Bob Nutting.

It's a ninety-minute trip down Highway 61, tracing the Mississippi, so I agree; it will give us time to talk. Nutting's car isn't one of the shiny Dodge Caravans from Hawkeye Hank's lot; it's not even a puke-colored 2005 Altima. It's a red 1987 Ford Tempo with red seats, red floor pads, and red upholstery faded pink from water damage. We wear face masks and keep the windows down. As Nutting punches it onto Highway 34, the engine adopts the high-pitched whine of a kitchen timer.

Permit me a page for Iowa in general, as surveys indicate a fair portion of you reading this can't find it on a map. For starters, Iowa is not Ohio, nor is it Idaho or Utah. Iowa is a three-hundred by two-hundred-mile rectangle just northeast of the center of the United States. It's flat on the top and bottom and squiggly on the sides, thanks to the Mississippi and Missouri Rivers. At 217,000 people, capital Des Moines (duh-*moyn*) is the largest city. Hardly a metropolis, but growing as young people abscond from rural areas. Mostly, they're leaving Iowa period, where the median income is $40,000 per household[28]—and, while they're at it, leaving the Midwest too.

After decades of agricultural losses and plant closings, Iowa's "brain drain" is a full-blown crisis, the stuttering of the Heartland's heart. Iowans identify themselves with rural living in a deeply emotional way. Two-thirds of the state identifies as Protestant, one in five as Catholic.[29] Yet you can chart the evangelical-liberal wrestling match in Iowa's reputation as the archetypal swing state. From 1964 onward, Iowa has voted for Republican and Democrat presidential candidates seven times each.[30] In election years, there are plenty of silent, stewing dinner tables.

To me, Iowa has always felt that way: silent, stewing. The fire-crackle of crop fields, the idiot hum of highways, the cloud continents sagging over fiery horizons. It wasn't until a cloudy day in 2017, while driving to Iowa for a funeral, that the beauty I'd heard about incessantly growing up

---

28 Reid Wilson, "Eleven Maps That Explain Iowa," *Morning Consult*, January 29, 2016.

29 Ibid.

30 Zachary Crockett, "How Has Your State Voted in the Past 15 Elections?", *Vox*, November 9, 2016.

revealed itself. Blame it on my mindset of death, but I interpreted it this way: the state's raw elegance only emerges under stormy skies.

We get to Jonny in late afternoon. We have to slow to a creep so we don't blow through it in thirty seconds. Jonny is located in the township of Sugar Creek, a minor civil division of Cedar County. It boomed in 1882 when the Rock Island Company built railroad tracks there to harvest dolomite lime from the bluffs. In the post–Civil War rebound, Jonny-Co. Lime built thirty-five-foot kilns capable of producing one hundred and fifty barrels of lime daily from rock quarried by European migrants. Keeping kilns white-hot day and night required staggering amounts of wood, and the lush landscape was razed. Five years after the millennium's turn, cement won out over lime-based mortar, and Jonny-Co. shuttered. To this day, the area feels as if in cancer recovery, its returning foliage sparse and sickly.

Through these ugly barrens runs Jonny. A single paved two-lane, Rolf Tonks Road, leads north off Exit 269 for one mile. Rolf Tonks is like the straight part of a dollar sign, crossed twice in an S-shape by the logically named 1st Street. (There is no 2nd Street.) There is a clump of seedy homes and exactly four places of business. Heading north, the first is Big M Auto Repair, a hill of rust with two smaller hills of rust in the shape of fuel pumps. Second is Empire Tattoo; don't go there. A bar called Pros is third. Finally comes a shack shedding blue paint called Jaime's Peaches. I don't know what to say about Jaime's Peaches.

It should be noted none of these places look open for business.

Jonny, Iowa, today (photo by the author).

"Last I heard," Nutting says, "all thirty-some people in Jonny were under the poverty line. Probably goes for everyone in a twenty-mile radius. Drugs, I guess. But that's only half the story. I bet your grandparents were farmers, same as mine. The CSR [Corn Suitability Rating] in these parts is still, what? Seventy-five? Eighty? Doesn't matter. Mega-farms own us jowl to loin. So what do you do if the bank's foreclosing on you and your kid needs her tonsils out, and you've got all this anhydrous ammonia fertilizer sitting around, which meth cooks will pay out the wazoo for? I'm asking. What do you do?"

The Tempo shudders through a five-point turn in the middle of Rolf Tonks Road, just in front of dinky Jane Galveston Park, where Scotty Flossen claimed he'd found Ash Muckells's Drive 8 switchblade. It is a good time to confirm what Nutting said in the Starz documentary. He still believes in the Burger City Poltergeist?

"Oh, yeah. Big-time I do. Don't bog me down in details if it was a poltergeist, or a ghost, or whatever Quin used to talk about. But if you tell me there wasn't *something* there, I'll laugh in your face." He does laugh, an angry snort. "At BCU, they taught us every little thing Burger City managers needed to excel in the QSR [Quick Service Restaurant] space. Employee accident forms, trade secrets, harassment policies...."

Nutting tucks away a top lip furred with the orange goatee he was never allowed to grow at Burger City. His eyes are wet.

"But nowhere in all the seminars and handbooks did they say a single thing about what to do if your Lil' Beefy standee starts moving by itself. Or if the situation in your walk-in freezer gets weird. Or if things escalate beyond your control until six people end up dead—in your *restaurant*, where you poured in all your blood, sweat, and tears for eleven years."

Passing Empire Tattoo, Nutting strikes the steering wheel with the flat of his hand.

"Why isn't there any sympathy, for crying out loud? Why doesn't anyone feel bad for Bob Nutting?"

The Tempo's plastic parts vibrate so hard I can feel it in my teeth. As mentioned, the trees in the Jonny area are sparse, so it's not long before I see the charred lot where Burger City #8 used to shine its yam-orange and royal-blue sign over an interstate of hungry hurriers.

By noon on September 4, 2016, Ash Muckells's body was on ice at Iowa City's Mercy Hospital, having been pronounced dead at 9:49 a.m. Scotty Flossen was seventeen blocks away at the Johnson County Jail, where he'd been processed, fingerprinted, photographed, and jailed, and none too gently from the look of the bruises displayed at his bail hearing.

Back at Exit 269, Burger City was a cop convention. For the first couple hours, Bob Nutting did himself proud. After following along to employee accounts, he'd picked up the sequence of events well enough to take over storytelling duties. He might have trumped up his heroism a bit, but who could blame him? He'd given Weltch and Bank access to the security system, which would exonerate him and his staff of wrongdoing. Nutting thought he might even come out of this smelling like a rose.

The performance was pure adrenaline. After being asked to take a seat in the Grand Room, he wedged himself into B9, the Geezers' booth, where the gravity of the mess hit him like a slushy Iowa snowball. This was a *murder*. In *his* Burger City.

He felt locked inside. Not just inside the building, but his career, his life. The endless phone calls he was sure to receive from Burger City brass pressed in on him. A visit from Regional Manager Beauregard Waterhouse seemed unavoidable. Every detail of Nutting's operation would be scrutinized. The cleanliness. The complaint file. Worst of all, the sales books. The numbers were bad.

He pulled out his cell phone. Thirty-one missed calls, twenty voice messages, forty-five texts, and one alert that it was his turn in Words with Friends. He thumbed past the notifications, opened his favorites, and pressed the name *Lisä*. (He never understood how that umlaut got there.)

His wife picked up on the third ring. "Bob?" she yawned. He knew where she was, roughly. Last night she'd told him she probably wouldn't be home. Nutting wanted to be furious. He wanted to peel the skin off her face with the force of his screams. While she was being fucked in interesting positions and enjoying post-coital coffee that made BC Deluxe Select Brew taste like liquid shit, he was trapped in his so-called restaurant by an ocean of blood.

Still, his wife's voice felt like home.

"Lisa, it's awful," he cried, hot tears sliding between the fingers he'd planted over his face. "Come home, please. Please, please come home."

Detective Craig Cookson,[31] handling crime-scene photography that day, snapped a picture of Bob Nutting on the phone to his wife. Nutting is sitting

31 Like all other Cedar County Sheriff's Office employees (possibly under direction from, and including, Sheriff Weltch, and with the exception of Detective C.L. Bank), Cookson declined to be interviewed for this book.

sideways against the booth's wall, knees to his chest, an arm coiled around his shins. Details give it poignance. The abstract, pastel "art" over the trash bin. The Burger City polo stretched tight over Nutting's gut. The cell-block white of the overheads giving the image the look of a William Eggleston.

I show Nutting the photo on my phone. He's busy picking up litter left at the Burger City ruins and dropping in into a plastic Hy-Vee grocery bag: beer cans, McDonald's cups, a condom wrapper. He's never seen this picture before. This surprises me until I put myself in his place. Would I scour the internet to relive my worst traumas?

"Just four years ago," he says. "Look at all the weight."

I ask him what he was thinking when the photo was taken.

"That's easy. I was thinking, 'I'm about to be fired from the only job I'll ever be qualified for. I'll be on the street. My wife will never come back. My girls will never go to college. I'm going to end up like that speed freak who just got stabbed in the neck.' I mean, I was having those thoughts before, but it's easy to push them away in the daily grind, you know?"

It's the first I've heard that Bob Nutting had been considering leaving Burger City prior to the September 4 murder. Nutting corrects me. He hadn't been planning to quit. It was Burger City Inc. that was considering closing #8.

"My understanding is independent QSRs can still make a go of it in towns. But exit-ramp franchises? They're ghost towns. If you're from anywhere else, you don't know what a Burger City is. You wait for a Wendy's or a Subway. You *piss* at a Burger City. Maybe."

Nutting hands my phone back and looks down. The gravelly dirt beneath his loafers is all that's left of the office inside which he'd spent forty hours a week for eleven years. The terrain here is uneven; even bulldozers couldn't fully erase what he'd done behind his locked door. He scuffs his shoe over the ash.

"This place was going to end up like this one way or the other."

He heaves a big sigh. Talk about ghosts: I swear I smell the tangy, smoky aroma of a Beefyburger. Nutting takes a long, loud sniff. He frowns and nods at his '87 Tempo.

"Let's get while there's daylight. Some of the old staff still live close. Seeing their homes, the *state* of their homes, ought to be educational. Just don't ask me to stop the car. None of them want to see me. Honestly, that's what I worry about most. Not what people think of me. Not how I keep losing weight for no reason. It's running into Amber Smyrna at the hardware store, Dion Skerry at the State Fair, that kind of thing. It petrifies me. Pe-tri-fies."

JODIDO

Kit Bryant's frantic phone call of October 2, 2016, made no sense to Bob Nutting. Something about Lil' Beefy being moved? Nutting failed to see why the repositioning of a cardboard standee—or even its outright theft, if that's what Kit was saying—necessitated interrupting his Sunday-night viewing of *NCIS: Los Angeles*.

But Nutting felt obligated to get dressed and check it out. Kit was what BCU trainers identified as a "Core Worker," the kind who might mature into a lifelong stalwart a la Cheri Orritt. The Manager's Handbook spent two pages on how to stimulate Core Workers ("Allow them to make their own mistakes, and when they fail, embolden them to learn from those failures").[32] It was a tricky balance in the QSR biz. Your worst employees got fired, your brightest employees quit. That left the middle: the dispirited, the apathetic, the trapped.

Nutting got into his car (back then, a blue 2014 Honda Civic), and made the twenty-minute trek from his and Lisa's duplex in Bennett, Iowa (population 405). Entering around 9:00 p.m., his gut take was, yes, Kit was high. The 19-year-old was tap-dancing with enthusiasm. Nutting glanced up at Cameras 2 and 3, a habit since the stabbing, and suddenly Kit was dragging him over to Lil' Beefy, who was right where she was supposed to be. Kit presented the faded old standee with a flourish.

"It's hopping," Kit said with a big grin.

Nutting surveyed the empty restaurant. "You mean busy?"

Kit laughed and pogo-sticked. "Hopping! Up and down!"

Nutting glanced at Amy Mold and Tamra Longmoor, who stood behind the counter looking embarrassed. Nutting exhaled, fixed his hands on his hips, and stared Kit in the face.

"Look at me," Nutting ordered.

"I am!" Kit laughed. "But you should be looking at Lil' Beefy!"

Nutting jabbed two fingers at his own eyes. "Right here. Let me see 'em."

"You need to get on the floor with me. I know that sounds weird."

"Page twelve," Nutting said.

32 *Burger City Manager's Handbook*, 2014, 11.

"Come on, man. Just get on the floor. There's some dust you gotta see."

Kit sounded crazier by the second. Nutting repeated it: "Page twelve."

Pages twelve through fourteen of the Burger City Team Member Handbook detailed the company's draconian drug policy, which asserted not only the right to perform pre-employment testing, but on-demand testing as well, based on the "reasonable suspicions" of "unsteady gait, slurred speech, volatile moods, excessive absenteeism, or violent temper."[33]

Volatile mood was the relevant descriptor here. Kit inhaled through his nose like only God's grace prevented him from going apeshit on this dumbass. He bugged his eyes so Nutting could get a nice, long look. No redness, no dilation, no skittering. Nutting shrugged to admit Kit looked okay.

"Now, don't shoot, officer," Kit snapped. "I'm going to take my phone out of my pocket, verrrrrry slooooowly."

"Why isn't that phone in the Break Room Bucket?"

Kit patted the air, begging for mercy. He got down on his knees, slid his phone from his pants, and tapped on the flashlight. Nutting leaned and squinted. Maybe he'd heard Kit wrong and there'd been a mouse hopping around back here. Mice were serious business, though Kit ought to know that, when it came to pests, you called Dez Mozley, whose janitorial cart housed all varieties of lethal poisons.

Kit ran through the whole thing. The six-minute disturbance took longer than six minutes to describe. Nutting asked for corroboration. Shrugging apologetically to Kit, Amy Mold confessed she hadn't technically seen it. Tamra shook her head, refusing to get involved. Zane Shakespeare meandered to the FOH in his apron, holding a guide to red wines, and smiled his enigmatic smile.

"Is this about the Crime?" Nutting asked. The Crime, capital-C, his euphemism for the Ash Muckells murder.

"No!" Kit cried.

"Because that's blood along the bottom of Lil' Beefy, is it not?"

"Yes! Probably!"

"Do you know how much a brand-new Lil' Beefy costs?"

"I don't care. I super-duper don't care."

"It costs one hundred and-sixty dollars. Out of my personal wallet."

"I'm not asking you to throw away Lil' Beefy! I don't *want* you to throw away Lil' Beefy! Can you get it through your head I'm talking about an unexplainable event here?"

---

33 Ibid., 18.

Nutting pinched the bridge of his nose. Headlights illuminated the southern windows; Amy switched on her headset and began walking and talking. Tamra parked herself before the order screen. Zane folded a page corner of his wine book and headed back to the grill. This left Kit and his pout.

"What do you want me to do?" Nutting asked. "Call Peter Vinkman?"

"*Vinkman?* Is that a Ghostbusters joke?"

"It's late. Tell me what you want."

Kit clasped hands in prayer formation. "The security cameras. That's all I ask."

Nutting was appalled. Kit should have expected it. Since the Crime, anything regarding the cameras had been touchy territory. The September 4 security footage had been combed over by BC Corporate, including that of Camera 1, which showed the safe in Nutting's office. His overall fitness as a leader was being judged.

"Just 4:24 to 4:30," Kit pleaded. "Six minutes."

"Official use only."

Kit sprung to his feet. "Six stupid minutes!"

"Over my dead body, Bryant."

"Six stupid fucking minutes!"

Nutting grimaced through the painful procedure of extracting his big, pointy key ring from his too-tight pants pocket. "Good night, Bryant. Tamra, Amy, Zane—180 percent, folks."

Proving he did, in fact, have a speck of good judgment, Kit waited for the exit door to settle shut before exploding.

"Six stupid fucking shit bitch minutes!"

The inside of Kit Bryant's head was fertile ground for ideas. The same held true for anxieties. Nutting, Tamra, and Amy thought Kit was off his nut, and for most of Kit's life, he'd believed it possible. No one had ever come up with a better reason why he'd been such a crappy student. No one could reconcile his agile imagination with his listless acceptance of the shittiest of shit jobs. Maybe he was simply, as Javi always joked, jodido—fucked up.

The next day, Monday, October 3, Kit wasn't scheduled to work, but traded shifts with Zane so he'd be operating the fryer at 4:24 p.m., replicating the conditions of the day before. The time came. Kit held his breath. Lil' Beefy didn't move. Kit made a sound like a sob, and was horrified by it. Only lunatics made sounds like that. He drank a sixer of Busch Light that night. The enterprise repeated itself on Tuesday: he traded his night shift for Cheri's day shift only to angrily slam his drawer at 4:30. Nothing. That night, two sixers.

He might have called in as "barfy" on Wednesday, his code for a hangover, but he was scheduled to be on the counter all afternoon with a good view of Lil' Beefy, so what the hell—he'd give it one last shot. He booted Assistant Manager Dion Skerry off Till 2 (Dion was Kit's boss that day, but a doormat) and spent the long day washing down ibuprofen with the hangover cure he called "the Necromancer"—half Coke, half Mountain Dew, a shot of pink lemonade.

By 3:00, he was making multiple runs to the men's room. It wasn't the Necromancers. It was worry over what would happen at 4:24. For three days, the staff had been giving him shit. Javi had tiptoed into the break room with his apron draped over his head like an old-timey ghost. Mickey had stood behind Lil' Beefy and thrust his hips, saying the bitch was only getting freaky with her ghost-dog boyfriend.

The sharpest blow came from Quin Arthur. This was typical. Both boys were people-pleasers in their own ways, and as such, did adequate jobs pretending to like each other. Privately, they did not. Kit saw Quin as a showoff, though some of that was jealousy. Quin didn't smoke, didn't drink, didn't procrastinate, didn't fail—like Amy Mold, his future success was guaranteed. What exasperated Kit most was Quin's infatuation with Amber Smyrna. During none of Kit and Amber's half-dozen romantic breaks had Quin grown the balls to make a move, which only lowered him in Kit's estimation.

Mostly, Kit didn't dwell on it. As we now know, Quin did.

Quin often bragged of his movie collection, so Kit didn't suspect trickery when Quin drew him aside in the break room and somberly told him he had a DVD that might help him. Quin handed over a copy of an old Bill Cosby comedy called *Ghost Dad*. Kit laughed but felt the pinpricks of tears at the corner of his eyes. They didn't know how close to the edge he was.

At 4:15, Kit washed his hands from his final restroom trip and retook his place at Till 2. All he could think of was how many times his coworkers had seen him stumble. The two or three occasions he'd publicly sworn to get better grades. The times he'd tried to take up jogging or weightlifting. His business plans—oh, the grandiose follies of his business plans. His monitoring of Lil' Beefy was a metaphor for every one of his wasted dreams.

Then, at 4:24, right on schedule, Lil' Beefy hopped.

Kit's gestures are outsized for his Chernow bunk. I worry he's going to crack a fingernail against a wall. A collector of bad habits, he was a smoker before the Burger City Tragedy, but now his nails look like those of a 40-year addict—long, thick, jagged, and yellow.

"Probably the most exciting six minutes of my life is how I'd put it! The customers all standing there? Poof! Darcy at the drive-thru? Poof! All the restaurant noise too, just poof, poof, poof, until it was just me and Lil' Beefy, all alone."

Customers were probably upset he'd left his station; Kit doesn't recall. He breaks into delighted laughter and describes Lil' Beefy's second through fifth jumps happening right under his nose. Every hair on his body stood on end, a million straightpins, as if the cardboard standee radiated electricity.

"Being that close to it, it's like a whole other universe opens up. Like a door—it just opens up. What's on the other side? Magic? Proof of the afterlife? Man, I don't know. The point is there's an *other side*. The stupid world you thought you know, it doubles. Or who knows? Triples, quadruples! And all cuz some dumb cardboard dog moves a few inches!"

There's a knock on the door. Kit turns, I turn; even Nuncio looks up. It's a woman in blue scrubs rolling a cart. She brings over two paper cups, one holding meds, the other water. Kit is unfazed. He jerks his chin at her as if to say *hey*, takes both cups, and keeps going.

"When it was over for a bit, 4:31, 4:32, I stayed on the floor, man, just collecting my shit. After everyone making fun of me, I knew I had to play it smart. If I asked Nutting to check the cams again, he'd fire my ass for real. So I was like, all right, Kit. Go slow. Do the Scientific Method. Like, okay, I've observed it, I've got a hypothesis. Now I need independent confirmation."

He pops the pills into his mouth, sips the water, and sets the half-full cup atop *Rotters*, which he's returned to his desk. I scan the other books in the vicinity, some unjacketed. Judging by color, dimension, and thickness, they are my other novels.

"What?" Kit asks.

I tell him it's nothing; let's continue. But his jolly eyes taper and darken.

"You think I'm lying?"

I assure him I don't.

"But I've—I've read your *books*."

He looks crestfallen. Unexpectedly, my heart goes out to him. No matter what he did on June 1, 2017, he did it when he was twenty. Now he's trapped here, and if he ever gets out, the trap will only tighten. My novels, I gather, have offered solace, and it feels cruel for the author to snatch that away. So I backpedal. I tell him I'm still figuring out if I believe. I say that's what my books are: attempts to figure things out.

Kit nods. I can tell *he* wants to believe that *I* want to believe.

"Maybe you don't think I'm being serious enough. Yeah, okay. I can see that. People died and whatnot. It's just, when I get talking about this stuff…it wasn't all bad, you know? For a while, the poltergeist—I mean, it was the best thing that ever happened to me. That ever happened to pretty much all of us. There was one article I read that said I was naïve. Well, yeah. Try spending your whole life in Jonny and not end up naïve. I was *excited*, man. I was just excited the poltergeist *was*."

A blue mood pours across the green room. I take the moment to measure the effects of Kit's weight gain. The three-inch scar on his forearm has paled as it has stretched.

"I'll tell you this," he says at last. "I wasn't so naïve I thought anyone would take my word. I needed a partner. Not an adult, no way. But also not a high-schooler who had lots of after-school shit, because school didn't let out till 3:30, and Lil' Beefy had her 4:24 thing locked tight. So I didn't really have a choice. It had to be Clem."

HOLY SHIT

Clemens Dumay clomped into Burger City on Friday, October 7, 2016, at 4:21 p.m. in his usual ensemble of black sunglasses, black T-shirt, black duster, and black army boots. It was just three minutes till the Lil' Beefy Show, and Kit conveyed his displeasure at Clem's tardiness by noisily dunking the fryer basket into the oil pan. Comic-book fanatic Clemens, who dressed like the Punisher but acted more like Deadpool, responded by wiggling his fingers at Kit as he might an infant. Kit sternly nodded at Lil' Beefy. Clem gave a thumbs-up from his fingerless black gloves, glanced around like a saboteur, and ambled in that direction, whistling innocently for effect.

In truth, Clem was right on time. The restaurant interior was a minefield. It was Burger City's busiest shift; Fridays after school attracted high-schoolers with cars, the ones Bob Nutting called "horseplayers." Nutting always chose the shift as part of his weekly forty, and at 4:21 was prowling the grounds like a headwaiter.

Nothing set off Nutting like employees showing up early, trying to steal a precious extra $7.25/hour. So why was Clem risking his skin? Because Kit asked him to. That was Clemens Dumay for you. His self-worth relied on being the one who'd do what your typical scaredy-cat wouldn't dare.

Typical scaredy-cat isn't a bad description of Quindlen Arthur. He, too, entered at 4:21, but instead of charging into the scrum along Clem, he slunk behind the condiment counter and its drapery of plastic ferns. He carried his Panasonic HC-V770 HD camcorder. You didn't see a lot of camcorders in 2016, but Quin, an accomplished video creator, scoffed at the one-size-fits-all qualities of phone cameras. The HC-V770, which retailed at $550, featured a tripod receptacle, 1/8-inch mic input jack, and manual exposure control, all of which would be useful in the upcoming Game of Pricks.

On October 7, the HC-V770's most relevant feature was its 20x optical zoom. Quin smoothly traced Clem's ducking, juking progress across the lobby. Anyone who has spent time behind a lens can tell you how hard it is to move and keep a steady picture at full zoom, but Quin knew how to use his body as counterweight and arm as gimbal. Very few of the 51,952 comments under Quin's YouTube video, titled "Burger City Ghost?", mention his technical prowess, but it's the unsung reason for the video's popularity (85,743,068 views as of this writing).

Clem's goal was to tape the Lil' Beefy Anomaly.

Quin's goal, however, was to tape Clem. If Clem got chewed out on the spot, or even fired, well, that would royally suck, but at least the friends could watch it on repeat until their gasping laughter leeched it of all anguish.

At 4:22, Clem slipped his shattered iPhone 5c from his overcoat, a surprisingly slick move. He was the kind of proudly clumsy kid who knocked people off their feet with hugs and entered swimming pools exclusively via cannonball. At 4:23, Clem nudged through the Till 2 queue until he was kissing distance from Lil' Beefy.

Clientele paid little attention. But Burger City personnel was rapt. Tamra, Dion, Javi, and Yesenia all understood what was happening. Even Darcy, who was in no state to follow plotlines (more on that later), grasped the stakes. For Clem: discipline, humiliation, his job. For Kit: the same job, but also redemption, restitution, and dignity.

Clem kneeled down, camera running, just as Nutting emerged from the restroom hall. All nine staffers turned to look. Nutting saw Clem and charged. Clem saw Nutting and winced. Kit called out to the boss, a last-second stab at distraction. Quin did the only thing he could do: zoom in on Bob Nutting's purpling face.

"Was I going to fire Clem?" Nutting repeats my question over the rattle of his Tempo. "You bet your butt I was. You're a boss, and your workers aren't giving you 180? You know what you got to do."

Clemens Dumay was born on May 22, 1998, making him 19 in October 2016, old for a high-school senior. The unfortunate reason goes back to February 13, 2010, when his father, Jerrod Dumay, was killed in a car crash on icy Highway 30 east of Cedar Rapids. The academic toll forced Clem to repeat eighth grade. His mother, Greta Dumay, wasn't cut out to take care of a fractious 14-year-old. A contract painter and handywoman by trade, she was, according to friends, a late-blooming lesbian with a major flaw: open regret at having had a kid.

After Jerrod's death, Greta became besotted with impromptu road trips, which often left Clem on his own for two or three weeks at a time. To make things worse, Jerrod had a long-standing arrangement with his sister, Cleo, to watch her mentally handicapped 21-year-old son, Lysander, on nights Cleo had to work. This task, too, now fell to Clem.

He did what he had to do. The day he turned 15, he got a job at Burger City, and put the money toward keeping his purple 2007 Toyota Corolla in working order, so he could travel between school, home in Ayresville (population uncounted), and the Walmart in Tipton to stock up on microwave meals for him and Lysander. If Lysander didn't get his Swanson Hungry-Man Salisbury Steak, he flew into destructive tantrums, one time ripping the door off the refrigerator. Clem kept the burden of Lysander to himself. Thus, it went unappreciated by teachers who attributed Clem's failures to laziness. They thought he was a clown.

To a degree, he was. Perusing the endpages of Clem's 2015–2016 RCHS yearbook shows he was renowned for it. Celebrity voices, teacher impersonations, reckless pratfalls—he did it all. Everyone at Burger City liked Clem, something you might be able to say about Cheri Orritt, but no one else.

Clem's best friend was Quin Arthur. Not even Kit and Amber's relationship compared to their bond—"a friendship so strong it was able to strangle."[34] Clem was the only reason Quin worked there. Quin didn't need to. His father, the splendidly named Garth Arthur, was a successful insurance man working out of Wilton, six miles south, while Quin's mother, Winnie, worked as head librarian at the Wilton Public Library. Quin Arthur was upper-middle-class, which probably made him the richest kid near Jonny. You didn't buy a Panasonic HC-V770 on a Burger City pittance.

Clem was short and stocky; Quin was tall and thin. Clem was explosive, garrulous, and like many jesters, depressive; Quin was dry, sarcastic, and quick to frustrate. Clem was easy to love, too easy to pity; Quin was easy to like, nearly impossible to know. Clem loved having a straight man, and Quin loved being one—it gave him the chance to play the intense intellectual, which is more or less what he was.

Most of their time together was spent in Quin's 2014 Ford Fusion "cruising," which, in Midwestern parlance, is the act of driving around town making periodic slow-downs at popular parking spots, where you

34 Rene Thurgood, "Meat Cute: Who Loved, Who Hated, and Who Killed in the Burger City Massacre," *Vice*, December 2, 2017.

can ask if anything good is going on. Usually it isn't, but often a beer or joint will pass from car to car. It's hard to describe what a bonding experience cruising can be. Night after night, the mileage rivals that of a year-long trek across Europe.

Clem and Quin gabbed about everything while cruising, with one exception. They avoided the topic of their post-graduation lives. It was too tender a topic. Quin was bound for NYU or USC. Clem was bound for more shifts at Burger City.

Survivors agree about few things these days, but they concur the Clem-Quin friendship was legendary. Amber Smyrna put it best: "They brought out the best in each other. Quin without Clem could be pretty harsh. And Clem without Quin? He just—you know, Quin had all the ideas. Without Quin, Clem just sort of sat there. He'd just sit there and rot."

Amber is dead-on. On October 29, 2020, I find Clemens Dumay rotting. No survivor has heard from him for two years, and no one I interview is harder to track down. It is his mother, the peripatetic Greta Dumay, who gives up the secret without a fight. I hate her a little for that.

Clem has strayed farther than any other Burger City employee, which still isn't far. I find him working the graveyard shift at Biff's Gas & Diesel & Store south of Exit 33, off of the very same Interstate 80. Except he's sixty-seven miles east, living in Hooppole, Illinois (population 204). It's the state line that has concealed him; the Burger City #8 that lives in the minds of the survivors cannot extend beyond Iowa borders.

He works in Annawan (population 878), a ten-minute drive straight south. Located a fatal 0.8 miles farther from I-80 than the Shell station, Biff's shows every sign of being dead and not knowing it. The restroom around back is spray-painted *KEEP OUT*. The pop tunes grinding from pump speakers have a slow-mo Black Lodge quality. The service bay light is too bright against a too-dark night; this cube of reality has been carved out of the normal world and offset in a separate dimension.

It's spooky. Clem, if I'm being honest, is spooky too. His curly black hair has expanded into a bramble undelineated from his knotty, chest-long beard, which piles around all sides of his face mask. It's a fuck-ton of hair, perfect for camouflage, yet it still fails to hide the gravity of weight loss—the 23-year-old's tree-trunk body has been whittled to a stick. His jewel eyes have extinguished. His cheeks are withered like dried apples.

He's reading a comic book. At least that hasn't changed. He meets my introduction with the grim nod of one receiving long-awaited bad news. He stands there as I deliver the talk I rehearsed on the drive over, the crux of which is that I've spoken to every living survivor except him. By the time I'm done, Clem looks defeated, as if we've reached the end of a decade-long legal battle instead of a two-minute pitch.

He lifts his left arm to take a tin of Kodiak Wintergreen off the rack. This betrays the limited shoulder motion he still suffers from his Burger City Tragedy injury.

"Chairs outside," he murmurs.

The chairs are plastic, half-busted, dappled with bird shit. Clem tells me a shipment is arriving around 2:00. He's going to get busy around 2:00. Do I understand? He pulls his hood over his head and his sleeves to his wrists, but not before I see them, further evidence of the tragedy.

I admit, they *do* look a little like bite-marks.

He slumps into himself, a furry bag of bones, and peers past the pumps to the streaking lights of the interstate. I listen to moths suicide against the awning and Clem packing his chaw. He slips off his mask and tucks a wad under his lower lip.

Clemens Dumay on October 29, 2020 (photo by the author).

"Is it back?" he asks.

My disquiet breaks into outright chills. No one else has suggested that the Burger City Poltergeist could reemerge. I try to picture it manifesting at another regional chain. The Maid-Rite Poltergeist? The Menards Poltergeist? The Happy Joe's Pizza & Ice Cream Parlor Poltergeist? If that's what Clem thinks, no wonder he's isolated himself in the kingdom of forgotten gas stations.

I tell him no, it hasn't returned. Clem spits tobacco juice into an old Snapple bottle. The spit looks bloody. I glimpse his mouth. His gums are brown. Three teeth on his right lower jaw, all in a row, are gone.

I start my recorder at 10:05 and we talk for almost four hours, during which two cars gas up but pay at the pump, leaving us undisturbed. In my opinion, Clem has a model case of survivor's guilt. His account is full of self-hating *I could've* and *I should've* prefaces. Yet talking about the tragedy seems to do him good. He crosses his legs and wags a boot. His voice surpasses a monotone. If he's concerned about the Burger City Poltergeist coming back, I ask, why doesn't he keep traveling? I-80 goes all the way to New York.

"Keep thinking I will." *Keef finking I whoa,* behind the dip. "But I wouldn't trust my ride to Indiana. Plus moving's expensive. I make $8.25 an hour. Not going to get my deposit back either cuz there's smoke damage all over the ceiling." (He won't elaborate.) "Plus who says I'm hiding? Maybe I'm waiting. Waiting for it come back and try and fuck with one of us again."

This also fits in to what I know about survivor's guilt, the compulsion to do anything that might bring him closer to the dead. Clemens Dumay may not be cutting himself or burning holes in his skin. But consider the loss of weight. The loss of teeth. The cancer that might be festering in his mouth, the mind-fuck of a graveyard shift, the suffocating solitude—especially for a guy who once thrived on attention. Even Clem's retirement of his all-black ensemble feels like surrender. He wears blue jeans and a faded Fighting Illini hoodie. He hates sports.

"None of us did any of the stuff they do in movies," he says. "I mean, Tamra put up those crosses, but there wasn't any priest, any holy water. Nine months of what we went through and no one held a single séance?" He's half-joking, an ounce of his old humor squeezing out like pus. "We could've tried. We should've at least given it a shot."

Could've, should've. What I took for a grin is a grimace. His spit now looks like pure blood. I ask him if he misses any of his old crew.

"Shit. I've known you for two seconds and I'll miss *you* when you're gone. All I *do* is miss people."

I ask about Quin specifically. He fidgets.

"Try not to think of him, mostly. Sometimes a guy will walk in here and I'll think it's Q, and for a second, I'll feel—not happy, really, but, like, relieved. Like I can joke again. Like *we* can joke again. We'll go out cruising. Make stupid videos. And if he says, hey, let's start taping the weird shit at work, I'll be like, 'Let's not.' But thoughts like that, what good do they do? What good does your *book* do? It's like trying to figure out the meaning of a school shooting. What is there to say? 'I'm glad it wasn't my kid.' 'I'm glad it wasn't me.' Well, it *was* me. We *were* kids. The meaning I take from it is I'm going to be there if it happens again. There's a shotgun behind that counter. At home I've got a revolver, an ax, knives. I'm ready. I mean, I'm not ready. But I'm willing."

Willingness has always been a large part of Clemens's appeal. Willing to try Mickey McCormick's improvised cocktail of Jägermeister and mayonnaise. Willing to dash naked (plus a luchador mask) behind the Graduating Class of 2014. Willing to risk public firing by Bob Nutting by hunkering down beside the Till 2 queue and taking cell-phone video of Lil' Beefy.

Clem's October 7, 2016, footage hasn't survived. But Quin's sure has. At the exact second Air Supply's "Making Love Out of Nothing at All" strikes its Soft Rock 95.6 crescendo, you see Lil' Beefy hop. *Hop* probably isn't the best word. The cardboard standee jumps three inches off the ground.

Clem jerks backward. Of course he does. Something inches from his face just leapt like a rat. Nutting recoils, not because he sees the jump (he doesn't), but because Clem backs into his shins. Who does see it, though, is Quin. "Holy shit," he says, in a voice of such incredulous, even hilarious, surprise that hundreds of YouTube comments simply parrot those words. Eventually the words will grace countless Burger City Poltergeist memes, some of them supernatural in nature, most of them just GIFs of Bob Nutting or Dion Skerry looking vapid above the words, in Impact font, *HOLY SHIT.*

Quin jockeys closer, braver now, establishing a closer shot in time for Lil' Beefy's second jump. By then, Clem is on the ground, Lil' Beefy between his feet. The queue ripples back. Nutting begins apologizing (in Quin's footage, you hear him offer certificates for free Chillees), but he is ignored, as customers angle past him to lay eyes on what must be a rodent.

Lil' Beefy's third jump is four inches, nearly enough to tip it over. That's when Nutting starts to pay attention. The fourth and fifth jumps are smaller, but on the upside, now everyone is watching. When it concludes at 4:30, Quin rushes from cover like the host of a hidden-camera show, waving his HC-V770 above his head. All staff (Kit, Darcy, Dion, Tamra, Javi, and Yesenia) abandon their stations in the sort of wholesale desertion only seen amid natural disasters. They gather around the camera. For Quin, it must be the Sundance Film Festival reception he dreams of.

Quin's footage ends there, but witnesses confirm the next few minutes. Quin rewinds the video and plays it for all to see. Burger City personnel huddle close. In his glee, Quin lets go of his Amber-related resentment and makes space for Kit. Even Nutting stands on his toes to get a peek. For half a minute, there is silence.

Then everyone gasps. Quin grins. Kit doesn't breathe.

Finally, squeals. Tamra cries out. Javi hoots. Darcy claps her hands over her face. Suddenly the whole crowd is hopping like Lil' Beefy and embracing Kit as if he's sunk a half-court basket for a million bucks. They clap his back, grab his shoulders. Clem knocks off Kit's Burger City cap so he can ruffle his hair. Kit keeps staring at the screen, eyes tearful with gratitude—that Clem and Quin pulled it off, and that everyone, including Nutting, has seen the irrefutable proof, both of Lil' Beefy's new habits and Kit Bryant's sanity.

From roughly 4:33 to 4:38 on Friday, October 7, 2016, as cars honk from the drive-thru lane and customers continue to enter, the staff (minus Nutting, inert with shock) gambol, holler, and hug without fully understanding why. Today the why is clearer. The workers of Burger City #8 sensed they'd found that illusive thing for which they'd always longed. The force moving Lil' Beefy across the tile was the thing that would move *them* too, all of them, in exciting new directions.

They could not have been more wrong.

NOVEMBER 2016

WE'RE IN THIS TOGETHER

Even ghosts can't exist in a cultural vacuum.

The backdrop of the poltergeist's arrival was nothing less than the election of Donald J. Trump as President of the United States. Ash Muckells was murdered on September 4, 2016, five weeks after Trump accepted the Republican Party nomination—two surreal events, neither of which boded well. By October 2, 2016, the day of Lil' Beefy's first move, the first debate between Trump and Hillary Clinton was six days in the can, and bettered the odds of a Clinton election night blowout. In the late afternoon of October 7, 2016, at the exact time Clem Dumay and Quin Arthur taped Lil' Beefy's five hops, the world was being introduced to *Access Hollywood*'s "Grab them by the pussy" tape.

Amy Mold should have been obsessed with Lil' Beefy. She'd been present for its October 2 debut and was vulnerable to Kit's charms. But she was also Burger City's most politically active employee. Posts still mineable from deleted social accounts show a 17-year-old deeply invested in Hillary Clinton. A July 22 staff memo from Bob Nutting warned against political propaganda at work, so Amy took her passion elsewhere. Her Burger City hours dipped as she volunteered for everything from door-to-door proselytizing to sliding campaign signs onto wire holders until her fingers bled. (There's a selfie of her looking pretty proud of those fingers.)

The mood at Burger City drastically changed the morning of November 9, the day after Trump's upset victory, which Iowa helped happen. Employees who paid little attention to politics were bewildered by the intense emotions infiltrating their workplace. Regular customers cut usual orders in half, complaining of stomach upset. A half-dozen women were spotted openly weeping. Customers in red baseball caps showcased a strut that made others retreat to their vehicles. To cover the edgy silence, Nutting went into the break room, where the radio was stationed, and cranked the Soft Rock Hitz. What was typically an abstract drone came out diamond-sharp, with Kenny Loggins and Juice Newton mocking 2016's state of affairs from their cool, comfortable 1970s.

The Amy Mold who arrived for her November 9 shift displayed emotions opposite to her usual wry humor and tsking disapproval. Her eyes were swollen, hurt, betrayed. Her nostrils were raw from tissues. One can only imagine the day she'd had at school, the target of proto-racists emboldened to one day grab pussies of their own. Burger City proved itself a family: Quin, no good at touchy-feelies, hugged Amy long enough for his yam-orange collar to darken with tears, while Nutting, a MAGA guy through and through, gently urged her toward the break room so she might pull herself together.

Amy Mold looked at Lil' Beefy differently from that day forward. So did other Burger City staff, and so did many of the regulars. The nation's dust had cleared. The coiling smoke of American turmoil had revealed itself to have been a python all along. Your neighbor was a villain. Your country wanted you exiled. Anything was possible, even the supernatural.

Amber Smyrna was no Amy Mold. She couldn't tell you Senator Clinton's position on bankruptcy reform, or what figure Clinton was pressing for the National Living Wage. All Amber knew was she *didn't* want a reality-show rapist leading the nation. Amber wept that afternoon too, but privately, inside a restroom stall. Amy Mold's superior grasp of what they'd lost shamed her.

Like millions of other women shattered on November 8, Amber had always been fiercely aware of her body, the way most men only are when their flesh is bruised. As a pre-teen, she'd leaned into the qualities that made her well-liked. By middle school, she knew those qualities included a pretty face and did not include scholastic or artistic ability. A January 1, 2011, diary entry, logged when Amber was 12, shows the results of a New Year's audit:

> *If I am honest I am 2 things: pretty (to be honest) & very nice & I think its important to focus on niceness & prettiness in the following year.*[35]

The Amber Smyrna of 2016 resembled actress Myrna Loy, her cheek-to-jaw structure nearly octagonal, adorned with a snub nose and rosebud mouth, with long eyebrows arched over blue-gray eyes. Naturally brunette,

---

35 Amber Smyrna offered me exclusive use of her diaries, which cover 2007 to 2017, but they were of little use for this book. Following the Burger City Tragedy, she incinerated the 2016 and 2017 volumes, and has kept no journals since.

she was enjoying her second year as a blonde. Her shoulder-length hair shagged down like the boughs of a pine. Even her dopey Burger City cap (when she deigned to wear it) couldn't contain it.

All indicators suggest Amber's 2011 New Year's Resolutions succeeded. Yet she had grace enough to know she'd been fortunate. She'd never been sexually assaulted, a significant thing in a state where one in six females have been raped, well above the 1-in-10 national average.[36] Amber had a cheery relationship her sister, Natasha, a senior at Northern Iowa University. Their parents had divorced in 2008, but remained on good terms, with her tax-attorney father, Paul Smyrna, living in Iowa City, where he'd married Erica Cerveaux in 2010. Amber's life with her mother, Darcy, was humble but happy. She was involved in cheerleading and swimming, and she liked books by John Green and Cassandra Clare.

One might guess that activist Amy Mold would be the vegetarian of Burger City, but it was Amber Smyrna. She'd stopped eating meat at age nine. She had no role model in the decision. The idea of meat simply struck her as cruel. In a way, her feelings about it presaged that 2011 diary entry: focusing on niceness was important, whether the object of that niceness was bipedal or quadrupedal. It was not a popular regional choice—99 percent of Iowan families eat meat[37]—but friends and family made allowances. She felt lucky. She *was* lucky.

The lucky streak ended in August 2016, one month before the Ash Muckells murder, when her mother, Darcy, was diagnosed with Grade III Anaplastic astrocytoma brain cancer. The prior eight weeks had been marked by what Darcy had brushed off as "zone-outs": ten- or fifteen-second lapses in attention. On Sunday, July 3, 2016, Amber was awakened by panicked cries from the living room. She barged in to find her mother thrashing about in her underwear, screeching that she couldn't see from her right eye.

X-rays revealed something in the left parietal space. No one said *tumor* yet, but what else could it be? MRIs, CT scans led to both the T-word and C-word. On August 4, University of Iowa Hospital's Dr. Pavel Bigham performed a CT-guided stereotactic biopsy that revealed the shape of the thing: three centimeters, grayish white, "moderately vascular."[38] Darcy had lost all vision in her right eye and could not walk by herself.

36 Kathy A. Bolten, "1 in 6 Iowa Women Say an Intimate Partner Has Raped Them, Survey Says," *Des Moines Register,* January 25, 2019.

37 Dirck Steimel, "Survey: Iowans Love Meat," *Iowa Farm Bureau,* October 27, 2017.

38 Over the phone on May 30, 2017, Dr. Bigham made an offhand comment to me that I haven't been able to shake, describing the tumor as "tarantula-shaped."

Amber tended to bury negative emotions, but she permitted herself to briefly rage against the dying of the light—in the style of John Green or Cassandra Clare, you might say. Cancer was endemic in Smyrna women. Both Amber's grandmother and great-grandmother had died of it. She saved some of her anger for her mother. Hadn't it been selfish of Darcy to give birth to two children—two girls—and pass along those doomed genes?

Amber's grudge became her own tumor. She begged her mother to come clean to Nutting. Days later, Darcy did, standing in the beige box of the manager's office, twisting her hands and holding back tears while her daughter spied from the hallway. It was awkward, with Nutting reciting lines from the Burger City Manager's Handbook. *Take whatever time you need. You need to take care of you.*

Darcy demurred and downplayed like Amber worried she might, allowing Nutting's real concerns to emerge. How much time did Darcy anticipate needing to take off? Had she thought about who might cover her shifts? Had she studied Burger City's Family and Medical Leave Policy?

Amber was her mother's daughter: she walked away, choosing melancholy over rage.

Dr. Bigham and his team performed brain surgery on August 13, removing what they could of cancerous cells. Amber got through it okay, only to lose it the next day when Betadine, a sticky antiseptic, made combing her mom's hair impossible. Darcy was in a fog; she only heard about the Burger City murder days after it happened. Because she'd displayed epileptic tendencies, she was on a dizzying regimen of Eptoin, Eltroxin, Levipil, Lamitor, Eslizen, and Amaryl, plus one Temodol a day leading up to fractionated stereotactic radiotherapy sessions on the Truebeam LINAC machine.

Darcy caught a break. A single month of this treatment did the trick. By the time Lil' Beefy moved on October 2, physical therapy had mostly weaned Darcy from her walker. She returned to Burger City, first one day a week, then two, and always on the drive-thru, where she could sit and use her left eye to full advantage.

Darcy wasn't the same. She dropped condiment packets. On occasion, she wandered from the window for no reason. Sleep remained difficult. Following TV storylines bedeviled her. Her eyesight improved, though she still had to sit along the right wall of movie theaters to see the full screen. She belonged at home. But the medical bills. The *regular* bills. Hers was an unwinnable situation.

Amber bore witness. Would she, so much like her mother, make all her mother's mistakes?

The question was at the forefront of her mind on November 9, 2016, at about 4:20 p.m., as she stood in the Burger City lobby, flat-footed and feeling flattened, and decided that she, and the rest of Election Day's ruined Americans, needed to take Lil' Beefy seriously. They needed something to believe in, no matter how crazy.

"Hey." She waved at the Till 2 customers. "Pay attention. You're going to want to see this."

Amber laughs, disintegrating the e-cigarette vapor.

"They listened to me. That felt good. I was an 18-year-old girl. People *looked* at me all the time, but they never listened." Her second laugh is more bitter than the first. "Now they don't even look."

Today Amber Smyrna lives in Rochester (population 133), six miles northwest of Jonny, in the tiny two-bedroom she once shared with her mother. Those only familiar with urban living might misconceive rural "apartments"; they are dominated by quirky, second-floor cubbies above restaurants, laundries, vet clinics, funeral homes, et cetera. Downstairs from the Smyrna place was Tobin and Mack's Septic and Sump. That meant low foot traffic, which was good, but also odors so bad they bordered on comical.

On the May afternoon I meet Amber at her place, both of us brandishing negative Covid-19 results, the sewage stench is so pervasive I wonder if airborne bacteria has played a role in her physical transformation. If Amber had been concerned, like many daughters, about growing up to resemble her mother, she needn't have worried. She looks much worse—and she's only 22. If it seems harsh to write that, know that Amber wanted it written.

"Back then, you'd want to fuck me," she insists.

Her manner of speech, too, has changed. But this bravado fades fast.

"Look at me now. Look at this body. Look at this face."

Amber doesn't use the meth that haunts this story. But she *looks* like she does. At 85 pounds, she is bone thin, but more than that, she's *loose*, as if the 50 pounds she's lost since 2016 evaporated overnight. She looks like a bad 40. Her skin, spotted with tattoos now, is jaundiced and blotchy. Her hair, dyed dark, has the cotton-candy quality of someone losing it in clumps. She has a sty on each eye. There is a worrisome cluster of fresh moles in the middle of her left cheek. She still wears a nostril stud, but it looks infected. Her underarm skin has lost elasticity, swaying when she moves jerkily, which, these days, is how she moves.

Then, of course, there are the alleged bite-mark scars. Same as Clem's but ten times as many. Her tank top shows off at least thirty on her arms

Amber Smyrna on May 17, 2020 (photo by the author).

alone, and when she sees me looking, she juts a wing closer so I can see the pinprick couplets. She knows I'm still dubious and raises an eyebrow.

"Plenty more I could show you," she says, "but we just met."

Her new habits have done her no favors. There's the vaping. Teenage Amber never smoked, and I suppose it's good she's made this marginally safer choice. Except that she drains two cartridges over the four hours that we talk, the equivalent of forty cigarettes. Meanwhile, she drinks. Not beer, wine, or liquor, but Seagram's Escapes Jamaican Me Happy wine coolers. At only 3.2 percent alcohol, it's another prudent selection. Except that she drinks thirteen of them. All the while, she's screwing and unscrewing medicine bottle lids. Abilify, Quetiapine, and Olanzapine, anti-psychotics to treat depression. Amber doesn't have insurance. She's living off SNAP, Iowa's version of food stamps. It doesn't allow for good vegetarian options.

"I'm fucked," she says each time she cracks open a Jamaican Me Happy. "I'm fucked, I'm fucked, I'm fuckity-fucked."

Her front door is gummed by the residue of landlord notes. She asks that I keep my voice down so Tobin and Mack won't know she's home.

Before we're an hour in she asks me for a loan. She's four months late on rent. I give her two twenties, which she squirrels away in an extravagantly complicated hiding place.

"I'll pay you back," she says, but it's just more vapor.

What the Amber of 2020 shares with the Amber of 2016 is anger.

"I didn't even *know* how I felt that day. That's how Mom brought me up. Little girls can be happy or sad, and that's it. But I was mad as a motherfucker. The future was so scary, our country decided to go backwards. But right there at Burger City, we had something that *felt* like the future. I was like, do you people see *this*? Are you going to deny *this* is happening too?"

As luck had it, the three people in the Election Day queue were women. They weren't going to refuse the request of a girl facing a lifetime of men's rule. Out came their cameras, as Amber directed. Inward they huddled, shoulder to shoulder like 200,000 more would be gathered two months later at the Women's March in Washington. Roused by the thrill of leadership, Amber wedged herself into the warm, female ranks. When Lil' Beefy hopped right on schedule at 4:24 p.m., the women gasped and pulled even closer in solidarity.

With a little work, one can trace Lil' Beefy's path to internet fame. It began with one of the three customers. Geneva Sheehan, 41, was a hairdresser at Great Hairz Salon in Durant (population 1,833). She had a brand-new iPhone 7 Plus capable of brilliant 4K video, which partially atoned for her fumbling operation—she wasn't yet used to the phone's six-by-three-inch size. Sheehan embraced the gossipy stylist stereotype, and posted on her socials between every haircut.

Back on March 29, 2016, Instagram had increased their maximum video length from fifteen to sixty seconds, which required Sheehan to slice her Lil' Beefy video into three chunks to upload it in full, finishing at 2:32 p.m. The posts served as a minor tonic against the overpowering national news, and the uploads received fifty-three likes and twenty comments, well above Sheehan's median response rate. Sheehan's 16-year-old son, Jennings, liked the posts three days later. Using the third-party app Regrammer, he downloaded all three videos to his iPhone 6s and used iMovie to edit together a dual-panel video. Above, the footage he'd grabbed from his mom's account. Below, the October 7 video he'd harvested from Quin Arthur's sleepy YouTube channel. Exploiting a temporary bug in Snapchat's iOS allowing users to add unlimited-length videos to their Stories by double-tapping the home button, Jennings presented his finished work at 10:05 a.m. on Saturday, November 12, 2016.

Pairing the two videos of the unexplained event had an immediate, explosive effect. Over the following days, at least two dozen of Jennings Sheehan's contacts copied Quin's video and disseminated it via socials, complete with commentary best described as "freaking out." Most viewers found the video cool, with several roughing out plans to visit Burger City #8 ASAP ("time to pound some beefyburgers bruh"). Hearsay suggests the loudest chatter was going down on WhatsApp and Kik.

If Amber Smyrna was gratified by the response, Quin Arthur was beside himself. In one week, his YouTube page rocketed from five-thousand views to fifty-five-thousand. The biggest bump was yet to come. On November 21, Brooklyn-based DJ HaXn, who grew up in Des Moines, tweeted "headin home for thanxgiving turkey but want a beefyburger just as bad." The tweet generated 23 replies, among them user @jmp239 asking, "have you seen this?" alongside a Storify link collecting ten customer videos of the Lil' Beefy Anomaly. HaXn retweeted the link to his twenty-million followers with the comment, "this cray."

Thanks to Quin's early start, Google's PageRank made his YouTube page the major beneficiary of all ensuing searches. Views shot up to forty million by November 23, by which time Quin had posted two additional Lil' Beefy vids. Though they lacked the heart-in-your-throat thrill of the October 7 footage, they were technically superior, and captured Lil' Beefy's five hops better than anything else out there.

Amber Smyrna felt like an integral part of the drama. When Lil' Beefy obliged the three women from Till 2 on November 9, after a whole nation hadn't, Amber smiled—God, what a feeling, to smile again—and turned her head, hoping that Kit was watching.

He was. His eyes sparkled with proud tears.

"I know, I know," Amber says. "One day after the men of America ass-plowed us, the first thing I do is turn to one for validation. Amy Mold would've killed me. A little earlier, she was telling me how all the women in the world could kill all the men in one night if they just organized. You ever see *Children of the Corn*? It was shot in Iowa. There's this scene where all the kids in town kill all the adults." She scratches her patch of moles and sucks on her Juul. "I pretended to agree with her. But I didn't. What about love? What about desire? I was a fucking romantic."

Amber doesn't seem aware that *Wired* used the movie's title for their March 3, 2018, feature on the Burger City Tragedy ("Children of the Corn: Teenage Madness in the Midwest"), and that's probably for the best. She holds aside her e-cig long enough to wash down a yellow pill with pink wine cooler.

"Kit wasn't like other guys. Now I sound like a battered wife. But Amy Mold would've said the same thing if she wasn't all fucked over Hillary. She had a crush on Kit. I didn't care. Everyone did. Except me. When you date someone, then break it off, then date, then break, that's not a crush. That's something you can't get away from no matter how hard you try."

Amber and Kit had known each other most of their lives. Little League games, skating rinks, carnivals. Even after they were thrown into closer quarters at Rose Community High School (average total enrollment: 175), they kept separate friend groups. It was only on April 18, 2013, the day Amber began at Burger City, that things took off. Kit had been at the restaurant only a year longer, but it felt like he'd been born there. He opened and closed refrigerators with elbows and feet, and executed complicated handshakes with coworkers who obviously adored him. It made Amber go wobbly.

She lets steam trail off her tongue. "We were on fire right from the start. The first time we made out was by the bathrooms when we were closing. His hands smelled like Clorox. Our feet kept kicking the mop bucket and sloshing out water. Yeah, I know, gross, but if that doesn't sound hot to you, you're the one with the problem. He pulled off my panties—look, I don't care. Print this. Those were the best times of my fucking *life*. He pulled off my panties and put his face between my legs, and it was the first time I'd ever come with someone else, with my socks soaking in Pine-Sol."

"I remember the soda fountain," Kit says from his room at Chernow. "We were on the floor behind the counter, butt naked, going at it. It must have been August or something because we were sweaty. Amber reached up and hit the ice tea lever and we just get doused with tea, and we're licking it off each other, and it's really great, and next she does pink lemonade, and after that, Coke. By the time we were done, there must have been five gallons of soft drink on that floor, which we had to mop up all over again."

"Always used a condom," Amber says. "Always, always, always. You know how rare that is? You know how few boys even have the baby balls to *buy* them? Kit felt competent. *Competent*. What a low fucking bar we hold our men to. If I was merely competent at something, I'd be fired. *Have* been fired. Repeatedly. Jesus. Nice self-own, Amber."

"Eventually it got out me and Amber were together," Kit says. "And

Nutting calls us into his office and I'm thinking, uh-oh, the security cams caught us, right? But he calls us in, and he folds his hands, and he's like 'I understand the two of you wish to enter into a romantic relationship.' It was the weirdest. Then he busts out these things called Burger City Dating Relationship Declarations. Amber and I looked at each other like, uh, are we getting married? I guess they were so Burger City wasn't liable for what they called 'hard feelings issues.' We signed it, and Nutting signed as witness, and then he smiled and said we were now allowed to go on a first date. I was thinking, dude, we've screwed against your office *door*."

"The dating contracts," Amber groans. "Our coworkers had a field day. There was something sketchy going on with Nutting's wife back then. Anything to do with relationships, his face got all red. But Kit was nice about it. He was always nice. I started noticing it at school too. I was no A student, but Kit was terrible. The good teachers, though, they loved him. He'd ask how they were doing. Like, how their sick dad was or did they get their car repaired. He remembered all this personal shit. About *teachers*."

"I wouldn't have graduated without Amber," Kit says. "Most people think I just made up a missing credit after graduation. That's not true. I was down like, I don't even know. Three credits? Four? No way I would have bothered. But Amber led me around to all my teachers a few weeks before graduation and begged them to give me last-second projects so I could skate by with Ds. And they did. Not for me. For her. Who was going to say no to Amber Smyrna? She had this way of—hey, are you going to interview her? Then you'll see."

Amber uses a jagged fingernail to scrape a scab off her lip as she chews on my question: Does she miss Kit Bryant?

"I don't know," she says, drooling vapor. "I think about what happened to me in the Biting Room. What he did to everyone. But fuck. Jesus. Motherfucking shit. He's hard not to miss. It's like the guy who did that awful stuff is wrestling in my head with the skinny boy who treated me so good. Four fucking years later and every morning I wake up, it feels the same: Kit Bryant, all over me."

Kit cocks his head as if I've asked something frivolous.

"Hm. I never really thought of it. Do I miss Amber. Do I miss her. Hm. Do I miss anybody? There's a question! An interesting question. I mean, I'm so busy these days. They pack your schedule pretty tight here. Am I right, Nuncio? Nuncio? There's meals. Exercise. Classes. Therapy. Group. Do I miss Amber. Hm. Let me think about that. Hey, man, you want a glass of water? In a yucky little paper cup?"

Technically speaking, on November 9, 2016, the day after the election, Kit and Amber were not a couple. The irrefutable facts of the calendar gave this breakup weight. In ten months, provided Darcy's medical expenses didn't bleed them dry, Amber would be starting at Kirkwood Community College or Indian Hills Community College. Though neither was far away, symbolically they were countries for which Kit Bryant had no passport.

Kit's support of Amber's college plans was unconditional, and he knew she needed to make a clean break—from Burger City, from Jonny, from him. The closer Fall 2017 came, the more deeply Kit understood his cornfield isolation. He might work at Burger City all his life like Cheri Orritt. He might become a bottom-feeder of broken women like Mickey McCormick. He might go completely off his rocker like Dez Mozley. His window of escape wasn't closing. It had closed.

After DJ HaXn's November 21 tweet, people began showing up from as far as Minnesota, Nebraska, and Kansas. And who was their maître d' to the fantastic? Not Quin Arthur, who was trapped at school all day, cursing his luck. It was Kit Bryant.

Kit's eyes, dull since the July breakup with Amber, roared back to full light. He'd always been good with customers; that's why Nutting put him on the tills, even though Kit could do any job in the building. He was instantly likable, but more than that, he instantly *liked*. Whether curious new customers came to Lil' Beefy from places of skepticism or belief, he respected their points of view. How about stick around till 4:24 and see for yourself?

Amber was heart-struck the same as everyone. This was her Kit. The Kit who would never let her drift away. The second she saw his tearful smile after she'd spurred three customers to record Lil' Beefy, she knew there was no keeping them apart, no matter what it meant for their futures. At 11:30 p.m., a half hour after closing, they had sex atop B6 in Burger City's southwest corner, near the enclosed Puppy Pen, in Camera 4's well-known blind spot.

"Of course we shouldn't have done it," Amber tells me. "We shouldn't have fucked on the table, we shouldn't have gotten back together, blah,

blah. But right then it felt like the antidote to the country collapsing. I could still feel young and sexy. And wanted. And valued. I remember thinking, while I was knocking salt and pepper shakers off the table, that the thing moving Lil' Beefy, maybe it was a force of good, you know? Maybe all this hateful shit Trump stirred up had triggered this *other* thing, this silly little thing that pushed a cardboard puppy a few inches across the floor, and that silly little thing was all the world needed to pull together again, to look at it and go, wow—there's so much shit we still don't know. We're in this together."

Amber pauses our interview to phone in a refill for Abilify. It goes poorly. She ends up calling the pharmacist a fascist and ordering him to call her back after he's gotten his "shit squared away." After ending the call, her hands are so sweaty they carry out a comedy of errors, dropping her phone, Juul, and eighth bottle of Jamaican Me Happy. She laces her fingers to steady herself, but the lax folds of her neck keep swaying.

I ask her if she's tried cognitive behavioral therapy.

"CBT? How about ECT? Electroshock? Fucking tie me to your car battery, I'm ready. I can't live like this much longer. It's not just the anxiety, it's the loneliness. I used to have dreams. About a husband, a little girl of my own. I don't care if it sounds old-fashioned. It's never going to happen anyway."

She presses the icy wine cooler to her swollen eyes. This puts her bent arm right in front of me, all those alleged bite scars, daring me to believe.

"Plus, if I had a girl, I'd only give her cancer. I don't know. Maybe it stopped with Mom. But I hope not. Because where's mine? I put every nasty kind of garbage I can into my body, and nothing. My boobs are bruised from how hard I check for lumps. Just one lump. I'm begging. I've got a whole plan. I've got this butcher knife. I'll cut them off. Left boob, right boob. It'll feel good. It'll be the only thing that does. I try to get Covid too. Every day. I go outside, no mask, like it's my job. But no. This thing's going to make me live a long time. To watch myself disintegrate. To watch everyone else from Burger City disintegrate. You think the fucking *videos* went viral? Nuh-uh. It's the *ghost* that went viral. It got inside us. It's eating us from the inside. What, you don't believe me? Look at me. My face. My body. Fucking *look* at me."

THE COLDEST COLD SPOT

Stu Blick, a bespectacled, blade-nosed, 73-year-old member of the Geezers, introduced the idea through a mouthful of Egg-a-Beefy, a $1.25 breakfast skillet dripping with grease and cheese. It's hard to date his comment more specifically than the second week of November 2016; Geezer breakfasts were all the same. Stu spent his adult life as a foreman at Bedrock International, a steel company producing truck axles, power tools, avionics parts, and, in the 1960s, nuclear missile components, until its Moscow, Iowa, plant closed in 2003, forcing Stu into retirement.

"It's a ghost," he said. "Plain as day."

The Geezers were big fans of slow conversations. Silas Ireland didn't reply for a few days.

"Ghosts, plural, probably," he said.

Silas was a thick-faced, 76-year-old retired farmer. Silas didn't tip his filthy, frayed Pioneer Seed Corn cap at the quotidian notion of a breakfast; his regular 5:30 a.m. order was a Grampa Beefy, fries with ranch, and a large BC Deluxe Select Brew, which he said tasted like turpentine next to Burger City's original church-basement-style coffee. Like lots of country folk, he'd never doubted the afterlife. Where there's one ghost, he explained, there's always more.

A day or two later, Zadie Budden, age 80, opined that the Burger City teens were begging for trouble. Zadie's profession had been the formidable one of keeping house for a husband and six kids. On doctor's orders, Zadie wasn't allowed to introduce Burger City slop into a digestive tract troubled by dysphagia, IBS, and GERD, but Zadie was no freeloader. She dutifully purchased a $1 carton of milk to add to the Grape-Nuts she brought in her purse. Her homemaker life had been filled with daytime talk shows, which had convinced her of the supernatural. Ghosts, she told her fellow Geezers, were harmless until aggravated, and aggravating was what these kids were up to.

It took Stu a full day to make a joke of it: "Harmless till aggravated? Sounds like she's talking about you, Vandyke."

Vandyke Elbutt, the 77-year-old former American Lit professor, huffed his disdain from lips covered in CinnaYumz icing. Even among curmudgeons, Vandyke was the curmudgeon, his surly mug barely visible behind his year-round swaddling of coat, scarf, and winter hat. By Thanksgiving 2016, Elbutt was eleven weeks into wearing the arm cast he'd won during the Scotty Flossen affair. "Elbutt's Elbow" was healing poorly, making the simplest dining tasks gloomily difficult.

Ghosts, he lectured, were the kind of backwoods bullpucky he expected from his gullible cohorts.

Vandyke knew about ghosts. All the Geezers did. Each had lost spouses over the past twenty-five years, either from catastrophic medical event or long-term illness; three of the five had lost children. Each Geezer had sought out the warmth, light, and conviviality of their local fast-food joint until they'd found one another. The raw nerve endings of their grief twisted together to form new family bonds.

Maxine Pinto patted Vandyke's cast with a liver-spotted hand. The 68-year-old former grade-school teacher was the Geezers' darling, a tiny human with eyes that twinkled behind glasses. She'd had a rocky decade—partial lobectomy of her right lung, urinary system reconstruction, pancreatic cyst removal, abdominal hernia repair— but you'd never know it from her prim posture, the way she held her purse with both birdlike hands, and the smile that made you crave a grandmother's embrace.[39]

Maxine gave it a day or two before gently bringing up what all the Geezers were thinking. What about what Vandyke had seen when he'd lost his heartbeat?

In 1998, Vandyke Elbutt had undergone ventricular restoration following congestive heart failure. Vandyke had flatlined for two minutes, and when he'd returned to Burger City after a five-week absence, he'd reported, to his own consternation, abstract memories of white-light-at-the-end-of-a-tunnel bullshit. It had taken the cynic months to rebuild his disbelief. He'd even showed off a book that asserted the white-light thing was just the brain losing blood and oxygen.

The Lil' Beefy Anomaly made Vandyke uncertain again. The Geezers heard it in his defensive huff. Knowing too well the old prof's sensitivity, they returned to their cold coffees and *Des Moines Registers*. Secretly,

---

39 This is according to Amber, who, it bears reminding, had never known her grandmothers, having lost both of them to cancer.

though, Maxine curled her old, trembling fingers around Elbutt's Elbow. She loved the old crank, and knew the old crank loved her back.

Maxine Pinto is dead and the Geezers think the poltergeist killed her.

Three years, ten months, and nine days after Lil' Beefy first moved, I meet surviving Geezers Stu Blick, Silas Ireland, Zadie Budden, and Vandyke Elbutt in the outdoor seating area of their new breakfast joint of choice, the Hardee's in Tipton. I'm wearing a face mask and keeping distant, but it feels dicey. Governor Reynolds refuses to mandate masks in Iowa, and in twenty days, the White House will confirm the Hawkeye State as suffering America's highest rate of positive coronavirus cases.

Like Amber, the Geezers aren't fighting against disease. Their trays, however, are stocked from the "Better for You Options"—Low Carb It Charbroiled Chicken Club, Trim It Big Hot Ham Sandwich, Veg It Side Salad, and Gluten-Sensitive Low Carb Breakfast Bowl. It's hardly health food, but one can only improve from Burger City's cholesterol-loaded USDA beef.

It's notable that Silas, the only Geezer who actually raised cattle, is eating the salad. He's gone vegetarian, and though he claims he's just following doctor's orders, I suspect that he's lost his taste for flesh. Truth be told, none of the four eat with gusto, which could be attributable to illness, age, or how I'm stirring up Burger City business again.

Unlike Burger City staff, the Geezers haven't lost undue weight. But they look bad. Not regular old-person bad either. They look like the lost causes you see being wheeled down hospital hallways, giraffe-spotted with inexplicable bruises, arms gummy from IV tape, hair nebular, spines sclerotic.

"We should've stopped showing up after that drug kid got killed," Silas Ireland sighs.

"The hell we should've," Vandyke Elbutt says. "No junkie had the right to chase us off."

"No ghost either," Zadie Budden reminds. "But it did anyway."

"Van, I recall you saying we ought to pack it up out of Burger City," Stu Blick says.

"Only because it was too crowded!" Vandyke insists. "All that riffraff showing up with their cameras and selfish sticks."

"Selfie sticks," Stu corrects.

"And the whole mob acting like they're about to witness the Moonshot. Thanksgiving week, there were kids in our booth three days straight. All because it had a good view of the cardboard dog."

"Van was very upset about that," Zadie confides to me.

"I had every right. That booth had a reserved sign."

"No one was reading Bob Nutting's laminated signs," Stu says.

"Van made himself a bigger sign," Silas laughs. "Didn't you, Van?"

"Hah?"

Silas cranks the volume. "Didn't you, Van? Didn't you go and make a bigger sign?"

Vandyke knocks his bony fist to the table. "I did, and it kept that riffraff out of our booth."

"Not out of the restaurant, though," Stu says. "I had a urinary thing and was using the men's room every thirty minutes. Suddenly there's a line. That's when I started wearing the incontinence briefs." He shrugs miserably. "I didn't know how good I had it. Back then all I had was BPH—enlarged prostate. Now it's prostate cancer. I get rectal exams like most people get their mail."

"You want that in the book?" Vandyke asks. "Your adult diapers? Your sordid medical history? Jesus H."

Their bickering feels heightened, an attempt to run out the clock on the worst topics. Silas clears his phlegmy throat. He's got more ailments than the others (PSVT heart arrhythmia, stage 3 rheumatoid arthritis, secondary hypertension, neuropathic fibromyalgia, severe COPD), but farm life taught him to master the art of concealing discomfort.

"For the longest time, I figured whatever was going on at Burger City had to do with the kids' gizmos, their phones. But Zadie finally got Amber to explain it."

"Amber," Stu says. "Now there was a princess."

"Heart of gold," Silas agrees.

"Legs of gold too," Vandyke says. "She used to come by our booth wearing the shortest cut-offs you ever saw."

"You want *that* on tape?" Stu asks. "You dirty old man?"

"If I had the figure," Zadie chuckled, "I'd wear those shorts too."

"You know about her mom, I guess?" Stu asks. "I don't think Amber's friends understood what she was going through. But we did. Van's wife had ovarian cancer. Maxine's husband had pancreatic. I've had non-melanoma skin cancer half my life. I don't know if we helped her. I hope we did. I hope Amber's okay." His worried eyes meet mine. "Is she? Okay?"

Zadie senses my hesitation. Perhaps to protect the old men hanging on my reply, she picks up her story.

"Amber told us there was a 'viral video.' Even before Covid, *viral* was a scary word, especially when you're getting on in years. But Amber said it would pass. That's why we kept breakfasting there. You have to understand, in the beginning, all the events—the ghost or what have you—happened in the afternoon. All we Geezers saw was how it changed the staff."

I ask them if they believe, as Amber does, that the presidential election played a big part in the Lil' Beefy obsession.

"Maxine sure believed it," Silas says.

"I think that's why she paid more attention than the rest of us," Stu explains. "Maxine voted GOP most her life, but Trump disgusted her. If we talked about him too much, she'd go check out the cardboard dog. She was the one of us really fascinated."

Zadie's shoulders shake. "Oh, Maxine."

"We think…" Stu sounds tentative. "Most of us think—"

"Let's not go through this again," Vandyke snaps.

Stu ignores him. "The rest of us were fine leaving things be. But Maxine…"

Vandyke picks up a white plastic knife. He does this often, for the same reason Senator Bob Dole used to clutch a pen. Elbutt's Elbow never healed right—so many Burger City injuries, both physical and mental, never healed right. It looks like Vandyke is threatening Stu with a plastic stabbing.

"Going down this route makes us look like old fools."

Stu picks up a plastic fork. Armed for a duel, the elderly warriors glare.

"Why should we be afraid to look like fools?" Stu challenges. "In our last, wrinkled, bedsore, no-good years, what does it matter? We all know it was the ghost that killed her."

"But to *talk* about it," Vandyke hisses, and with that, I understand. If the Geezers believe Maxine Pinto's interest in the poltergeist got her killed, it's no stretch to believe that airing *their* interest in it might have similar effects. It's the precise eventuality that Clemens Dumay guards against seventy-five miles away.

Stu's lips, darkened by angiokeratoma, tremble. "I don't care. Let it come. We're all going to die, friends, and soon. Wouldn't you rather die without fear? Wouldn't you rather tell Maxine up in heaven we didn't run from death with our tails tucked? That we told that ghost to fuck off? For once, let's not be the fearful old shits we've always been. Let's tell the truth."

What really caught Maxine Pinto's fancy was the ghost's second purported manifestation, soon to be known as the Coldest Cold Spot. Like most fast-food outfits, Burger City was open three hundred and sixty five days a year, but only a skeleton crew was present on November 24, 2016—Thanksgiving Day—when Javier Villareal first reported the phenomenon around 1:15 p.m.

"Something's wrong with the freezer," Javi griped to Dion Skerry. "Too cold."

It's as absurd as the Burger City Poltergeist itself. Can a freezer be too freezing? With Bob Nutting at home sharing a turkey carcass with his estranged family, 21-year-old Dion was in charge for a five-day stretch, the longest to which he'd ever been entrusted.

It's difficult to imagine an assistant manager commanding less authority than Dion Skerry. Most Core Workers at a place like Burger City have a story of how they got there—dramatic misfortune, bad luck, dashed aspirations. Dion Skerry represented the worst possibility of all: he seemed born for it, vacant of ambition, imagination, backbone, or independent thought.

After peeking at the other two workers (Cheri at the register, Yesenia on drive-thru), Dion waddled his 330 pounds back to the walk-in freezer and checked the gauge. It read -2, barely off from its 0 degree setting. Dion, as was his habit, didn't give it another thought.

Two hours later, Dion noticed white vapor oozing from the ajar freezer door. Inside, he found Javi and Yesenia. They faced one another like dazed boxers, staring at the floor. Nutting had molded the boneless Dion in his own image, complete with a distrust of Latinos. Two Latinos together, in private? They had to be up to something.

Burger City's walk-in freezer (photo by Kit Bryant).

"What are you guys doing?" he asked.

"I said it's too cold," Javi said.

"It's fine," Dion insisted. "I checked."

"Not there." Javi jabbed a finger at the floor. "*There.*"

Dion followed the finger. At some point, chicken blood had leaked from a box into the center of the floor. It was pink, glossy, and frozen. Dion looked back up and noted that Yesenia still wore her B1099 headset.

"I don't think that'll work in here," he said. "You better go back out."

"I don't want to walk through it," Yesenia said.

"Through what?" Dion asked. "The chicken juice?"

"Just go around it," Javi suggested.

"What if it touches me?" Yesenia asked.

"If *what* touches you?" Dion asked.

"Cuidado," Javi said. "*Cuidado.*"

"Okay," Yesenia said. "But I might scream."

"Whoa," Dion said. "Please, nobody scream."

No staff member was more big-hearted than 34-year-old Javi, but few suffered fools with less patience. He broke eye contact with the frightened 16-year-old girl and glared at Dion.

"You are not helping. Come here. Sí, into the freezer. Rápido, rápido."

Bob Nutting was infatuated with signage, and doing as he was told, Dion had plastered the BOH with posters. *The Top 10 Dirtiest Spots in Your Kitchen. Correct Dishwashing Procedure. Deep Fat Fryer Safety.* As he stepped into the walk-in freezer, Dion's eyes landed on a two-foot-long vertical poster called *Degrees of Doneness*, showing, in microscopic detail, the colors and textures of beef at six standard temperatures.

The images bit down on him like a bear trap. The merlot mash of "Raw 40°F (4°C)." The ruby jelly of "Rare 125°F (52°C)." The magenta fibrils of "Medium Rare 135°F (57°C)." The swollen tongue of "Medium 145°F (63°C)." The congealed bubblegum of "Medium Well 155°F (68°C)." The arid, fat-rippled brown of "Well Done 165°F (74°C)."

Suddenly the chill of the walk-in didn't matter. Dion exuded sweat so forcefully his clothing glued to his skin. He became overwhelmed with visions of long, thick, glistening tubes of meat snaking from a pitch-black void, piling over his legs and belly until it reached his face—a cold salt-lick of blood, a sharp, rank stench.

Dion tripped on a frostbit box of bacon and stumbled forward. Javi caught him, but not before Dion plunged into the center of the room. The sweat of Dion's forearms crystalized into needles of frost. The tissue inside his nostrils flash-froze, his eyeballs watered, his scrotum tightened. He cried out. His body was so cold, yet all he could see and smell were hot, stinking, rolling hills of meat.

Javi yanked Dion back. Dion gasped, rubbed his cold eyes, noticed Yesenia under Javi's other arm. She'd made her escape during the confusion.

"You okay?" Javi asked Yesenia, then Dion. "You okay?"

"Gonna barf," Dion said. A good assistant manager, he flopped into the hallway before he did.

Dion would avoid entering the walk-in freezer for another five months, quite a feat for a man with inventory duties. If he felt the barest finger of cold air as he passed the freezer, he experienced paralyzing visions he came to think of as "Meat Grief": beef at all levels of doneness squirting toward him from the darkness.

But on November 24, 2016, he was still in charge, and after a single day of recovery, he took steps to remedy the freezer's malfunction.

Bob Nutting was fortunate to have two mechanically-minded men on staff, and the next morning, Dion Skerry called them both: Zane Shakespeare and Mickey McCormick. Zane, of course, arrived first. Tamra Longmoor might be the most musclebound of Burger City employees, but the peaceful, head-shaved, 40-year-old Zane was health personified, dedicated to urbane habits like bicycling to work, snacking on carrots, and waking at dawn to meditate with his girlfriend of fourteen years, Wendy Exley. Zane and Wendy had rehabbed their old farmhouse, and in the process, he'd learned to fix about anything.

By 6:30 a.m. Zane was outside Burger City's walk-in freezer, toolbox in hand. After checking the outer gauge, he explained to Dion how setting the thermostat to -10 degrees could shorten the life of the compressor and freeze the coil. In other words, the dip in temperature might signal a defrost.

Dion didn't care about any of that. "Go inside," he said.

Zane did. The freezer door clicked softly shut behind him, the cluck of a tongue. Dion cowered beside the *Degrees of Doneness* poster, the smell of Beefyburgers on the grill making him want to puke again. Seconds passed. Dion heard nothing from the freezer. What if Meat Grief had gotten Zane too, and he'd frozen to death against a bag of frozen fries?

He gasped when the freezer burst open. Zane exited in a hurry, slamming the door behind him. His long brow, usually so smooth and placid, was rumpled.

"It is *very* cold in there," he said.

"I know," Dion said over the thump of his heart.

Zane reapplied his coat and gloves, raided the lost and found box for a scarf, and went back in. He examined the wiring and fuses. He checked the fan motor. He drained excess refrigerant. He cleaned the suction filter and drain line. The freezer's four-inch walls prevented him from hearing the modded exhaust pipe of Mickey McCormick's red 2013 Harley Street Glide. When the 44-year-old Mickey ambled into the freezer, the overhead bulb's light shining off his black-dyed hair, Zane looked more perturbed than anyone had ever seen him.[40]

"Give me your hand," Zane said.

"It's 8:45," Mickey yawned. "I don't engage in homosexual acts till nine."

By 9:00, however, the odd couple was befuddled and fascinated. They found Dion at the counter, shrugging at the questions of Maxine Pinto. Zane and Mickey presented their report. Neither could find shit-all wrong with the walk-in. The ultra-coldness was limited to the direct center of the room. Could be an electrical surge. Maybe underground tremors were narrowing coolant patterns. Dion didn't absorb any of it. There was only one person left to call.

Because he weighed 330 pounds in 2016, Dion Skerry sits at a frame-appropriate 170 in 2020. In other ways, too, he has fared better than most Burger City survivors. He's found part-time work handling scheduling at Atkins Roofing in West Branch (population 2,322), the kind of unchallenging job for which he was born. He's also taking business management classes two nights a week (online during the pandemic) at Muscatine Community College. He's neither a good student nor bad one, but keeps going in that passive Dion Skerry way, and one of these days he'll graduate. What business does he want to manage?

"Anything but food," he says.

Dion's spells of Meat Grief went away after the Burger City Tragedy, but it's not a result he's inclined to stress-test. Like most of the survivors, Dion has gone vegetarian. The sight of meat has become a full-blown phobia. It's gotten so bad he's had to get creative (never his strong suit) and plot circuitous paths through Dewey's Jack & Jill grocery so he can shop without laying eyes on vacuum-packed pork or film-wrapped chicken cutlets. And beef?

"I'd drink bleach before I ate beef," he says.

---

40 As described by Dion, who lurked and peeked.

It sort of looks like he has. His weight might be modest, but like Amber, he has the look of an addict. His eyeballs are yellow eggs buried in bruised hollows. His nostrils are chapped. His purple lips look raw. He's losing hair at a malignant rate. When I interview him on August 5, 2020, he's a portrait of beige in recline, slouched into a tan sofa, clad in too-short chinos, a cream-colored polo, and a khaki face mask.

He's thinking of managing a movie theater, maybe. Maybe a laser-tag place. Possibly a video game store. These dull musings don't inspire confidence. They never did. No one at Burger City particularly liked Dion Skerry, but a benign cyst like him didn't seem worth hating. I don't agree. Back in 2016, Dion Skerry followed Nutting's every order. He also did whatever Nutting's nemesis, Kit Bryant, said. Dion Skerry is the type of person who takes no sides, which doesn't work if you give a shit about anything at all.

It's possible he's on some kind of tranquilizer. After only two hours of interviewing, I've had it with his daftness. People he knew *died*, I remind him. Doesn't that upset him at all? He pouts like I've turned the TV channel to a show he likes marginally less.

"I guess," he says. "I don't know," he amends.

While I'm packing up my shit, he asks me if I'll go with him to Kum & Go, a regrettably named Midwestern convenience store chain. The one on South Downey Street stocks Swiss Miss Creamy Milk Chocolate Pudding, Dion's favorite, but Kum & Go puts the pudding beside the packaged roast beef, which Dion cannot bear to see. The request infuriates me, but I can't pinpoint anything Dion has actually done wrong. So I follow him in my car and together we enter the store, keeping six-foot social-distance guidelines. We're met by an arctic blast of air-conditioning. It staggers Dion a bit. I wonder if he's reminded of the Coldest Cold Spot.

To see Kit Bryant stride through the Burger City door, scarf flapping, peeling his winter gloves and slinging off his old backpack, was to see a hero returning to save his embattled kingdom. Kit wasn't who Dion had called to help, but Dion was relieved to see him. It might be Bob Nutting's restaurant, but it was Kit's ghost.

He flipped the hinged counter, marched through the kitchen, and faced off with the walk-in freezer. Only Darcy Smyrna held her post at the drive-thru; Dion Skerry, Tamra Longmoor, and Mickey McCormick gathered in the hallway to watch Kit roll his neck like an MMA fighter. He removed from his backpack a digital hygrometer, a full plastic water bottle, a piece of chalk, and three Hot Wheels cars.

"Give it hell, Bryant," Mickey cheered.

"You all are nuts," Tamra scoffed.

"Don't get hurt," Dion said, thinking of his own liability.

Kit stepped inside the freezer and let the door click shut behind him. The normalcy of the space was unnerving. Supplies in their usual disarray, the wan scents of frozen foods, the cold-milk odor of ice-encrusted cardboard. Kit unscrewed his water bottle and shook droplets onto the floor near the frozen chicken blood. Dion wouldn't like it—a slipping hazard—but fuck Dion.

The drops flash-froze into white ice and floated down to the floor. Despite the cold, Kit's body burned with the thrill of finding another paranormal aberration.

Kit was nothing if not a gonzo reporter. He stuck his bare hand into the coldest area. Once at a party, he and three other boys had plunged their hands into a steel tub of ice-cold beer water to see who could hold them there the longest. The other boys bailed before two minutes were up; Kit held on for four. His hand had ached for hours afterward, and days later, patches of dead skin were still flaking off.

In the walk-in's focused cold, he lasted four seconds. He withdrew with a gasp and tucked his hand into his armpit. With his other hand, he took up the hygrometer. At home, he used it to keep his bedroom humidity below 38 percent, anything over which attracted a microscopic insect called the springtail, which made Kit break out in bedbug-like swellings. The hygrometer also had a temperature gauge, and Kit clocked it at -2 degrees Fahrenheit before using his shoe to push it next to the frozen chicken blood.

The digital numbers began to peel away: -5, -10, -15. Kit recalled Cheri Orritt regaling him with a story about making it to Burger City barely alive in February 1996, when temperatures in eastern Iowa dropped to -47.[41] What if the walk-in freezer was about to set its own kind of record? He rooted for the LED digits as they faded from black to pale purple: -20, -25, -30. If it beat -47, he'd impress the hell out of Cheri.

Kit Bryant had no mother; Cheri Orritt had no child. This is the most obvious reason why the prickly but beloved 53-year-old had become the 19-year-old's adoptive mom, and Kit her adopted son, with all the revelations, delights, broken hearts, and failures thereby afforded. That wasn't the only reason, of

---

41 "U.S. State and Territory Temperature Extremes," *Wikipedia*, December 20, 2020.

course. Plenty of kids with fucked-up lives had entered and exited Cheri's workplace over the past twenty-seven years. It was only Kit she loved.

Cheri scolded Kit when necessary, and it was often necessary. Like when Kit relied too much on Amber for homework, or came to work with a hangover, or smelled like pot, or was caught selling Mickey pot, or really anything having to do with pot—Cheri often painted a picture in which Kit ended up behind bars. Kit's investment in Cheri's opinions was obvious. He'd snap back, call her a bitch, or retract into a sullen shell. But when he had good news, it was Cheri to whom he ran. Kit had done a good job pretending his Summer 2016 graduation was no big deal, but from the drive-in window, Amber Smyrna saw the two-minute embrace he shared with Cheri in the parking lot, and how Kit's back, under Cheri's hands, had hitched with sobs.

Cheri had so far chuckled along with the ghostly endeavors, but her tinted glasses didn't prevent Kit from reading her true mood. She saw Kit investing too much energy into this thing, the same way he'd invested too much energy into restoring the 1973 Dodge Challenger that sat rusting in his dad's driveway or sketching out the snow-plow business that never escaped a red, beaten-up Mead spiral notebook labeled, on a blue strip of painter's tape, *IDEAS*.

But this walk-in freezer thing confirmed the Lil' Beefy thing! Cheri would have to admit that! Kit leaned close to read the paling LED; he felt the ultra-cold column of air scrape his nose. The gauge ticked down: -35, -40, -45—and that's as far as it got. Shrouded in frost, the gadget winked out and Kit exhaled the lungfuls of air he hadn't known he was keeping. His breath powderized and drifted downward. He thought of the *IDEAS* notebook. He knew where it was. He'd brush off the dust, start taking new kinds of notes.

Before he left the walk-in, Kit Bryant dribbled more water to establish the frigid area's dimensions, which he outlined in chalk—a circle fourteen-and-three-eighths inches in diameter. He pushed the Hot Wheels cars into the circle, aimed in different directions, to see if they might move over time. Later checks revealed the cars frozen solid and nothing else. Kit made a mental note to log these facts in his notebook.

I grab two six-packs of Swiss Miss Creamy Milk Chocolate Pudding from the Kum & Go cooler and hand them off the beige smudge known as Dion Skerry. I turn to leave, and that's when I see her enter. If it were anyone else, I'd have to study her for longer. But one thing you can say about Desdemona Mozley is that she's utterly unmistakable.

If Dion is as unspecific as a pile of putty, Dez crawls straight out of a Dungeon Master's Guide, a scraggly-haired, gap-toothed, hunch-backed woman dangling tin trinkets from wrists and neck. She's wearing dirty jeans bejeweled with plastic rhinestones and a black blouse fringed with tassels. On her feet are what look like deerskin moccasins, worn down to pale hide. She wears a face mask, but it's well below her nose. Is she as skinny as the rest of the survivors? Through all the clothing and hair, it's hard to tell.

Burger City's janitor from 2006 till the awful end, Dez looks a lot like she did in the dozens of photographs published after the tragedy. Unlike other survivors, Dez wouldn't shut up, and her allegations were so bizarre people couldn't resist printing them, thereby intensifying the circus. Warlocks were to blame, she said.[42] Someone should check area cemeteries, see if any bodies have been dug up.[43] Everyone around Jonny was fearful of evil spells except her, she said, and don't you wish you knew why?[44]

But Dez slid off the radar in summer 2018. No one found her for comment after Kit got sent to Chernow. She didn't appear in *Blood at Burger City*. I've wanted to contact her but didn't know how. I raise a hand in hopes of making a non-threatening introduction, but she's glaring at Dion. *Glaring* isn't a strong enough word. She's a cartoon, eyes popped huge, arms thrown to either side like a burglar caught in a searchlight.

I'd almost forgotten. Dion and Dez: bad blood. Right there, in the center of her left palm, is the pale scar from their April 22, 2017, clash.

"Oh," Dion says. His pale face drains paler. "Hey, Dez."

Dez screeches.

"No, you don't, Maggot Boy!"

Her hard, heavy purse arcs over her head and bashes the left side of Dion's face. He's knocked into a display advertising *3 FOR $.99* chips. Like a martial-arts warrior, Dez whirls her purse strap around her fist for better control and comes at Dion with a series of quick blows to the head, shoulder, and back. He retreats into the candy aisle, plows into a shelf, and falls. Starburst, Werther's, and Jolly Ranchers scatter.

I chase Dez along with another customer, but the chip display has toppled, and honestly, we're both a bit astonished. Dez's purse has gotten caught in the display, so she grabs two handfuls of candy and hurls them at Dion.

"This is my place!"

---

42 Riley Walshe, "Burgers, Fries…and Witches?", *Waterloo-Cedar Falls Courier*, July 1, 2017.

43 Jodie Baldock, "Burger City Janitor Sounds Off," *Hawk Eye*, July 10, 2017.

44 Jorge Lumb, "The Burger City Story Keeps Getting Stranger," *Webster Daily Freeman-Journal*, August 20, 2017.

M&Ms and Skittles make poor projectiles. Dion's getting up. Dez spins, grabs some Tic Tacs, and starts zinging them. These are plastic and hurt. Dion cries out and starts crawling away on all fours. His pants are slathered with Swiss Miss Creamy Milk Chocolate Pudding. By now, the customer and I have negotiated the chips rack, but Dez, a wild-haired cyclone, goes a step further than anyone imagined. She grips a shelf with both hands and rips it off the aisle wall.

It's flimsy but metal, with sharp edges. Dion has flopped to his side, his cream-colored polo halfway up his cream-colored torso, and it's easy to imagine Dez punching the end of the shelf right through Dion's stomach, forcing him to confront his worst nightmare: his own raw meat. But the customer beside me lassos Dez around the waist, allowing me to wrench the shelf from her grip.

The register clerk shouts about police. Dion rolls onto his back, heaving for breath. Dez bursts for the front of the store, snatching up her purse. She's in worse shape than Dion. I hear the sucking noises of her jagged inhales. The thoracic deformity of her spine has gone a horseshoe shape, forcing her to crane her neck upward just to see straight ahead. She grips the Kum & Go door like it's only thing preventing her from collapsing, and manages to turn.

"You never come here again! Maggot Boy! Maggot!"

Dez nurtured slights like Bonsai trees and had special names for those she believed had crossed her. Bob Nutting: Boss Man Bob. Dion Skerry: Maggot Boy. Cheri Orritt: Ice Cream Cone. Tamra Longmoor: Toll House Cookies. I have thought on the origins of those names, but let's concentrate on what was shared by the objects of her scorn: one manager, one assistant manager, two shift managers. In short, anyone whose job included criticism.

Her beef with Dion predated their April clash, but Dion's commentary on it is colorless. I'd love to hear Dez's take. I find her on the sidewalk outside Kum & Go, pacing a figure-eight on the sidewalk. Another hyperbolic reaction, like she's performing for an audience. Dez's mad energy is endurable in the bright wide-open, but must be nerve-wracking in enclosed spaces—say, Burger City while you're closing.

The sunny day allows me to better define what others have danced around. Dez's homeliness borders on deformity. Her masses of tangled, ink-black hair swell the size of an Easter Island head with features that are just *too much*. Too much chin, too much nose, too much cheekbone, like she's wearing movie prosthetics. Here's what strikes me hardest: Dez Mozley has the worst complexion I've ever seen. She's Caucasian, but her skin is a ripe-apple red. It has an apple's shine too, though it sure isn't apple-smooth.

I realize her skin looks like ground meat.

When Dez sees me, she does a Looney Tunes double-take and waves her hands like she's begging for one single break in life. Again, the left palm, the glowing, once-inch scar.

"Hold on! Are you the manager, sir? Sir, are you the manager?"

It's unfortunate that Dez has the stereotypical look of a witch, as witches were her favorite culprits on whom to pin the Burger City Tragedy. According to her, the Cedar View Village Estates trailer park where she lived seethed with diabolism. It seems clear to me: once you cross Dez, *you* become a witch.

"Maggot Boy in there assaulted me, sir! Go ahead and check your video cameras! Dez Mozley is a law-abiding citizen that believes in peace and justice, I swear!"

It's a straight-up lie, but that's not my concern. I explain to her who I am, why I was at the Kum & Go with Dion Skerry, and that I'd like to speak to her about the Burger City Tragedy, if she'd be willing. She shakes her head so hard her long mats of black hair whip her red face.

"You're trying to trick me. Make me say forbidden words."

I assure her I'm not. I pull someone else's business card from my wallet and write my information on the back. I give it to Dez and tell her to call if she'd like to get her opinions on the record. She stares at the card like it's on fire, then stares as me like I'm on fire too.

"You don't know what you're dealing with. I ought to carry a gun instead of spells, a big old gun. You don't know about the dead birds on my doorstep. They're wrapped in corn leaves. Do you know what that means? It means *be careful*. You listen to what Maggot Boy says, it's your ass. I'll tell the cops the same thing. You think that many birds fall out of the sky on their own? When I go outside my trailer, it's crunch, crunch, crunch. No, sir, I won't say forbidden words. And if you chase Dez Mozley in your devil car, she'll drive straight off a cliff, you hear?"

Around 4:45 on November 25, shortly after Lil' Beefy did her thing, Kit texted Clem to swap shifts so he could monitor the walk-in freezer. Unable to help himself, Kit texted a picture of a frozen Hot Wheels car.

Word spread quickly among employees of a new abnormality. Clem texted Quin, who texted Amber, who texted Amy, and so on.

One of the frozen Hot Wheels (photo by Kit Bryant).

Kit arrived for his morning shift at 5:00 a.m., gripping his *IDEAS* notebook. At 6:45, Maxine Pinto got up from B9, ostensibly to get a fresh cup of BC Deluxe Select, but really because she'd overheard Kit and Amber discussing the freezer. Stu Blick and Zadie Budden took note. Maxine was speaking to Kit the instant Quin Arthur paraded through the door.

He held a book like a pennant. At two hundred and thirty four pages it was slender, with a plastic-coated jacket and numbered spine identifying it as property of the Wilton Public Library where his mother worked. Maxine Pinto, being partially deaf, didn't hear Quin enter, and finished her question to Kit.

"Has our friendly ghost moved to the cooler?" she asked.

Quin halted at Till 2 and slapped down the book.

"That circle in the freezer? It's called a *cold spot*." He glanced at Maxine Pinto. "And we don't have a ghost. We have a poltergeist."

DECEMBER 2016

THE SHOW AND THE MEAL

On December 3, Kit devoted the whole of his thirty-minute break to hearing out Quin's theories. Joining them at B5 at 10:45 a.m. that Saturday were Clemens Dumay, who'd arrived with Quin, and Cheri Orritt, who'd just clocked out. Normally she bolted outside for a smoke. Perhaps she was drawn by the peril of the two young rivals facing off.

Sailing into his senior year with a 4.0 GPA, Quin Arthur was editor of the school paper, *The Rose Bugle*, Debate Team member, National Honor Society inductee, RCHS Film Club founder, a not-bad tenor in both chorus and chamber choir, and heavily involved in drama, where he continued playing Clem's straight man on stage. Quin's way of wooing Amber was to impress her with his videos. She was always impressed, that was true. Also true: she was never wooed. Yet the popularity of Quin's "Burger City Ghost?" video had given him the biggest confidence jolt of his life.

The Lil' Beefy Anomaly had put Quin and Kit on a collision course.

The book Quin displayed to the others was *The Poltergeist* by William G. Roll. He insisted, quite correctly, that the 1972 text remained the central pillar of poltergeist inquiry forty years after it was written. It was published with the tacit endorsement of the relevant quarterlies of the day: *Journal of the American Society for Psychical Research*, *Journal of Parapsychology*, and *Journal of the Society for Psychical Research*. The book introduced Roll to the public as the world's leading investigator of poltergeists—or, if you were a skeptic, the word's most dupable apologist for attention-seeking adolescents who liked to bump lamps off tables and cry ghost.

Quin set his phone on the tabletop and hit record on the Voice Memos app. He was a post-millennial trained to gauge the social-media potential of any given situation, and high on YouTube fame, he wasn't going to let this meeting go undocumented. He cleared his throat, paused dramatically, and unleashed Roll's central premise.

"Poltergeists have nothing to do with ghosts. They have to do with a person."

Kit frowned. It sounded like Quin was trying to drain wonder from events Kit considered wonderful. Cheri laughed once, gruffly, her way of indicating she was listening. Clem, meanwhile, popped fries and calibrated punchline placements.

"You mean a *person's* haunted?" Kit asked.

"Roll came up with this thing, RSPK—Recurrent Spontaneous Psychokinesis. Psychokinesis is moving things with your mind. That's what a poltergeist is, a physical manifestation of a person's PK. Roll calls the person with PK 'the agent.'"

The deckled edges of Roll's book were brightened by a week's worth of colored page markers, tokens of Quin's study methods. He flipped to one of them and paraphrased.

"'Apparently some people function rather like batteries, giving energy to such occurrences…there's nothing bad or evil about this energy.'"[45]

"I agree with that," Kit said. "I don't feel anything evil about any of this stuff."

"Here I thought I only had gas," Cheri snickered.

"Did none of you see the movie?" Clem interjected. "We're going to have clown toys coming to life here. I don't mean Ronald McDonalds either. I'm talking sharp-toothed clown monsters with long, strangly arms. There's also probably going to be a man-eating tree. Don't sugarcoat this, Q!"

"The bad news is poltergeists can be violent," Quin said. "People really get hurt by these things. There's biting poltergeists recorded way back in 1762. It gets confusing, because some people react psychosomatically. They'll get rashes and hives just from being around it."

"I *do* have a rash I'd like to show everyone," Clem offered.

Quin continued. "Lil' Beefy and the cold spot fit perfectly. Poltergeists are all about repetition. They do the same things over and over. Objects fall off the same counter every day at three. Screams come from the attic every forty-eight minutes. Whatever."

"Well, nothing's more repetitive than Burger City." Clem adopted a robotic voice. "Bun toasting: eleven seconds. Burger cooking: thirty-eight seconds. Assembly: twenty seconds. Wrapping: fourteen seconds. Full customer service in under ninety seconds. Bleep-bloop."

"What I'm saying is, you can't quantify ghosts," Quin said. "But poltergeists can be *measured*. Look, this is a chart Roll made of things moving around a warehouse."

The diagram Quin displayed did more to convince coworkers of a poltergeist in their midst than anything he could ever say. The warehouse in question was Tropication Arts, a wholesale novelty-gift business in

---

45 William G. Roll, *The Poltergeist* (Doubleday, 1972), 153.

Miami that William G. Roll observed in January 1967, logging two hundred and twenty-four instances of highball glasses, back scratchers, plastic fans, and other tchotchkes flying from storage shelves. It's dizzying to look at: blueprints slashed with solid and dashed lines, each of them arrowed and meticulously numbered, tracking every movement.

My personal copy of Roll's book (photo by the author).

The rigor of Roll's cataloging made Kit and Clem instant believers. Their credulity should not surprise us. A 2003 Harris Poll of two-thousand Americans showed that 90 percent believed in God, 89 percent in miracles, 68 percent in the devil, and 51 percent in ghosts.[46] Cheri Orritt was a different story; a Gallup poll confirms that 56 percent of people between the ages of 18 and 29 believe in haunted houses, but only 26 percent of those 65 and older do.[47]

"We can do the same thing," Kit realized. "We can do it up scientific."

"Like my dad says," Quin replied, "darn tootin' we can."

If only those who lost loved ones in the Burger City Tragedy could see this golden moment: Kit and Quin, galvanized by possibility, willing to work together, straddling the edge of cooperation and competition. It's easy to speculate on the lives that might have been saved had the two been able to maintain this balance.

"I don't want to call the cops on your party," Cheri said. "But this is your [Quin's and Clem's] senior year. There's maybe, just maybe, something to be said for focusing on school, grades, your future—you know, all that boring shit? And you, kid [Kit], you got energy to spend, that's for sure. It's just where you choose to spend it, am I right?"

---

46 Michael Clarkson, *The Poltergeist Phenomenon* (New Page, 2011), 11.
47 Ibid., 11.

Cheri said her piece lightly, but today it feels heavy. While Kit was thinking of the Roll-style diagrams he could draw inside his *IDEAS* book, Cheri was thinking of the busted dreams of the notebook's earlier pages.

It was a hot six seconds of silence.

"Also," Clem said, "this is your friendly reminder of killer clowns."

The tension-breaker worked too well. Everyone laughed, even Cheri, and the bad idea rampaged free. Quin flipped through the book and tapped a page with a finger.

"Roll says here, 'Genuine poltergeists are nearly always short-lived.'[48] They usually only last a few months. So, you know, it can't take up *that* much of our time."

"That's so quick!" Kit cried.

"Don't say I didn't warn you assholes," Cheri sighed.

"So who's the agent?" Kit pressed.

"Well, it's not like someone is Carrie," Quin said, citing the Stephen King novel. "No one's throwing fireballs with their mind or anything. RSPK is totally unconscious."

"I'm calling it now," Clem said. "Dez is the agent. No question."

"I did read that ghosts are attracted to people interested in the occult," Quin said. "But this isn't occult. This is science. PK usually centers around a young person. Lots of times a girl going through puberty."

"Who's the youngest employee?" Kit asked.

Cheri pointed a finger. "I don't want you dumb fucks bothering Yesenia."

"Age is just one variable. Roll says someone's PK ability can be set off by a troubled life. And here's the kicker. They don't even always have to be *around*." Quin skipped to a red tab and read aloud. "'A rare but important poltergeist phenomenon is the occurrence which takes place when the agent is absent.'[49] People who produce PK leave it *behind*."

"Troubled life," Kit repeated softly. Even on audio, his yearning is laid bare. Kit ached to be the special one, and for the first time in his life, he had all the qualifications. Quin humphs. If one were to believe Roll's theories, and Quin did, Kit Bryant did look like the most likely agent. Therefore, Quin couldn't let the role feel too desirable.

"There's a story in here about a girl in Scotland back in the sixties," he said. "Furniture flying around and all that stuff. And her sister-in-law's excuse to people was that she suffered from 'an obscure ailment.'[50] See, the

48 Roll, *The Poltergeist*, 201.

49 Ibid., 193.

50 Ibid., 103.

person at the center of this is basically sick. He's got a disease. He or she. I hope it's not me, is all I'm saying."

Kit leveled Quin with the steady, bemused look he always did when Quin exposed his jealousy. If it had been Amber next to Kit instead of Cheri, Kit would've snaked his arm around her waist to confirm the pecking order. Five years from now, Quin Arthur would probably be making fifty times Kit's salary. But right now, Kit had the only thing Quin wanted.

Cheri smelled trouble. "All right, boys. Daggers on the table."

Kit snorted derisively. Like he'd need a dagger to take down this geek? Quin, for his part, didn't stand down. His smugness is audible.

"When Lil' Beefy first started moving, she didn't do it very often," Quin said. "But when people started *waiting* for her to move? It started happening all the time, every day. Then I upload my video and the hits go through the roof. What does the poltergeist do then? It turns toy cars into ice cubes. It makes a cold spot *inside* a cold spot—the walk-in freezer. This thing is fucking with us."

Kit was won over. "Because we're fucking with *it*."

"Exactly. The more attention we give it, the more it responds. So what do we do? We publicize it. Post about it. Tag celebrities. DJ HaXn was great, but imagine if we got, like, LeBron James or Jimmy Fallon."

"Mickey says he knows a guy who knows Pitbull's dad's step-kid," Clem said. "So that's pretty dope."

"Everyone use my YouTube page to link to," Quin said.

"Right." Kit smirked. "I see how it is."

"You got a better idea? All my best videos are pinned there, plus I'm keeping playlists of every customer video that gets posted."

"So what are you going to call this thing?" Cheri sighed. "This tiny little no-big-deal thing that definitely isn't going to detract from schoolwork and staying out of trouble and all that?"

"Jerry," Clemens suggested. "Can we call it Jerry?"

"If we want to stick to convention, usually they have location names," Quin said. "The Enfield Poltergeist, the Thornton Heath Poltergeist."

"It's like Nutting says," Kit giggled. "A good product name sells itself."

"The Burger City Poltergeist?" Cheri chuckled. "You want to call it the Burger City Poltergeist?"

There is another six-second pause filled with customer scuttle and the distant croons of WKES's Soft Rock Hitz.

"Badass," Clem said.

"Hell yes," Quin said.

"Ba-boom!" Kit Bryant cried, angling a skinny arm around Cheri Orritt's shoulders, bringing her close, her frizzy red hair interlocking with his greasy black locks. Even in his ill-fitting blue-and-orange uniform and dorky cap, it's hard to picture the kid ever looking cooler, or happier, or healthier. If he had an obscure ailment, it sure didn't look like it.

Bob Nutting had managed to forget about Lil' Beefy for the extent of his Thanksgiving vacation, if "vacation" was what you called a five-day festival of groveling before a wife who'd lost twenty pounds, streaked her hair pink, and gotten a snake tattoo down her left arm. Lisa Nutting had an arsenal of new behaviors that mesmerized Kristina and Brandine—confident swaggers, sexy pouts, carefree laughter—leaving good ol' dad alone in the kitchen, perspiring over a bird no one wanted.

Nutting returned to work on November 28 in no mood for the picture-taking gawkers bottlenecking his lobby at 4:00 every afternoon. BCU instructors had rammed home the rule of keeping queues moving above all else. A customer standing idle is a customer likely to notice a dozen other failings.

The challenge for any QSR manager was reconciling this directive with the precept of "the customer is always right." Nutting was paralyzed with indecision. Should he beg the Lil' Beefy groupies to get into queues? Should he chuck the blood-stained standee into the dumpster? By the second Monday of December, he made the radical move of avoiding the 4:00-5:00 hour altogether, preferring to monitor the fray from his office computer.

It was during one of these caesuras that he read the latest sales report.

When Bob Nutting took the reins of Burger City Franchise Location #8 in 2006, it was producing a yearly profit of $60,200 at a profit margin of 16 percent. Ten years into his tenure, the location was on life support, generating a $48,000 profit at an 8 percent margin. Ticket averages were down across the board. Neither the relentless upselling of 50-cent Beefyburgers to pricier options (BeefBoat, BeefBowl, Reefy Beef, and Big Beefy at $4; Grandpa Beefy at $5.25; BeefBomb at $7.25), nor the steady 90 percent soft-drink profit margin could pull #8 from the off-ramp quicksand. After the Crime, things only worsened.

As Bob Nutting keyed figures that December day, the arithmetic shocked him. POS data showed table turns doubling. Overall ticket sizes were up 40 percent, with Friday and Saturday tickets up a staggering 60 percent, numbers unheard of outside of grand openings.

The evidence was undeniable. Lil' Beefy rubberneckers were staying to buy. And buying big, like you might indulge yourself with a meal after a show. Nutting recalled seeing a production of *Nunsense* with Lisa in Iowa City, all sorts of habit-wearing singers twirling about while he gnashed the matinée menu of Pineapple-glazed Ham, Scalloped Potatoes, and Vegetable Medley. "Dinner theater" it was called—and that's what he had on his hands right now. He had the show *and* the meal.

Suddenly he was sweating so badly he had to switch off the space heater. He had mental recalculations to make, and fast.

Thank Christ he hadn't tossed that cardboard dog!

He cursored through his email trash. Days earlier, he'd junked a message with the subject line *TV9 Inquiry*. He recovered it and read it. An anonymous Burger City employee had sent Cissie Patmore, a reporter from Davenport's WNOG-TV9, a playlist of videos documenting something called "the Burger City Poltergeist." (Today we know this was Quin Arthur, launching his PR push.) As much as Nutting hated the idea of a staffer doing anything behind his back, this could not have worked out better.

He called the reporter that instant.

At 3:00 p.m. the next day, Patmore and videographer Gillespie Hendy set up camp in B5 to tape interviews. It was small-market local news: a clunky, first-gen, digital-format camera; a charred Fresnel light; a reporter with hair shellacked into a solid piece. Nutting was to be interviewed, followed by Dion Skerry and Darcy Smyrna, the two workers he'd deemed least likely to go rogue or steal the spotlight.

The video is gone from WNOG's site, but it's pirated all over the net, including remixes that slow or stop moments to facilitate conspiracy-theory analyses. Doesn't the murk in the Grand Room look like a woman's face? Doesn't the wall above the water fountain seem like it's bleeding? Can't you hear in this section of audio an Indian chief's ancient curse?

Let's stick to the original version. From the opening voice-over, Cissie Patmore's "spooky" tone brands the story as the D-block puff-piece it is, and the interviewees play along. Dion relays the sequence of events well enough, and manages to mention the cold spot without buckling from Meat Grief. Darcy, in a shoulder-length wig, wins out over her damaged brain cells, charmingly nervous, a blush pinkening her cheeks.

"I just never saw so much excitement," Darcy says, adding proudly, "My daughter Amber works here too, you know. We're all just excited."

Bob Nutting gets top billing. What a difference a day makes. In his sit-down, he's animated and playful, doing his best Vincent Price, and when he leads the camera through the narrow BOH halls, it's with the bouncy step of someone showing off their homemade haunted house.

"No one can explain it," he intones, sweeping a Dracula arm at Lil' Beefy.

"Who can say who goes there?" he asks rhetorically, side-eyeing the Coldest Cold Spot.

In the weeks after the June 1 Tragedy, a whisper campaign suggested the whole thing had been a hoax perpetuated by Bob Nutting to save his restaurant. The idea had precedent. In 1761 England, Richard Giles faked a poltergeist to lower property value.[51] In 1948 Illinois, Wanet McNeil blamed a poltergeist for the fire that consumed her farm, when really she was just sick of living there.[52] Nutting, however, wasn't inventive enough to pull off such shenanigans. He saw the upswing in sales as the first step in repairing his broken family—that's it.

With the Ash Muckells murder only three months old, Nutting had so far kept the whole Lil' Beefy thing close to the vest. Anxious over how his TV appearance might play to Burger City brass, on December 7 he sent a note to Regional Manager Beauregard Waterhouse framing the attention in a jovial light.

Hello Mr. Waterhouse!

Bit of excitement down here in Jonny as our #8 has become famous for a ghost! I gave an interview to a local TV station, and what fun everyone had. It is great POSITIVE publicity and the sales results prove it! Please see the attached numbers. I think it will make you have a Lil Beefy sized smile!

Have a spooky day!

Bob Nutting
Manager, Burger City #8
2953 N. Rolf Tonks Road
Jonny, Iowa 52778

---

51 Clarkson, *The Poltergeist Phenomenon*, 122.
52 Ibid.

For me, the best part of TV9's kicker is the final bit, naturally shot at 4:24 p.m. When the camera swings toward the swell of phone-holding onlookers, you see Cheri Orritt, arms folded by the fry cooker, having had just about enough. You see Amber Smyrna fluffing her hair. You see Quin Arthur grabbing surreptitious behind-the-scenes shots. Finally, you see Kit Bryant at Till 2, and he's *glaring*, not at Lil' Beefy or Bob Nutting but directly into Gillespie Hendy's lens. This is *his* ghost, and the fact that he's been kept from the news, small as it is, is un-fucking-acceptable.

THE MEN'S ROOM BULLY

Hanford Pendergast is the aforementioned 77-year-old who loves bitching about dark tourists visiting the Burger City ruins near his house. It was Pendergast who alerted the Tipton Fire Department of the November 14, 2017, blaze that guaranteed the place would stay closed for good.

"Made me a nice stiff drink first before calling." Though Pendergast's face mask hides his lips, a smile tightens the baby-fists of his eye flesh and lowers his snow drift of hair.

During my time in and around Jonny, I get a lot of smiles like this. It's the Midwestern-nice version of a conspiratorial wink. Pendergast's innuendo is clear. He waited until fire was pouring from shattered windows before calling in the clean-up crew. I find it offensive. In our third unwelcome conversation, Pendergast reveals he's the guy who shot up the *FOOD EXIT 269* sign on I-80. I know the one he means. The Iowa Department of Transportation removed Burger City's placard from the sign in 2018, leaving it blank but for the spray of bullet holes.

Another nudge-nudge smile. "I did it for Cheri."

Finally, Pendergast has my attention. I regret never having met those who died on June 1, 2017, and Cheri Orritt is at the top of that list. She was a lifetime older than some of those who died, yet it is her I hear mourned at diners, stores, and parks. She was the emotional spine of this swath of Iowa, and I don't think anyone knew it until she was gone.

"I used to see her at Bloom's Pub couple times a month," Pendergast says. "We'd line up the High Lifes, literally line them up, and when I started doing the penguin walk, Cheri would still be drinking and smoking. Smoking isn't even allowed no more. But Cheri, she'd situate herself in a booth with a pillow for her bad back, and she'd just puff away, and all night long people would come visit."

Cheri Orritt was held dear in the opposite way of Darcy Smyrna. There was nothing soft about Cheri. She had a fried shrub of frazzled red hair, gnawed fingernails, an indifference to fashion that became its own rural-bohemian style (including her ubiquitous shaded glasses), and the foulest mouth along I-80. It wasn't just Bloom's Pub she frequented.

It was Beer & Billiards in Ayresville, Classy's in Wilton, Yesterdays in Rochester, and Ye Olde Alehouse in West Liberty. No one suggests she had a drinking problem. These were simply places that felt like home to Cheri, the same way Burger City, for all its pitfalls, did too.

Her actual home, a crumbling five-room bungalow near Crooked Creek off IA-38, must have felt lonely in comparison. No one I spoke to had ever visited. Today it is boarded up but still reeks of Cheri, which is to say Newport menthols.

Rumor: the great love affair of her life ended tragically. Rumor: she used to play backup bass for the Allman Brothers. There's little about Cheri Orritt that *isn't* rumor. She didn't talk about herself. She talked about you.

"She had this quality," Pendergast says in the moment I like him most. "You wanted Cheri to like you. And when she did—gosh, it made your troubles feel far away."

With a twenty-eight-year Burger City career behind her (and the *KILL ME NOW* plaque to prove it), Cheri was the only employee able to confirm that #8 had never closed a shift before, not even during the Puppy Pen rebuild of 2001.

But on Tuesday, December 20, Bob Nutting did the unthinkable. At 7:30 p.m., he began dropping by tables and booths to politely refer diners to the signs taped up everywhere: *CLOSING AT 8PM FOR TEAM MEMBER TRAINING.* At 7:45, he flipped the *CLOSED* signs, stationed Mickey McCormick at the door, and sent a bundled-up Javi Villareal to place a sawhorse in the drive-thru lane. By 8:00, the lights of the pole sign and drive-thru menu went dark, the door was locked, and Nutting herded his entire staff into the Grand Room, minus Darcy Smyrna, whose exhaustion kept her at home.

Most of those present were drinking Chillees. They paid the usual employee half-price and were happy to do it. Burger City might be known for the Beefyburger, but the Chillee was its real innovation. Wendy's Frosty, McDonald's Shamrock Shake, and even Shake Shack's mighty Black & White couldn't compare. Chillees were the ideal consistency, the perfect temperature. The malty texture was sprinkled through with explosively tasty sugar crystals. Chillees were not especially sweet; in fact, some speculated the secret ingredient to be a pinch of salt.

Employees lived on the stuff. They depended on it. A cold, creamy Chillee could turn around a bad day, instill hope in an otherwise blighted future. Health-nut Zane downed them as frequently as anyone, and Amber, the staff's sole vegetarian, was fully addicted. As she liked to quip, there was no evidence Chillees contained animal matter, including dairy. By law, in fact, Burger City couldn't use the word "milkshake"; its prime components were corn syrup, whipped cream, and something called "Chillee fluid."[53]

The problem, and it was a gnarly one, was the Chillee Shake Machine. Burger City workers all over the Midwest cursed these belligerent shit-heads. Each one resembled a five-foot-tall espresso machine with rubber tubing pumping the ingredients. One suspects the "Chillee fluid" was what so frequently gummed up the mechanics. Fixing, cleaning, and sanitizing a Chillee Shake Machine was an all-night nightmare requiring total disassembly. Dez Mozley was the only human near Jonny who could do it, and often a full week would pass before she got around to it. During those times, morale dangerously dipped.

The night of the meeting, Chillees helped calm a staff anticipating some serious shit. Most had a fair idea of Bob Nutting's agenda. He paced a drill sergeant's line in front of T1, T2, and T3. At precisely 8:05 p.m., he stopped, tapped three pieces of papers against his thigh, and surveyed the staff seated across T4, T5, and T6.

From T4, Quin Arthur secretly taped the whole thing on his phone.

"I hope everyone here appreciates the dramatic steps I've taken tonight," Nutting began. "We ought to have another three full hours of business yet. It's 14 degrees out there. When it's this cold, people don't go to restaurants. Where they go is drive-thrus. We're missing a big Tuesday take."

Nutting's sigh played to the cheap seats.

"I don't get it. I really don't get it. It feels like a few days ago, our team was working together stupendously. Wasn't it going stupendously? I put that velvet rope around Lil' Beefy and doesn't it add a certain razzmatazz? It's like I always say: KPIs [Key Performance Indicators] tell us the best action items combine focused marketing with our team's passion for the Burger City experience."

Nutting shook his head, a gravely disappointed dad.

"Then comes this week. I get here yesterday afternoon, cold as heck but thinking about our customer-centric mission, and go back to my office to sit in front of the heater for a minute, and what do I see taped to the break room door? Anyone care to answer that? Kit? Clemens? Javier? Yesenia?"

His suspicions laid bare: a nemesis, a prankster, a blur of Latinos.

No one answered. Nutting's neck blotched with a pinkness that Dion Skerry, in the grips of Meat Grief, might have described as "Medium Rare."

"I guess I'm going to have to show you what I'm holding here. If

53 *Burger City Manager's Handbook*, 20.

anyone would like to *prevent* me from doing so with a confession, I'm sure we'd all appreciate it. No? Fine. You know what? Fine. It truly brings me no pleasure to have to show you this, I hope you know that."

"I could have watched that dude squirm all day. He was like Mr. Gottschalk [from your novel *Rotters*], one of those dudes who thinks he's some kind of genius, but has never met a challenge in his life. And the poltergeist was a big, huge challenge. Of course he was going to fail it."

Kit Bryant is wired inside his room at Bruce P. Chernow Medical Health Institute. I've been holding my need to use the restroom; I don't want to interrupt his flow. Behind me, Nuncio's breathing has gotten louder and steadier, making me wonder if he's fallen asleep. Should I be worried about that?

"At that point, I was royally pissed about TV9. He gets Darcy to go on camera? And Dion? *Dion?* Are you shitting me? Are you actually physically shitting on me? At least that was small-time. That was local. No way I was going to let Nutting keep me away from *national* TV."

There is no use tracing the path of the TV9 kicker to internet fame. In 2016, the online promulgation of funny local TV spots was a well-oiled machine. Quin's video had a lot of views, but it's not like it had spawned a trending hashtag. The TV9 piece did. For the weekend of December 9–11, #BurgerCityPoltergeist was an official trending topic on U.S. Twitter, right alongside #NationalPastryDay.

Reporter Cissie Patmore's off-tune naïveté was bait for slavering trolls, but videographer and editor Gillespie Hendy seemed to appreciate the golden turd he was polishing. He holds closeups longer than he should, allowing that extra beat of silence that makes everything twice as funny.

"Just because Nutting knew words like *ROI* and *smarketing*," Kit says, "he thought he deserved all the credit. The Monday after we trended, we started getting job applications. Truckloads. This was Jonny, Iowa. This was Exit 269. Usually we had to make calls when we needed a fresh body. Suddenly I'm seeing applications from Des Moines. By Wednesday, it was Peoria and Omaha. We got one in from Boston. People *wanted* to work there. To be one of us. Us!"

That *us!* hurts, a pin headed for an inflated balloon.

"Everyone knew when Nutting got the call. We heard his office door bang open. Dude had no chill. I was working kitchen with Cheri and he comes in, and just kind of looks at us, and then starts talking real quiet, which was a thing he'd do so you'd have to stop what you were doing to hear what the fuck he saying. So we lean close, whatever, and he says, 'I just spoke to…the Travel Channel.'"

Founded by Trans World Airlines in 1987, the Travel Channel (these days restyled as Trvl) made its name with programs like *Anthony Bourdain: No Reservations*. By the time of the Burger City Poltergeist, smart programming had gone down the tubes[54] and the Travel Channel had gone all-in with spooky bullshit. As of this writing, the Travel Channel runs the following supernatural programming: *The Alaska Triangle, Alien Highway, America Declassified, The Dead Files, Destination Fear, Expedition Bigfoot, Famously Afraid, Ghost Adventures, Ghost Adventures: Serial Killer Spirits, Ghost Adventures: Haunted Houseguests, Ghost Loop, Ghost Nation, Ghosts of Morgan City, Haunting in the Heartland, The Holzer Files, Hometown Horror, Kindred Spirits, Most Terrifying Places, Mountain Monsters, My Horror Story, Mysteries at the Castle, Mysteries at the Monument, Mysteries at the Museum, Mysteries at the National Parks, Paranormal Caught on Camera, Portals to Hell, Strange World, Trending Fear,* and *Witches of Salem*. It's a depressing but successful[55] lineup.

"So Cheri goes, 'Travel? You taking a trip? Thanksgiving must've gone pretty good, huh?' But Nutting acts like he's on another plane. Like nothing we mortals can say could penetrate his exalted bubble. He goes, 'It was a producer from…*Spectral Journeys*.' Cheri just stared, but damn, I knew that show, and as dumb as Nutting was acting, I kind of felt it too."

The *Spectral Journeys* call came on Tuesday, December 13. Producer Marsella Nixon had seen the online buzz and wanted to bring her crew to Burger City to do "some gentle ghost-busting." What had rattled Nutting was that a cancelation in their shooting schedule dictated that they tape on January 2 and 3—just two weeks away.

"Everything went into hyperdrive," Kit says. "Dez was called in during the daytime, which freaked everyone out, and he said he'd pay overtime to anyone who helped with a top-to-bottom scrub—except inside Lil' Beefy's velvet rope. Dude never paid overtime in his life. A bunch of us got in on it. Clem, because of Lysander. Amber, because her mom. Javi, Mickey. We made that shit-hole gleam. Did we get a thanks? A *yay, team*? All we got were personal invites to a suck-ass emergency meeting."

It's a wonder that Bob Nutting didn't consider the image he displayed to his staff at 8:10 pm. on December 20 as possible infringement of the

---

54 Another example: consider how the Learning Channel's programming progressed from such shows as *Paleoworld* and *Captain's Log* to *Jon & Kate Plus 8, Hoarding: Buried Alive,* and *Here Comes Honey Boo Boo*.

55 "Travel Channel Earns Best Year in Network History," *Travel Channel,* January 4, 2019.

sexual harassment policy in section 3 of his cherished Burger City Team Member Handbook, particularly the fourth bullet:

> 'Visual Harassment.' Examples: obscene notes, unwanted 'love letters', staring at an employee's anatomy, leering, sexually oriented gestures, mooning, derogatory photographs, sexual cartoons or drawings, videos or 'GIFs.'

"The Haunted Dick Pic" is what staffers would come to call it, though for obvious reasons its existence was not made public until well after the Burger City Tragedy. As you might anticipate, it was a photo of an erect penis. It was circumcised and Caucasian. It looked to be roughly five inches in length. The pubic hair was black or brown, hard to tell due to the camera flash.

Nutting had adhered a pink Post-it note to hide the penis's head. Hilariously, this left the shaft in full view, as if that part was PG. Nutting's display of the photo established that he was the police chief here and this penis was Public Enemy #1.

"*Spectral Journeys* will be here in a fortnight. Translation: two weeks. Do you know what kind of hoops of fire I had to jump through to get BC Corporate to sign off on it? I will not—will *not*—allow one of you to humiliate my restaurant on national television. If this were a random obscene photograph, that would be one thing. But this?" Nutting rotated the dick for all to enjoy. "You recognize the location? That's a stall in the men's room. This was taken right here, printed out—in color!—and disseminated."

There was a snort, probably due to the closeness of *disseminate* and *inseminate*.

"I'm sure everyone who worked yesterday saw this picture on the break room door. I'm sorry for that. I'm genuinely sorry." He slapped the paper face-down on T3, then held up the next paper. It was the same print-out, except in this one, the penis was festooned with glitter glue. "Those of you who went into dry goods storage also saw this one. I'm sorry for that too." Slap! The final paper was the same except with something drawn on it. "And this one? On the door to the Puppy Pen? *The Puppy Pen?* Just because someone drew a Santa Claus hat on top does not make this male member any less offensive."[56]

Multiple snorts this time, and loud enough that you can identify the snorters: Cheri, Clem, Mickey. There are also a couple tsks of disgust, probably from Tamra, the devout Christian, and Dez, quick to take affront to anything. It was enough to embolden Amy Mold.

---

56 Tragically, none of the copies of the Haunted Dick Pic survive.

"I don't think we should be calling them 'offensive male members.' There's nothing offensive about a penis. Or a vagina."

Nutting's color went "Rare."

"Please don't say *vagina* in my Grand Room," he said.

"This is how body dysmorphia starts. The human body is natural."

"Amy," Nutting pleaded. "All I'm asking is you don't take pictures of your natural body and hang them on my walls!"

"How do we even know that chile belongs to one of us?" Javi asked.

"That's right," Mickey added. "Could be a customer who got in the mood."

"Those are Burger City slacks," Nutting insisted.

"Hmm," Clem said. "You'd have to be looking *really hard* to know that."

Snickering from pretty much everyone now. Nutting was losing control. Quickly, he ditched his plan for a patient siege and turned on his prime suspect.

"Kit Bryant. You're awfully quiet."

Kit shrugged. "Not my dick, man."

"And I'm supposed to believe that."

Kit laughed. He couldn't help it. "You're going to have to take my word."

"Can you tell me to my face that's not you in the photo?"

"Trust me," Amber said, quite saucily for her. "That's not Kit's dick."

The joint blew up. Laughter, gasps, cheers, hoots, and that *haww* noise you make when someone just got owned. Nutting's blush hit its final stage: "Raw."

Watching Quin's footage, I find myself sympathizing with Nutting. Cheri Orritt apparently felt the same. With seventeen years of seniority on Nutting, she was the only one able to serve as conduit between the king and his serfs. Her interruption was calm and generous.

"Bob," she began—she always began with the *Bob*. "I hear you. That's a lot of cock for one Burger City. But I think we're focusing on the wrong thing. We all saw the pictures. But the *point* of the pictures isn't that very natural male member, is it?"

To this day, the penis goes unidentified. But the alleged sequence of events goes like this. Around December 18, a male entered the men's room stall, sat on the toilet, and began to masturbate. At some point, the self-pleasurer heard a noise strange enough for him to crack open the stall. He saw something, fumbled for his phone (possibly already in use for porn), and snapped a shot. This, as Cheri Orritt said, was the point: not the dick, but what was *behind* it.

The auto-focus racked to the foreground penis. Though this flaw gives the photo a sense of authenticity, it doesn't mean it's authentic. Digital artists regularly use this technique to insert all sorts of ghoulies into existing photographs.

The creator then used a digital pen to draw emphatic red arrows pointing at the phenomenon. All Burger City bathrooms had hand-cranked dispensers that begrudgingly emitted useless scraps of brown paper towels. But behind this penis, a long banner of towel effortlessly rippled through the air, as if reeled out by an invisible hand. You could even see the reflection of these towels in the bathroom mirror.

Unwilling to fess up to public masturbation, the photographer printed and hung up three copies of the photo, most likely to make staff aware of a new spectacle to add to the Lil' Beefy Anomaly and the Coldest Cold Spot. Nutting was probably right that it was a staff member (excuse the pun); whoever hung the pictures exploited security-cam blind spots.

Believers consider the Haunted Dick Pic to be the first manifestation of the Men's Room Bully.

Nutting's meeting dissolved at 8:50 following a half hour of employees exchanging theories about what the heck was going on with those hand towels. Taking Amy Mold's cue, they showed surprising maturity by ignoring the penis for the rest of the discussion. Nutting, however, had anticipated fear and trembling. By 8:30, he'd folded like an introvert at a party, dejectedly taking a seat at the T3 two-top. He looked like he might cry; one imagines this is how he looked when Lisa went out with other men.

Quin's covert footage is below his usual standards, but the last three seconds catch something fairly incredible, and there's nothing ghostly about it. Everyone is up, putting on coats, finding keys, gabbing as they head for the door. Quin's camera swipes across the Grand Room as he reaches to turn off the recording. Right before he does, we catch a glimpse of T3.

Cheri Orritt has joined Bob Nutting at the two-top. She has lit a cigarette, a violation not even Amber could get away with. Her free arm, meanwhile, has snaked behind the salt and pepper shakers, sugar packets, napkin holder, and an advert for 33-percent-off Grandpa Beefys. She holds Nutting's wrist. It's not sexual, it's not condescending. It's the act of someone who has slugged out enough battles with Nutting to hold him in weary affection. It's like Hanford Pendergast said: *You wanted Cheri to like to you. And when she did—gosh, it made your troubles feel far away.*

Cheri Orritt was the best of Burger City #8.

It was a shame she had to die.

JANUARY 2017

TRY TO HAVE FUN WITH IT

The *Spectral Journeys* shoot happened the day (mostly the night) of January 2, 2017, with January 3 reserved for general Iowa B-roll. Producer Marsella Nixon stressed that no changes to the restaurant's regular operations should be made, and order-follower Nutting followed orders. Interviews with staff would be held down the road in a portable soundproof shed. Kit was among the scheduled interviewees. He was flying high.

From the time Nixon power-walked across the lobby in five-inch heels, Kit was spellbound. He took his break as quickly as possible, while certain members of the eight-person crew set up for interior daytime shots. He'd been fascinated by TV9, but this was production on a different scale. The camera was sleeker, rigged with monitors and meters, and often mounted to a jib arm or slider rail. The lights were LEDs, atop aluminum stands, clipped with colored gels. The crew functioned with cool efficiency, cordoning off space, taping down cables, and weighing down stands with sandbags like they'd done a thousand times before.

Darren Husselbee on January 2, 2017 (photo by Kit Bryant).

The *Spectral Journeys* crew had criss-crossed the country for three seasons. They were skilled at deflecting inquisitive small-towners. But they took a shine to Kit Bryant right away, particularly fifteen-year camera veteran Darren Husselbee. While Kit took notes in his *IDEAS* book, Husselbee educated him on all the jargon Quin Arthur had internalized years ago. Key lights. Fill lights. Match cuts. Rack focuses. Swish pans. MOS shots. Outside, a guy was prepping a drone for aerial footage. Did Kit want a look?

He did, but there were burgers to sling. When Quin rushed over after school, he observed the rapport between Kit and Husselbee and got competitive. He weaseled up to Husselbee and asked if he used "free run timecode," if he was shooting "60i," if his "cam" had a "built-in filter wheel." By then, things were hectic with the B-crew shuttling staff members to the interview shed. Husselbee shooed away the show-off.

Everyone noted Quin's look of humiliated fury.

Terrified of a resurgence of the Haunted Dick Pic, Nutting had forbidden his staff to utter a word about the men's room. Kit broke the gag order around 3:45 p.m., telling Husselbee how cool it would be to get footage of the paper-towel dispenser. Quin overheard and overheated. It was *his* footage that had launched Lil' Beefy; *he'd* been the one to call TV9; *he* was the film student the crew ought to be adopting.

So Quin tattled. To Nutting, this was further proof that Kit was behind the Haunted Dick Pic. Nutting needed the day to go off without a hitch if he was going to impress Burger City Inc.—and Lisa too. He collared Kit and ordered him to go home or get fired. Kit was crushed. If he left now, he'd miss the arrival of hosts Gaetan Goodricke and Roxie Stoyle! Nutting didn't budge. Kit turned red, grabbed his coat, swatted a column of drink cups to the floor, and stomped off. He knew who'd fucked him. He glared at Quin as he hit the exit door.

Husselbee wrapped up with some dusk shots around 5:00. One of these shots made it into the aired episode, and if you look close, you'll notice a lanky, bearded man stroll into the restaurant. It takes a mighty sharp eye to recognize this as Kit Bryant, back at Burger City, this time fully incognito.

It's the happiest moment I share with Clemens Dumay. He laughs once, a nice sound. But the laugh appears to rattle him. He applies his palms to his face. His sleeves droop and I see the alleged bite marks. He scrubs his face with hands that stink of gasoline. That might be the point: when he removes his hands, his eyes shine with tears, and now neither of us can say for sure what caused them.

"That's right. I forgot. Kit called me from his car and told me his idea. I had this fake beard left over from *Carousel*. It's a musical we did when I was a junior. I played this guy Jigger Craigin and they let me keep the beard. Thing was itchy as fuck and had adhesive gum all over it."

It's hard to imagine Clem ever needing fake hair. Light from Biff's Gas & Diesel & Store glistens on the chaw in his beard that failed to reach his Snapple can.

"I did him up with the beard, some shades, a hoodie. He looked like the Unabomber. It was funny, man. I laughed so hard I couldn't get the beard on straight. Kit was *not* laughing. He wanted me to hurry up. He thought the TV people might be able to find out if he was the PK agent, you know? He wanted answers. While the rest of us, I think, we just wanted attention."

I ask him if he means Quin. Clem adjusts in his seat.

"Yeah, I felt weird about it. Like, plays and stuff were Q & me's thing. Now here I was putting a beard on Kit. It stressed me out. We all should have been working together. I don't know why we couldn't. I don't know why *everyone* can't. Half the people who come to this gas station are mumbling how they're going to show that bitch or fix that asshole. What the fuck is wrong with us?"

Spectral Journeys interviewed every employee save Cheri Orritt, who declined, and the visually unappetizing Dez Mozley. Those who didn't make the final cut make sense: Yesenia, too shy; Zane, too abstruse; Dion, too dull. Amy Mold's failure to appear sticks out. No one at Burger City was a better extemporaneous speaker. But that very day, while Kit Bryant whispered to Darren Husselbee about the Men's Room Bully, Amy was having her first experience with the Drive-thru Phantom.

Amy Mold's interview wasn't scheduled until 5:45 p.m., but she rushed to Burger City right after school. She didn't want to miss Gaetan Goodricke and Roxie Stoyle. She was also, as it happened, scheduled to work the window. For a Wednesday, the crowd was thick; word had spread that something was happening off Exit 269. Amy took the headset from an exhausted Darcy Smyrna, strapped it on, and studied the register to make sure it had proper change. Darcy had been absent-minded lately.

Within one minute, noise snarled through the headset static. Snowy interference was typical, but this was more forceful, starting with a plosive *P* and crashing through consonants, a sound Amy Mold, describing it to me years later, would replicate as *PPPRRRTTTSHHKKKXX!*

She tapped the headset. The sounds went away. She rang up BeefBoats, Healthy Cowboy Salads, Chik-N-X-Tremes. Twenty minutes later, the noise returned, louder and longer, this time with vowel sounds rounding the buzz.

Amy knuckled the headset harder. She asked a customer to repeat himself. She rang up Beefy Melts, Hog Heavens, Chik-a-Chunkz. The noise was not to be ignored. Next time it went for ten seconds, with recognizable morphemes bobbing through the electric swamp. *Pro,* she heard. *Her,* she heard.

She asked a drive-thru orderer to hold (a major Nutting no-no), tore off the malfunctioning headset, and replaced it with the backup charging on the knee-level shelf. She couldn't believe her rotten luck. Having to squash her hair with a stupid cap hours before a big-deal interview. The stupid zits on her temple, probably from these headsets. And now the crappiest of Nutting's gear crapping out.

Five minutes after swapping headsets, again the noise jabbed Amy's ears, as if angry that she'd tried to repudiate it. "Sorry," she apologized, without meaning to.

The two-way drive-thru intercom system has been a QSR staple since the late 1940s, when In-N-Out Burger used carhops to deliver food to waiting vehicles. HM Electronics took the idea wireless in 1984, but it was 3M that freed drive-thru workers from annoying and fatiguing belt packs.[57] Tech-forum geeks tend to agree that the B1099 model was 3M's worst. It was made of chintzy plastic that got brittle when cold—and drive-thru alcoves are often cold. The rubber coating of the flexible mic peeled off within months of use and the ear foam disintegrated in greasy environments, forcing workers all over the country to improvise with cotton balls to prevent chafing.

Burger City's customer frequency ran at 469.0125 UHF, their clerk frequency at 464.0125 UHF. Exit 269's desolation made it unlikely that anyone but passing semi-truck drivers could interfere with transmission. But an idea hit Amy as she watched a production van ferry Quin off for his interview. The film crew! Who knew the kind of wireless signals they were using? They must be overpowering the B1099.

The noises spaced out as the night progressed. When it was time for Amy's interview, she handed off the headset to Tamra. Would Tamra act like there was nothing wrong with it as Darcy had? The bumpy ride down Rolf Tonks Road took three minutes, enough time for Amy to know she was going to choke at the first question. All she could hear, all she could

57 John Wilks, "Drive-Thru 101: History," *Dr. Drive-Thru* (blog), February 13, 2010.

think of, was the noise. Its initial shouts had gentled, with each iteration refining until Amy thought she could make out the words being said.

PROTECT HER.

By 10:00 p.m. on January 2, activity in the soundproof shed was finishing up. Back at Burger City, most of the *Spectral Journeys* gang had packed up for the night, leaving behind the crew of three that worked with Gaetan Goodricke and Roxie Stoyle during their overnight ghost-hunting.

While they installed GoPro cameras on walls and tested their thermal- and night-vision functions, Unabomber Kit was hunched over an untouched tray of Beefyburger and fries in B6. He'd bought the food from Cheri, who'd recognized him right away. She'd laughed so hard she had to brace herself on Till 1, and commenced referring to him by the names of famous bearded men: Grizzly Adams, Paul Bunyan, Santa Claus. When she gave him his tray, she also gave a warning.

"I'd get while the getting's good, Abe Lincoln."

But Kit ran hot on the fuel of unfinished business. He pecked at his paw-shaped burger, biding his time. When Darren Husselbee finally pulled on a coat to fetch something from the equipment truck, Kit dumped his tray and hurried after him. In the parking lot, Kit withdrew his *IDEAS* book like a machete. Husselbee whirled around.

"Easy, guy!"

"It's me. It's Kit." He held up the notebook. "From before."

A light snow dimmed the lot's sodium lights. Husselbee leaned and squinted.

"I thought your boss sent you home."

"He did. But I didn't get to finish telling you."

"Telling me what?"

"I wanted to tell Gaetan and Roxie, but they're still not—"

"What are we talking about here?"

"The men's room," Kit said. "There was this picture—you have to put a camera in the men's room. The paper towel holders, it was bonkers, it was like—"

"Kid."

"—*violent*, the way they flew out, like something was pissed—"

"Kid, kid, listen."

"And I'm the one—you know about RSPK? Well, there's this guy, William Roll—"

Husselbee gripped Kit's shoulder. Kit shut up. Husselbee gave Kit a pained look.

"Look. Kid."

"Kit."

"*Kit*. You're a good egg. I mean that. I hope you get out of this job and all that."

Kit was baffled. "Why would I get out? Everything's *happening*."

"I'm going to be straight with you. Gaetan and Roxie…they don't want to hear what you have to say. They're not interested. They've got their thing they do. They do it, they get out of Dodge, and go do it again."

"But if they knew…"

"Marsella's a tyrant. She's got a breakdown for the whole night, and Roxie does not deal well with last-minute changes."

"But how can you schedule anything when you don't even—"

"Plus Gaetan's a germaphobe. He's not stepping one foot inside a fast-food bathroom." The man gave Kit's shoulder a hearty slap. "Buck up, kid. Buck up, *Kit*. Show's turnaround is six to eight weeks. Six to eight weeks and all your friends will see you on TV. Remember, these shows are *entertainment*. First and foremost. It's fun. Try to have fun with it. Can you do that for me?"

Kit could *not* do that for him. He walked to his car, which he'd parked way on the other side of I-80, and got inside. He ripped off the fake beard, ran the engine, and puffed warm breath into his cupped hands. He was stewing. Regardless of what Husselbee had said, meeting Gaetan Goodricke and Roxie Stoyle—that would be something! He scribbled down what he needed to tell to the hosts and tore the page from *IDEAS*. If he could get close enough to one of them, he could press it into one of their hands.

It got less likely by the minute. Kit was group-texting with the night's closers, Amber, Clem, and Javi (Cheri was there too, but had never texted in her life), and word was that Nutting was shoving them out the door. No one but him was going to meet the show's stars. Kit's reply was instant: *Fuck that*. He was going to stake out the place and meet them. Who was with him?

Not Javi; he had a wife and three kids. Shenanigans like this were Clem's raison d'être, but he'd already irked Q more than he liked. That left Amber, who only agreed in hopes that she could convince her boyfriend to change his mind.

Nutting emptied the joint by 11:20. Amber tromped through overpass snow, got into Kit's car, told him this was a bad idea, then steamed the windows with him for fifteen minutes. She suspected this was mainly to shut her up, but she didn't mind.

Bundled up again, Kit and Amber skulked back across the overpass, angling into an island of skeletal winter trees. At 11:35, Nutting's Civic lit up and crept north, wipers swatting snowflakes. Kit skittered across the Exit 269 ramp, mitten-in-mitten with Amber. Already there was evidence of exciting goings-on. Burger City's windows had been covered with Duvetyne (a black fabric filmmakers use to block out light), but swirling white, green, and red lights leaked out. Was it the crew setting up spirit-sensing doodads? Or was every device in Burger City going haywire from the poltergeist?

Kit and Amber huddled against the restaurant's north side. Amber's better judgment evaporated in the exhilaration. She blinked away cold-stung tears and grinned at her best friend, lover, hero, and inspiration through the gray swirls of their intermixed breaths.

Amber has moved to her windowsill, all pretensions of ducking her landlords forgotten. This stretch of my audio file is riddled with the blasts of a backfiring car and a low *chug-chug-chug*, probably one of Tobin and Mack's sump pumps. Amber blows vape steam into the springtime air. The falling afternoon sun softens her emaciation, evens out skin textures, hides scars.

"I remember Kit wiping my nose with his glove because I couldn't feel anything. I remember being honestly worried about frostbite. I had a whole panic attack that Mom's cancer was going to come back and I wouldn't be able to help because I wouldn't have any fingers. They call that catastrophizing."

Nevertheless, Amber's recollection of those subzero hours are warmed with affection for Kit. The Duvetyne didn't perfectly fit the drive-thru window, making it the peepers' best vantage point. By crooking their necks, Kit and Amber made out a Burger City interior darker than they'd ever seen it, though occasionally striped by the light of a passing camera. They both thought they spotted Gaetan and Roxie, though it might have been wishful thinking.

Most of the action seemed to be taking place in the windowless BOH. Kit had a key to the back door, but Amber drew the line there. There was a lot of noise behind that door. A woman talking. People arguing. Voices crackling through a walkie talkie. Gaetan Goodricke shouting, followed by Roxie Stoyle chanting in a singsong tone. Opening the door might ruin some important discovery. Kit agonized to miss it, but knew Amber was right.

Shooting wrapped around four. Kit and Amber high-tailed it back to the car, unsatisfied but energized. It was going to have to be like Darren Husselbee said: *Six to eight weeks and all your friends will see you on TV.*

"Until that night, I didn't really think Kit was the whatever-you-call it, the poltergeist agent." Amber tips her head back, and in the loose bands of her neck, I see a trace of a graceful arch. "But he was on fire. Which set everyone else on fire. Isn't that alone proof he had some kind of power? To have that effect on so many people?"

Normalcy resumed at 5:30 a.m. At least that was the goal. Staff displayed bloodshot eyes, stubborn bedhead, mismatched socks. Addled from sampling the Hollywood drug, no one had gotten much sleep. Geezers watched in amusement (or consternation, in Vandyke Elbutt's case) as the yawning workers took twice as long to piece together the old folks' rations.

The night had offered no chance at cleaning, so Dez Mozley was present. No degree of Soft Rock Hitz could drown out her grumbling. The TV crew had tracked mud all over the floors. The restrooms were filthy. There were scuffs on the walls. One of the invaders had managed to knock the knob off the break-room door. The Travel Channel had promised to pay for that, but for now, Nutting ordered Dez into the cellar. He had a vague memory of a couple extra knobs down there, dating back to his 2006 overhaul. Hard to be sure, though. No one ever went into the cellar.

While leaving hours later, Maxine Pinto, Zadie Budden, Stu Blick, Silas Ireland, and Vandyke Elbutt tiptoed around a *SLIPPERY HAZARD* sign, carefully as old folks must. There they encountered Dez stocking napkins, her head inside the condiment station cabinet. Her masses of black hair lashed with every vehement mutter.

"Won't listen to me...won't take one second to see what's in front of your stupid eyes...I'm telling you, Boss Man, that cellar...maybe you don't want to know...but there's something down there...and that thing's got *teeth*."[58]

---

58 At that moment, Quin Arthur was at school, but if he'd been there to hear Dez, he might have been reminded of a story told on page 56 of Roll's *The Poltergeist*, in which Roll, as well as several police, witness manifestations of "mysterious bat-like bites" on Lina Gemmecke in 1962 Indianapolis.

THE TRUCKER'S NEW TESTAMENT

Seventeen miles due east of Jonny, a straight shot down I-80, off an exit a great deal more carnivalesque than 269, lords the Iowa 80 Truckstop, aka the World's Largest Truckstop, aka the Trucker's Disneyland. It's not hyperbole. The 24/7/365 facility has yet to close a single day since its 1965 opening. Iowa 80 services nine hundred trucks per day and five thousand people. You can wash your truck, wash your clothes, wash your dog, wash yourself, pump iron, get a haircut, visit a chiropractor, play arcade games, enjoy a movie theater, and even get that aching tooth addressed. If your pains are of a different sort, you can attend 9:00 a.m. Sunday Services at Trucker's Christian Chapel Ministries. The day I visit Iowa 80, an ex-Marine pastor explains why it's okay to cry to five truckers seated at the back of the room.

The Iowa 80 Truckstop (photo by the author).

Most of these points of interest are on the small upper level. The sprawling, 130,000-foot ground floor is dominated by two spaces. To the east, the 67,000-foot Super Truck Showroom, bedazzled by three tricked-out trucks (America the Beautiful, the Blue Ox, and the Cornpatch Cadillac). To the west, a vast grocery and gift store with the wood-finished polish and girdered ceilings of a modern Whole Foods. Anchored by a three-hundred-seat food court with the perilous options of Wendy's, Pizza Hut, Taco Bell, Dairy Queen, and Einstein Brothers, the place is stocked with gifts penitent long-haulers bring home to alienated spouses (lots of jewelry) and children (personalized everything: magnets, mini license plates, even pocket knives).

Mostly, though, the place sells food. Yogurt, popcorn, donuts, chips, candy, beef jerky, nuts, cheese, soda, coffee, caffeinated drinks. These energy-blast options, plus the fact that Exit 284 was just far enough from Jonny to offer anonymity, made Iowa 80 the perfect place for the teen contingent of the Burger City drama to get together and plot their eventual ruin.

The gang met five times from January to April,[59] with their prime directive being to channel and shape the Burger City Poltergeist goings-on into a variety of social-media channels. Quin recorded all meetings on audio. High on possibility and feeling official, he logged the date and time at the start of the first four recordings. (The tumultuous final meeting of April 23, 2017, lacks tagging but witnesses reliably date it.) The transcripts that follow are abridged to remove superfluities.

January 6, 2017

Quin: —B-C-D-E-F-G. This is the first meeting of the, I guess, the BCP[60] group? It's January 6th, 2017, at exactly…11:51 p.m. and zero seconds. We're in the food court of the Iowa 80 Truck Stop in Wolcott, Iowa. Present are—

Kit: Not student council, dude.

Quin: —Quin Arthur, Amy Mold, Amber Smyrna, Kit Bryant, Yesenia Ruiz, Clem Dumay.

Clem: Always last. I'll be but an asterisk in history books.

Kit: Are we all quorumed up? Can we vote on the prom theme yet?

Amy: Student government requires a 3.0 GPA, Bryant.

---

59 It has been suggested that Jonny's geographical isolation, specifically its dearth of local psychotherapists, prompted the need for the Iowa 80 meetings. I think there is some truth to this.

60 Despite Quin's attempts to make "BCP" happen, the others never picked it up, sticking with the more laborious, but less embarrassing, seven-syllable "Burger City Poltergeist."

Amber: Aw, baby. It's not the size of the GPA. It's how you use it.

Amy: Yeni, you should do student government.

Yesenia: Oh, no. No, no, no, no.

Amy: We're 100 percent white right now. It's worse than Congress.

Quin: I don't want to intrude…

Clem: Narrator: "Quindlen Arthur loved to intrude. 'Twas his passion, his lust for life."

Quin: But let's remember what we're doing here.

Clem: Narrator: "They had gathered to consume great quantities of Red Bulls and Flamin' Hot Cheetos…"

Kit: It was my idea.

Quin: Huh?

Kit: Getting together like this. We won't know what Gaetan and Roxie turned up till next month. But if they found something big…we need to be ready to jump on it.

Quin: That's right. That's why I wanted to divvy—

Kit: It was *my* idea. Just saying.

Quin: Uh, okay. We'll find you a blue ribbon later.

Kit: Dick.

Quin: Anyway. I've talked to all of you separately, but here's how we're divvying up the BCP socials. Amber: Twitter. Yesenia: Instagram. Amy: Facebook. Clem: Tumblr. Kit: Google+. I've got YouTube.

Amber: But we can all post everywhere, right? We've all got the passwords.

Quin: Yeah, but let's try to stick to our beats.

Kit: Don't you think this is a little…much?

Quin: [*Pages turn.*] This is from Roll's appendix. "Since there are so few trained investigators in this field, the student of poltergeists and ghosts can make important contributions by exploring cases on his own."[61]

Amy: "His." Might we lowly womenfolk serve coffee? Offer handies?[62]

Quin: "He should keep an eye on news reports in the papers, radio, and television."[63]

Clem: Ah, yes. "The papers."

Quin: He wrote this in 1972. But you get the drift. Roll's begging us to keep going. It's been, what? Three days since *Spectral Journeys*?

Kit: Yep. Three days since you got Nutting to kick me out.

---

61 Roll, *The Poltergeist*, 199.

62 This sarcastic joke echoes one of Amy Mold's earlier complaints about William G. Roll's *The Poltergeist*, namely his dismissive use of the term "housewives" on page 20.

63 Roll, *The Poltergeist*, 199.

Quin: Whatever. Three days and already we've had—

Amber: The lady screaming in the Puppy Pen for no reason.

Kit: If you'll allow me to participate, Supreme Leader Snoke, I've got it all in my notes. *[Sound of ruffling pages.]* January 4th, the Puppy Pen lady—

Amber: But that was Kim Comerford's mom. She's got...issues.[64]

Kit: January 5th, guy comes in, says there's stuff flying out of the dumpster.

Amber: Javi and I checked that out. That guy had slime up to his elbows. I think he was flinging it out himself.[65]

Kit: Later that same day, we have the seventh-grader who says an invisible force flung her drink in her face.

Amber: That kid was trouble the second she walked in. She just wanted attention.[66]

Kit: Amber! You're killing me! They're not *all* fakes!

Clem: There was that old fogey who said he got shoved around by the Men's Room Bully.[67] Old people don't lie, do they?

Quin: Yeah, that one feels real. You go in there alone, it's like someone's shoving.

Kit: Which is exactly what I was trying to tell *Spectral Journeys* before dick-head here sold me out.

Quin: Fake news is the problem now. I expected the TV show to kick the poltergeist activity up a notch. But now we've got all these idiots flooding our socials, trying to get famous. It's noise in our data.

Yesenia: Maybe we overdid it. The Facebook group...I don't like some of the comments.[68]

Clem: What do they say?

Yesenia: Some say we're lying. That we're liars.

Amy: Lying sluts, lying hos, lying cunts. You ever *been* online, Clem?

Yesenia: I don't want to run the Instagram anymore. Someone else take it.

---

64   When I reach Mrs. Comerford for comment, she literally screams into the phone and hangs up. I do not know what to make of this.

65   Seeing how the Exit 269 overpass had a history of sheltering the homeless, it makes sense this man might be one of them, simply hunting for food.

66   My best research efforts suggest this was 12-year-old Nadia Flanders. When I speak to her mother, Karina, I am told only that Nadia "is our own little Meryl Streep."

67   This was not one of the male Geezers, though all three of them admit to thinking they felt something in the Men's Room.

68   A representative example, posted January 4, 2017: "this is just bitchies [sic] trying to get attention. it's pathitic [sic]."

Clem: Who would have guessed we'd become influencers! *[English accent.]* "Consider pairing that frisky Burger City uniform with this fun, flirty ghost."

Amber: I'll do the Instagram, Yeni.

Quin: You sure? You've already got Twitter. And that's the busiest one.

Amber: I'm an old pro.

Quin: Okay. That's great, then. I've got some ideas. You want to get together tomorrow? I think we need longer captions. PR firms say longer captions on IG get maximum engagement.

Clem: I'm about to maximally engage these Funyuns.

Kit: First things first. We gotta debunk the hoaxes. Or no one's going to believe anything we say.

Amber: How are *we* supposed to know what's real? Our expertise is greasy beef.

Quin: We'll do everything according to *Theta.*

Clem: Enough with your imaginary girlfriend, Q.

Quin: Theta is the journal of the Psychical Research Foundation. It was edited by Roll back in the day.

Kit: You and Roll. Get a room.

Quin: [Rustle of papers.] Here. Issue 16, Winter 1967. Developed with Dr. J.G. Pratt, President of the Psychical Research Foundation. They came up with thirty-two questions[69] to test if a poltergeist is real. When people post suspicious stuff to our socials, we just need to calmly present— *[Paper rustles.]* Hey.

Clem: "Have any of the persons who witnessed the phenomena had telepathic dreams or other psychical experiences in the past? If so, state who and describe the experiences. Have there been instances where the ghost, footsteps, etc., were experienced by some persons in the room or area but not by other?"

Amber: So the plan is boring them into submission.

Kit: No, I get it. I get it. Lil' Beefy does her 4:24 thing every single day. That's the standard new phenomena have to meet.

Clem: "Anything less than the best is a felony."

Quin: Exactly. We make them show their work. Right there on the socials. Let them expose themselves as fakes.

Clem: That was a Vanilla Ice quote. No? No Ice Ice Babies here?

Quin: Amy Mold. You draft stuff like this for student gov, right? You think if I gave you guidelines you could whip something up? Amy?

---

69 These questions are reproduced in the appendix of William G. Roll's *The Poltergeist.*

Amy: Hm?

Evident in the Iowa 80 records is a hard downtick in Amy Mold's moxie. She felt scared, frightened, and alone. Each time she strapped on the B1099, a rasp sizzled through the static, the Drive-thru Phantom's whisper: *PROTECT HER.*

Her Saturday morning shift. Sunday night shift. Wednesday night shift. Thursday afternoon shift. It distracted her all day and kept her eyes blinking half the night. She asked the other drive-thru workers if they'd heard anything weird, but if she kept that up, she'd start to sound like one of Quin's despised attention whores. She had to accept that the voice spoke only to her.

This left two possibilities.

The first was that the voice was a fluke. Amy's grades began to sink as she spent her homework hours trawling the internet. She haunted message boards for home-scanner enthusiasts. Some reported picking up fast-food drive-thru signals from two miles away. Reversed interference had to be possible. Given the glitchy nature of the B1099, it might even be likely.

The second was that she was being punked. Someone might be waiting for her to put on the B1099 before speaking through a gadget with a voice modulator. But who? It was too nasty a trick for Clem. Kit had the aptitude, but as the likely RSPK agent, he was fixated on authenticity. Javi, Zane, and Mickey, all accomplished tinkerers, had no motive. That left Quin. Amy wanted to think he was beyond ginning up a ghost. But she wasn't sure. Quin craved the biggest circus possible and had anointed himself ringleader.

A third possibility came lurking.

Amy Mold might be losing her mind.

She wasn't destined for RCHS valedictorian. She habitually challenged sexist teachers, rebelled against whitewashed history lessons, skipped class to join University of Iowa protests. But in any realistic intellectual appraisal, Amy Mold towered over her contemporaries. She found their fandoms trivial, their opinions jejune, their jokes predictable. She'd visited the Mensa site enough to have it bookmarked; she longed to pay the $60 Admission Test fee and be certified brilliant once and for all.

Only with the arrival of the Drive-thru Phantom did Amy feel fissures in her granite sense of self. Was she cracking up? Before she got a Mensa card? Before publishing her first book of critically-acclaimed essays? Before founding a paradigm-shifting org that staved off environmental cataclysm?

To pursue the meaning of *PROTECT HER* was to scratch a rash. Amy Mold resisted for eighteen days. It was during a spell in the break room, tired from the evening's phantom messages, that her red eyes happened upon the shift schedule. She yanked it from the bulletin board. She scratched the rash and it felt good.

If someone needed Amy Mold's help, she figured, it had to be a woman. She ticked down the alphabetical list. Tamra Longmoor: she could tear a phone book in half, but she *was* Black and this *was* rural Iowa. Dez Mozley: Who knew what kind of sinister characters roamed her bizarre life? Cheri Orritt: working as hard as she did, her heart might be ready to give. Amber Smyrna: her sunny smile must be hiding anguish over her mother's health. Darcy Smyrna: in grave peril, for sure, but what could Amy do about cancer?

Yesenia Ruiz was the final name on the list.

Yesenia Ruiz. The shy, 16-year-old sophomore. Who lived with a factory-worker mother and three siblings. Whose non-estranged father lived in North Carolina for some reason. Who took every shift she could to help support her big, struggling family. Who'd suddenly begun showing up to work last August with pretty flowers delicately inserted into her polo's button holes. Who'd seemed so happy then, but now seemed so apprehensive.

Amy scratched the itch till it bled.

January 11, 2017

Yesenia: This is too much. My mom tells me to quit. Maybe I should.

Amy: Yesenia. Doesn't listen to Quin. You don't have to do it.

Clem: Me and my neighbor did it when we were little. See this scar?

Kit: They've only got plastic knives here. But I'm up for a little Civil War sawing.

Amber: No one is cutting themselves. Quin? Yes? Agree?

Quin: When I said *oath*, I only mean *pact*. No bloodletting. Jesus, people, relax. Here, I typed this up. Last night, after closing.

Amy: [Sighs.] I meant to do that. I just didn't…I couldn't…

Quin: I didn't say anything.

Amy: You didn't have to.

Quin: Whatever. Everyone just read it. Basically it says we all agree that, no matter what happens, we don't go blasting it out before discussing it. No one knows who's running our socials and we need to keep it that way. Especially don't tell parents. It's like Yesenia said. They might make us quit. Any serious talking we do right here.

Amy: I like it up here. It's quieter.

Kit: Wait till truckers start singing in the showers.

Amber: Or getting teeth yanked at the dentist.

Clem: Or holy rolling in the chapel.

Kit: Speaking of holy rolling…

Amy: [Reading aloud.] "The Trucker's New Testament Bible."

Clem: That bible has a sixteen-wheeler on the front. You don't see that everyday.

The Trucker's New Testament Bible (photo by the author).

Amy: [Reading aloud.] "By opening this book, you will learn your life's purpose as you truck down that long road to your eternal home."

Quin: Guys. Guys.

Amy: "Trucking friend, this New Testament will explain how you are a unique and loved child of God."

Yesenia: [Reciting from memory.] "My God is my rock, in whom I take refuge, my shield and the horn of my salvation. He is my stronghold, my refuge, and my savior."

Quin: Enough with the God stuff?

Yesenia: "The Lord is my shepherd, I lack nothing. He makes me lie down in green pastures, he leads me beside quiet waters, he refreshes my soul."

Amy: That's nice. That's really nice.

Yesenia: Do you want to hear my favorite?

Quin: No offense, but—

Amy: Yes, I do.

Yesenia: "I lift my eyes to the mountains—where does my help come from? My help comes from the Lord, the Maker of heaven and earth. He will not let your foot slip."

Amy: [Softly.] He will not let your foot slip.

Amber: Amy. You okay? I've got a kleenex.

Amy: [Through tears.] Yeah, no, I'm—it just sounds good right now.

Clem: Here. The books are free. Take one. Take ten.

Amy: I'm sorry, everyone.

Amber: Don't be. It's a weird time.

Yesenia: He won't, you know. Let your foot slip.

Quin: That's good. The stairs to this level are very steep.

Kit: You suck, dude.

Quin: I'm not begrudging anyone their God talk. I'm just saying, that's not what we're here to talk about.

Amy: How do you know that? Maybe it's *not* a poltergeist. Maybe we're talking about life after death here—the afterlife. What if the most important book we've got is this *Trucker's New Testament*? And not your Mr. Roll?

Quin: If you read Roll's book like I asked, you'd know he's fine with religion. RSPK manifests in the form of your beliefs. If you believe in My Little Pony, you'll have My Little Pony disturbances. *[Pause.]* You're *all* taking copies now? Not leaving any for spiritually bereft truckers? *[Sighs.]* Whatever. As long as we agree on these basic points.

Kit: You actually want us to sign this thing.

Clem: Thankfully, I keep my lawyer on retainer. Dez Mozley, Attorney at Law.

Quin: Just read it and absorb it. Is that too much to ask?

Amber: It's fine. Kit, baby, this is fine.

Quin: Thank you, Amber.

Yesenia: I am okay with it too. I don't want to tell anyone.

Amy: Hard agree.

Clem: Then shall we lift our tankards in hearty accord? Hoist thy Diet Dr. Pepper! Raise thy goblet of Arizona Mucho Mango Iced Tea! *[Beverages cans and bottles tap.]*

Amber: Come on, baby.

Kit: I just don't give a shit about this, is the thing.

Clem: We at Burger City value your feedback.

Quin: Yeah, we know you don't give a shit. That's why our Tumblr engagement is zilcho.

Kit: Let people think what they want to think. All I care about is the poltergeist.

Quin: That's like saying you want to make a movie but have no publicity plan.

Kit: Well, isn't that why movies have big-ass crews? Go work on publicity if you want. I'm focusing on the movie.

Quin: So in this metaphor, are you the star? Or the director? Or is this an Orson Welles type deal and you're both? You're so positive you're the PK agent, you're just that special.

Kit: Will you ever stop? For one second, stop and look around? It's amazing, isn't it? To be there? At Burger City? Right in the middle of it? To feel Lil' Beefy move, or how cold the Cold Spot is, or the things pushing in the men's room? We are the luckiest people in the *world.* Let's not forget that, while we're making all these pacts and plans. This thing—it's a beautiful, rare fucking thing.

Until he took up reading Daniel Kraus novels at Chernow, Kit Bryant's only use for books was as a surface for rolling joints. Not once in the nine months of the Burger City Poltergeist did he pick up William G. Roll's *The Poltergeist.* It's too bad. Numerous passages address what Kit tried to articulate at the January 11 Iowa 80 meeting.

Roll believed psychic destruction released an agent's interpersonal tension.[70] Following an argument at Tropication Arts, an alligator-themed ash tray leapt from a shelf and crashed to the floor. (This is "Event 176" in that wild-looking chart Quin originally showed Kit, Clem, and Cheri.) Instantly, the mood of one of the arguers, Julio, improved.

---

70 From page 175 of William G. Roll's *The Poltergeist:* "Sometimes the objects that break express this theme. In one home where the main conflict was between mother and child, two phonograph records broke. One of these had the title 'My Mother'; the other was 'At Home with Me.'....In general, we find hostility in the agent, which cannot be expressed in normal ways, the main target for the anger being people with whom he is associated on a daily basis."

I asked [Julio] how he felt. "I feel happy; that thing [that broke] makes me feel happy; I don't know why."….[A]fter a series of four incidents in the early afternoon of the 27th, Julio looked unusually cheerful and I asked him how he felt. He replied, "I feel good. I really miss the ghost—," he caught himself, "I mean—not the ghost, but I miss it when something doesn't happen."[71]

Julio is introduced as an anxious[72] "19-year-old Cuban refugee who worked as a shipping clerk."[73] Kit, too, was 19, and his anxiety was the stomach-turning dread that Burger City's drudgery would last the rest of his life. Quin knew these passages; in January 2017, he was one of the world's authorities on *The Poltergeist*. He disinclination to cite them had to do with what he, and he alone, saw as a triangular relationship between him, Kit, and Amber.

January 30, 2017

Quin: Thanks, Amber. I guess it's safe to say Twitter isn't letting up.
Amber: You're welcome. Is now a good time to ask for a raise?
Quin: I wish!
Kit: Whoa, did anyone feel that?
Amber: What?
Kit: Quin's hard-on bumping the table.
Quin: Ha, ha. Update on the Coldest Cold Spot?
Kit: Well, I put a rock in there. It shattered the rock.
Clem: That's why Sasha quit.[74] Took one look at those pebbles and arrivederci.
Amber: Who's Sasha?
Clem: New hire. Restaurant's a little busy, if you haven't noticed.
Kit: Sasha replaced Cameron. Who also quit after one day.[75]
Amber: I met Cameron. I found him throwing up in the men's room. He said it smelled like roadkill, but I couldn't smell it.

---

71 Roll, *The Poltergeist*, 169.
72 Ibid.
73 Ibid, 115.
74 Sasha Wrenn worked at Burger City #8 from January 20–23, 2017. Over the phone she tells me, "Being in that place felt like being buried alive under living things."
75 Cameron Judge worked at Burger City on January 17, 2017. Over the phone he tells me, "When I flushed the urinal, blood came out instead of water. You think I was just going to keep working there?"

Kit: Our poltergeist's not real welcoming to newcomers.

Quin: We don't need them. Furthermore, we can't trust them.

Amber: Well, we can't go on like this! Twice the customers, but the same number of staff?

Kit: It's not going to get any better. Nutting thinks the place is going to blow up after *Spectral Journeys* airs. He's thinking about a second entrance, a second drive-thru window.

Quin: Have you guys thought about it? What it's going to be like?

Clem: Having a second drive-thru window?

Quin: Being on TV. Being…famous.

Amber: I'm going to get a killer college-entrance essay out of it, that's for sure.

Clem: I just hope it monetizes, man. I can't eat many more Swanson dinners.

Quin: It could snowball. It really could. Jimmy Kimmel. Good Morning America.

Clem: Dr. Phil. Pleeease, Dr. Phil.

Quin: We just need to be realistic about it. It might not happen overnight. It may take a few weeks to gather steam.

Kit: Our lives are really going to change.

Amber: Thank God.

Clem: Stick a fork in this old one. It's done.

Quin: Yeah. *[Pause.]* So where's Amy and Yesenia?

At 4:40 p.m on January 31, 2017, six minutes after Lil' Beefy did her show, the Burger City buzz was pierced by a sustained cry, like a weight-lifter straining for one last rep. If it belonged anywhere, it was dry goods storage, Javi or Mickey lifting an overstuffed box. But it came from the drive-thru cubby. Kit and Cheri, working the tills, stared at each other for a long second. A repetitive snapping noise joined the cry. Kit and Cheri abandoned their stations.

Inside the cubby, they found exactly who was supposed to be there: Darcy Smyrna. She held a broad stance, one you might use to keep upright after a punch. Her face was wrinkled into a red, sweaty grimace, lips curled back from clamped teeth. The straining noise came from the depths of her throat. Her wig, cap, and headset had fallen off to reveal the silk scarf she wore to cover her scalp ulcers, burned there by stereotactic radiosurgery.

The snapping noise was Darcy striking the cash register with a metal stapler. Kit thought of Darcy's daily anti-convulsives. They must have failed.

"Oh, no," he said.

Cheri lunged and took Darcy in a straitjacket embrace. The stapler attack stopped. Darcy's groan segmented into thick disbelieving grunts.

"I...can't...see...from...my...right...eye..."

FEBRUARY 2017

SOUNDS PRETTY FAR-OUT TO ME

Bob Nutting's apartment in Burlington, Iowa, reflects the poignant optimism of the novice bachelor. A dusty bowl of mixed nuts designated for no-show family and friends. An alphabetically arranged shelf of unwrapped Blu-rays. Too much attention paid to the wet bar. Singeing the air is the burnt odor of aggressive vacuuming. He's prepped for my arrival, but the breeze of the opening door still wags a dozen dog-hair thatches. Instantly I'm body-checked by five chubby one-year-old beagles.

"Down, Hillary," Nutting says.

He confirms the pooch is named after Hillary Clinton. I'm surprised; Nutting is a Trump guy. He smiles for the first time since Hawkeye Hank's Pre-Approved Used Auto and points at the dog's collar. I thumb past velvety chub for the name tag: *CROOKED HILLARY*. The whole cuddly quintet, rescued en masse by Nutting from a local shelter, is named after Trump political rivals. Here's Lyin' Ted, licking my chin. There's Low Energy Jeb, scratching a floppy ear. Little Marco gnaws my shoelace. Slurping at the water bowl is Lightweight Senator Kirsten Gillibrand; her name barely fits her tag.

"Ran out of good nicknames," Nutting admits.

This dog-based attempt to amuse his politically engaged daughters backfired. They are avowed Democrats. Nutting grabs two Miller Lites from the fridge and we head for the outdoor balcony, the driest port in the pandemic storm. On the way, I notice a shiny blue plaque propped up on a Blu-Ray shelf.

I ask if that's it. Nutting swipes it, tosses it to me, and takes a seat on the balcony. I sit six feet away and read the plaque while Low Energy Jeb attempts to chew its lacquered corner.

BURGER CITY MANAGER OF THE YEAR
2016
Robert Nutting
Burger City Franchise Location #8

"Ought to junk it," Nutting mutters.

Seeing anyone this despondent makes me despondent. I remind Nutting that Hawkeye Hank just named him Salesperson of the Month yet again. He may have faults, but he's a good worker.

"Yeah. I guess. The praise of my peers used to mean everything. Everything. But I *have* no peers. Not anymore. No one's been through what I've been through. No one understands."

Bob Nutting drains his beer in two minutes. It's worrisome, but in his defense, it's been a long day of conjuring sooty demons. He crushes the can in a fist, drops it to the carpet, reclaims the Manager of the Year plaque, and tosses it back inside like a steak. Lyin' Ted and Lightweight Senator Kirsten Gillibrand pounce after it, hungry for tasty varnish.

"You know how many Burger Cities there were in 2016? Thirty-eight. Thirty-effin-eight. BC Corporate didn't spread the love just for kicks. Most years, the same two or three managers won. So when Bob Nutting took Manager of the Year, I'm telling you: shock waves."

Bob Nutting's long-lost swagger briefly resurfaces. It's how he looked doing his Vincent Price act on TV9. It's probably how he looked the night he kissed Deirdre Benji.

"Everyone was talking. Bob Nutting's place *doubled* its net? Bob Nutting's going to be on TV *again*? I was hiring workers over and above the recommended margin. No Burger City in 2017 was doing that. Those new hires didn't stay, but that's a different story. I had the *resources* to do it is what's important. I made sure my staff knew. I made sure Lisa knew. Give me one goddamn reason I shouldn't have been proud."

The beagles are making short work of the plaque. Morsels of wet wood pepper the carpet. Crooked Hillary, the pick of the litter, sits off to the side, munching freebies.

"All of it was a yellow brick road leading straight to *Spectral Journeys*. Excitement was off the charts. I was getting calls from the top. I'm not just talking CEOs. I'm talking *Edwina Hucklebridge*. Widow of *Aldo*.[76] She gets on the phone, nicest old lady you can imagine, and tells me how proud Aldo would have been about how I turned things around. She told me stories about Lil' Beefy, the *real* Lil' Beefy, the pup she and Aldo had. I'm on Cloud Nine. Cloud *Ten*."

---

76 On September 29, 2009, Aldo Hucklebridge died at age 65 of a crushing coronary, which one suspects was brought on by off-the-charts cholesterol levels. On page 45 of his self-published autobiography *Hail to the Beef*, he writes, "To this day, I eat beef three meals a day—and as rare as possible!"

If there was a fly in Nutting's soup, it was Amy Mold.

"Sometime in February, Amy started taking these long breaks. Team members were allowed one break per shift and she was taking three or four. She'd wander from the drive-thru and go spying on Yesenia. Sure, we know why *now*. But at the time? Unprofessional behavior. Amy Mold was losing it. Oh, I see your look. You're thinking Bob Nutting lost it too. Well, maybe so. But you try being Burger City's golden boy for a whole month and then February 26th rolls around and it's gone, it's all gone, it's all the eff gone."

It is rare and chilling to be able to pinpoint the precise high point of someone's life, much less several people's lives. For the staff of Burger City #8, that day was Sunday, February 25, 2017. We can do ever better than that. Their best *hour* was from 8:00-9:00 p.m., meticulously scheduled so that everyone could get back home and situated for the 10:00 *Spectral Journeys* premiere.

Like the teens' secret meetings, the festivities unfolded at the Iowa 80 Truckstop. The younger staff was used to going there, and suggested it when Dion surveyed staff regarding a location for Burger City's first ever employee party. Iowa 80 was close, had a lot of grub, and as long as they didn't go the sit-down buffet route, they could get in and out rapidly.

The snowy night didn't stop anyone, though a bare-bones trio did have to stay behind and pilot the ship: Tamra at Till 1, Dion at the window, and Javi on the grill. Dez, of course, didn't come; it isn't clear she was even invited.

Darcy was also absent.

The resurgence of Darcy's cancer was more volcanic than any Dr. Bigham had seen. Hours after the right-eye blindness of January 29, Darcy checked into the Iowa City Cancer Treatment Center for a round of new scans. The results were shocking. Her Grade III Glioblastoma multiform (GBM) was now a raging Grade IV brain tumor, knots upon knots of abnormal astrocytic cells and blood vessels rooting into the right cerebral hemisphere's frontal lobe. Edema fluid swelled Darcy's brain within days. Her whole head throbbed with fever. She threw up everything until there was only bile, and was too weak to aim it anywhere but her own neck.

GBM kills 95 percent of patients within five years.[77] Amber knew this and, having taken cancer's sucker-punch before, was better able to absorb the impact. Never, though, had she anticipated her mother not

---

77   Robyn Stoller, "4 Must-Know Facts About the Deadliest Brain Tumor," *National Foundation for Cancer Research,* May 30, 2017.

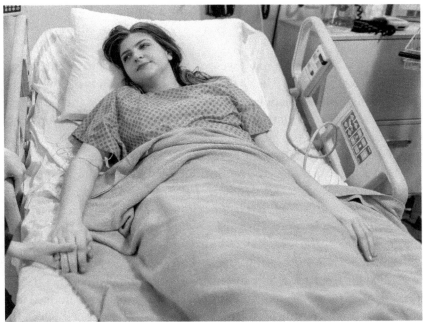

Darcy Smyrna in August 2016 (photo by Amber Smyrna).

recognizing her. By mid-February, Darcy was calling Amber "nurse," "nice lady," or, when the delirium was worst, "Bambi."

Bambi, leave me alone, Darcy moaned.

Bambi, please, it hurts, Darcy sobbed.

Amber felt it all. Frustration. Humiliation. Fear. Fury. She'd never known anyone named Bambi. Was *Bambi* a jumbled version of *Amber?* Or was it a reference to the 1942 Disney movie? Amber's best hypothesis was that her mom had been affected by the film as a child. Regardless, Bambi had become a negative force; Amber loathed being mistaken for her, or it.

Darcy had no such problem identifying Kit. Among visiting family, friends, and medical personnel, Kit alone was the lighthouse through cancer's fog. Amber was jealous at first, then grateful. When Kit visited, Darcy's turbulence settled. And Kit was a prince. Darcy's knobby limbs, the needle bruises, the tang of sweat and piss—none of it bothered him. He let Darcy's injection-spotted talons grip his hand, and when she pursed her scabrous lips, he'd lean over to let her kiss him, never recoiling from her sour breath.

Darcy didn't need to worry about Amber, Kit said. He'd take care of her.

My guide, Darcy would call him. *My protector.*

Darcy couldn't leave the bed—in fact, her wrists and ankles were strapped to it—but Amber took frequent advantage of the adjoining restroom. It was the perfect place to cry.

So Darcy was twenty-five miles west of Jonny the night of the premiere. There was no chance she'd be watching from her hospital bed. She'd spent the morning violently slapping at unseeable aggressors. By afternoon, she was knocked out on fentanyl and in the throes of what specialists privately call "death breath"—the hitching, slurping, dying drones that sound like muffled conversations from the other side.

Kit visited earlier that day. Amber mumbled that she should stay with her mom. Kit pointed out that Darcy had death-breathed before, and besides, she'd want Amber to celebrate the TV event. Amber let herself be pulled along. It was easier when the only discernible word Darcy gasped was *Bambi*.

Amber was no introvert. Groups recharged her. Just feeling the puff of canned air from Iowa 80's automatic doors improved her mood. She inhaled deeply—no rotten-fruit hospital odor here—and noticed her body parts anew: healthy, resilient, sexy, defiant. She gripped Kit's arm and saw Clem waving from the food court. Her face ached with the force of her grin.

Her *friends*. They had their differences. But they were her *friends*.

You couldn't drink alcohol in the food court, but you're damn right alcohol was present. Everyone had fountain drinks and Mickey McCormick flashed Amber the flask he had tucked into his vest. Kit was driving, so why not? Mickey poured, Amber drank. She shut off her phone. God, it felt good. Cut off from the Cancer Center's bed of nails, she was at ease, yet never sat down. There were too many friends to hug, too much squealing at candids they'd taken during the *Spectral Journeys* shoot, too much razzing about which of them had "gone Hollywood."[78]

No one asked after Darcy. It was like they knew Amber needed the night off.

Of course they knew. They were her *friends*.

Cheri, of course, went out nightly, but to joints you needed an ID to get into. The younger staff was overjoyed to see their dark-lensed, frazzled-haired hero in the bright lights of Iowa 80. They behaved just like Hanford Pendergast at Bloom's Pub, each taking a turn to pay their respects as

---

78   The only one not using their phone was Amy Mold, who was witnessed continually referencing *The Trucker's New Testament Bible* placed on her lap.

she sipped a Brisk Strawberry Melon Iced Tea spiked with Mickey's hooch. Most interpreted Cheri's attendance as approval of the poltergeist enterprise, but Kit knew the truth. Cheri had only hardened from the position she'd taken against Quin's initial proposal; she'd been the only staff member to refuse *Spectral Journey*'s interview request. Worse, she had yet to praise Kit's fastidious note-taking. That hurt. He thought it was the best work he'd ever done.

Not wanting a scolding, he tried to avoid her. But at 8:55, as people were fist-bumping, high-fiving, and confirming plans to group-text through *Spectral Journeys*, Cheri's look snatched Kit like a grabbing hand. He inhaled, steeled himself, and walked over. Cheri was bathed in Dairy Queen's blue light, while the Taco Bell sign bestowed her split ends with a purple halo. The look she gave Kit wasn't angry. It was gentle and imploring, with an edge of caution too. Cheri's lecture was ten words.

"I hope this brings you what you're looking for, kid."

Kit's room at Chernow receives natural light from a small grid of glass-block windows. When his mood gets dark, the whole room seems to dim. The mint walls go a crocodile green. The pink scar on his forearm looks like a cockroach.

"I know people like to say how great Cheri was and how they all loved her and yippety-skippety. But nobody should be praying to her like some a saint. I was just a project to her. A little cross-stitch. *Oh, here's this messed-up, lonely kid, maybe I can exercise my ovaries by telling him how to live.* I was feeling really good that night and Cheri ruined it."

It is near the end of the first of our two scheduled interview days. Nuncio is yawning and stretching, and through the walls I hear other patients fussing. Kit, too, must be getting tetchy. These comments are the meanest he's made, and feel out of step with what I know about his relationship with Cheri. I ask Kit if it's possible that he, like a child who has lost a parent, has refashioned grief into anger as a form of self-protection.

"Who are you, my shrink? Stick to the book-writin', Kraus! Ha, ha. Just look at what she said. *I hope this brings you?* All formal like that? Like we're strangers? *What you're looking for?* Like I'm a baby who wants his binky? I wasn't Quin. I wasn't after some cheap ego boost. I was after, I don't know. Transcendence? Is that the word? That's why I never gave Amy Mold shit about her trucker's bible. At least she was looking, right? Searching? Attempting? All I wanted was to get *beyond*. Beyond Burger City, beyond Jonny, beyond all the fucking walls."

Kit gazes around.

His room is three paces wide.

S4 E04 begins as all episodes do, with the dropped-pan crash of the show's percussive score. "On tonight's episode of *Spectral Journeys*," the narrator booms over rapid-fire flashes of Gaetan Goodricke and Roxie Stoyle whipping their heads around at unseen surprises. A fake lens flare segues into an aerial shot tracking along Rolf Tonks Road. If it's the road you drive every day, you probably cry out in delight. A pickup truck rumbles the opposite direction down the I-80 overpass, billowing dust in its wake. It's a cool effect: our view is obscured until the drone exits the cloud and reveals a familiar restaurant.

Gaetan Goodricke and Roxie Stoyle (via the Travel Channel).

Gaetan's voice now: "Burger City. A small Midwestern fast-food franchise. Practically the last place you'd expect to find…a haunting."

Cut to Kit Bryant (the first person to appear!), lit through Giallo gels, practically wiggling off his interview chair with enthusiasm: "First I thought I was crazy. But then it kept happening, and happening, and happening."

Cut to Bob Nutting, a decade fresher from makeup: "I run a tight ship at Burger City. Nothing happens here without me knowing about it. Nothing."

Cut to Tamra Longmoor, crossing herself: "In these times we pray, *The cross of Christ be with me; The cross of Christ overcomes all water and every fire…*"

Cut to Amber Smyrna, pink nostril stud gleaming: "All I know is, since it started, *nothing* here has been remotely normal."

Cut to a hand-held night-vision shot of Gaetan gripping the door handle leading to the Puppy Pen as Roxie presses a hand to her forehead. "This is the locus of the malevolence," she moans. "Don't open it. Gaetan, I'm telling you, don't open it!" Gaetan, of course, opens it.

Another lens flare transitions to the show's ten-second title sequence: a leather-jacketed Gaetan shines a flashlight and steps from between fake gravestones aswirl with glycerin fog. "I'm Gaetan Goodricke, science-based skeptic when it comes to the strange and unexplained." On a witchy-looking set with a steaming cauldron, Roxie whirls around, lips pursed in a pinup's faux-surprise, long black hair spinning. "And I'm Roxie Stoyle, paranormal channeler and psychic medium." Suddenly, the two are striding down a fake-cobwebbed hallway. Roxie crosses her arms like a TV cop as Gaetan points aggressively at the camera and says, "Join us—if you dare—on a spectral journey." Animated lightning explodes the image to dust, which reforms into the slithery title: *SPECTRAL JOURNEYS.*

A new aerial shot traces a shiny black SUV zooming down I-80's Fred Schwengel Memorial Bridge over a gray Mississippi River. Music is pumping. Gaetan speaks from inside the SUV: "Usually we see ghosts—if that's what you want to call them, Rox—manifesting in domestic spaces, or areas where communities once gathered."

A dashboard cam takes us inside the vehicle. Everything you need to know about the driver, Gaetan Goodricke, is digestible in seconds. A stocking cap reading *SPECTRAL JOURNEYS* sits fashionably askew atop his head. He wears a silver tracksuit zipped to his chin. If it were 1999, he'd be fronting a rap-rock group.

While Gaetan wears the same toolish getup every episode, Roxie Stoyle cycles through closets of vintage dresses, often with stylish corsets and matching ribbons. Her spacier presence fits her psychic role. There is a trace of an old lisp in her voice as she recites what sure sound like memorized lines.

"That's correct, Gaetan. But let's remember that restaurants are perhaps the most potent of all community centers. They are where we gain sustenance, break bread, share the meat of brave hunters."

Gaetan smirks. "Brave hunters? We *are* talking about a fast-food place, aren't we?"

"In modern times, chain restaurants play the same role."

"Sounds pretty far-out to me, Rox. I know Iowa is home to the World's Largest Cheeto…but who ever heard of Iowa ghosts?"

A pan flute signals a shift to ye olden times. Another lightning effect kicks off a montage of sepia-toned photographs: creepy-looking homesteaders, ramshackle farms, rural graveyards. There is no evidence these photos were taken in America, much less Iowa, but Roxie doesn't let that stop her.

"Iowa is actually the Midwest's paranormal hotspot. Oskaloosa was the site of America's first crop circle back in the 1880s. In 1893, Scranton residents spotted a forty-foot serpent suspected of gobbling their livestock. In 1948, a man named Paul Weekley fell victim to SHC—Spontaneous Human Combustion. 1966, UFO sightings. 1979, Bigfoot sightings. As recently as 2008, there were reports of a cemetery cult possessing people via demonic ritual."

Dissolve to a painting of a red-and-green-painted Indian chief.

"Most of Iowa's phenomena seems connected to the Native American tribes who once claimed these fertile fields. The word *Iowa*, in fact, derives from the Iowa tribe, once led by the fearsome White Cloud. After avenging his father's death against enemies, White Cloud led a violent raid against the Osage tribe—only to be mortally shot in the back by a fellow Iowa."

Apparently random depictions of American Indians follow.

"Elkader, Iowa, natives claim their Lover's Leap is visited by a lovelorn Indian woman who threw her body off the cliff. Algona, Iowa, was the site of the 1857 Spirit Lake Massacre, in which the Gardner clan was slaughtered by a tribe of Sioux, and where psychics report overwhelming waves of sadness. Listen closely at Vegors Cemetery in Stratford, Iowa, and you might hear children's laughter emanating from transplanted Native American graves."

Back to the white people: Gaetan and Roxie pulling off Exit 269.

"I still say a burger joint is different," Gaetan says as the SUV rumbles into the Burger City lot. He gives the dash cam his trademark smirk. "I guess the PhantasmaScope will tell us what's really going on."

The most incredible thing about Gaetan's "revolutionary"[79] all-in-one ghost-hunting gizmo isn't its purported ability to make subsonic audio from beyond the grave audible to human ears. It's that the show has never once pretended to explain how it works. To learn anything about the black, pyramid-shaped doohickey edged on all sides with colored LED lights, one has to study all forty episodes of *Spectral Journeys* (a doleful fate) and grasp at whatever nonsense Gaetan Goodricke blurts. Thus, we

---

79 *Spectral Journeys*, "S1 E1," 46:00, January 16, 2013.

know the PhantasmaScope features "high-sensitive infrared laser motion detectors"[80] and "temp and motion sensors"[81] to "scan static electricity,"[82] "sweep EVP fields"[83] and "measure SDD shadows."[84]

What does this all mean? *Spectral Journeys* prefers we don't ask. After Nutting races across the Burger City lot with hand outstretched (Marsella Nixon told Nutting that germaphobe Gaetan doesn't shake hands, but Nutting forgot), the first thing he asks is "Can I see the black pyramid?"

"First thing's first, buddy," Gaetan replies gamely, but he floats his hand away from his body to await disinfecting.

The quick tour that follows resembles WNOG-TV9's except that these hosts don't laugh. Roxie Stoyle holds one palm to her heart and the other flat to the air, and periodically makes oblique utterances like "I don't feel safe." She shouldn't, considering there are BeefBombs on the premises.

Beside her, Gaetan holds the PhantasmaScope in a leather-gloved hand and makes a show of consulting a fluttering blue light. "I don't know, Rox, EMF levels are pretty low," he says. It's standard patter. Like Dana Scully of *The X-Files*, Gaetan begins each episode rejecting all paranormal falderal only to close out by wondering aloud if there *are*, in fact, things beyond the reach of science.

Gaetan and Roxie escalate their act upon reaching the walk-in freezer.

The PhantasmaScope's lights blink rapidly and minor-key notes bleep and bloop. "Whoa!" Gaetan cries. "Extreme spike in activity here!" Meanwhile, Roxie feels the air around the door. "I feel a tug on my dress," Roxie says. "Something doesn't want us here, Gaetan." Roxie turns on Nutting. "I'm seeing blood. Lots of blood. Was some kind of violence perpetrated here?"

Bob Nutting's sober description of Ash Muckells's murder plays well to a general audience. Unlike most of the series's ancient misdeeds, Muckells died just five months ago. Gaetan and Roxie, of course, knew all this before arriving. It was Marsella Nixon's hook. Every staff member was asked about the Crime during their interview.

Spectral Journeys always runs forty-six minutes, the first half devoted to backstory and preparation, the second detailing the night the hosts spend in the haunted location. There's not much more to say about the

---

80 Ibid.

81 *Spectral Journeys*, "S1 E4," 46:00, February 19, 2013.

82 *Spectral Journeys*, "S2 E5," 46:00, August 26, 2014.

83 *Spectral Journeys*, "S2 E7," 46:00, September 9, 2014.

84 *Spectral Journeys*, "S3 E10," 46:00, May 3, 2016

first half; they are twenty-two minutes of TV only Burger City staff can adore. It's fun to see yourself and friends under makeup and lighting. In that way, it's sort of like prom.

In contrast to the bright, smooth, high-definition visuals of the show's first half, the latter half is a punchy mishmash of night-vision, thermal-imaging, and infra-red shaky-cams edited for high ambiguity. It would not behoove audiences to get a clear view of what is (or is not) happening.

You have to hand it to *Spectral Journeys* for transforming the small, familiar confines of Burger City #8 into a convoluted haunted house. Gaetan spends most of the time twiddling his PhantasmaScope in dark corners and hissing things like "You hear that?" to an unidentified videographer. Eventually, Roxie cries out in distress. The soundtrack crashes. Gaetan sprints heroically, hollering to Roxie to hold on, he's on his way! (These were the shouts Kit and Amber heard the night of the shoot.)

Gaetan grips Roxie by the shoulders. They're hunched beside B5, near the entrance to the Puppy Pen. The hosts have paid respects to Lil' Beefy and the Coldest Cold Spot, but curiously, most of their attention has focused upon the kiddie playground, where absolutely no one at Burger City has ever reported a disturbance.

Roxie tosses her hair. "We're not wanted here."

Gaetan's gadget is aswirl with colors. "Just look at the energy fields!"

"Something sharp," Roxie gasps. "Feels like a blade."

"You think it's related to the murder they told us about?"

Roxie shakes her head. "No. It's...older...somehow less refined..."

"Is it a knife? An axe?"[85]

Roxie grimaces, strains. "I think...it's teeth."

Before their TVs, the Burger City staff is collectively breathless. Even Kit in his basement, impatient to hear about RSPK, is enthralled.

Gaetan bugs his eyes. "Human?"

"No." Roxie looks at him spookily. "Dog."

My theory is that Marsella Nixon acquired a copy of *The Iowa Road Guide to Haunted Locations* by Chad Lewis and Terry Fisk, published in 2007 by Unexplained Research, a company whose website, as of this writing, prominently advertises their MySpace page. The book's entry

---

85 This is likely a reference to Iowa's most famous haunted house, the "Axe Murder House" in Villisca, Iowa. In June 1912, eight people, including six children, were chopped to pieces in their beds. The crime was never solved.

for the Thirteen Steps Cemetery in Palo, Iowa, just one hour northwest of Jonny, includes this bit: "The cemetery is guarded by a ferocious phantom dog."

Phantom dog, Nixon must have mused. *We haven't done that one before.*

A smash-cut takes us back to the Lil' Beefy standee—Lil' Beefy, you know, is a *dog*—and to a clip of Bob Nutting explaining how Lil' Beefy was inspired by Aldo Hucklebridge's pooch. This is followed by a clip of Nutting acknowledging that, yes, the Puppy Pen had been an outdoor facility before being damaged in 2001. Roxie's off-the-wall conclusion is that a child who once played here had been protected by a loyal dog, whose canine spirit was drawn back by the doggie visage of Lil' Beefy.

Instead of laughing explosively into her face, Gaetan strokes his chin, and then, despite his co-host's pleas, enters the Puppy Pen with his gadget. Most episodes of *Spectral Journeys* end like this, with the PhantasmaScope hissing "*HHSSSHHHMMMFFF,*" which subtitles generously translate as something like, *"I'M LOST, MOMMY!"* Gaetan then loses his shit and it's up to Roxie, with a dramatic hitch in her voice, to command the lost soul(s) to begone.

In this case, the lost soul is a dog—a goddamn *dog*—and the hilarious subtitles read *"BARK GROWL BARK!"* I have slogged through every single episode of *Spectral Journeys,* an exercise in insult, and S4 E04 is the program's absolute nadir, the laziest hour of television I've ever seen. The show jumps a whole ocean of sharks, and even if the bad press of the Burger City Tragedy hadn't dirtied the show's rep, it's hard to imagine it recovering.

If I believed in psychic energy, I'd bet that at 10:55 p.m. on February 26, 2017, a noxious blast of bad feeling shook through the Jonny area as the employees of Burger City #8 realized their great big dreams had just been shredded into tiny pieces.

"I'd gotten the whole family together," Nutting says. "Brandine, Kristina back from Ames. Lisa, too—I pretty much begged her to clear her calendar. I made popcorn, and me and Lisa had champagne. Fuck me, I bought *champagne.* I'd built it up, you know? Nationwide TV? Manager of Year? Then it's like…a *ghost* dog? Brandine laughed. She wasn't being mean. She was 14. It was just funny to her. Kristina covered her face. She'd told her college friends to watch. And Lisa—she just set down her champagne. She got up, got her purse, gave the girls pecks on the cheeks, and gave me this look. On my deathbed, I'll see that look. Like, *Well, Bob, what did you expect?*"

"It was a Lysander night," Clem recalls. "It was his birthday the next day and I was late from the Truckstop, and he was…he was like he got sometimes. There were pots and pans all over, and cushions everywhere, and he'd busted all the lamps. He wanted his Hungry-Man Salisbury Steak. I missed the first ten minutes of the show making it. When I finally got to watch, I felt so *good*. For Q, for Kit, for everyone who'd worked so hard. And then…the dog? The demon dog? There was one lamp Lysander didn't break and when he was in the bathroom, I went over, and I fucking broke the fucking shit out of it."

"You know that scene in [your novel] *Bent Heavens* when Doug has his big show? It was like that. In just a few seconds, the poltergeist was a laughingstock. *I* was a laughingstock." Kit says this as Nuncio is gesturing for me to follow. It's dusk and visiting hours are over. "I knew they were TV people and all that. But they were also supposed to be experts. When I did my interview with them—Mr. Kraus, they told me they *believed* me. But they didn't even listen. When the show ended, I ran outside and threw up till there was blood. All this bright red blood on all that white snow, but I couldn't hardly see, and I couldn't hardly breathe, cuz all I could hear was Cheri going, *I hope this brings you what you're looking for.*"

"Well, I didn't see it, did I?" Amber hisses harshly. "I wanted to. I'd planned to. I'd just had the best hour I'd had in a year. But it was a trick. The universe's trick. It was Satan, if you believe in Satan. First I had this shitty ride home with Kit, crybabying about how Cheri was trying to bring him down. He didn't kiss me when he dropped me off. Right then, I should have known. I went home, turned on the TV, and figured I'd text Clem and Quin so it'd be more fun, and I realized I hadn't turned my phone back on yet. So I did. And there was a voice message. I don't remember the exact words. Satan would have said it better anyway. He'd be honest at least. None of that sad-voice hospital bullshit. *Darcy Smyrna died alone.* That's what the devil would have said. *While you were out whooping it up, I slipped in and killed your cunt mother.*"

MARCH 2017

DECLINE PATTERNS

Darcy's death was a slap-to-the-face wake-up call. Burger City staff had splendored in the sun for a while; black skies had returned. They'd been awed by infinite possibility; the finite had re-bricked its walls. They'd believed themselves chosen to participate in the historic; they were suckers, a discredit to family, friends, and one another.

Monday workers overrode Sunday night's raw burn by slurping Chillees and shifting into sympathy mode. Oh, Darcy—she'd been their shining light. Poor Amber—at least she had Kit. When the Geezers heard, they cried out in unison. Maxine Pinto and Silas Ireland napkined tears while Stu Blick and Zadie Budden sputtered ideas to raise funds for Amber. Vandyke Elbutt rubbed Elbutt's Elbow and scowled into the murky depths of his BC Deluxe Select.

Spectral Journeys S4 E04 wasn't exactly the *Mad Men* finale. It took weeks for clips to gain traction. But they did. Television recap sites, Reddit threads, and more reacted with glee. Clearly, the Burger City Poltergeist was a hoax perpetuated by pathetic yokels. Lightheaded with grief, Amber didn't check the @BurgerCityPoltergeist Twitter and Instagram accounts until March 7, at which point they'd been tagged over two-thousand times.

Amber was in no mood. She deactivated both accounts.

Bob Nutting fared no better. He was spotted thumbing his phone from the back row of Darcy's service. Beginning less than an hour after the Travel Channel premiere, he'd been deluged with calls and emails from Burger City brass aghast at how the PR stunt had gone awry. They'd signed off on *Spectral Journeys*, but it was Nutting's feet held to the fire.

Things kept degrading. On Saturday, March 11, Dion Skerry arrived at 5:00 a.m. to open, concurrent with Zane Shakespeare, Javi Villareal, Yesenia Ruiz, and Kit Bryant. Dion clomped across the lobby, yawning, and disappeared into the BOH to switch on the kitchen lights. What Dion entirely missed, Javi, the second to enter, saw instantly.

"Ay, mierda," he said, as Yesenia and Kit joined him.

The place had been turned into a church—or at least a church basement. Old bibles were stacked at the condiment station. Tall candles were spaced between the tills and, more crazily, actually lit, the melting purple, blue, and pink wax a pastel echo of Ash Muckells's red blood. Five tables in the Grand Room flickered with red votive lights. A nylon Christian flag had been tacked below Camera 3. A poster of a praying family beneath the words *SHARE JESUS* was taped to the soda dispenser. *INRI* decals had been applied to both tills. White plastic mini-crosses had been liberally scattered. Directly above Lil' Beefy hung a shabby, four-foot-tall wood-and-plaster crucifix, Jesus's face angled demurely at Till 2.

"Holy moly," Kit said.

Yesenia crossed herself and murmured prayer. This was captured by Kit, who'd taken out his camera to document the redecoration.

Zane strolled in, stopped, and stared in disbelief.

"You have got to be *kidding* me," he hissed.

Zane Shakespeare was the staff sphinx. Though he was not vegetarian like Amber, he only ate meat he confirmed as free range with his own eyes. That was only the start of his clean-living commitment. He biked to work. He meditated three hours a day with his girlfriend, Wendy. They took dewy dawn constitutionals to commune with deer and quail. They practiced neotantric sex featuring yoni and lingam massage. His favorite musician was Sting. He was the only employee able to discuss foreign films with Quin or speak a bit of Spanish with Javi and Yesenia. Three days after Darcy's death, he moved Amber to tears with a Thornton Wilder quote: "The highest tribute to the dead is not grief but gratitude."

Zane's humanist code was shot through with intensely anti-religious beliefs. Nothing ran him redder than church-state muddying. He was also human. The joke his workplace had become likely stirred a long-dormant shame for holding the crap job in the first place.

He charged the counter, ripped down decals and posters, grabbed the trash bin from under the tills and shoveled into it all the plastic crosses. He dipped his fingers into a blast of Sprite, used them to extinguish the candles, and pitched them into the trash too. His shaved scalp had gone pink with rage. He tore down the Christian flag and chucked the votive lights.

Finally Zane dragged a chair from T6, hopped atop it, gripped the crucifix with both hands, and yanked. It hinged outward, but was firmly slotted onto a nail. Zane was out of patience. He pulled, and twisted, and heaved. Suddenly, a foot-long crack jagged through the wall.

"Hey!" Kit cried.

Zane yanked once more, big muscles bulging, and the crucifix wrenched free. The nail shot to his left, clacking against a credit card reader. Atoms of plaster poofed. Zane toppled off the chair, hit the floor, and rolled rightward to dodge the falling crucifix. Jesus struck Lil' Beefy's cardboard head.

The fallen crucifix beside Burger City's dumpster (photo by Dion Skerry).

"HEY!" Kit screamed.

On video, it's dizzying. Kit dashes forward, dropping his phone. Momentum hockey-pucks the phone across the lobby floor, skidding to a halt at the condiment station. We see only the ceiling, but hear the fall of the crucifix, the crunch of Lil' Beefy, Kit shouting "Watch it, watch it!", and Zane shouting "Off off off off off!" This is followed by the rat-squeaks of sneakers over tile and the meaty slaps of palms against bodies. Then, as perfectly as if staged, Kit's body flies into view and lands directly atop the phone, blocking it out and, two black seconds later, killing the video. Against Zane, Kit never had a chance.

Most staff (and patrons) of Burger City staff considered themselves Christian, albeit that Heartland variety that attended Sunday services mostly out of nebulous notions of civic obligation. Tamra Longmoor, though, was a passionate Evangelical.

She was the one Burger City employee you didn't fuck with, didn't even joke with. She had no detectable sense of humor, and if you pushed her an inch further than she liked, she turned on you with the wrath of God, spitting chapter and verse.

The Longmoor family needed that strength. Iowa is 87 percent white, 5.5 percent Hispanic. Clawing for purchase in the surplus 7.5 percent are Blacks.[86] Still wounded over Tamra's disappearance, the Longmoors declined to speak with me. But it doesn't take extended interviews to suppose that Tamra and her three siblings didn't have the easiest upbringings.

Roughly once a month, the Longmoors made the four-hour round-trip trip to the Lutheran Church of Hope in West Des Moines, a megachurch boasting average service attendances of over ten-thousand,[87] making it one of the country's fastest-growing churches.[88] Closer to the Longmoors' home in Springdale (population 2,857), they attended Redeemer Evangelical Lutheran Church in West Branch three times a week. Minister Kurtis Madgwick recalls Tamra fondly, though his nervous laughter suggests Tamra's devotion was a bit much even for him. "She was often, very often moved to tears," Madgwick says. "It was very normal for her to occupy the Crying Room, which, you know, is typically used for children."[89]

If Cheri Orritt held the Burger City Poltergeist at arm's length out of concern for Kit, Tamra did so for feeling hell's heat singe her fingertips. This explains her heavy presence on *Spectral Journeys*; her pious rancor juiced up the proceedings. My theory is that seeing the show made Tamra feel she'd played a part in a heathen affair.

She always gave the 180 percent Nutting asked for. She was the best shift manager on payroll. She was one of six (along with Nutting, Dion, Cheri, Kit, and Dez) to have keys to the joint. At 1:20 a.m. on March 11, after Dez finished cleaning, Tamra entered and gave the restaurant a holy makeover. It was was overdue. Whether it's Jay Anson's *The Amityville Horror* or Robert Curran's *The Haunted*, there's usually a point where God drops by.

The Zane-Kit fight barely qualified as such. Kit stepped on Zane trying to save Lil' Beefy from the crucifix, and Zane grabbed Kit's leg and hurled him away. Both rolled onto their knees, glaring and panting. At some point, WKES switched on, providing a Blood, Sweat, and

86 "Race and Ethnicity in Iowa," *Statistical Atlas*, December 22, 2020.

87 *Hartford Institute for Religion Research*, December 22, 2020.

88 Patt Johnson, "West Des Moines Lutheran Megachurch Eyes Expansion in Metro Area," *Des Moines Register*, January 7, 2014.

89 Via a phone interview with Magdwick on September 25, 2020.

Tears soundtrack. Dion strolled into the lobby, blinked at the fallen warriors, the fallen crucifix, and fallen mascot. Lil' Beefy's head was severely bent.

"What happened?"

A confusion of allegations exploded. Zane demanded that Tamra be fired. Burger City had a legal responsibility, he cried—this was no place of worship! Dion replied that Nutting wasn't due in until tomorrow. Then get him on the phone, Zane ordered. No one had seen Zane like this; Dion did as he was told.

Zane took the call in Nutting's office, slamming the door for privacy. Dion crept away like a scolded mutt. Kit, Javi, and Yesenia, on the other hand, Scooby-Doo-ed their heads around the corner and heard it all. Zane citing some Iowa law. Zane freaking out. Zane quitting too, which no one saw coming.

The office door flew open, crunching into the wall. Zane barreled past the eavesdropping trio. He swiped up his bag from where he'd dropped it in the lobby and barged through the doors for his bicycle.

Zane expressed regret that night when telling Wendy of his resignation. He had no idea that abandoning Burger City was the best decision he'd ever made. It really should have saved his life.

March 14, 2017

Quin: March 14. 10:20 p.m. Quin, Clem, Amber, Kit. No Yesenia. I knew she wouldn't show.

Kit: She's creeped out. Lay off.

Quin: And Amy Mold? Anyone able to get more than a grunt from Amy Mold?

Clem: She's…pretty into that trucker's bible.

Amber: Something's weird. She keeps begging for drive-thru shifts.

Clem: You think it has to do with…?

Amber: My mom? She barely knew my mom.

Clem: Your mom did so much drive-thru, through. Maybe Amy thinks those shifts need the most—

Amber: I doubt it, okay? Amy didn't even come to the funeral.

Quin: Screw Amy Mold. We don't need her.

Clem: Q coming in hot.

Kit: Nice 'tude, dude. It's not Amy's fault those TV fucks fucked us.

Quin: Tough talk *now*. You were practically planning your *Spectral Journeys* tattoo.

Kit: If they'd listened to *me*, maybe they wouldn't have had to invent their stupid-ass dog!

Amber: Great meeting. Great meeting.

Quin: That show…really set us back. My YouTube? Did anyone see the comments? People are being really…

Clem: Don't read that stuff, Q.

Quin: I turned off the comments. I didn't think I'd do that in a million years.

Amber: People are mad. They're mad at *us*.

Quin: And we didn't do anything wrong! All we wanted was to—

Kit: We wanted to show people. Because it's fucking *incredible*. We know that. We *still* know that.

Clem: Preach, Brother Bryant.

Kit: And we can't let some piece-of-shit scam artists make us stop.

Clem: Can I get an amen?

Amber: But can't we? Can't we stop?

Kit: Quin, how many cameras you got?

Quin: Well…I mean, they're not all state-of-the-art…

Kit: How many, how many?

Quin: Two handheld. One GoPro.

Kit: Plus your phone. You have that twisty little stand for your phone.

Quin: Yeah. Yeah, that's right. Actually, you know what? There's gear. Special gear. I know where to get it. Give me a week.

Amber: Isn't this a sign, though? To do the opposite?

Kit: Great, so we've got the cameras. You know what else we've got?

Clem: The passion? The never-say-die attitude?

Kit: [Jangling keys.] Keys to the kingdom, baby.

Amber: No one's listening to me.

Quin: We can build the YouTube back up. Win them back over. One video at a time.

Kit: No, no. You put anymore stuff online, Nutting will bug out.

Quin: Right. Okay—how about this? Listen to this! We approach it like a *documentary*, right? Shit, yeah. Of course! I make a feature fucking film about this thing.

Kit: We. Not I.

Quin: I'm the director. There's no way I'm not going to be the director. You all can be whatever else you want. Producers.

Clem: Hey, better than Key Grip.

Kit: Whatever. How does it work?

Quin: First, we assemble the footage. Only after we've got everything do I do the edit. Then we blow people's minds. By then, it won't matter if Nutting sees it. We'll be at Cannes. We'll be at Toronto, Telluride.

Clem: You think you can keep your finger off the upload button that long?

Quin: The shooting part won't take a long time. We don't *have* a long time. *[Pages flipping.]* "When these smaller sections of the experiments were examined, decline patterns were found."[90] Roll gets into all this. Vortex fields, exponential decay. It's what I said at the start: poltergeists don't stick around. We're on month five already.

Kit: If we're going to do it, let's do it. Charge your cameras, Quin. Buy whatever other gear you want. But let's not wait for it. Let's start tomorrow.

Clem: What about Dez? She'll be creeping around the joint till one or so.

Kit: Let's say two then.

Amber: Two? Two in the morning?

Kit: You don't have to come.

Amber: Gee, thanks.

Kit: I don't mean it like that. It's just, honestly, the fewer of us there, the better. Nutting keeps the Grand Room lights on all night. We can't have people driving by and seeing us.

Clem: Low-prof. I dig it. But I've got Lysander tomorrow.

Quin: Well, I *have* to be there. It's my gear.

Kit: Well, I'm *definitely* going to be there.

Quin: Fine. Tomorrow night, you and me.

Clem: You two? You sure you won't need a referee?

Amber: Hold on. What are you two actually going to *do?*

[Long pause.]

Quin: We take our *own* spectral journey.

Amber: To what end? What's the point?

Kit: Amber. Think about it. You can even think about it in terms of your mom. If we can get people to see there's things beyond this world? Then all the loved ones they lost—that *we've* lost too—maybe they won't seem lost anymore. Maybe we all can exist together if we find the right wavelength. You know?

Clem: I'm not crying, you're crying.

Amber: Fine. Whatever. Just be careful. Will you please be careful?

Kit: *[Pats notebook.]* Nobody worry. I'm going to note-take the shit out of this. All those teachers who gave me D's? Wait'll they see *this* Kit Bryant.

---

90 Roll, *The Poltergeist,* 5–6.

GAME OF PRICKS

The demarcation line between Kit's excited, jumbled theories and his strict, orderly recording of events happens on page forty-one of the *IDEAS* book, with three words penciled thick enough to cut through paper: *GAME OF PRICKS*.

As mentioned before, the guitar in Kit's room had been used exactly once to impress Amber by playing two ballads by Guided by Voices, stalwart heroes of the indie-rock scene since their breakthrough 1994 album *Bee Thousand*. A year later, GBV released *Alien Lanes*, and among its twenty-eight tracks is the 1:33 power-pop ditty "Game of Pricks." Like most GBV songs, the lyrics make no sense, which is one of the things Kit still treasures about them.

"They're not singing about girlfriends or break-ups or any of that. Nothing's what it seems. 'Blimps Go 90' isn't about blimps. 'My Valuable Hunting Knife' isn't about knives. 'Tractor Rape Chain' isn't about rape. Or tractors! Or chains! Everything's just a feel, you know? Like, here's thirteen story elements—*you* piece them together."

It's April 19, 2020, the second and final day I have with Kit at Bruce P. Chernow Medical Health Institute in Decorah. I'm in the same chair marked *MR. KRAUS*. Kit, of course, wears the same beige scrubs and sits on the same bed. The biggest difference in the room is that the stack of my novels has sprouted dozens of scraps of paper to mark pages, the neophyte reader's version of Quin Arthur's colored tabs.

He spent the whole night preparing questions for *me*.

Is Boggs in *Rotters* a cannibal?[91] Is Bridey's screenplay the key to understanding *Zebulon Finch*?[92] Do the houseflies in *Blood Sugar* represent good or evil?[93] Are people's last names in *The Monster Variations* clues?[94] They are great questions. It pains me to remind Kit that Chernow's Sunday visiting hours are short. We have to focus.

---

91 Yes.
92 Yes.
93 Good.
94 Yes.

He doesn't like this. He crosses his arms and looks suspicious. I attempt to save the day by telling him my favorite GBV album is *Tonics and Twisted Chasers*. This deep cut gets him back on my side. A real mid-tempo stunner, that one. Fan-club exclusive for a long time. I pivot and ask him why he called the Burger City experiments the "Game of Pricks."

"Oh, geez, I don't know. Maybe because I was mostly working with Quin? Who, you know, was a prick? And we're in the BOH half the night doing things that were probably illegal. Which I suppose is a pretty prickish thing to do. So there you go. A couple of pricks."

Did they consider it a game? A portion of Kit's 355 pounds slides down his brow.

"Of course not. People saw that word in the notebook and assumed— do I wish I would've chosen different words? Well, sure, *now*. Back then, I wasn't thinking whatever goofy thing I wrote down was going to be analyzed to pieces. No one took the poltergeist more seriously than me. But you're there, it's late, you're experimenting, and you get certain results? Sure, you celebrate. You hoot and holler. It looks bad on tape, but that doesn't mean I considered it a *game*."

Kit seems earnest now. But in 2017, the young staff of Burger City was well aware of the genre of YouTube videos featuring fast-food employees cutting up behind the scenes. These videos all have a similar feel. It's at McDonald's, or Wendy's, or Taco Bell. It's night and teen staffers asphyxiate with punch-drunk laughter. Then the antics go too far. Someone wipes the kitchen floor with a bun, then builds a burger on it. Someone else urinates into a nacho basket.

To people like that, workplace misbehavior *was* a game, and to know Kit Bryant is to have a solid hunch he'd done a handful of gross things in his time at Burger City. The early Game of Pricks videos have a touch of this flavor, filled with up-too-late foolishness, even when adversaries Kit and Quin were the only two present.

Occurring one or two nights at week from March 16 to April 28, the Game of Pricks was, at the very least, energetic and industrious. Take, for instance, the care taken in fooling Burger City's security cameras. Quin devised a simple method of using clothespins (which he called "C-47s," as they do on film sets) to deflect camera angles slightly upward, just over their heads. If you were Bob Nutting, fast-forwarding through night footage, you'd never notice.

They began with the grill.

The kitchen's twenty-by-fourteen-foot dimensions were cramped with the heated prep station, industrial toaster, order monitor, bun racks, warming cabinets, sinks, supply shelves, and grills. The "grills" are not what you are picturing. Burger City #8 cooked frozen patties on a three-phase electric Taylor Clamshell Grill, manufactured in Rockton, Illinois, circa 1997, a 700-pound steel behemoth originally designed exclusively for McDonald's. They operate like giant George Forman grills. You hinge open a lid, place your patties (you can fit ten per lid for a max of twenty at once), close it, and latch it. Once the timer hits its limit (two hundred and ten seconds for a Beefyburger), the lid unlatches with a pneumatic hiss. Upkeep is simple: change the teflon sheets each night and dispense the grease from the trays.

A busy McDonald's might have two or three grills going. Burger City #8 had just the one. Though the grill was destroyed in the November 14 fire, survivors generally concur it was lopsided; the left grease tray never filled while the right grease tray filled too quickly. A few nights before the first grill experiment, Kit had been working Till 2 when he heard Javi eject a string of Spanish curses. Kit poked his head into the kitchen to find Javi scraping a patty off the floor. Kit kidded him, but Javi's good humor was gone. It was the second paw-shaped piece-of-shit that had slid off the grill that night.

Kit had a hunch. Around 3:00 a.m. on March 16, Quin set up his HC-V770 while Kit fired up the grill, fetched a frozen patty, and held it above the hot surface with a bare hand. Lowering the lid would hide the patty, so they left it open and started recording.

Grill X1, 3.16.17 (*X* for experiment) is an intensely dull video. If there's anything eerie about it, it's the absence of the Soft Rock Hitz that has suffused hundreds of other Burger City videos. In cadaverous silence, we see a medium-shot of the grill surface. A patty is placed on it. Nothing interesting happens. Once it's good and scorched, Kit frees it with a spatula and waves away the smoke. A jump cut takes us to their next try. Same thing. Eventually Quin zooms in. Still nothing.

Well, almost nothing. The burger *does* get cooked. It's really something, cooking meat, when you stare at it, and *Grill X1* gives you nothing else to do. There's that first sob of released moisture, the patty going glossy. Nodules brown and harden, reminders of the flammability of flesh. Fat blobs cling and wobble, then break like blisters, releasing juices that crackle and spit. This close to meat, it's easy to lose your bearings. Maybe

The Living Grill (from Grill X1).

it's a hamburger, maybe not. You can almost feel the scalpel manipulation of kitchen tongs ripping melting skin from sticky steel.

If you're a carnivore, you can't help it: it makes you hungry.

Grill X2, shot on a different night, adds a tape measure. It's a toolbox antique, and a good thing, for by the end of *X2*, it's scorched black. Through clever rigging we don't get to see, Quin's camera now points straight down at the grill. Burger smoke whips sideways, courtesy of a break-room fan we hear but don't see.

Now there is progress. One burger slides one-tenth an inch. Another burger moves a couple inches. The burger of the hour moves four-and-a-half inches. All of them in a northeastern direction. But again, the lopsided grill; the patties might just be sliding on their own grease.

Grill X3 introduces obstacles. A metal bolt is placed onto the teflon in the way of the predicted northeastern movement. An interesting idea. If the poltergeist wants to move all burgers in the same direction, will it expend the extra energy to get burgers around the bolt?

It takes three tries, but it does. The first few times I see it, I laugh aloud. By this point, our testers are breaking frozen patties into chunks to conserve meat, and just when you think the chunk is grounded, it does a sideways glissade and clears the bolt. You hear Kit, Quin, and Clem (that night's group) murmur excitedly. Next, two bolts: a bigger ask for the poltergeist. A few tries later, the meat executes both turns.

How does a skeptic explain this? Still gravity, still grease. Chunks of meat weigh less than full patties and are more mobile. There's also the possibility that, consciously or not, our Burger City scientists may be placing the chunks so as to give them better shots. That's how it looks to me, but Quin's changing camera angles, while visually interesting, do my analysis no favors.

Usually sequels don't match the original, but *Grill X4* is the best of the series. Added to the two bolts are two snippets of metal wire and a nail. There's something about the delicacy with which these items are placed that is touching. Kit's *IDEAS* book reveals the consideration put into the arrangement, the page gray and wrinkled from erasing, revising.

Kit's arrangement gives the meat chunk two options, one that leads to a dead end, the other which allows it to proceed. The correct choice leads to the first wire, which guides the meat chunk to the right. The second wire guides the meat chunk to the left—but only if the meat doesn't overshoot it. If it executes the turn, the meat meets the nail. There's no way around the nail. It's two inches long and 0.0999 inches in diameter, a significant speed bump for a humble bit of beef.

Eight meat chunks make the run. The first two make the wrong choice of entrance. The next makes the correct entrance, but gets caught on the first wire. The third and fourth clear the first wire, but overshoot the second. The fifth, sixth, and seventh make it all the way to the nail, against which they halt and burn to smoky crisps.

You could call these failures. You could also call them progress. You could even credit them to a learning poltergeist. The eighth wad of meat creeps for that nail roadblock at the same sluggish pace as the others, but this one conquers it, its grease *slorping* in the HC-V770's sensitive mics.

The three-man crew explodes into cheers. High-fives smacks resound. "Night of the Living Grill!" shouts film enthusiast Quin, which supplies the phenomenon its name. He's probably already imagining how he'll edit it, how he'll score it, the gasps of his first film-festival crowd. The three young men party so hard the camera's audio peaks and distorts. It's like hearing them go insane in real time.

OUT OF ORDER UNTIL FURTHER NOTICE

Clemens Dumay squints at a box elder bug scaling a tire air pump, screws up his lips, and spits chaw. Direct hit. The insect waggles drunkenly and flops to the gas-station sidewalk. It's both impressive and sad. How many teeth has Clem lost perfecting that spit? He starts packing his container of Kodiak Wintergreen for another pinch.

"You gotta remember, it was March. All this was happening the same time as school. I'm there for maybe half the experiments? Amber once or twice. The couple times Amy Mold shows, you know what she does? She wears the drive-thru headset the whole time. So it was Kit and Quin's show. You could tell too. Both were ragged, man. Kit didn't have 8:30 school but he had 5:30 shifts."

Clem gestures at the unbroken night, the galaxy.

"See all this? All this nothing? It's what I expected for me. It's *better* than what I expected. I figured I'd graduate, but what was I going to do after that? Besides run people's credit cards or load boxes? My wildest fantasy was to not have to take care of Lysander four nights a week. So falling asleep in class? Who cared?" He laughs, a self-critical sound. "The whole galaxy awaited me."

For the others, he says, the stakes were higher.

"Q had a 5.0. Or a 4.0. Whatever the highest is. I think it was March when he didn't get an A on some paper. He got a B-*minus*. He lost it. Lost it. We were cruising, doing our Red Bull thing, and he was, like, shaking and crying. We were besties—Hobbs and Shaw—but I'd never seen the dude cry. He started trying to convince himself. He said that if his grades slipped, that was okay, colleges wouldn't mind because they'd be wowed by the Game of Pricks film. Suddenly he was depending on the poltergeist to fix everything. And who does that sound like? Huh? His name rhymes with Shit Pryant."

The profusion of programs like *Spectral Journeys* has fostered a cottage industry hawking paranormal tech to amateur ghost busters. It should go without saying (but clearly does not) that these businesses are full of shit. Their doohickeys might gauge electricity, temperature, whatever. But to think your

$130 "P-SB11 Ghost Box" will allow you to eavesdrop on the hereafter is absurd. A Magic 8-Ball works just as well at a fraction of the price.

What stuns me is the mental contortions Quin Arthur had to perform to justify his purchases. He'd be the last person in town to click on a phishing link or forward a conspiracy theory. What had thrilled him about *The Poltergeist* were the scientific elements, Roll's use of electroencephalographs, electrostatic voltmeters, and more.[95]

Too effortlessly, probably desperately, he made the leap from legit devices to the garbage pile of modern supernatural gadgetry. Quin was a sucker for tech. His closet was a production equipment depot, his bedroom an editing suite. Tamra had the Lutheran Church of Hope; Quin's cathedral was B&H Electronics.

B&H was too reputable to sell this kind of junk. With Clem watching nervously over his shoulder, Quin visited websites with "spooky" designs and dragged device after device into online shopping carts. A Digital Dowsing EM Vortex Pump ($325). The coffin-shaped Para4ce Paranormal Music Box Poltertune ($349). An Infrared Thermometer ($29.99). The Phantom Lite IR Flood Pro Illuminator ($72.99). The REM POD EMT ($179). The Trifield Natural EM Meter ($249). The Ovilus 5b EVP translator ($429). Clem talked down Quin from getting a Boo Buddy ($359.95), a spirit-sensing Teddy Ruxpin that registers disturbances and, in a child's voice, replies with statements like, "Brrrr, it's cold in here," and "That tickles!"

The more than $2,000 Quin spent on this specious shit is indicative of the corner into which he felt painted. Bump-in-the-night ghosts were a far cry from RSPK-based poltergeists. Exhausted, stressed, and up against a competitor who didn't like to lose, Quin had at last conflated the two, or else had decided anything was worth trying to get the finished film he needed, no matter the cost. Indeed, the cost would prove to be extreme.

Meanwhile, strange events continued to beset Burger City #8. The ice machine went haywire, spraying ice chips like broken teeth. Three shelves in dry goods storage collapsed over three consecutive days. The bun warmer caught fire. The beam of the Puppy Pen seesaw broke, bruising the tailbone of a young rider. The drain hose of the dishwasher kept spilling water, a sure sign of mice, yet traps caught nothing. Registers zeroed out,

95 I believe it likely that Quin also read about eccentric electromagnetics innovator John Hutchinson, whose 1979 "poltergeist machine" created zero-point energy (this is quantum physics stuff) to suspend gravity, leading to all sorts of phantasmic wonders, from glowing orbs to levitating objects to shattering mirrors. See Clarkson's *The Poltergeist Phenomenon*, 95.

enraging customers and pushing Nutting to berate innocent employees. Most noticeably, the lights in the Grand Room went on a strobing fritz that would persist until Burger City's terrible end.

None of these irregularities were imbued with any sense of fun. They didn't inspire customers to gasp and whip out cameras. Lil' Beefy hadn't budged since getting her noggin bent by the crucifix. The Coldest Cold Spot had become old hat; staff simply stepped around the chalk circle. Spectacle had been replaced by a series of wearying irritations.

True disaster descended on Sunday, March 19. That was the day the Chillee Shake Machine quit working. Starting off her morning right, Amber went for a breakfast Chillee at 5:15 a.m. only to receive a cup full of sticky sludge. She screamed, literally screamed. Javi rushed up, expecting gore. His good attitude had thus far proven impervious to the melancholy spreading among Burger City staff. But one look at the gloppy cup and he lost it. He covered his face with sanitary-gloved hands.

A large Chillee (photo by Amber Smyrna).

Dez Mozley, the only one capable of fixing the Chillee Shake Machine, refused to give it priority. There were a hundred other bullshit calamities mewling for her attention at Burger City, plus the place was giving her bad vibes. No way was she spending six or seven hours, in the dead of night, dismantling and rebuilding that motherfucker. And so the unthinkable came to pass.

OUT OF ORDER UNTIL FURTHER NOTICE, read the sign.

There was actual sobbing. Desperate embraces. Tearful reassurances, which no one believed, that everything was going to be okay.

Robbed of the palliative and solace of Chillees, the Game of Pricks crew might have folded. Instead they worked twice as hard. They could only film the Living Grill so many times. That left the Men's Room Bully as the next target. Ever since the Haunted Dick Pic heralded its arrival, it had been the most aggressive phenomenon. Every male employee of Burger City had felt a light shove at some point, and several customers backed the claims.

There is, of course, zero proof that the Men's Room Bully was anything but a suggestion passed from one person to the next. There is also zero proof that the Men's Room Bully caused the poltergeist's first fatality, though that is what the survivors believe.

Biff's Gas & Diesel & Store has an Olde Midway Electric 18 Hot Dog 7 Roller Grill capable of keeping fourteen franks rolling at once. Capable is the key word. The residue of a million hot dogs past (ghosts in their own way) so badly mucks up the purportedly non-stick rollers that Clem has to scrape it clean with a chopstick every couple hours. The chopping action brings him physical pain—the shoulder injury from the Burger City Tragedy.

In addition, Clem says, cleaning the Olde Midway Electric disgusts him—shades of Dion Skerry's Meat Grief. Even here, at the edge of nowhere, Clem cannot escape cheap, greasy food.

He returns outside munching Corn Nuts. He underhands a bag into my chest. Clem is yet another of the Burger City crew who has gone vegetarian. I see it as a form of fighting back. He falls back into his chair and telescopes inside himself, hiding behind his beard.

"Write that we faked it if you want. I mean, what do I know? Maybe I'm Sheeple #537 and I just followed the herd. All I can tell you is when we were in that bathroom, we were scared. I know that's not how the videos sound. But why do you think we were laughing so hard? *Because* we were scared."

I ask him to describe what the Men's Room Bully felt like. Without hesitation, he strikes my shoulder with an open palm. I drop my Corn Nuts.

"Like that. Physically, anyway. Mentally or whatever, it felt like— look, I was pointing at the stars before, right? You cannot look at those and not believe there's other dimensions, planes of existence. Being with the Bully was like those brown paper towels when you dried you hands: our world got all soggy and see-through. We sensed it. It sensed us back. The question was, how did it feel about us?"

I push for clarity. Is Clem an adherent of Roll's RSPK theory or just straight-up ghosts? He crunches a Corn Nut in frustration.

"You're asking shit that doesn't matter. Did a shark evolve from tadpole? Or did it just emerge from the goo fully sharked? Either way, it's sharking its shark ass your way. If you're too busy getting theoretical, brother, you're about to get got."

The men's room footage does include a lot of reverberant laughter. It's not all male; Amber and Amy are sporadically present. The teens try all sorts of stuff. They spread flour on the floor, then hoot and holler, hoping the invisible visitor will leave tracks. They tape the strings of twenty helium balloons to the floor and scan for motion. They turn off the overheads and use a strobe light. Colored light. Night vision. Infra-red. A fog machine from school. They use Quin's old Kinect to layer the room with a three-dimension grid of green dots.

Things happen. But what kind of proof is a recoiling balloon or swirling nebula of glycol fog? The only truly dramatic instant is from *Mens X6, 3.31.17*. At what Quin's exhausted voice later tags as 2:57 a.m. on March 31, the men's room door blows opens as if kicked from inside. The camera and tripod shudder. Everyone present—Kit, Quin, Clem, Amy—cries out simultaneously. Seconds later, the door starts to swing back shut, and right before it does, Amy darts for it, arms over her face, shouldering her way out.

She's wearing a 3M B1099 headset.

It's good theater. The other three wander into view, saying *Holy shit* and *What the fuck, man?* and *Is she okay?* If you'd like to see more good theater, I suggest tuning in to the Travel Channel's *Paranormal Caught on Camera*, which features this sort of thing every single episode. After seeing a dozen of these, they begin to lose their magic. Either we live in a world mobbed with meddlesome spirits or these are fakes. Only one answer is logical.

Naturally, the Game of Pricks players chose the other.

I suggest to Clem that someone on the other side of the door yanked it open. He gives me a pitying look.

"Well, let's review who else had keys. Dion, who couldn't move that fast if he was on fire. Dez, that lighthearted, goofy prankster. Cheri? Up *that* late? And Tamra. I suppose you could make a case for Tamra. Zane tore down her Jesus stuff, Nutting almost fired her. So, fine. Tamra whipped open the door for some reason and ran out of the building, and Amy Mold, who ran out two seconds later, didn't see her. Makes perfect sense."

Clem is a statue.

Then he rockets to his feet and shouts into the night.

"BUT I KNOW WHAT I SAW! AND I'M SORRY! ALL RIGHT? YOU HEAR ME, MR. GHOST, SIR? MS. POLTERGEIST, MA'AM? WE'RE SORRY FOR WHAT WE DID! ALL OF US ARE SO FUCKING SORRY! SO YOU WILL PLEASE LEAVE US THE FUCK ALONE?"

The cries echo, their own ghosts, undying, returning. The hairs on my arms pinprick. It's a tragically cinematic vision that might have appealed to the old Clem's imagination. He's the omega man, the last person on Earth, raging against his fate.

He sits, grabs his Snapple can.

"We made the Men's Room Bully leave the men's room. Not bad, huh? We hip-hip-hoorayed all fucking night. But where did the ghost go? Where did it make *sense* it would go?"

Seven hours later—Friday, March 31, 2017, at what EMS logs later state as 9:50 a.m.—a shriek blistered from the direction of the restrooms. A subsequent *clunk,* somewhat like a fallen toilet seat, was audible beneath the Soft Rock Hitz and workaday drone. A second later, a softer, lower *thump* concluded the series of sounds.

Bob Nutting was by the french fryer, Yesenia Ruiz to his left, Cheri Orritt to his right. The look he gave them was not so much shock as it was weariness—so much weariness. Yesenia took the shaky backward step of someone used to being beaten. Cheri's wrinkled forehead fell toward her tinted glasses, yielding to the weight of anticipated despair. It didn't last; she set her lips into a determined line.

The shredded muscles of Nutting's pride contracted. This was *his* restaurant. That *he'd* saved from ruin. Now it floundered, with sales bottoming 20 percent lower than where they'd been pre-poltergeist. He thought of his family, all that lost respect. He pictured his newly arrived Manager of the Year plaque, already a joke.

He flung up the end of the counter and, with a loafer squeak, pivoted into the restroom hallway. The fluorescents flickered, gateway to a horror funhouse. His peripheral vision caught Cheri, Tamra, and Mickey behind him. He balled his fists and moved faster.

He'd felt the Men's Room Bully before. Now he swore he was going to fucking end it.

Nutting grasped the cold knob, yanked open the door, and leapt inside. *"Get the fuck out!"* he cried.

A gawping man peeked from inside the toilet stall. Quickly, the man closed the stall door and locked it. Nutting panted, blinked, gazed about. Nothing else was there.

"Oh, lord!"

Cheri's voice. Nutting whirled around, elbowed the door back open, and bumbled into the hall. Cheri was holding open the women's room door staring down. Nutting couldn't breathe. He crossed the four feet between restrooms and placed his body in front of Cheri, shielding her, maybe the bravest move he'd ever made. He looked at the floor. It seemed a long way down.

It's 11:00 a.m., past time for the Geezers to vamoose from the Tipton Hardee's. The yawning morning patrons are being replaced by their louder, pushier lunch-break counterparts. Stu Blick, Silas Ireland, Zadie Budden, and Vandyke Elbutt have held down this outdoor table for five hours. Repeated restroom trips requiring the Covid-19 procedures of masking up and scrubbing down have tired them. Medicines wait at home. So do naps.

But Zadie Budden once carried a child with a broken leg two miles to the nearest neighbor. Vandyke Elbutt once tackled a student who'd held his class at gunpoint. Stu Blick and Silas Ireland had both enlisted to fight in Vietnam. They keep pushing. No other part of their story is this important.

"Sticking with Burger City seemed like the right thing to do," Silas says. "Bob Nutting needed our money. His electricity was on the blink. The Chillee machine was kaput. In hindsight, we should have headed for the hills."

"Hindsight is a construct made up by people who like to wallow," Vandyke seethes. "There is the future, the now, and the past. I will not live in the past."

"We're Geezers." Silas shrugs. "That's all we got."

"You may not live in the past," Zadie says, "but the past lives in you."

Stu, as usual, rights the ship. "I never saw that ghost program. If memory serves, none of us saw it."

"*60 Minutes,*" Silas says. "That's what I watch on Sundays."

"Maxine, though—she said she watched the show, and then watched the whole staff fall apart. Bob Nutting was in a 24/7 panic. Amber, with everything she was going through, looked about to crack. Maxine just soaked it up, like it was her burden. She wanted to help so bad. Kit was upset about the cardboard dog getting bent, so she brought in...what were they? Popsicle sticks?"

"From her grandkids," Zadie confirmed. "To tape to the back of Lil' Beefy. She wanted it to start hopping again. Not for herself, mind you. For Kit. For Amber. For everyone who seemed so downtrodden. When the lights started flickering, Maxine thought she could be helpful again. Kit took notes all the time, so Maxine thought, wouldn't it be nice if she did some record keeping for him? So while we all jib-jabbed, she watched the lights, and timed them, and wrote down the data. She really thought she had something."

"Heart of gold," Silas mourns.

"Platinum," Vandyke insists. "Palladium."

Maxine Pinto (photo by Zadie Budden).

Their trays are gone. Their coffee cups have been stuffed with napkins. There is nothing left to fidget with. Stu lets out a long, sad sigh.

"To hell with it," he growls. "You can say Maxine had an accident all you want. The fact is, she messed with it. She got up in its business. Doing that, with a *force* like that? It's gambling, plain and simple. You gamble enough, it doesn't matter if you're as pure-hearted as our Maxine. There will be a time when the bill comes due."

Maxine Pinto lay dead on the restroom tile. Blood from the back of her head wormed along the grout, making right-angle turns, a bright-red grid. Her short white hair wicked up blood, turning pink. Her glasses had been jarred to the side of her face. Her dentures had popped onto her chin.

Where did the ghost go? Clem asked me three years later. *Where did it make sense it would go?* Having been chased from the men's room, the

Bully entered an adjacent room indistinguishable but for the lack of urinals. When Maxine, no friend to the poltergeist, presented her frail body alone in that room full of sharp corners and hard flooring, her fate was sealed.

Or she simply suffered a heart attack and fell. Maxine Pinto had CAD and lowered neutrophil levels, and had been living with a heart murmur for five years. Her official cause of death was type-2 acute myocardial infarction. It's right there in black-and-white.

None of that softens the blow of finding a corpse in your restaurant. Bob Nutting, filled with purpose seconds before, peeled away from Cheri, tilting into the hall with an elbow crooked over his damned eyes. Tamra and Mickey filled his space, leaving Dion Skerry, loyal sycophant, to follow his boss's staggering path.

Customers asked Nutting what was wrong. He stared through them. He lurched behind the counter and through the kitchen, where Yesenia asked if someone was dead. He nodded, kept stumbling. In the BOH hall, Nutting swayed like he might faint, and Dion felt a dim pulse of courage telling him to catch his mentor. But Nutting was beside the walk-in freezer, and Dion didn't dare linger by the Meat Grief epicenter. He waited until he heard the familiar springing sound of the office chair.

Before Dion could move, he was knocked aside. He expected Mickey, maybe Cheri, but it was some old man. Dion cried out in nameless fear. An ancient spirit had materialized to kill Dion and Nutting, just as it had killed Maxine Pinto!

It was Vandyke Elbutt. He bulled past Dion and into Nutting's office. The manager was just sitting there, staring at the floor. Vandyke stood in front of him, liver-spotted hands in fists, tricky knees flexed to pounce. He shook a white-haired finger at his target.

"You killed her!"

Nutting squinted, as if hearing a distant bell.

"You and all this ghost shit, you made her believe!"

Nutting noticed the old man. He cocked his head.

"You scared her to death and now she's dead!"

Stu Blick and Silas Ireland burst into the office, taking hold of the trembling Vandyke. The second Vandyke felt his friends' hands, he raged, legs cycling, arms pinwheeling, civilized professor turned wild animal. He knocked the phone handset into Nutting's lap. He toppled the desktop monitor. Eventually the Geezers' weight prevailed. Vandyke fell, and the three became a pile of bad hips, creaky joints, and aching backs.

Nutting discovered the handset in his lap. He picked it up, and after a moment's consideration, dialed 911. As the boss, it was the least he could do, but to hear Dion describe it, it wasn't worth the three digits.

"Dead lady," Nutting sobbed. "Lady's room."

After that, nothing else was intelligible.

Dion backed away, helped up the Geezers, and closed the door. When 911 responders arrived, Nutting spoke to them from his office. When Yesenia requested to go home early, Nutting assented from his office. And though Bob Nutting went home as usual that night, and most of the nights that April, he never really left his office again, not in any way that mattered, not until the night of the Burger City Tragedy.

APRIL 2017

HEXES, PLAIN AND SIMPLE

For the next part, Amy Mold wants to relocate. There's not another denizen within a hundred feet of us in Fairfield's town square, but that's not good enough. Face-masked people outside Cafe Paradiso gaze in our direction. A man talks into a phone outside Davis and Palmer Real Estate, and who's to say he's not reporting our movements? This kind of paranoia is rampant in the survivors. Their spines ache from cowering.

She tosses her Kapha tea, my signal to finally dispatch my Vata. I follow her in my car to OB Nelson Park at the south side of town. I remember the park from childhood mostly for its public swimming pool, a piercingly loud, cement-hot, chlorine-fogged prison of direct sunlight, where I, a terrible swimmer, always felt on the precipice of death. Today it's gone, buried. We pad over the grass and I hear my own ghosts: summer screams, the thwap of the diving board.

"People always focus on Quin's B-minus, poor baby. But I was an A-student too. And you know what I was suddenly getting? D's. F's. Meetings with teachers and counselors. I was in free-fall. And I couldn't tell anyone."

I ask why she didn't tell Kit. Surely he would have believed. Amy breathes through her nostrils. A particular inhale likely taught by her TM instructor.

"It's like you're not listening. Of course Kit would believe. And then what? Then it's a group project? *Protect her,* is what I heard. *Her,* Mr. Kraus. You think those boys' club screw-offs would have actually *protected* anyone? They'd turn it into a three-ring circus. This was three months into Trump. Women were on their own."

A sudden breeze nearly knocks over her 126-pound frame. She careens and I reach out to grab her. For a split second, my fingers graze her left hand and I *feel* the burn scars—slick, lumpy, strangely supple.

She doesn't want that. Amy retracts her hand, finds her footing, and takes a steadying inhale at the nexus of two softball fields and a tennis court. It's June 2 and 74 degrees. But all three sports areas are vacant. It's like the whole town got buried in the pool behind us. It fits the mood. Amy Mold has felt alone since the first blip from the Drive-thru Phantom.

She places her scarred hand over her heart.

"*The Trucker's New Testament* had this little diagram. At the bottom was a box labeled 'Sinful People.' At the top was a box labeled 'Holy God.' There were arrows showing us how to get there: 'Religion, Morality, Good Works.' All my homework time went into studying those options. I decided I couldn't do much with Religion and Morality. But Good Works? Do you see how it all came together?"

The nature of those Good Works crystalized at 5:15 a.m. on April 8, 2017. Until then, the Drive-thru Phantom had repeated two words. That morning, just as Amy situated the headset over her ears, the voice said more—without static or interference. This one instance, the crappy B1099 might have been a luxury Bose or Sennheiser.

Amy, dear, the voice said.

She recognized it now.

It was the voice of Darcy Smyrna.

The Trucker's New Testament Bible had Amy Mold pondering sacrifice and resurrection. It made sense she'd pine for the part of Mary Magdalene, first witness to a martyr's return. But it had been forty-two days since Darcy's death, and the Drive-thru Phantom had begun speaking ninety-seven days ago. So it made no sense that it had been Darcy all along—unless you bought into the chilling notion, as Amy did, that the excised cancer cells of Darcy's brain had allowed part of her to cross over.[96]

Amy gasped. Her heart felt full; she'd heard the idiom before but never understood it. Here was the religious experience she'd pined for since picking up the truckstop bible.

He's hurting her, Darcy said.

Amy hid in the drive-thru cubby's corner, nose flattened to the stacks of Puppy Pack boxes.

"Darcy? Who? Who's hurting who?"

Darcy did not make her wait.

Mickey, she said. *Yesenia.*

Softly, a *whump*, a shovelful of grave dirt falling to a casket lid, and like that, the Drive-thru Phantom, whatever it was, was gone for good.

Amy Mold trembled. The tower of Puppy Packs swayed. She made herself sit. For the next ten minutes she prayed. For Darcy, wherever she

96 As a high-schooler, Amy Mold had been deeply invested in abortion rights, and today, she believes her younger self, under the grips of the poltergeist, had managed to confuse a woman's owership over her own body with the weird notion of a woman's actual body parts—including lost pieces of it—being semi-sentient. There is also evidence that Amy had the flu in April, which could not have helped her thought process. And, of course, she could be lying to me.

was; for herself to be strong; and as soon as it occurred to her, for Yesenia Ruiz, who was in some kind of trouble with Mickey McCormick. Yesenia— she was there right now! Twenty minutes ago, she'd greeted Amy, her new sister in Christ, with her usual, "We can do all things through Him!" Yesenia had helped Amy so much. Now it was Amy's turn to help Yesenia.

"It's 5:32." Dion Skerry's voice. "You should unlock your till."

Dion was busier than ever. Darcy was dead. Zane had quit. Tamra had been docked a week of shifts. Back in January, staff would have fought for those open shifts, but not now. In the past, Bob Nutting would fill in the gaps. But Nutting had more or less vanished. He entered and exited Burger City through the back, unseen. He kept his office door locked. Double-locked, in fact: he'd installed a sliding bolt on the inside. The last time Dion had dared knock, he'd received a muffled, irritated response from Nutting:

"Busy!"

Noises began to emit from the office. Difficult to identify. Low, splintering noises, as if Nutting was snapping twigs. He made occasional grunts, leading Mickey McCormick to posit that Bob Nutting, accepting his inert marriage, had discovered phone sex.

Soon a sulfurous smell joined the noises. As April wore on, it thickened into a rotten-egg stench. Like an interminable fart, it leaked into the break room until staff began to avoid it. The upside was that the Break Room Bucket sat empty. No one was policing phone use now.

Staff turned to Dion to bitch about the smell. If he didn't do something, soon it would reach the kitchen, lobby, and Grand Room. The whole joint needed cleaned. Scrubbed. Disinfected. They were paying someone to do that, weren't they? On April 19, 2017, Dion Skerry marshaled his fortitude and called Dez Mozley.

Forty-nine days pass between Dez's attack on Dion at the West Branch Kum & Go and the call I receive on September 22, 2020. It's the unmistakable growl of Dez Mozley. She says she has things I need to hear. I try to get more details, but she claims wireless signals can't be trusted. She tells me where she lives, warns me not to be late, hangs up, and doesn't pick up when I call her back.

I'm in the midst of a pandemic-times PR blitz for my book written with George A. Romero, *The Living Dead*. But I get in the car and make the four-hour trek to Cedar View Village Estates near Stanwood, Iowa (population 684). Located alongside U.S. 30, the trailer park is carved from an acre of cornfield. It has no signage. A cracked cement path the width of two sidewalks winds between car-tire entry towers. The path makes a wobbly oval from which twenty-nine trailers extend onto grassless strips. I'm always struck by how low to the ground trailer parks are. The blue Iowa sky is vast.

But the people I see stare at their feet or, worse, straight at me. Some have haunted red eyes, sparse teeth, the scratched-up skin of Ash Muckells and Scotty Flossen. A clean, new rental car in their midst: I'm there either to buy or sell.

I circle the lot three times before noticing a vacuum cleaner in the backseat of a car. I park, get out, and peer into the vehicle like a carjacker. The backseat is piled with cleaning materials, some of them ancient. The trailer is small. Once upon a time, it had been pink. The rotten stairs up to the door don't creak. Instead, they give beneath my shoes like sponges.

The door before me requires scrutiny. A big, foreboding sigil has been scratched into the old paint. Small brass bells dangle from dozens of rusty nails. A semicircle of salt has been poured at the door's base, and inside that border sit three plastic twenty-ounce soda bottles filled with a dark yellow liquid.

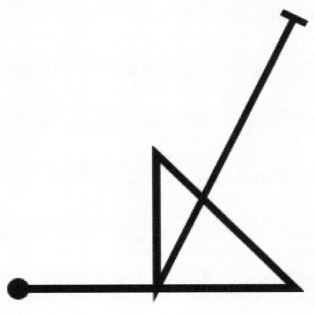

Reproduction of the sigil.

Urine, it turns out—a folk remedy to keep witches at bay. Dez tells me this after throwing open the door like she's trying to rip it from its hinges. The meaty red sausage of her face startles me anew. She scowls around the park, then motions me indoors with her talons. I don't like my Covid-19 odds and ask her if we can talk outside. She ducks back inside and returns with an official-looking piece of paper.

"I get tested," she barks. "Every day I can. Everywhere I go. What else am I going to do? You don't have any idea how hard they're trying to get me."

Her Covid receipt checks out but I stay masked up. The inside of Dez's trailer is dark for a sunny afternoon. This is due to musty blankets nailed over the windows. Not that the ceiling lights are especially vibrant. Each leaks a lightning bug's worth of illumination. On the floors I make out rough contours: dunes of clothing, hoodoos of stacked dishes, promontories of carpet miscellany.

The living space reeks of urine, possibly by design. I take a seat on a dry-looking padded chair beside a sofa-sized pile of junk while Dez peeks through the blanket-curtains. I ask her what she's looking for.

"Warlocks. When someone visits, they think I'm distracted, I'm weak. But Dez Mozley's always one step ahead of those suckers. I've been drinking salt water all day. That pee out there is high-octane. Those bells on my door came off of cats. *Dead* cats."

Lots of potential followups here that I don't ask. But Dez doesn't need the ammo of questions to keep firing.

"They don't know who they're dealing with. I had water allergy as a kid. Acquagenic urticaria, mister. Dez Mozley beat it! When I was 14, I had total facial paralysis. I let kids punch me in the kisser for five bucks. How you think my face got like this? Dez Mozley beat that too! It only made me stronger. Binding spells, banishing spells—no black magic can stop me now. One time I fought off a spy and got eleven stitches in my lady-parts. I healed in six days, mister!"

I ask her to rewind to the black magic part.

"You think I'm lying? I should be dead right now! Since Burger City, let's see. I've lived through bullets, firebombs, deadly arrows, acid sprays, raccoon armies, devil deer, gassy slugs, murder hornets." She grins, half her teeth gone, the other half terminal. "I've defeated so many lesser witches, I've ascended. Since last time you saw Dez Mozley, I became the most powerful witch in the Mississippi Valley."

I offer congratulations and ask if she thinks witchcraft has anything to do with the Burger City Poltergeist. She flails her arms.

"Anything? *Everything!* There's a whole coven to blame."

Here in the trailer park?

"They're too clever to gather in big numbers. They're all over the land. They carry lightning rods. They hold meetings in cemeteries. I've infiltrated them. I'm a powerful witch so they invite me out of respect. They don't know I'm plotting against them."

Dez sits in what I think is a chair, but might be a heap of afghan blankets. In the gloom, her apple-red face burns like fireplace embers. She pulls from a pocket of her denim blouse a purple pouch. She unknots the drawstrings with warty fingers.

"Before my ascension, Dez Mozley had to play ball, you understand. I had to play ball or my ass was grass! I wouldn't dare tell you to come here. I'd have your blood on my hands! Now it's them that are afraid. Oh, they might try to scare you off. They might slash your tires or bust your windshield. But you're safe with me."

I glance toward the blanketed windows. The prospect of vehicle debilitation isn't great. Neither is the idea of the whole trailer being encircled by a hooded cult. When I look back at Dez, she's pouring sparkly powder from the pouch onto a blackened piece of tinfoil. I ask why she decided to call me.

"To set you straight! If you're listening to Maggot Boy Dion, you're being fed a meal of lies. There never was any poltergeist. No ghosties, no goblins. It was hexes, plain and simple."

I follow the logic; it's the only flashlight I have. Was Burger City #8 cursed because an Iowa coven had a beef with Dez? She shakes her head. Plaits of matted black hair flop.

"I don't know what brought the hex down on that place. But I was the only one who saw what was happening! You think anyone listened? Dion Maggot Boy? Boss Man Bob? They treated me the same as ever, like a booger shot out of their nose."

Despite her belief the joint was cursed, Dez continued to do her job in 2016–17 and I'm inclined to believe her work was adequate. How else could she have managed to keep her other gigs at Godfather's Pizza in Wilton, Tres Hermanos Restaurant in West Liberty, and the Durant High School in Durant? In addition to a mastery of the mop, she had a knack for fixing things—the Chillee Shake Machine is just one example. She says that's where the April 21 conflict with Dion took root.

"He told me fix the Chillee or else. And I said, *Or else, little maggot!* I had too much to do. There was a hex in that walk-in freezer—and I had to mop up the freezer! There was a hex in the little boys' room—and I had to clean the pissy floors! While everyone was having a party about the whole thing, Dez Mozley was taking all the risks. I did salt pours from those tiny little salt packets when I forgot my Morton Salt at home. You think that was easy? I drew secret signs behind the toilets and hid the dead birds. Your Chillees will have to wait!"

I want to know about those dead birds, but Dez rages on. Meanwhile, she's pulled a matchbook from her pocket.

"I was looking out for their *lives*. It wasn't just Morton Salt I was bringing. Look around, mister. I'm not made of money. But my supplies don't cost me nothing. I have piles and piles."

The match lights, she drops it, and the powder on the tinfoil bursts into a foot-tall lance of white flame. I rear back and make decisions regarding which window to kick through. But Dez has done this before. The flame shortens and fattens, spreading an orange glow across the lower half of the room. It catches the scar in the center of her left palm, a remnant of her Dion altercation.

"There," she sighs. It's the gentlest sound she's made.

The light brings definition to the nondescript pile to my left. It's not trash. It's what Dez said it was: piles and piles of cleaning supplies. I've read about this stash, but seeing it is something else. The brands hail from the post–World War II era. A chalky tin of Simoniz Kleener. A wilted box of Oxydol. A water-damaged pack of Bab-O Soap-Filled Scouring Pads. A carton of something called Sunlight Zeep.

"Daddy's stash. He taught me all there was to know. People think any monkey can mop up scum. You know how painting's an art? Well, cleaning's an art too. The opposite art. You're taking junk away instead of adding it in. Daddy told me nothing they make today works as good as the old stuff. He stockpiled it."

I can't believe Dez has been allowed to keep these. The urine odor hid it before, but now I feel a chemical prickling in my sinuses. Forget Covid-19; here's a better reason to get out of this trailer quickly. I take out my notebook and get down to business.

April 19, 2017: Dion Skerry calls her, says there's a stench. What does she remember?

"Dez Mozley's memory's like a fist. Maggot Boy called me in and, even though I should've been sleeping, I gathered some of these special cleaners here and headed out. There were rose petals all around my car.

You see any rose bushes around here? I should've known there was going to be blood."

Darcy's beyond-the-grave voice, aided by the righteousness of a fresh Christian faith, pushed Amy Mold to uncover a secret I believe she'd sensed without the aid of supernatural help. On the night of April 10, 2017, Amy Mold trailed Yesenia Ruiz from Burger City to her home in the unincorporated township of Downey, Iowa (population uncounted). Her unfamiliar vehicle drew stares. By April 15, she'd learned to park by the railroad tracks off Baker Avenue and skulk to the Ruiz house, where she hid in a variety of places: the grove of trees alongside the house, the broken-down pavilion in the backyard, under the living-room window once all had retired for the night.

Yesenia Ruiz and a sibling (via Twitter).

Amy learned a lot about Yesenia during her two-week surveillance, things no one else at Burger City had bothered to learn. Yesenia had three younger siblings. Her mother, Graciela, worked at a daycare facility in West Liberty. Her father, Marcos, lived way the hell in North Carolina, yet seemed to have a great relationship with the family, speaking to all four of them nearly every night.

Yesenia wasn't a shrinking violet at home. As the eldest child, she bossed around the others with a cocked hip and lots of gesturing. She said bad words (when her mother wasn't around). She wore tube tops. She bellowed pop songs and shook her ass all across the yard. She cooed at what seemed to be a dozen outdoor cats. Amy wondered if Kit would have emptied his coffers to pay for Yesenia's cat's surgery if he'd known she had an infinite supply.

Some nights, Yesenia snuck outside, started the car, and drove off. The first times she did this, Amy was caught off-guard. Her own car was by the railroad tracks. She had to learn to anticipate Yesenia's escapes by the sequence of doors being softly shut.

Eventually it paid off. Amy trailed Yesenia for twenty minutes to a modest white house in Moscow, Iowa (population 403). There Amy hunched under a different window to overhear new noises, these ones sexual in nature. She positively identified the two voices as Yesenia and Mickey.

Amy had so far cultivated a detective's composure. Now her emotions exploded. Yesenia was 16. Mickey was 48. Nothing could excuse the predatory 32-year age difference. New Testament imagery flashed through Amy's mind, with her playing all the wrong roles: Pontius Pilate whipping Jesus, Romans nailing him to a cross, Longinus spearing the corpse. She wanted to kick open the window, crawl through it, grab hold of glass shards, and stab the man inside until he was a purple mash.

She tore herself away, got inside her car, and slugged the steering wheel until the rubber grip was feathered with blood. She wasn't thinking about the poltergeist per se. She thought only of the long-put-upon Darcy Smyrna, an older woman urging a younger one to take the revenge their gender was owed.

Amy went home. She didn't sleep. She stewed. Morning came. It was only because she'd driven to and from Burger City multiple times a week for three years that she was able to pilot her car onto I-80 and off at Exit 269, and park without crashing, and pull open Burger City's door at exactly 9:10 a.m., and duck under the register counter, and fling open the ice bin, and extract the metal scoop, and sink it into the boiling fryer, and ladle up a half a pint of sizzling-hot grease, and lurch into the kitchen, and hurl the full, deadly load right at Mickey McCormick.

One hour before the Kum & Go brawl, while Dion bores me with inadequate answers, my mind wanders to what links him and Amy Mold. Both believe that outside forces (Meat Grief, Darcy's ghost) controlled their willpower, dovetailing their violent acts into a single twenty-four-hour period across April 21 and 22.

I wonder if there might be value in getting the two to hash it out. Dion shrugs when I ask permission, so I dial up Astral Adventures and am glad to hear Amy answer. She's still employed, though her doshas, she reports, remain volatile.

When I suggest talking to Dion, she sounds appalled. But no survivor is fighting harder to right their wronged life. Speaking to a fellow survivor might be healthy and Amy knows it. After setting parameters (speaker phone, on tape, ten minutes max), she agrees. I explain all this to Dion. His expression doesn't change, not even when the call begins.

"Dion?" Amy is quiet, tentative.

"Hey," he replies.

"Hey. How…are you? Are you…functioning?"

"I guess. Are you?"

Amy pushes a laugh through teeth that sound clenched. "I don't know what you'd call it. I'm living, I guess. Barely. Every day is hard. Don't you think? Don't you think it's harder than it should be?"

"I don't know."

"I mean, it's been three years. We have to get over it. What it did to us. What *we* did to other people. Don't you think? There's, like, a self-forgiveness, a grace that has to happen if we're going to move forward. It's overdue, Dion. Neither of us tortured anyone. You know what I'm saying?"

"I think so."

"So this writer guy wants us to talk about what happened that April. Like what was going on in our heads. It's a big question! Don't you think? When you try to situate yourself there again, mentally, and take a hard look at your decisions? It's like trying to catch yourself by surprise in a mirror. You're always *this* close, but you can never quite pull it off."

"Huh. Yeah."

"I can blame what I did on the Drive-thru Phantom and you can blame what you did on your whole meat thing. But maybe the writer is right. Maybe those are excuses. He doesn't believe any of it. And he's talked to Amber. He's talked to *Kit.*"

"He's, uh, listening."

"I know. I know he is. I'm just trying to be honest and *talk* to you, Dion. For once. Because back when it was going on, sure, we talked. All of us talked. But we didn't *communicate.* We were all off on our own little missions. We weren't *connected.* What if that was its goal? To divide us? To make us doubt and suspect each other? Or do you think we did that on our own? We just had all that hatred waiting inside us."

"Boy. I just…"

"You're not making this easy. You never made anything easy. 'Unlock your till.' That's what you told me right after I heard Darcy. Couldn't you tell I was upset? Tears on a girl's face meant nothing to you? Do they now? That's one of the things I that I hope for. That we're better now. At least somewhat improved. But I don't *feel* better, Dion. I feel—what I feel is anger. At you."

"Oh. Uh…"

"And I shouldn't! You said three insensitive words three years ago. That's no reason I should want to beat your face in right now. So what gives? Is the ghost still inside us? All I can see right now is your face, and my fists, and lots and lots of blood. I feel sick. But wild too. Is that what it felt like for you? Your meat thing?"

"Sort of."

"And *alive*. Fuck, why does the ghost always make me feel so *alive*? Think about how Kit was. How Nutting was at the start, Manager of the Year. Do you know about TM? Transcendental meditation? There's proof, scientific proof, that enough people doing TM together can lower violence levels. They call it the Maharishi Effect. That's the kind of communication I want. We have to pull ourselves back together again."

"That sounds nice."

"We could generate the Maharishi Effect right here. Over the phone. Do you have a mantra? Of course you don't. Well, if you did, you could chant it, and I could chant mine, and maybe we could call up Kit and Amber and Nutting, and Clem and Dez if we can find them, and all of us could meditate as one. We can't change what we did. But we can change ourselves moving forward."

"Okay. So do I…?"

"Except I can't. All I can think of is your face, Dion, just blood, blood, blood. You know what? I changed my mind. There's a reason we don't talk, Dion. Why none of us talk. When we do, the little pieces of the poltergeist inside us wake up and start getting bigger. You want to talk about April 21, Mr. Kraus? Right now I feel *exactly* like I did on April 21! So I need to hang up. This was a bad idea. I'm sorry but if I don't hang up I'm going to strangle the next fucking person I—"

Dial tone.

The sun falls. The tinfoil fire dies on Dez's trailer carpet. No longer can I make out details of the cleaning-product foothills. Dez has gone silent and still in the smoky gloom, a state of being I didn't expect. The only activity is the night-scavenger twinkle of her eyes.

I ask her to take me through the events of April 22.

Silence for a half a minute. Then a chuffing sound. Several points of light, a minor constellation: yellow teeth emerging from a grin. Dez is laughing.

"All right, Angel Boy."

At some point during her fire ritual, Dez decided she likes me, and lovingly refers to me as Angel Boy for the rest of our talk.

"I'm going to show you something. I tried to show Maggot Boy back then but he wouldn't look. If he would've looked, he would've understood, and everything would've gone better. Can you see good way over there? You want to come closer, Angel Boy?"

I tell her I can see just fine. She grins, additional teeth catching the light, and with both hands takes hold of the bottom of her denim blouse. It's not teasingly, how she lifts it, but there is a certain drama. The hem strains, then pops free over a bluish-white belly that is, indeed, emaciated. My hearts pounds. Dez pulls the shirt up higher, and she's leering, daring me to tell her to stop, but I don't, and she keeps going, and suddenly the shirt is wadded against her neck.

Her breasts are covered with the same sort of scars I saw on Amber Smyrna, that I will soon see on Clemens Dumay. Pink divots the shape of incisors. Chunky purple marks where molars chomped down on wads of flesh. It's the worst around the nipples. Dozens of razor-thin scars, as if on April 22, 2017, Dez had been suckled by a pack of small, rabid dogs.

YOU'RE ALL GOING TO DIE

On October 3, 2020, I take a half-empty flight to John F. Kennedy International Airport. At this point, I have yet to find Clemens Dumay and believe I'm down to my final interview. So I double-mask and take the risk. It is a slippery moment in America's Covid-19 calamity. After a summer slump, cases have spiked to around sixty thousand per day.[97] Sadly, it's no fluke. Cases will not fall until January 2021, when the rate has reached two hundred and forty thousand per day.

As with Amber and the Geezers, disease declines to touch me.

Darren Husselbee, former *Spectral Journeys* camera operator, opens his Queens apartment door. He's double-masked too. There is a reason we're meeting in person. Two months before the cancelation of *Spectral Journeys*, Husselbee sensed which way the wind was blowing and quit. This allowed him to maintain possession of certain batches of raw footage. It was common, he says, for *Spectral Journeys* videographers to use their own gear and tapes.

Stressed from pandemic travel, I'm far less amiable than I was during my first interview seven months ago. I let loose with my opinions on Gaetan Goodricke and Roxie Stoyle: preening, narcissistic, pouty, insufferable, ungracious charlatans who gleefully preyed on people's anxieties to glorify themselves and pad their pockets.

He makes two gestures: one, at a bottle of Maker's Mark, and two, toward a closed room.

"Gonna get along fine," he says, and gets to pouring. "Gaetan and Roxie can suck a donkey's dong."

Husselbee leads me into the apartment's second bedroom, restyled as an editing suite. From the central screen glows the ubiquitous editing-software timeline. Husselbee may not have kids, but these pieces of equipment are clearly his babies. He proudly rattles off their names. 3.32GHz Intel Core i9 1700X 10 Core processor. 64GB DDR HyperX Predatory Memory. Kingwin SuperSpeed USB 3.1 Gen 1 Mini Combo Card Reader. Audio-Technica ATH-M50x headphones.

---

97 Morgan McFall-Johnsen, "6 Months Into the Coronavirus Pandemic, 9 Maps and Charts Show How It Took Over the World," *Business Insider*, July 1, 2020.

He hands me the headphones and starts mousing. Blue lights dance across his LaCie RAID Array external drive. Footage leaps to the BenQ EX3501R monitor and I gasp. I've watched every piece of available Burger City footage multiple times. Suddenly, here's more. It's junk footage shot while Husselbee left from the break room. But look! There's a glimpse of the ceiling! I've never seen the break room ceiling before! For me, it's like seeing a new angle on the grassy knoll.

Clack: Husselbee thumbs the space bar. New video plays. The perspective tells me Husselbee's camera is on the floor, facing the walk-in freezer. The image is the sort of black you get when a camera tries to see in the dark, which is to say, not black at all, but a boil of blues, browns, and grays. The visuals, however, are not important.

"Headphones on."

I shut my eyes and squeeze the ear pads. The audio is enveloping. I am at the center of a rumbling cymbal the size of Saturn's rings, a lion's roar slowed down to last forever. Wave after wave of slow-motion tones sludge by. I feel the pulses in my dental fillings.

Clack: the footage pauses.

"Yamaha SKRM-100 Subkick. Usually used to record bass drums. Bottoms out a 100Hz. Lowest mic in my kit. Now check *this* out."

Clack: Back into the grumbling vortex, my skull, jaw, and finger bones vibrating. The sounds are a blanket—and that blanket begins to twist. Threads of echo twine into a fine rope, string after shrieking string. It's not feedback. It's not a moan. It's words, scrabbling along my ear canal on metal-wire legs.

five more five more five more gone

Husselbee shouts over it. "You hear that?"

I'm five I'm five I'm five minutes gone

I shout back something affirmative.

gone and I'm gone and five five gone gone gone

Clack: I rip off the headphones, the cord catches, and they drop to the PVC chair pad. Husselbee doesn't hold it against me. He raises his eyebrows.

"Right? Is that the weirdest thing or what?"

I take my time gathering the headphones, cooling myself in the editing suite's dark. I ask Husselbee why he never shared this with anyone.

"I didn't find it until I went back to it, after the Starz doc. I have two theories, if you want to hear them. Theory one is audio bleed. Some completely unrelated audio track seeping in. That's more common with analog sources, but stranger things have happened. Theory two involves the fact that the Subkick wasn't faced outward. It was faced straight down at the floor. That raises the obvious question. What was *below* the floor?"

There might be no one alive in late 2020 with a firmer grasp of Burger City #8's blueprints than me. Tucked between the break room's west wall and the walk-ins was the cellar door. The Geezers told me what they'd overheard Dez Mozley mutter after the *Spectral Journeys* shoot. Now the words spook me, a puzzle piece clicking into place.

There's something down there…and that thing's got teeth.

At 10:15 a.m. on April 22, Dez Mozley hulked into Burger City in response to Dion Skerry's call. She planted her gorilla frame in the cramped junction of walk-ins, break room, manager's office, and janitor closet. Dion lurched from the break room. He'd felt sick all morning. WKES's Soft Rock Hitz were cranking out all gnarled, making it sound like Hall and Oates were being tortured. It was loud like Nutting liked it, but Dez's voice was even louder.

"Yeah, it stinks! What am I supposed to do about it? I can't get into Boss Man Bob's office!"

Dion scooped sweat from his skin, squeezed it from his eyebrows. It wasn't fair. That Dez could stomach this stench while he was so susceptible to it. That he had to wheedle with this medusa. The stench changed, like a carnivore had opened its mouth mid-chew. Dion coughed, tenting a hand over his nose and mouth. Did he smell raw meat?

"Don't think it's coming from the office," he managed.

"I got bleach. You want me to squirt bleach under the door? Is that what you want?" She pulled out her keys and rammed one into the closet's keyhole.

"*Below* the office," Dion gagged. "I think a dead animal died in the cellar."

The supply closet swung open but now Dez stared, white eyes against a red face.

"Oh, no. No, no, no. I told you. I'm not going down there again."

Not raw meat. *Spoiled* meat. Dion took a step away. His back hit the walk-in freezer. Ice seared through his clothes, frosted his skin, froze his bones.

"You have to," he said.

"Dez Mozley doesn't have to do baloney! None of you know what's down there!"

"A dead animal." The nausea, the gorge sloshing in his gut.

"I *hope* it's dead! For your sake, I hope!"

Couldn't a single thing go simply? Nutting had been a shadow for weeks. All ordering, all scheduling, all disputes fell to Dion alone. Lawyers at BC Corporate had begun calling about Maxine Pinto. Did the old lady *die and fall,* or *fall and die?* The distinction made all the difference.[98]

Dion didn't fucking know! He only remembered Nutting's 911 call. *Dead lady,* Nutting had said. From the smell of it, there was a whole pile of dead ladies downstairs. His sweat was hot movie-theater butter. His stomach gurgled gelatinous contents. But he was in charge. He gasped between dry heaves.

"You won't. Clean the freezer. You won't. Go in the cellar. Why are you. Even working here?"

Dez's facial muscles helixed with fury.

"You can't fire me, Maggot Boy! Only Boss Man Bob can! And he won't! You know he won't! Who else but Dez Mozley is going to clean this evil pit?"

Magically, Dion saw inside his own body cavity. It was packed not with organs but ground meat, squirming up his neck to be forced from his mouth like sausage. He cried out while clamping a hand over his mouth.

"I can! You're fired! You're fired!"

Dez's face was a slack patty of meat, her arms tubes of meat, her breasts sacks of meat. She reached into the closet—the bowels of a building built of bricks of meat—and withdrew from her cart an object that cut through all delusions, because it was, in fact, sharp: a box cutter, two inches of silver blade gleaming in front of Dion's face.

Mickey McCormick was born in Kabetogama, Minnesota, near Voyageurs National Park on the Canadian border. His post-high school life resembled that of Ash Muckells and Scotty Flossen, except that Mickey majored in pot with a minor in cocaine. Through it all he played guitar and nurtured what photographs assure us was a series of lamentable pompadours.

At age 29, he drove to Ames, Iowa, to crash on the sofa of his older brother, Waylon. Their plan, hatched during high times, was to resurrect their band, Flat Armadillo, in Davenport, Iowa, which Waylon swore was the country's next rockabilly hotspot. It wasn't. Waylon, though, made a decent wage working construction and brought Mickey into the fold until he'd saved enough for his own place.

---

98 In a rare piece of good fortune for Burger City, a judge deemed in November 2018 that Burger City Inc. was not liable for Maxine Pinto's death.

Shortly after Mickey moved to Moscow, Iowa, he and Waylon purchased a thousand-square-foot cabin three miles south, where the Little Mosquito Creek threads off the Cedar River. Accessible only via a ten-minute walk, the cabin was isolated inside velvet woods, the only sounds being the river and the animals it drew. The brothers played music out there till their amps broke and strings snapped, none of which they bothered to replace. From there, they focused on drinking. The benders they shared there were mythic. To them, anyway.

While working a highway job in 2006, Waylon was sideswiped by an SUV, tossed forty feet, and killed. Mickey lost his taste for the work, saw the *Now Accepting Applications* sign at Burger City, and within the week began his eleven-year run as the joint's resident asshole.

Until 2014, he'd regularly hung out with Burger City's revolving bill of teen employees. He'd never, to anyone's knowledge, done anything illicit, but his behavior felt wrongish, sitting too close to girls, convincing boys to imbibe more liquor than advisable. It was Cheri Orritt who ultimately had a sit-down with Mickey. We don't know what was said, but no one administered tough love any better.

Few survivors ascribe malice to Mickey. He was just fixated on remaining the hard-rocking, lady-bedding bad boy that, to be honest, he'd never been. By 2017, his hair had gone gray, and the ink-black severity of his dye job was the equivalent of a comb-over. Kit reports once barging into the men's room to find Mickey flexing long-gone muscles in the mirror and softly crying.

Even Amy Mold confesses that Mickey and Yesenia's post-coital chats were gentle and affectionate, but here Amy overcorrects for her past mistakes. Mickey McCormick knew the illegal and immoral things he was doing with Yesenia Ruiz. If there's a sad element to his life, it's that he did not consider it worth protecting.

Fast-food chains do their best to idiot-proof their kitchens with automation, but they are still chockablock with danger. Knives get dull, which makes them slip. Gas ovens get left on overnight. Old Teflon pans emit toxic smoke. Unwashed cutting boards, of course, are the real killers, petri dishes for harmful microbes.

Hot grease requires fewer warnings because the danger is so blatant. Beneath every french fry basket roils a 325-degree-Fahrenheit vat of pale, liquid fire. Fast-food joints report twelve thousand burns annually.[99] In 1991,

---

99 "10 Restaurant Safety Tips to Prevent Oil Injuries," *Restaurant Technologies,* June 2, 2017.

a 20-year-old worker was cleaning an overhead exhaust filter when she fell
and dunked her arm in the deep fryer. Her second- and third-degree burns
required four days of hospitalization and eventual plastic surgery.[100] Incidents
involving skin removal, skin grafting, and permanent scarring are common.

You can't fill a metal scoop with white-hot grease without getting it
all over your hand. Yet Amy Mold wouldn't notice her burns for several
minutes. Every cell in her body was fixated on Mickey McCormick. When
she chucked the grease, he was five feet away at the prep station, facing
her dead-on, clad in apron, hair net, beard net, and the infant expression
of the truly startled.

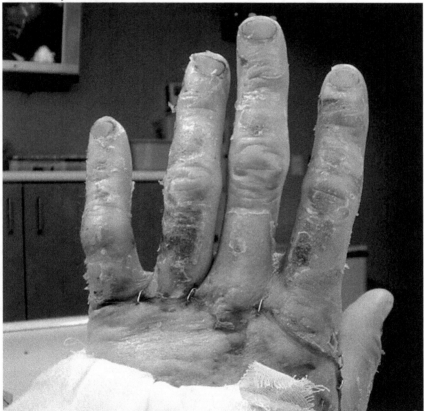

Amy Mold's blisters (photo by Amy Mold).

The matter of Amy's aim remains ambiguous. She recalls it dimly, like
a half-forgotten scene from a scary movie. If her aim was for Mickey's face,
it made sense that she missed. She couldn't throw for shit. She was one of

---

100 "Occupational Burns Among Restaurant Workers—Colorado and Minnesota,"
CDC.gov, September 24, 1993.

those kids who considered gym class a caveman farce, and had lobbied for its eradication. It might be what spared Mickey's face.

Given the nature of Mickey's crimes, it's just as possible that Amy hit her target dead-on: his groin. No one else witnessed the throw (Cheri was present but facing the grill) but it's easy to picture. Amy's weird speed and skidding halt. Her left arm's outward jerk. The scintillation of grease as it wobbled through the air, an amorphous blob.

Mickey actually laughed, probably believing it was water, just another kitchen prank. Cheri turned at the noise and it's her later detailing of the scene that sources our account. Mickey looked down and saw a splattery line of droplets on the tile, writhing and crackling. This wasn't water. This wasn't even coffee. Mickey's neck crooked further. The brown stain on his apron looked alive, hissing and steaming. A hole widened like a mouth. Hot grease was burning right through it.

Now Mickey screamed. He yanked the apron's neck loop over his head as he backpedaled from his assailant. He struck the bun rack, creating a hailstorm of sesame seeds. By now, Cheri was moving. *Everyone* was moving, and if it took an extra beat for them to arrive, it was due to fatigue: another day at Burger City, another scream.

Cheri didn't go for the sink. Water on grease would envelop Mickey in an inferno. She dropped to her old knees and threw open a drawer of pots and pans. Mickey shouted a stream of obscenities as he tried, and failed, to unknot the apron strings at the small of his back. The apron's lap had disintegrated. Beneath, the crotch of his faded jeans had grown a pelt of orange flame.

It was the one time in Mickey's life that he welcomed a steel pot slamming over his genitals. It was Cheri, teeth bared to the heat, flames reflected in her glasses, trying to smother the burn. The pot bit at Mickey's fingers as he tried to undo his jeans buttons. He wore them tight, naturally, and several seconds of total panic passed as he couldn't manage it. At last, down went the pants: it was Tamra, depantsing Mickey with both hands. Mickey kicked off his shoes, then jeans. Tighty-whities and a half-apron, that's it—and the briefs were yellow. Urine from fright? Or an active burn? Mickey didn't fuck around. He tore off the briefs and finally undid the apron strings, and stood in the kitchen naked from the waist down, checking his penis and scrotum for damage. (Side note: he was instantly exonerated from taking the Haunted Dick Pic.)

He turned disbelieving eyes at his crumpled jeans, still aflame.

Mickey's head snapped upward at Amy Mold.

"The fuck, bitch?!"

Amy hadn't moved since tossing the grease.

"I know what you did." Her voice cracked like ash.

"*I* did? You almost burned my fucking dick off!"

"Darcy." Amy sounded hollow, crumbling. "She told me..."

"You're crazy! This psycho bitch is crazy!"

"Yesenia," Amy managed, and then her legs gave out, and she folded to the floor.

Cheri rushed over, saw the flesh of Amy's left hand melting like cheese, and ran to call 911. Tamra darted to the break-room and returned with her black leather jacket to cover Mickey. He didn't accept it. Everyone tensed for a counter-attack on the fallen Amy. Instead, Mickey's face fell—and fell, and fell, eroding like his jeans under the greasy flame. He dropped his face into his hands and staggered; Tamra held him aloft and whispered prayers. For a while, those prayers (and distorted Soft Rock Hitz) were all anyone heard.

No customers called 911. That they fled was their final verdict: there was no more helping Burger City #8 and the souls caught in its trap.

Dez Mozley shook the box cutter in Dion Skerry's face. A single thrust and the blade would be buried in his jugular. He could picture it, feel it, hear it, taste it, the thin metal blade in his palate, cold against his jawbone. He visualized a thin funnel of oily meat extruding from the gash.

Stabbing Dion was not what Dez had in mind. She raised her empty left hand as if testifying in court, and without looking, jammed the blade directly into the center of her palm.

Box cutters are designed so that you can snap off a dull blade to free the shaper blade beneath. That's what Dez did, hinging the cutter's handle ruthlessly, stretching the cut wider, until the cutter broke free and clattered to the floor, leaving the blade embedded in her palm. Blood spurted, soft as milk, sliding down Dez's forearm and onto the floor.

"Why'd you do that?" Dion gasped.

Dez's eyes bored into Dion's as thick drops of blood cracked down like marbles. Her lips, the same magenta as her skin, parted to reveal a graveyard of teeth and the sea monster of a pale tongue. It was a smile.

"You're all going to die," she croaked. "Unless you let me save you."

Quiet, steady, assured: it didn't sound like Dez at all.

The severed nerves struck pain receptors. Dez screeched and whirled, her left arm arcing through space, blood chasing like a ribbon. Hot liquid struck Dion's face as Dez, directly above, ran her palm over the freezer door with the frenzy of an inspired painter. The blade was still caught in her flesh. Dion wiped blood from his face, gagged, and rolled away.

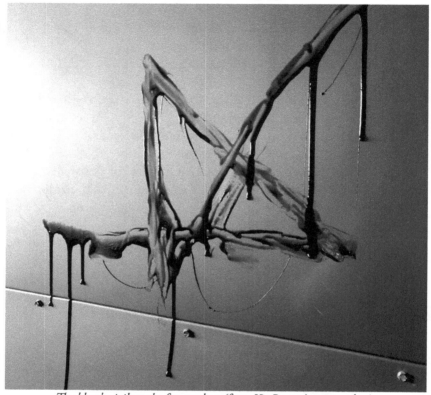

The bloody sigil on the freezer door (from Kit Bryant's secret videos).

"Dez Mozley's going to save *all* your ungrateful asses," she panted.

The only image powerful enough to break through Dion's Meat Grief was Section 24 of the Burger City Team Member Handbook, regarding the handling of biohazardous waste: urine, feces, mucus, sewage, and blood. He was doused with it, and it had come from Dez, disease personified. He crawled away from her, toward the cellar door, only for his hands to slip in the blood and send him sprawling.

Dion felt the fallen box cutter beneath him, fished it out, thumbed up a new blade, and rolled over, ready for defense. But Dez was finished. She stood there, her hunched back rising and falling, blood pouring from her hand. Cheri Orritt rounded the corner, followed by Javi. Less than a day had passed since Mickey had torn off burning clothes and Amy had torched her hand. As strong as Cheri was, she withered at the sight of another calamity.

Dez didn't give Cheri or Javi the chance to do a thing. She bolted down the hall to the back exit, hitting the push-handle at full speed. She disappeared into blinding sunlight. When the door crashed shut, there was blood smeared on it too, though it showed none of her previous work's design.

Mere blood wasn't going to stop Javi from helping Dion. Vomit was another story. Javi slid to a halt as Dion unleashed his cargo of nausea. Puke unrolled like carpet over his chest and lap, dripping down his legs and swirling into Dez's blood. Javi drew back; Cheri held him steady; together they looked at what Dez had drawn in blood on the freezer door.

Four months later, the legal team prosecuting Kit Bryant interviewed Dez Mozley. She did it with enthusiasm. She had a lot to say and wanted it to be heard. The transcripts are public record. In them, Dez comes off so batshit crazy that both prosecution and defense teams abandoned the idea of using her. Dez's transcript ends like this:

> You're just like everyone else. Your suit and tie don't mean diddly. I'm trying to tell you I didn't draw that sign to warn the staff. They wouldn't listen to old Dez Mozley if I sewed my lips to their ears! I drew that sign to warn *the thing*, whatever the warlocks raised up and was hiding in our cellar. Warn it I had my evil eye on its ass. You don't give one diddly shit. Take off those suits and ties and you know what's under there? Maggots.

Dez was sadly right: no one at Burger City cared why she'd done it. Through his locked office door, Nutting told Cheri to find Dez to clean up the blood. Cheri had to tell him a second time that it'd been Dez who'd spilled it. The next person Nutting suggested was Zane, who, of course, had quit forty-three days earlier.

Finally Nutting said "Kit," which at least made sense, as Kit had done janitorial tasks before. Having already missed the Amy-Mickey fiasco, Kit would probably *want* to see this mess. Sure enough, Kit sped over and tromped into the crime scene with *IDEAS* jutting from his pocket. He wrestled Dez's mop bucket from the closet, and shooed everyone back to work.

He did not, however, start cleaning right away. Instead, he took out his phone. For the first minute, he doubted himself. He didn't have Quin's equipment. He didn't have Quin's shooting skill. But with every pan across the blood-spattered hall, his confidence built. He found that he relished recording the evidence by himself. No bullshit, no laughing, no squabbles. He should have been working like this all along.

Kit's footage of the Dion-Dez aftermath became the first of his private videos, which no one would know about until I acquired them. While the overheads flickered, Kit's camera lingered on the pattern Dez had slopped across the freezer door. It felt a bit like one of Tamra's Christian symbols, except this time, it was Dez who'd developed stigmata.

Three years later, I'd see the same sigil on Dez's trailer door.

GAME OVER

April 28, 2017

Kit: —sound like "decline pattern" to you? People are going totally mental in—

Clem: Whoa, whoa, whoa!

Amber: Kit! Sit down! Kit!

Kit: Oh, great, roll tape, right? You wouldn't want to miss a word!

Amber: Quin, really?

Quin: Yes, really, if this fucking psycho boyfriend of yours is going to come at me! I'm recording every fucking word so I can sue your ass if you even touch me!

Kit: I don't see how you could possibly come to that conclusion! Look at the evidence. Zane attacks me—

Quin: Oh, *he* attacked *you?* That's not how any of us heard it.

Kit: —then—excuse me—then Dez wipes her blood over everything, and let's not forget Amy here flinging hot fucking grease at Mickey!

Amy: I *told* you. That's not what I—look at these bandages, I—

Quin: Will you listen? To a single word you're saying, Kit? It's shit. Total shit. Decline patterns, man! Nothing's happened since the old lady died. Except a bunch of stressed-out wage-slaves yelling at one another in the cornfields.

Amber: Like you two are right now!

Quin: Don't tell that to *me!* Tell it to Romeo! He's—hey—do not—

Clem: Kit, dude, I don't want to, but I outweigh you by about five hundred—

Kit: I can't even fucking—do you not feel it, Quin? The energy?

Quin: No! I don't!

Kit: You really think Dez and Dion and Zane and Amy all woke up on the wrong side of the bed and that's it?

Quin: Yes! I do!

Amy: Listen to me. I know what I did. But that wasn't me.

Amber: It's the new you.

Amy: What do you mean?

Amber: What do you mean, what do I mean? Look at that bible.

Amy: What's wrong with my…?

Amber: You don't think it's related? One day out of the wild blue yonder you become a Jesus freak and *that's* when you start trying to boil people's dicks off?

Amy: There's no—one thing doesn't have anything to do—

Amber: That's one thing I'll *never* get over. Those people visiting Mom in the hospital, they weren't visiting for her. They just came to say, "Oh, God has a plan" and "Darcy's going to be with Jesus." You know why?

Amy: But God *does* have a plan—

Amber: They said it to make *themselves* feel better. So when they look down at what's left of my mom, they don't have to actually feel *anything*, they can just revert to their Sunday School fairy tales and feel all smug that they're part of some whoop-de-do grand design.

Kit: Amber.

Amber: There is no grand design, Amy. We're rats in a maze. And there's no fucking cheese! Ha! I guess we'll have to eat each other.

Amy: If you don't want me here, why don't you just say it?

Quin: This is what I'm talking about.

Amber: I don't own this truck stop.

Quin: We *are* going to eat each other. Listen to us. *Listen* to us. There's nothing supernatural here, nothing paranormal, nothing psychokinetic!

Amy: Screw this. 2:30 in the morning? What was I thinking?

Quin: "We should expect our data to follow a curve such as the exponential delay function."[101] Remember that?

Kit: William Gee Willikers Roll, ladies and germs! He's helped so much in the past!

Quin: We're there. The end. That's all I'm trying to say. While everyone was fucking fighting, the RSPK went and dried up.

Kit: I'll tell you when it's dried up.

Quin: You're in charge now. I see.

Kit: Now? The RSPK has been coming from me all along!

Quin: You are obsessed with that! It doesn't matter, Kit. Can you get that through your head? *It does not fucking matter.* If it's you, if it's me, if it's some mouse that lives in the dumpster. When was the last time the Living Grill deviated from the same old shit?

Kit: Maybe you don't appreciate that the Living Grill's *same old shit* is still the most miraculous thing any of us have ever seen!

---

101 Roll, *The Poltergeist*, 163

Amy: *[Inaudible.]*

Kit: What?

Amy: If the grill isn't just crooked, I said.

Kit: Slippery goddamn slope, Amy.

Amy: Oh, come on! When did this become the Third Reich? Can't someone have a dissenting opinion here?

Clem: What's the slope? Why's it slippery?

Amy: Because what Kit's worried about is, if we admit the Living Grill was just crooked, then maybe we're not so sure about the Men's Room Bully either.

Kit: Cut it out.

Amy: And then maybe we're not so sure of the Coldest Cold Spot.

Kit: What kind of counterargument can you even—

Amy: And then maybe we're not so sure of Lil' Beefy.

Kit: That's just crazy! There's a thousand, million videos!

Amy: Of what? Of what, really?

Kit: You're just trying to stir up trouble.

Amy: Then call the Gestapo on me, Herr Hitler!

Quin: You think I want to agree with Amy? But she's right. That's all that's left at Burger City. Uneven grills. Malfunctioning towel dispensers. Maybe that's all there ever was. Fuck. My GPA. *[Emotionally.]* My whole fucking future.

Clem: Guys. It's Yesenia.

Quin: It's over. We're over.

Clem: She's really booking it. *[Louder.]* Yeni, hey.

Amy: *[Alarmed.]* Who invited her?

Quin: I just texted our usual group—

Clem: Oh, shit!

Amy: No, no, no, no!

[Audio peaks as everyone yells unintelligibly. Furniture upends. Sounds of assault.]

Yesenia: How dare you! How dare you!

Amy: Stop! Please!

Clem: Yeni!

Yesenia: I'll kill you! I'll kill you!

Amy: Help me! Help me!

Quin: Help her! Somebody help her!

Clem: I got you. Yeni, I got you—

Yesenia: Voy a matarla, ese puta de mierda!

Amber: You're bleeding—

Amy: Don't touch me, Amber! Don't you fucking touch me!

Yesenia: You could have killed him! Hijueputa!

Clem: Who?

Yesenia: Mickey! My Mickey!

Amy: I'm sorry, all right?

Yesenia: No! I want your hijueputa throat!

Amber: The bitch deserves it.

Clem: Jesus, Amber. What is your problem?

Quin: We all fucking deserve it.

Clem: Q? Man, what is *all* your problems?

Woman: You kids better clear out. Security has been called.

Amber: Napkins, please—napkins for the blood—

Amy: Yeni. I did it to protect you. To protect all women. Darcy—she told me—over the headset—

Amber: Wait, what?

Amy: Amber…she talked to me. Over the headset. She told me—

[Fleshy thump, a yelp of pain.]

Amber: You think Mom would come back and talk to *you*? *To you?*

Kit: Amber! Amber!

Amy: I don't know! But she did!

Amber: Get off me, Kit!

Kit: You have to stop—

Yesenia: "All women?" Then why didn't you ask me, a *woman*, if I wanted your hijueputa "protection?"

Man: Hey! Leave that girl alone!

Clem: Out! Everybody out!

[Sounds of running.]

Man: You okay, miss? You okay?

Amber: She deserved it, officer.

Kit: Amber, will you come on?

Man: You think this is a game, young lady?

Quin: *[Distantly, laughing wildly.]* Yes, sir! The Game of Pricks, sir! But don't worry, it's over! Game over! Game over!

MAY 2017

I DON'T THINK IT'S HUMAN

By 10:00 p.m., Bob Nutting is leaning on the balcony railing, dangling a seventh Miller Lite over his building's four-story drop. The vista below boasts garbage bins, dumpsters, and rusty bicycles padlocked to a chain-link fence. I'm still seated, my feet buried by the sand-bag bodies of Low Energy Jeb and Little Marco.

"Why I did this. Why I did that. And where. Always where. All of them, just like you, with clipboards and laptops. What precise minute and second blah blah blah? Even in normal times, I wouldn't be able to answer good enough for you. And those were very un-normal times."

The badgering questions Nutting refers to are variations on *Where the hell were you during all this?* His presence during Burger City's final two months has been well corroborated. He was there when Amy Mold flung boiling oil and Mickey McCormick stripped naked. He was there when Dez stabbed herself and coated the BOH with her blood. He just wouldn't leave his office.

The single most astounding thing that happened in April 2020 was that everyone returned to work—save Mickey, who quit, probably anticipating a lawsuit. Even Dez returned. Though she'd violated roughly two-hundred company policies at once, she'd been right about Nutting's non-reaction: *Who else is going to clean this evil pit?*

The tension of May 2017 was stifling. Often Amber, Yesenia, and Amy (hobbled by a big ball of bandages around her left hand) worked the same shifts, shouldering past one another in frigid silence. Quin was a faded facsimile of his former self, quiet and sad, studying for finals every free second he had. Clem escalated his antics to smooth the place's edges, but his shenanigans felt misplaced, even vulgar. Dion avoided closing to prevent run-ins with Dez, and conferred with Nutting solely through email and text.

"The Chillee Shake Machine," Nutting slurs. "If that thing hadn't busted, those frosty fuckers might have pulled us through. But it was the camel on the haystack. The straw on the back. You know what I'm saying. It's never the big stuff that kills you. It's the little things, all added up until you just can't take it."

He sniffles and wipes his bleary face, and just as I'd feared, the Miller Lite slips free and shatters below. He tilts his head as if reading the pattern of busted glass like tea leaves. It appears to make sense. He turns toward me and his wobble isn't too bad.

"Electrics."

Pardon me?

He waves an impatient hand. "The flickering lights. The POS system going weird. The radio. All those wires, you know, were right under my office floor. Who was going to fix it? Mickey and Zane were gone. Dez hadn't even gotten to the Chillee Machine yet." Nutting jams a thumb against his sternum. "Me, that's who. I was going to fix it. Fix all of it. *All of it.*"

Nutting was rarely spotted in April, but he still slept at home. That changed in May. He no longer left the premises. He was there when closers left. He was there when openers arrived. He was known only by the cracking, chipping, clinking noises from the office, as well as the stench that staffers fought back with an arsenal of air fresheners. How was Nutting eating and drinking? There was evidence he raided the kitchen at night. How was he holding bathroom needs all day? That one, no one could figure out.

Amber and Kit had gone through many a spat, but the Iowa 80 Truckstop blowup shook her up. Prior to the divorce, Amber had watched her parents attempt to "reconnect" on romantic getaways. In May 2017, Kit was 20 and Amber 19, both living on Burger City wages. There were limited places for broke young lovers to go.

Kit knew all about the secluded cabin Mickey had once shared with his brother. In fact, Kit had partied there before. With rumors flying about Mickey and Yesenia, it stood to reason that some of their affair had transpired at the cabin. Teens, though, are generally unbothered by locational ickiness. Amber begged for Kit to take her somewhere and so he did.

On May 13, Amber told Paul Smyrna she was sleeping over with friends. Kit didn't tell Caspar Bryant anything; he just took off. They drove south along the Cedar River, pulled off near Little Mosquito Creek, and, with a night's worth of provisions, hiked to the cabin. Despite everything, they were still hormonal teens who got excited in the absence of adults. They had sex outside. Later, they had sex inside, after which they ate, loafed around for a while, and eventually prepared the pull-out sofa bed.

Mickey McCormick's cabin (photo by the author).

There was a single change of plain white sheets in the cabin and Amber used them. They turned off the lights. Amber drew the topsheet over her naked shoulder and snuggled until she felt the pulse of Kit's neck in the space between her eyes. The forest did its lulling. The walls above the sofa were tacked with cheesecake posters from Mickey's adolescence. Kelly LeBrock in a half-shirt and panties. Elle Macpherson in a star-spangled bikini. Shannon Tweed posing in lingerie.

Amber was glad for the company. Kelly, Elle, Shannon: forever impervious.

"Don't go back," she said softly. She meant Burger City, of course, but she also meant Kit's basement room, where she knew he hatched his riskiest schemes.

"Where else would I go?" he whispered back.

"My dad's place."

"He's not like Darcy. He never liked me."

"He doesn't know you. I can talk to him. Talk to Erica."

Kit's resignation broke Amber's heart.

"I have to go back. It's not done."

"It is."

"It's not."

"It's done if we say it's done," Amber insisted. "I don't like who we've become."

Kit stared into the ceiling dim. The room smelled of smoke and tar.

"We haven't hurt anyone," he said.

"You could have hurt Quin. I could have hurt Amy. We're all so close to hurting someone."

Kit appeared to change the topic. "When you had Mr. O'Ryan, did he talk about the Salem Witch Trials?"

"Yeah, I think."

Kit matched his voice to the sylvan stillness, softer than Amber had ever heard it. It was impossible, she thought, that a voice so gentle could ever lie.

"There's this theory he told us. That all the witches' visions, their convulsions and all that, was caused by rye bread. There was this fungus that grew on rye. It was like LSD. Made you see things that weren't there." He shivered, but it might have been the night, their cooling sweat. "What if that's all this is? Somewhere in the Burger City supply chain, fungus got into our food. None of this is happening. We're not even here."

"Baby, we're here."

"I guess. For now. Soon it'll be just me."

"What do you mean?"

"It's May."

RCHS graduation was in twenty-one days. Shortly after Quindlen Arthur, Clemens Dumay, and Amy Mold crossed the stage for their diplomas, Amber Smyrna would do the same. No matter how broken their collective had become, it was still sad to see it end.

"I told you, I'll make it work. *We'll* make it work. Baby, I'm *yours*." Risking life and livelihood for another person was what heroes did, Amber thought.

"You're a good person," Kit said. "If getting away from Jonny would help…"

"You're a good person too."

"I don't know. Most of the PK agents Quin used to talk about…they really weren't. Most were fakers. Most just wanted attention. And every time, people along the way got hurt."

"You believe it's real. That makes it different."

"It *is* real. But lions are real too. And I'm not sticking my head in their mouths."

"That's why I wanted to come here. A clean break. Let's stop. Baby, we can just *stop*."

"How? If it's coming from inside me, won't it follow?"

For some time, Amber had wanted to address this. But it had been a topic so difficult to breach. The gut-punch of *Spectral Journeys*, Darcy's death, the daily tumult—there was never a good time. Now, with Kit's rare hush and her supermodel support team, she dropped herself into those cold waters.

"I don't think it's you."

Amber braced for the stubble scrape of Kit's head turning in surprise. It didn't come. Instead, Kit held his breath for what felt like a year.

"Clem?" he whispered. "You think it's Clem?"

"No, baby."

"Yesenia? Sometimes I wonder about Yesenia."

"None of you. William G. Roll—I don't believe in him."

The hesitation was heavier than bedsheets. Roll had been part of Kit's calculations for so long, it took effort to recall it was only because of Quin. Amber listened to Kit breathing. Maybe ideas settled into his brain more gently when he had a soft girl nestled close.

"If it's real," Amber said. "It's a ghost."

"Is this because…Darcy?"

Amber sighed.

"I know how it sounds. Like I'm hoping my mom is still out there, watching over me."

"Sure. It's a nice thought."

"Except it's *not* nice. Imagine seeing someone you miss, but not being able to reach them. That's not someone looking out for you. That's a haunting."

Kit grappled with the idea. "So you think this ghost…isn't…benevolent?"

Amber shook her head. Strands of her blonde hair stuck to Kit's lip.

"It's mad. It's really mad."

"Do you…have a theory? Who is it?"

"I do," Amber said nervously. "I don't think it's human."

She felt Kit grin—and felt the same flash of anger that had incited her attack on Amy Mold at Iowa 80. She spoke sharply, cutting off whatever dismissive snark Kit might say.

"I didn't say it was a *monster*. I said it's not *human*." Spelling it out only got harder. Kelly, Elle, and Shannon gave her bedroom eyes of courage. Amber filled her lungs with night breeze and plowed ahead. "It's animals."

Various individuals get portrayed as the key thinker in the Burger City Poltergeist. Kit Bryant and his raw instinct. Quin Arthur and his scholarly scrutiny. Even Dez Mozley and her necromancing insight.[102] Forgotten amid these candidates is "the pretty one,"[103] "Kit's girlfriend,"[104]

---

102   As you might imagine, this is a hard position to take, which seems to make it irresistable to certain contrarian sorts.

103   Margo Loft, "Burger City Strife an Argument for Freezing Minimum Wage," *Chicago Sun-Times*, February 20, 2018.

104   Darryl Nartey, "Midwestern Fast-Food Under Fire," *Omaha Daily Bee*, July 3, 2017.

the "relatively insignificant"[105] Amber Smyrna. Yet it was Amber who formulated the most creative explanation for the unexplainable events.

Amber described when the idea first walloped her. It was early March. She stood at Till 1 at 4:24 p.m., watching watchers watch Lil' Beefy. Many held cameras with their dominant hand, leaving their clumsier hand to cram food. They gnashed wads of fries. Smashed burger patties into upper lips, the bottoms of noses. Amber saw rolling boluses of beef, bacon bits stuck to teeth, pink tongues working through strands of cheese.

S4 E04 of *Spectral Journeys,* which she'd finally watched, had begun with Roxie Stoyle listing the reasons that "Iowa is actually one of the Midwest's paranormal hotspots." She'd done that because Burger City #8 itself was devoid of lore. Exit 269 hadn't been built on an Indian burial ground. The plot hadn't been the site of a mental hospital. In short, prior to Ash Muckells, no people had ever died there.

But there *had* been deaths. Uncountable deaths.

"Cage-free" and "humane meat" are empty, undefined phrases used to pat the heads of queasy carnivores. Each day, 25 million chickens, 4 million pigs, and 800,000 cows are slaughtered.[106] The "lives" that precede these slaughters don't earn the term. Chickens that never feel sunlight are genetically designed to mature in forty days,[107] so rapidly their legs buckle beneath the weight. Sows spend years in pens too tight to turn around in, birthing piglet after piglet, vending machines of new meat. Cows are valuable as beef, but not enough care about their pain; one veterinary assistant reports a cow's infected eye being pried out over a period of hours without anesthesia.[108]

Livestock weren't slain at Burger City #8, but they were slain *for* Burger City, and the franchise's obsession with meat made it the fast-food exemplar of livestock's demotion from thinking, feeling creatures into edible insults called BeefBoat and Grampa Beefy. Believing Burger City's ghosts had to be human was typical human arrogance.

Once this idea gets its hooks in you, it's hard to shake. Rising far above I-80 are towering pole signs for fast-food joints, gas stations, and assorted combos. It takes only the mental subtraction of, say, McDonald's golden arches to see these signs as giant crosses populating thousands of

105 Shannon Lockie, "Getting Grilled," *Ottumwa Courier,* November 20, 2017.

106 Matt Zampa, "How Many Animals Are Killed for Food Every Day?", *Sentient Media,* March 1, 2020.

107 Matt Zampa, "The World's Largest Fast Food Companies Are Failing Chickens," *Sentient Media,* 2018.

108 Benjamin Aldes Wurgaft, *Meat Planet: Artificial Flesh and the Future of Food* (University of California, 2019), 69.

View from Interstate 80 in Iowa (photo by the author).

miles of cemetery, the only gravestones factory-farm animals are allowed.

Today, Amber credits vegetarianism for shielding her from the visions that affected Amy Mold,[109] Dion Skerry, Bob Nutting, Kit Bryant, and presumedly others who didn't survive to confess them. This leaves an awful question fit for an awful world. Was the blood of Ash Muckells, Maxine Pinto, and all those about to die in the Burger City Tragedy a fair exchange? Both animals and children are frighteningly easy to exploit. If we call the young employees of Burger City "children" (and legally, most were), the parallels leap out: they were fed crap, shoved into tight spaces, and ordered to produce.

And the rich got richer on their suffering.

I don't believe Amber's theory, but she's right that we should be haunted by what we've done to children and animals, and damned by the guilt of binding the two via mega-farm fast food.[110] If you look past the vest-wearing puppies and red-haired clowns, you might find one of the worst things we have ever done to the world, and therefore, to ourselves.

On December 13, 2020, I visit Aldo Hucklebridge's grave at Highland City Cemetery just northwest of Aldo's hometown of Highland, Illinois.

---

109   Amy Mold might have gone vegetarian earlier if she, the zealous new Christian, had happened across Psalms 40:6: "I hate, I despise your feasts....Even though you offer me burnt offerings and cereal offerings, I will not accept them."

110   The notion here is that centuries of animal cruelty has created a sort of bottleneck of souls regurgitating into our reality. If this were true, we might turn to books like Wurgaft's *Meat Planet*, where he envisions a future of stem-cell-originated "cultured meat"—free of cruelty, innocent of environmental harm, vegeterian by default.

He was a meat-and-potatoes guy; there's nothing fancy about his headstone, no cow statuettes, no engraved Beefyburger. It is a polished, bevel-edged, three-foot-tall hunk of granite. *Let My Beloved Come Into His Garden And Eat His Pleasant Fruits* is etched at the base in Zapf Chancery font. Above are two rectangles, one left blank for Edwina Hucklebridge, the other filled with the following data:

Aldo J. Hucklebridge
February 1, 1944
September 29, 2009

The stone itself is classic gray. But from rows away, it looks to match the light-pink hue of other stones. This is because it has been defaced. Many times, from the look of it, each new round of red spray-paint scrubbed off by some diligent caretaker. The vandal might be a persistent local activist. It might be someone connected to the Burger City Tragedy. The day I visit, the spray paint is bleeding fresh, as if the defacer knew I was coming. They left behind a single word.

MURDERER

The vandalism reminds me of the Burger City arson. It reminds me of the bullets Hanford Pendergast sprayed into the *FOOD EXIT 269* sign. Of Caspar Bryant's torched home. Of Clem Dumay, who incinerated his whole life so he could escape under cover of smoke. The poltergeist destroyed so many lives, and keeps on destroying them, that Clem's first question to me—*Is it back?*—wasn't really necessary.

It never left.

If Amber envied anything about carnivory, it was the ritual of it. Everyone in a circle. A particular knife. A technique for tidy dismemberment. Watching her dad carve up dinner carcasses as a little girl, she'd sensed how meat was proof of humankind's mastery over Earth, and she'd wanted that strength. Aldo Hucklebridge had felt the same thing, though his phrasing was different: "There's just no better feeling than seeing a sizzling slab of beef on your plate—that's how you know you're boss!"[111]

Hesitant throughout Amber's theory, Kit perked up at the idea of ritual.

"Maybe that's what we've done wrong," he whispered.

---

111 Hucklebridge, *Hail to the Beef,* 169.

Unburdened, Amber felt like putty, drunk on the wine of love, greedy for sleep so she could lose track of her body. She sensed danger in what Kit said. But she yawned too.

"We keep trying to measure the poltergeist," Kit said. "Or the ghost. Whatever. Maybe what we should have done is tell it how willing *we* are to be measured. But how am I supposed to know the thing's rituals? I can't. Any better than I can know a chicken's rituals, or a pig's, or a cow's. I'd have to meet it halfway."

"Let it go, baby. The world is telling us to let it go."

"Yeah. I guess you're right."

Kit yawned, and Amber, even from slumber's ledge, had the feeling he'd faked it.

The following two days, May 14 and 15, are the only days in the whole nine months of the Burger City Poltergeist story for which Kit's whereabouts are unknown. Scribbled shift schedules make it obvious he took off the days in a hurry, but that's the extent of the evidence. To this day, Kit pleads ignorance. He says he simply doesn't remember.

HARUSPEX

The final day of my interview with Kit Bryant, March 8, 2020, has to wrap up by noon. Chernow packs Sundays with activities so cleaning crews can get into the barracks and do their anti-bacterial sweeps. The thunder of vacuum cleaners has already made me toe my recorder closer to Kit.

Honestly, though, I'm ready to leave. If May 14–15, 2017, are the only days of Kit's blanked memory, the rest of May—the critical sixteen days before the Burger City Tragedy—qualify as faded. Kit's energy flags when speaking of them. He offers no elucidations, only listless confirmations of comings and goings. Famished for evidence that institutionalization has given him a glimmer of insight, I press him for a concluding statement. Kit frowns at the floor.

"Huh. Well…I guess I'm, like, sorry for everyone who got hurt? And who died? I mean, you know, I didn't really have any problems with them. With any of them, really. I liked them. I really did. I…guess I don't know what else to say."

That's it. I'm done.

When I turn to ask Nuncio if I can get the hell out of there, he's already standing, looking alert. What if his two days of apparent slumber had been an act to coax honesty from Kit? I give him a nod and start collecting my gear. I don't turn off the recorder, though, an old trick I picked up from my days in TV news.

"Bummer, man," Kit says. "There's so many things I wanted to ask."

I mutter that he can mail a letter care of my publisher. It's what you say to an off-putting fan whose missive you hope never to read.

"Oh, yeah. I totally will. That'd be amazing. Especially *Rotters*. I have so many questions about how you wrote that. Did you actually dig any holes?" He laughs. "Probably not! There's just so many great details about how the robbers can tell where something's buried."

It's an odd thing to bring up in our last seconds. But not was weird as what Kit does next. He opens his arms wide for a hug. His forearm scar stretches.

"All right. Bring it in, bro."

In that instant, I'm certain that nothing in the world is as perilous as a proffered hug. You hesitate a second too long and it's an insult. I give my new best friend Nuncio a glance, hoping he'll say personal contact isn't allowed, not with this Covid thing creeping closer every day. But Nuncio only supplies an it's-your-funeral shrug. Time's up: I fabricate a smile, open my arms, and step in.

Kit is quite the hugger. He presses me in hard, lodges his chin over my shoulder. His 355 pounds are even softer than they look; I feel like I'm sinking deep enough to find his bones. He growls affectionately as he gives my body a side-to-side waggle.

Right before he lets go, he whispers something in my ear.

"Tapes are behind the stone."

A loud clap on my back and then we're separated, and I stop the recorder, and head for the door while Kit blathers that he'd have me sign his books if they weren't from the library. I probably laugh; I don't recall. I'm gone, down the hall, following Nuncio's broad back. My mind is swirling. *The tapes.* What tapes? I thought I'd seen all the tapes. *The stone.* What stone?

Over my subsequent six months of interviews, *the tapes* and *the stone* are never far from my mind. When I visit the Iowa 80 Truckstop after interviewing the Geezers, I spend a while pacing the grounds, searching for notable stones. For a while, I play with the idea of a capital-S *Stone.* There's an Old Stone Church in Muscatine, twenty-seven miles from Jonny; it's rentable for $100/day, but has no relevance to Kit. In late September, I find Mickey McCormick's abandoned cabin. The foundation is stone and I spend the balance of the afternoon belly-crawling beneath, batting spiders with my flashlight.

I conclude my interviews with Amber, Amy, Nutting, and Dion by asking them if they have any idea what Kit meant. They don't, and seem to be disturbed by my interest. That's probably why it's Darren Husselbee who solves the mystery as I'm leaving his Queens apartment. He's trained in story, unblinkered by personal investment.

"Stone—it's gotta be a gravestone," he says. "People died, right?"

Quindlen Arthur is buried in picturesque Oakdale Cemetery in Wilton, memorialized as *Loving Son.* Yesenia Ruiz is buried in Iowa City's Oakland Cemetery near the superstition-laden Black Angel statue, a good fit for *Spectral Journeys.* County Home Cemetery north of Tipton is where you'll find Javier Villareal's marker, heartbreakingly small. To visit Mickey McCormick, you'll have to drive all the way to Forest Hill Cemetery in International Falls, Minnesota. Zane Shakespeare has no resting place aside from the urn Wendy Exley keeps on the hearth Zane restored himself. It shouldn't surprise you that Cheri Orritt's grave is always festooned with flowers; strolling up between the tall cedars of West Branch Municipal Cemetery, you can't miss it.

Tamra Longmoor's family still holds out hope that she'll be found.

Eventually I visit all of the above sites, out of respect and my completist nature, but not to find *the stone*. As soon as Husselbee keyed that lock, I knew directly where it led.

Death came slowly enough for Darcy Smyrna to manage her final wishes. She believed cancer had made her emaciated and ugly, and requested cremation. But she also wanted Amber to have a place to visit. So she set aside a chunk of her limited funds and arranged for her cremains to be buried under the simplest marker possible on the cheapest grave she could find.

That ended up being Rock Creek Cemetery, a twenty-minute walk from the Smyrna apartment in Rochester. It's a rinky-dink operation. Headstones poke their chins above waist-high weeds pernicious with ticks and undulating from rabbits. Darcy's stone lays flat on the ground, the size of a paperback book. I only find it because its overgrowth is thinner.

This is why Kit asked me about *Rotters*, my novel about grave robbers.

He wants me to rob a grave.

Subchapter §5231.316 of the Iowa Cemetery Code cautions that anyone who "damages, defaces, destroys, or otherwise disturbs an internment space commits criminal mischief in the third degree." I am stating here, for the official record, that I did not dig a shallow hole into the ground behind Darcy Smyrna's gravestone. Three feet down, I did not find a black garbage bag secured with packing type, and inside that bag I did not find a waterproof Rubbermaid cargo box containing two individually bagged and foam-insulated USB drives marked simply *#1* and *#2*.

I acquire Kit's secret tapes three weeks before finding Clemens Dumay. I ask him if he knew they existed. Clem leans forward and squints down South East Street for a sign of the shipping truck's headlights. Nothing. He leans back, spits into his jar, and, to my surprise, nods.

"And I'm the only one who did. Kit called me one night, middle of the night. Don't ask me the day. Close to graduation. Maybe three in the morning. He's all zombie-voiced, saying he needs help, he needs help. I say, 'Where are you?' and he goes, 'Your driveway.' So I put on pants and sure enough, his junk-ass Chevy's out by the road. I go out and look inside and there's just blood—blood all over him." Clem grits his teeth. "If that truck doesn't get here, we won't have any milk."

It happened during the pre-dawn morning of Friday, May 26. The dark wrappings over Kit's forearm couldn't conceal its bloody payload. Kit was pale, eyes half-lidded. Clem got him onto the grass and unrolled the cloth. It was, in fact, Kit's Burger City polo. Beneath was a three-inch gash. It was actively bleeding. Clem made Kit press the wound and ran back inside. Greta Dumay was gone as usual, allowing Clem to make all the noise he wanted finding clean towels and tape.

He wrapped the wound, got it propped above Kit's head, and fetched chocolate and Gatorade. When Clem recounts it, he focuses on the shoddy job he did, but it's possible he saved Kit Bryant's life. It's also possible Clem doesn't know how to feel about that. If Kit had bled out that night, lots of other people would still be alive.

Clem believes it was only because Kit was light-headed that he answered so many questions. What happened? *Cut myself.* How? *Knife.* Where? *Cellar.* The Burger City cellar? *Yeah.* What were you doing down there? *Pricks.* I thought we were done with that. *Not yet.* You should stop. *I will. Don't tell, Clem. Promise?*

"It felt good to be trusted," Clem confesses. "But I was a chump. The only reason he came to me was I didn't have family to tell. The only thing Kit had to worry about was Q. But he covered that too. He reminded me Q was trying to save his GPA, studying all the time, and if I told him Kit was still making videos, it'd screw him up all over again. I couldn't do that to my best friend, right? So I promised not to tell anyone. Feel real good about that today," he says sarcastically. "Feel *great* about it."

Clem changes around 2:30 a.m. He quits monitoring for the cargo. He stops chewing, spitting, waggling his feet. He settles into his chair, massaging his bad shoulder. I wouldn't call it relaxation. More like acceptance. I showed up and the truck didn't: proof that his life's order has been jarred. He doesn't seem to hold it against me. He gazes into the night and sighs, as if finding serenity in the used tires, the odor of spilled gas, the thwack of moths against the lights.

"Glad you came," he says.

I'm surprised. I thank him.

"You remind me of Q. I mean, if he was gobs older."

It's a gentle jab at me, twice his age. It's also heartbreak: I've lived twice the life Quin Arthur was allowed. I feel what I didn't feel at the end of Kit Bryant's interview: I want to hug this guy. If we weren't social distancing, I would.

"Come back tomorrow. This place will be dead by midnight. Can you come back at midnight?"

Even though the shipment didn't arrive, Clem's still on the clock and there's shit he's got to do. Of course I'll come back. There are a few things I still need to ask. But the real reason I'm nodding is that I'm flattered. Walking back to the Best Western Annawan Inn, twenty minutes north along IL-78, I don't think about how spooky it is that I don't see a single vehicle. I don't appreciate the eeriness of the dozen deer flashing silver eyes from the parking lot of Shirley's Coffee Bar & Diner. In my final interview, I have made a human connection. Maybe I could be the friend Clem lost in Q.

I sleep well. Never does it occur to me that I've been duped by Clem's flattery, the same way Clem was duped by Kit. The reason Clem wants me to return at midnight on October 30, 2020, is beyond anything I can imagine.

All told, USB #1 and #2 hold just over seven hours of footage shot by Kit Bryant from May 20 to May 26, 2017. (Time and date tags are nonexistent, but the *IDEAS* book helps.) I turn over the drives to Detective Bank a week after receiving them, along with a note that I made my own copies. He will not like that, but my lawyer advises that I'm legally in the clear.

Viewing these final Game of Pricks tapes, one misses Quin. Kit's footage is underlit and poorly handled. Half the time he props the camera up to free up his hands and ends up cutting off the subject, if the camera doesn't fall over altogether.

What is visible, however, is disturbing.

Thanks to Amber's theories, Kit homed in on what other Game of Pricks participants hadn't noticed. The key to the Burger City Poltergeist was blood. Ash Muckells's blood on Lil' Beefy. The chicken blood on the Coldest Cold Spot. The raw-meat blood on the Living Grill. Inevitable traces of blood in the restrooms, followed by Maxine Pinto's blood.

The first video is a shocker. The camera rests on the condiment station, giving a full view of the lobby floor. (Kit has already done the usual adjusting of security cameras.) Kit enters frame left in an apron and gloves, and removes the lid from a twenty-six-quart styrofoam cooler. He tips the cooler until a thick pile of guts flop onto the tile with a soggy smack.

After months of blink-and-you-miss-it incidents, it's practically a relief. Here is the gore we are owed. Beneath stretchy nets of tendon and tissue are piles of gray intestine, a blood-slicked liver, black kidneys, a marbled brown heart, the ribbed protrusions of a windpipe, and oddments of viscera—everything left over after the good venison was harvested.

Kit acquired the guts from a place called Frank's Locker in Tipton. He didn't do it under cover of night. He strolled right in and said he was a U of I student shooting a horror film and looking for realistic splatter. It's definitely fresh. Dark blood extends from the pile like fingers of a leather-gloved hand. Kit returns to the camera, reframes, and zooms. He gets too close; the guts become an inscrutable purple wad. For an hour, nothing changes except for the quality of the shine as the innards start to dry.

Kit grows impatient. He hunches next to it and whispers. Then he stands and shouts. Simple provocations like *Move!* and *Do something!* progress to would-be call-and-responses, as if the offal were a Ouija board. *Ash Muckells, you're back in Burger City! Maxine Pinto, if you're there, give me a sign! Darcy, it's me, Kit, and I miss you, we all miss you!*

It's strange and tender. Two hours in, all tenderness is gone. The footage jump-cuts and Kit's bearing has changed. Now he's Bad Cop. He holds a frying pan with an oven mitt. The pan is smoking and fire-engine red; Kit has cooked it until it changed colors. Slowly he lowers its bottom surface to the gut pile.

Imagine a ball of raw hamburger flattened to the grill with a spatula. Kit squashes the innards downward. Organs swell and burst, ejaculating fluid. Slurping, sizzling sounds overwhelm the audio. White smoke streams from where the red-hot pan meets the guts, and as bad luck has it, the smoke heads straight for the camera, obscuring everything.

Another thirty seconds and we hear Kit's voice:

"Yes! Yes! I see you! I see you!"

Another forty-five seconds and the camera is switched off. Thankfully, the *IDEAS* book doesn't leave us in the dark. Kit took copious notes on his private experiments, though he will tell investigators he doesn't recall writing them and can't decode them. Furthermore, he *doesn't* tell them there are seven hours of video to go along with them.

The first page of notes read as follows.

May 20
Pos: 3–4
Neg: 6? <u>*WHAT WAS SOUND*</u>
BURNS MARKS = SPECIFIC SHAPES…WHERE HAVE
I SEEN BEFORE???
  - & very hard to scrape off floor

Haruspex (from google)
  - Shax from in English class???
  - research at library (NOT WILTON)
  - replicate!!!!!
blood or something else? the way it burned
<u>what is the taste of my own mouth</u>

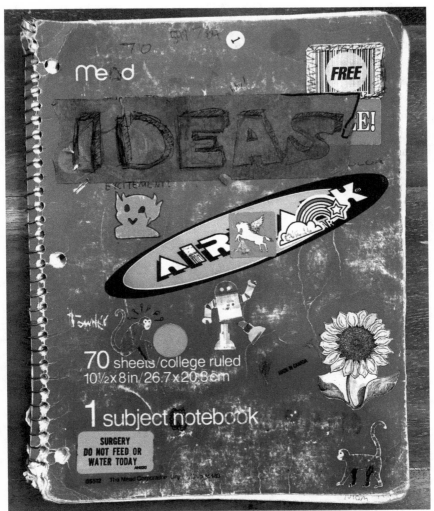

Kit's IDEAS book (courtesy of the Cedar County Sheriff's Office).

The second sequence one-ups the first. The angle is from the walk-in freezer floor. Kit kneels into view, breath pluming in the cold. He's wearing latex gloves and holding a dead squirrel by its front legs. Its puffed tail tickles the floor. One of its flanks is magenta with blood. We can take some comfort in that Kit probably didn't kill this animal; its limbs jut with rigor mortis.

He gently lays the stiff squirrel on the floor, belly up. Using kitchen tongs, Kit pushes the corpse closer to the camera, into the chalk circle of the Coldest Cold Spot. Instantly, the animal's pelt whitens with a layer of frost.

Kit again proves he's no Quin Arthur. He's sort of terrible at this. He doesn't notice when one of the squirrel's stiff legs bumps the camera. We lose the chalk circle. All we see is Kit. He doesn't realize his face fills the screen, which makes his unvarnished reaction even more compelling. His eyes, couched in bruised-looking flesh, are comically wide, blue irises flicking between points of focus. His chapped lips twitch with aborted exclamations. He must be running a fever; despite the cold, his long hair is pasted to his forehead.

He catches his breath. He sees something we can't. The video rolls on for another eighty-nine minutes, yet it's never dull to watch. No kid this animated could possibly self-destruct. He's too intelligent not to find a way out. He's going to be okay.

> *May 21*
> *Pos: 5*
> *Neg: ~6*
> *THE SHAPE:*
> * - Coincidence? Run tests? More insertions, see % that are same?*
> * - Draw & do image search*
> * - VERY FAMILIAR – compare with old vids?*
> *Problem: Q has vids!!!*
> * - Ask nicely*
> * - Steal?*
> * - Get Clem to steal?*
> ****BUT THERE IS NO LIFE*** Feels dead.*
>
> *Same taste? Diff taste? Is the taste of my mouth even a taste?*

The May 22 experiment (undated in *IDEAS*) involves another dead animal. It shouldn't matter that it's a rat, but it matters. What does it take for someone to jam a dead rat into their bag? Bring it into their workplace? Set its fat, black body beside their boss's closed office door?

One of the most startling aspects of Kit's secret footage is the volume of Nutting's noises. He really lets loose in there at night. Later evidence makes it clear that Nutting knows Kit is out there. He simply doesn't care. In madness, the two enemies finally find common ground.

Kit slides into frame beside the rat. He's holding something that looks like a TV remote. Kit points upward to acknowledge the strobing overhead lights.

He adjusts his posture, back to the camera. A blue light flashes near his hands and we hear a loud crackle, like the sparking of a subway rail. What Kit is holding is a stun gun. As entered into evidence for Kit's July 10 grand jury hearing, it is an Avenger Defense ADS-10, a personal protection device capable of a 1.3 µC charge and 30 KV voltage, which online videos suggest can put a grown man on his back for ten minutes.

The hallway lights respond by going wild. We glimpse Kit's smile as he cranes his head to the ceiling. Most viewers, though, will rightly focus on the rat. When the Avenger fires, the dead rodent's paws ball into tiny fists and its tail coils tight. Its body bumps off the floor half an inch, a real-world descendent of Lil' Beefy.

It feels like a Victor Frankenstein moment. But even if the stun gun did set off the overheads, so what? My office lights flicker anytime I use my printer. And maybe a 30 KV voltage is enough to make any dead rat tighten. (I did not test this.) Finally, of course, we can barely see the damn thing. Kit again botches the staging, placing his body in front of the camera. I believe Kit later discovered this himself. His notes feel embarrassed.

> *Pos: 2*
> *Neg: 7*
> *Rat: Electrical — ok*
> *Rat: Smell —nothing*
> *No signs. No blood = the problem?*
> *fuck it*

Viewers of the secret tapes might wonder if Kit will ever shoot a video in which we can tell what's going on. It is a classic case of be careful what you ask for. The next sequence (undated but clearly set in the early hours of May 24) kicks off with a perfectly framed shot of the Living Grill. A small wad of meat is on the grill surface. Per usual, Kit appears from camera left, but instantly exits the frame. There is a distant squeak of metal springs and Kit's soft, sweet murmur.

He enters the frame holding a living cat.

Those clinging to the idea of Kit Bryant as the bad-boy anti-hero should see this video. The cat is orange on top, white on bottom. Its dirty feet and lack of collar suggest it's a stray. Kit's fabled gentleness with animals is on display. He cradles the cat's ribs with his left arm while tussling the fur behind its ears. He whispers to it. The cat's ears are perky and its hackles are smooth. It licks its whiskers like Kit has been doling out goodies all night.

The cat makes eye contact with the meat on the grill.

Kit stops petting the cat long enough to switch on the heat.

The meat starts to sizzle. The cat watches hungrily. The heat rises until juices sizzle. Kit slowly shifts his grip so he has the cat between two hands as he begins to guide it toward the grill.

What the fuck are you thinking? Each time I watch it, I shout the question. A cat isn't going to let itself burn. All I can imagine is that Kit intends to pin the cat to the grill with the lid until its flesh melts like Amy Mold's hand and blood—real, living, pumping blood—spreads across the allegedly haunted surface.

Kit's repellent plot fails. Six inches from the surface, the cat flips out. It's a cyclone of fur, paws like rotary blades, fanged head striking three times in rapid succession. Kit holds on through six seconds but the pain is too much. He lets go and the feline vaults over Kit's shoulder. Kit lets loose.

"OWWWWW! FUCK! GODDAMMIT!"

He flaps his injured hands in midair. Eventually he bares his teeth and slits his eyelids to examine the damage. There are cuts. A runner of blood slugs down his forearm.

Kit's face relaxes a bit. He eyes the trail of blood as it reaches his elbow. He angles his arm so the blood gathers there, a thickening bead. Kit looks to have forgotten his pain. He arranges his elbow atop the grill and shakes his arm. The drop of blood falls on the meat. There is is a hiss and a spit and a high-pitched sibilance.

The video continues for another twenty-eight minutes. Kit stares as the kitty-sized serving of meat burns to black crud. He can't be jodido. He can't, he can't. It's hypnotic in all the worst ways. Kit's bottom lip is glossy with idiot droll. What is he hoping to see? Or, worse, what does he *think* he sees that his camera *doesn't* see?

This might be a good time to consult Burger City's May 2017 schedule to see who's handling Kit's day shifts during this six-day stretch in which he labors all night, every night.

The answer is Kit Bryant.

May 20, 5:30 a.m. to 4:30 p.m. May 21, 5:30 a.m. to 4:30 p.m. May 22, 11:00 a.m. to 11:00 p.m. May 23, May 24, and May 25: each are the dreaded seventeen-and-a-half-hour triple-shift, 5:30 a.m. to 11:00 p.m. And each night, he parks his car in a field entry a quarter-mile down Rolf Tonks Road and waits for Dez Mozley's car to depart, at which point he's back inside Burger City.

Eventually Kit switches off the grill and remembers the camera. He reaches over, picks it up, turns it off. But if the viewer pauses one second before the end, they will see Kit staring straight into the lens, fully illuminated, perfectly in focus. He doesn't just look bad. He looks *wrong*. It's not the sweat, the gnawed lips, or the bugged eyes. His coloring is off. His complexion is bad. His gums are scarlet. There's only one way he's pulling off his sleepless schedule. You know what's coming.

"We call it ice," Detective C.L. Bank says. "First-wave meth, law enforcement got pretty dang close to shutting it down. Took a decade. Lots of lives lost. Law enforcement lives too. But the whack-a-mole never ends. Mexican cartels started shipping new stuff. That's where we are today: twenty-, thirty-pound shipments every week. They send up operators too. Get the supply chain going. These operators, you can't scare them like local batchers. They'll choose prison over the cartel's wrath every time. And the ice is good, buster. Twice as pure, twice as potent. If you've got a steady stream of it, you can fly like Superman for weeks. I don't need a toxicology report. That's what Kit Bryant was using near the end, no question."

The U.S. saw nearly ten-thousand psychostimulant overdose deaths in 2016 (of which meth represented the vast majority), nearly doubling 2015's deaths.[112] Kit would have preferred to use what kids called "study drugs": Adderall, Concerta, Vyvanse, Phenylpiracetam. But he had no way to obtain them, particularly on short notice. Meth, though, he knew just where to go. Everyone liked Kit, including the addicts loitering in area parks, plenty of whom would happily peddle him ice. My hunch is that this is what Kit was doing over the MIA days of May 14 and 15.

Kit had tried a lot of drugs by age 20. Roughly in descending order of frequency: pot, alcohol, nicotine, ecstasy, mushrooms, acid, DMX, cocaine, Vicodin, nail polish remover. Meth was a new one, and whoever

---

112 Lee Rood, "20 Years After the Meth Crisis Began, Iowa's Addiction Is Worse Than Ever," *Des Moines Register,* 2018.

sold Kit his first $50 rock threw in a glass pipe and diabetic syringe. Kit chose the pipe. The high took ten seconds to kick in. Sparkly, dizzying, like ultra-jacked caffeine. He felt spectacular. Happy, confident, creative, hopeful—all the qualities he'd felt when Lil' Beefy's fame had first hit him like rays of sun.

Smoking ice got him through the gut-bucket, the squirrel, the rat. The issue with meth is that the effects fade in a day, if not half. To stay powered and avoid tweaking, you need to binge. These binges can keep users going for ten days straight on only the barest amounts of food and drink.[113] By May 23, an exhausting day—find the fucking cat, lure the fucking cat, catch the fucking cat—Kit was already requiring a harder, faster, longer-lasting dose.

The best analogy for Kit's swift acclimation to injecting ice is how he'd mastered the Guided by Voices songs for Amber. He learned what he needed online and didn't waste time. He liquified a third of a shard in the concavity of an upside-down soda can, wrapped his bicep, plunged his syringe, and went for it, popping the needle into an elbow vein and plunging. He pressed a dish towel over the wound, flexed his arm to get the blood flowing, and then flopped to his bed. While the cat meowed from an old pet carrier, gasoline roared through Kit Bryant's veins.

The early hours of May 25 were, in Kit's recollection, "difficult." At 2:00 a.m, he was still waiting to see Dez's car. He got out of his Chevy and stomped to Burger City, where he spied Dez rooting through her purse in the Grand Room. The bitch was just screwing around! Kit's mood had been all edges since starting meth. He considered punching his fist through the glass just to scare the shit out of her.

Then Dez got down on all fours. Kit crouched by the Puppy Pen and watched. He was too far to see the pin she wielded, but not too far to see the welling spot of blood on her finger. With her tongue stuck out in effort, Dez contorted her body and wiped the bloody finger across the bottoms of T4, T5, and T6. Kit shuddered in revulsion. Gum, boogers, bugs—who knew what was under there.

Ten minutes later, Dez was gone and Kit was inside. He checked under the three tables. Beneath each, Dez had smeared a smaller version of the symbol she'd painted on the freezer door. On a hunch, Kit looked under the booths. Dez, it seemed, had spent the past hour filling the restaurant with this bloody motif.

113 "Methamphetamine (Meth) Addiction," *Hazelden Betty Ford Foundation.*

The following video documents Kit's hunt. He finds the symbol on Lil' Beefy's base. Behind toilets. On the 3M B1099 charger. Behind the kitchen grill. Along the top edge of freezer door. Kit found the biggest surprise by standing atop a chair. The ceiling-facing surface of the cellar door's header board was adorned by thirty miniature versions of the sigil painted in feathery blood.

Kit sat in the break room, breathing the stink, listening to Nutting's noises from the office, just thinking. Finally he unlocked the janitorial closet, pushed aside Dez's cart of obsolete supplies, and dug out an old Black & Decker tape measure. He began to run lengths between the five known major disturbances: the Men's Room Bully, the Coldest Cold Spot, the Living Grill, the Drive-thru Phantom, and the Lil' Beefy Anomaly.

He overlaid these five points onto a hand-drawn map of Burger City in his *IDEAS* book. Then, simply enough, he connected the dots. It formed a star, or, if you prefer, a pentagram. Inside the center space, Kit scribbled a dark black circle.

What if this dot was the heart of it all?

Kit's hand-drawn map of Burger City #8
(courtesy of the Cedar County Sheriff's Office).

The dot indicates the kitchen, near where Mickey McCormick was struck by Amy Mold's boiling oil. Kit enters the frame and stands there. Refers to his sketch. Shuffles a few inches to his left. He closes his eyes, dangles his arms (he's got band-aids where he shot up), shakes loose his shoulders, and tries to *feel*. After a couple minutes, he scratches his arm violently and wipes away sweat. He begins to nod.

But I don't think he's feeling shit. His scratching is the tip-off. That's Meth 101—the sensation of bugs beneath your skin. Kit places his palms on the floor as if searching for a heartbeat. Three minutes of this—and he gasps. He grins. He looks up, searches off-camera, exits, and comes back with the sharpest item in the kitchen: a 9.6-inch Ginsu Yanagiba Sashimi Knife.

What was an ultra-sharp sushi knife doing in Burger City? All staffers knew the story. In 2014, Burger City cooks began complaining there wasn't a single good knife in the kitchen. Though Amy Mold had just started, she was already an able prosecutor, and reprimanded Nutting on the dangers of dull blades. Nutting folded and told Cheri Orritt, the only employee he trusted, to buy a block of new knives, anything under $50. Clem joked to Cheri that it'd be hilarious to get a set of Ginsu knives—the mail-order mainstay of late-night 1980s TV. Quin didn't hesitate. He got on eBay and found a "like new" eight-piece set, $49.40 with shipping. It ended up being a damn fine set of knives, and included the samurai-like sashimi knife, which came to be known in the kitchen as simply "the Ginsu."

Kit shows as little pause with the Ginsu as was did with the meth pipe.

He rolls the sleeve of his shirt to his collarbone. Lodging his thumb in his armpit, he pulls the blade around the lateral curve of his left shoulder, the motion used to peel an apple. He pumps his arm, as he does after injecting ice, and leans so the blood falls onto the designated portion of the floor.

Deer guts weren't going to cut it. Neither were dead rodents. Even live animals weren't going to suffice, especially if Amber was right about the ghost being animal to begin with. Human blood had to spill, in sacrifice, in ritual, and right into the ghost's open mouth.

Kit bleeds for forty minutes. As is so often the case with Kit, it's hard not to be swept up by his elation. You half expect to hear a slurping noise and see the blood sucked right through the tile.

May 24/25
Pos: 9
Neg: 2
INCREDIBLE THINGS!!!
The signs are <u>IN MY HEAD NOW</u>
Haruspex is a State of Mind — ha!!!
QUESTIONS/STEPS:
    1. Why weak return?
        BECAUSE THE FLOOR

2. Where is true center?
>   DIRECTLY BELOW
3. How much blood needed?
>   I DON'T KNOW — PROBABLY A LOT!!!

<u>Also:</u>
The taste of my mouth = the sight of my eyes = the smell of my nose
which means
ITS ME
IT IS ME

It was the next night—the early morning of Friday, May 26—that Kit ended up bleeding in Clem's front yard: *Don't tell, Clem. Promise?* Clem *did* promise, and for the next seven days, all that remained before the tragedy, he was beset by guilt. He was so consumed by it that he forgot to pick up Hungry-Man Salisbury Steak dinners for Lysander, who retaliated by breaking every mirror in the house. Clem didn't want to see his own face anyway.

At 11:35 p.m. on October 30, 2020, I text my wife a nervous goodnight and depart the Best Western Annawan Inn on foot. I carry nothing but my phone, recorder, and a travel cup of hotel-room coffee. It is an uneventful walk, but like everything else that happens that night, I can still feel every detail of it. The vibration of the *Live Bait* sign outside the Shell station. The Lynchian drone from the electrical pole outside Jackson's Collision Repair. The gray tornado of moths beneath the parking lot light of Annawan Banking Center.

Biff's Gas & Diesel & Store is as deserted as Clem promised. The white lights of the service bays flicker the way I imagine Burger City's lights once flickered. But the gas-price sign is unlit, a signal that something is wrong. Biff's is desperate for customers, but tonight, wants none of them but me.

I don't see Clem until I'm under the center service bay.

"Stop. Mr. Kraus. Stop."

The door to Biff's is propped open. The interior lights silhouette Clem's gaunt form. He wears yesterday's ensemble of jeans and a hoodie. Except both are a darker color. His hood is down and his hair is matted and shiny. I stop as requested, confused for only a few seconds.

He's darker because he's wet.

Slowly, almost shyly, he shows me the lighter in his hand.

"I don't want you to get hurt," he says.

I am speechless, motionless.

"I used Pump 4. There's no gas near you. All you have to do is run. When the time comes, run."

He holds out a hand and nods, assuaging a complaint I can't yet verbalize. The gasoline on his arm, beneath his rolled-up sleeve, highlights the bite-marks.

"Just turn on your recorder. Will you turn on your recorder?"

I do, anything to keep him talking.

"Good, thank you, because I want everyone who's going to hear this to know I don't blame you. This isn't your fault. I mean, it *is* your fault but you didn't mean it. You just wanted to tell the story. You were doing a good job. You cared. I really do believe that."

The pop songs grinding from pump speakers sound deranged.

"But it doesn't care if you care. This is how it works. When it showed up at Burger City, we *talked* about it. Nutting had that all-staff and we *talked* about it. We went to that truck stop and *talked* about it. And after we finally wised up, Kit broke ranks and kept on going. What's that? That's *talking* about it."

I pat my pockets for my phone.

"So Burger City burns down. We split up. Quit talking. It should have gotten better for us, right? Except what happened? The articles. The documentary. More talking, more talking. It keeps it alive, you get it? Now it's three years later and you show up. You didn't mean it. I know that. But you're spreading it like a virus. Put down the phone."

I have thumbed *Emergency*, thumbed the number *9*.

"Put down the fucking phone!"

It goes back in my pocket. Clem's torso heaves. He coughs. His eyes water. He stands in a six-foot-wide puddle. Behind him are red plastic gas cans and a sales floor slick with liquid. The store lights flicker like those of the service bay, like those of Burger City, and when they flash, I see that everything inside is soaked. Each pair of sunglasses on the spinner rack drips with gas. The Monster Energy Drink cooler is obscured by a golden wash.

"It followed you here," Clem says.

I start to apologize, but he waves it off.

"No, that's good. It's here with us. Right here at Biff's. Look at the lights—you see? You did good. I mean, you did bad, but it's going to end up okay. That's about as good as you can ask for. With this thing. With life too. Whoever burned Burger City had the right idea. It almost worked."

His smile is heartrending. His tobacco-stained teeth. His cheeks tight, skinny, translucent. The tearful hope of his bright, wide eyes.

"I finally got this fucker right where I want him."

My stupor breaks. I rip off my face mask. I shout. I beg. I apologize. I cajole. I pretend to hold answers that I'll divulge if he'll just stop. When he lifts the lighter, I accuse, I curse, I tell him this will hurt every old friend he says he's trying to save. If he doesn't care about his own future, think of theirs.

Clem laughs, an airy sound.

"The future's getting shorter every day."

Only a fraction of a second exists between the lighter's spark and the pillar of flame. Yet for me that instant holds a whirlwind of black questions. Will Clem be buried beside his father, his corpse so cooked that it never enriches the soil? Did all the laughter he inspired still exist in others, imbuing their breaths with hope? What is the price per gallon of a human life?

He goes up like Mickey McCormick didn't.

You can see the fire for miles. I watch from across the road, red heat against my face, cold corn at my back. I don't remember fleeing there. Gas tanks go up as individual screams. When the fire finds the gas reservoirs beneath the station, white flame shoots from manholes, gutter drains, cracks in concrete. Annawan has a volunteer fire department ten blocks away. Someone called them. Was it me? Sirens shriek as the small squadron is dispatched. They perform admirably. They battle back the blaze before addressing the smoldering black pile by the door. Clemens Dumay is dead, and it's terrible, though I feel certain his last seconds were ecstatic.

He loved comic books, you see.

All he'd ever wanted was to be a hero.

JUNE 2017

THE LAST SUPPER

None of those who died on Thursday, June 1, 2017, could have dreamt of such a fate. But they especially didn't expect it after one of the quietest days the little fast-food joint had had since Lil' Beefy's opening move of October 2, 2016. Flickering lights were the last vestige of the unexplained. Whatever had set coworkers and friends against one another had slipped away.

All that remained was to minister to the ailing patient until the official time of death. In this case, it was Burger City #8 hooked to the ventilator. Unlike Darcy Smyrna's private demise, this was death-breath everyone heard. It creaked from the front door when it opened, which it rarely did. It groaned like the Puppy Pen's unoccupied seesaw. It sighed like the walk-in freezer, tired of its own impossibilities.

Personal items that had crept into Burger City over the years were gradually taken home. Workers didn't talk much, but when they did, it was about finding new jobs. Yesenia had filed an application at a hotel in Iowa City. Javi was talking about detasseling corn—hard labor, decent pay. Tamra, not usually one to divulge fantasies, spoke dreamily of becoming a lay preacher.

Not everyone had good options. Cheri Orritt was 54. She'd spent her last twenty-eight years at Burger City. While sharing a cigarette with Clem, she showed a rarely seen vulnerability, wondering if she'd be able to hack it anywhere else. She had shit eyesight. A crap back. A smoker's cough. Clem didn't know what to say. He sensed the true source of her ennui. Burger City—for better and worse—was the only family she had.

Cheri's biggest concern, as usual, was Kit. All blood seemed to have drained from his body. The hollows of his skull looked bruised. He'd taken to wearing long-sleeved shirts beneath his Burger City polo, right when the weather was heating up. Cheri asked what was up. Kit said he was cold. Cheri asked if there was something wrong with his arms. She was sharp as a diamond. Nope, Kit said, but no one could read him like Cheri.

Any other time of year, others might have shared Cheri's concerns. But these were the final two weeks of school. Amber, Quin, Clem, and

Amy were graduating. After a big bastard of a year, they had senioritis bad. There was a parade of final exams, scholarship events, college visits. Rose Community High School's final day was Tuesday, May 30, with commencement set for five days later: Sunday, June 4, at 2:00 p.m.

Dion Skerry had yet to receive word from Bob Nutting to scare up replacement teens, and that was the clearest sign of all that it was over.

Amber barely saw Kit that week. That was unusual, but she was busy. She had dozens of friends to whom she needed to distribute hugs and solemn oaths to stay in touch. After Sunday, diploma in hand, parties attended, and gift envelopes opened, she could spend time with Kit. A lifetime, in fact. Since the night at the cabin, she'd felt swaddled in the certainty that they'd be together forever.

The Burger City staff, therefore, was caught off-guard by Kit's announcement. At 5:00 a.m. on Sunday, May 28, early-shifters Javi Villareal and Amy Mold shuffled into the lobby after Dion Skerry unlocked the door. To their surprise, the fourth opener was already inside: Kit Bryant, whistling to Soft Rock Hitz and mopping behind the counter.

He gave them a winning grin and leaned on his mop, Fred Astaire with a dancer's cane. Kit hit Dion, Javi, and Amy with the befuddling news that Nutting was throwing a party for the departing graduates, right here at Burger City. That's right—Nutting was going to shut down a night shift. As Friday, June 2, was too valuable a business day, the celebration was set for June 1.

There was disbelief. Nutting hadn't done anything for weeks. Dion, Javi, and Amy stared skeptically. Kit raised his eyebrows, amused by their doubt, then held up a Burger City cup like he was a magician about to do perform a trick. Indeed, he was: he placed the cup under the Chillee Shake Machine's spout and poured the thickest, yummiest Chillee any of them had ever laid eyes on.

Kit jabbed a plastic spoon into the shake, set it in front of Dion, and winked.

"Manager first."

The trio stared at the cup as if it were the Holy Grail.

Kit had fixed the Chillee Shake Machine.

Now they saw, lying beside Till 1, the stained, faded, wrinkled Chillee Shake Machine Care Manual. Kit had actually read it. He'd spent God knew how many hours here dissecting the beast, repairing it, puzzling it back together, and cleaning up what Dez's previous repair jobs had proven to be a crime scene of oil, grease, and fluid.

Amy laughed, true birdsong. Javi cursed in jolly incredulity. Dion picked up the shake and tasted it. One swallow and the downtrodden dude lit up like Burger City's pole sign. Kit poured three more, including one for himself. They gobbled, and gasped, and laughed, never noticing the state of Kit's hair, skin, gums, and teeth. All doubts about the June 1 party evaporated. They thought it before Kit, through a mouthful of Chillee, said it:

"Anything's possible."

No one knows why Dez Mozley wasn't invited. Most likely she was quietly ignored, as her erratic presence ruined any get-together. Aside from her, the party had perfect attendance. And why not? School was through. The graduates were feeling their first flexings of freedom, like staring down a long, empty stretch of I-80. From here on out, the exits they chose were up to them. The older workers, meanwhile, felt a surprisingly reciprocal emotion. A bad chapter was ending. The next chapter could only be better.

Kit didn't tamper with the security cams this time. Either he forgot or no longer cared who saw what happened. Combined with the recollections of survivors, the tapes allow a nearly complete record of how the Burger City Tragedy played out.

Camera 2 time-stamps the first arrivals at 6:55 p.m., a trio that had met at Bloom's Pub just prior. We'll never know for sure, but the discussion likely centered on how the heck this shindig might unfold. It's Cheri, Javi, and Zane, the last of whom happily accepted the invite after three peaceful months away from Burger City. They step inside as if for the first time, dubiously eyeing the limp celebration crepe looped from Grand Room ceiling lamps. One wonders if the three of them considered reversing course.

Noises sizzle from the kitchen. Camera 3 catches Kit Bryant lowering a tray of fries into bubbling oil. That fast, Cheri, Javi, and Zane are doomed. Kit's sheer delight at seeing them is overpowering, even for Zane, whom Kit had fought the last time he'd seen him. Kit booms a hearty hello and the newcomers cheer back the same. As the fryer sizzle subsides, they realize music is pouring from the speakers. It isn't WKES 95.6 either. It's the Rolling fucking Stones!

The tunes aren't distorted either. Word has spread about Kit's miraculous repair of the Chillee Shake Machine. Has he fixed the speakers as well? Come to think of it, the lights aren't even flickering! Everything feels *normal*, at long last, and whether that's Kit's doing or luck finally bending their direction, they'll take it.

Kit isn't wearing his uniform, but he's dressed in his best: a kitchen apron over clean army-green pants and a vintage long-sleeve Guided by Voices shirt advertising their 1997 album *Mag Earwig*. He waves the trio toward the Grand Room. Obediently, they rollick, happy and getting happier. This is a party after all.

Quin and Clem show up at what Camera 2 tells us is at 7:04, in tears over something funny. It doesn't matter what. What matters is that their happy and carefree feelings flood over everyone else. Clem spots the adults and gives them a whoop, and they huzzah back. The freshly minted grads, ladies and gents! Clem bows; Quin basks. Everyone embraces.

At 7:08, Dion arrives concurrent with Tamra. He holds the door for her, a big step beyond his usual interpersonal ignorance. Their arrival is mostly drowned out by Clem and Quin's hullabaloo, which is probably how Dion and Tamra prefer it. The water has been warmed; they have only to drift into it.

Amy Mold and Yesenia Ruiz are spotted outside around 7:10, and there is some worry about that, but at 7:15 they enter together, two young women choosing unity, smiling and holding hands (not Amy's bandaged one), eyes pink from tears. Another miracle: their Iowa 80 altercation wiped from the record. The whole staff has been holding its breath for a month: they exhale as one and cover the girls in hugs and kisses.

At 7:24, Amber enters alone, befitting a princess. She veers behind the counter and, barely visible from Camera 3, pops to her toes to kiss Kit's cheek, not minding—or perhaps not noticing—his pale color and patches of aggravated pimples. Kit has his hands full with a tray of frozen, paw-shaped patties, so he can only smile. But the smile looks good, looks real. Amber prances off to the party, shaking her hips so her skirt fringe dances, raising her arms in victory over high school, to which she receives applause.

The last person to arrive is the potential grenade.

Mickey McCormick slips inside at 7:32. He stands by the water fountain until Amy Mold notices, and her stare gradually notifies everyone else. Camera 4 makes it look like the revelers have trouble identifying Mickey. He looks nothing like the man who has been motorcycling into the Burger City lot for eleven years. In place of a sleeveless flannel, knotted bandana, jeans, and boots are pleated khakis, a white button-up shirt, brown loafers, and a black tie. None of it fits right; it's the ill fit, in fact, that gives it emotional force.

The clothes are nothing next to his face. He has shaven off his goatee. Even in Camera 2's low-res gain, you can see the milky negative where his skin hasn't felt sun in decades. Exposed, his features are confusing. His lips are thin and meek. His chin is receded and quivering. The hair on his head is gray at the roots, trimmed and ruthlessly combed.

Mickey opens his mouth but says nothing. Has he ever before shown restraint? He stretches his neck and makes sure the guillotine rope is within everyone's reach. Some eyes turn to Amy, but most to Yesenia. The 16-year-old need only give the slightest negative response and this villain shall be cast out. It is the expected reaction.

Nothing about this night goes as expected. Just as Burger City had long been suffused with the odorous effluvium of greasy meat, splattered ketchup, sticky children, and restroom diarrhea, tonight it is suffused with hope. It was hope that led someone to tell Mickey about the the party. It was hope that compelled Mickey to show up. Everyone present that night has failed their comrades in some way, and from these strands of failure a short rope of grace is woven.

No one says Mickey McCormick *can't* stay and that's enough for Mickey. His face crumples along age lines no one had seen before, and he nods in voiceless gratitude. He looks down at the floor, maybe to hide the tears, but the floor leads to the counter, the kitchen, and Kit, who stares just like everyone else. Mickey inhales hard, nostrils flaring.

"Help you out," Mickey says. "How about?"

Kit doesn't say Mickey *can't* help. So Mickey hurries into the kitchen, where he finds both an apron and a way to participate without participating too much. He gets to work on the patties Kit laid out, while Kit gets an eyeful of the man's strange, hairless face. Mickey once told him he'd had that goatee since high school. Maybe this is graduation day for Mickey too.

Meat hits the grill, serious business now, cooking cranked loud. Above, the Stones can't always get what they want. Someone cracks a joke, someone snorts at it, someone resumes a stalled conversation. Collectively, *they move on*, which is all this night is about. It takes the coming together of these thirteen souls for them to realize they aren't just coworkers, aren't just friends. United, they are exorcists too.

A couple people notice Kit crossing to the front door and locking it. Sure, why not? It's best to ensure a traveler doesn't barge in. Aside from Dez, the whole gang is here, right? Not quite—there is one missing character. Shortly before 8:00 p.m., they hear Kit's and Mickey's startled greetings, and they turn en masse to see a man no one has seen for two months: Bob Nutting.

"Well, 8:00 p.m. is what your notes say. When they asked me later—Detective Bank, all those dickheads—I didn't know, and you can imagine how that went over. Maxine Pinto died March 31. This was June 1. Two months. I swear to Christ I was in that office for two *years*. When I came out that night, it could have been 8:00 a.m. for all I knew. 8:00 a.m., December 2040."

It's near midnight. The dogs have been out for their final pee. They're inside now, snoring through the screen door, except Lyin' Ted, who is especially attached to Nutting. The chubby beagle has wedged himself between Nutting's feet. I feel bad about the hour. Nutting is expected at Hawkeye Hank's Pre-Approved Used Auto in eight hours. But he radiates that burned-fuel vibe of someone who doesn't sleep much.

I ask why he emerged the night of June 1.

"There were messages. I remember that much. Dion would text. Sometimes I'd text back. There were emails too. Some I answered. Most I forwarded to Dion. He was running the joint. And I didn't care. I had one thing on my mind and I kept at it."

Metamorphoses were going on inside that office. One of them was how Nutting felt about Kit Bryant.

"In May, I started hearing Kit show up late. I didn't know what he was doing. I heard the grill going. I heard an electric buzz, found out later it was a stun gun. Weird thing was, I was *glad* when I heard him. I had a feeling he was doing the same thing I was doing. I knew I was right when he started communicating. His way was so much better than Dion's. He slid notes under the door. Hand-written notes. Written simple so I didn't have to think too hard."

One of these notes still exists, found crumpled in the dry goods room when investigators combed the place two days later. It is an astonishing artifact. Much of what Nutting recalls from his time spent locked in his office feels unreliable, yet this note suggests at least some of it is true. Cross-referenced from the *IDEAS* book, Kit's handwriting is unmistakable.

Nutting doesn't recall this particular note. He claims to have no idea to what Kit was referring, nor any idea why he replied *yes*. He does, however, vaguely remember replying to a series of notes in the days leading up to June 1. The word stuck in Nutting's brain is *mass*.

"Everything Dion asked was so complicated. Then there was Kristina and Brandine and Lisa too, texting and calling all the time. How long had

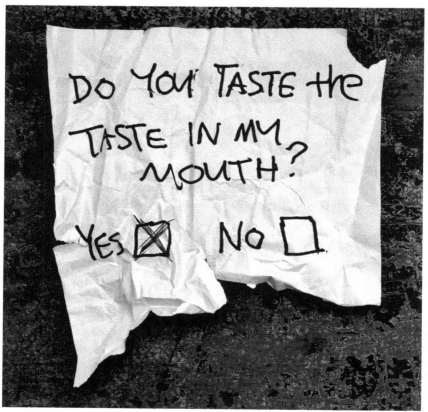

A note from Kit Bryant to Bob Nutting
(courtesy of the Cedar County Sheriff's Office).

I waited for that, you know? But their questions were complicated too. Saying yes to Kit—it just took X'ing the box. 'Can we have a party June 1?' *X.* 'Can we close the restaurant that night?' *X.* Kit's last note asked if I would come. By then, I was just so used to making that X."

At 7:41, Camera 1, the one in Nutting's office, records him crawling naked to his computer, shoved into the southeast corner. He spends ten minutes logging in to the security interface. When he manages it, he sees from Camera 4 a lot of motion in the Grand Room. At thumbnail size, it looks like maggots.

He enlarges the window. Not maggots. People. People buzzing about, gesturing broadly, grinning largely enough to read on camera. He smiles. It cracks a glaze of filth. It is good to see these people. He gazes around the office. For the first time in, well, a long, uncertain amount of time, the state of the place concerns him. He looks for his clothes. They are wadded along the periphery. The wilted, waxy cups of water he smuggles in every few nights are full enough for him to wipe himself down. Rinse out his mouth too. There is a strange taste in there.

Nutting dresses and exits the office. He isn't sure it's really happening. He doesn't recognize the first person he sees. Looks a bit like Mickey McCormick. But Mickey has a goatee. Plus, didn't Mickey quit? Nutting considers retreat, but then sees Kit Bryant. His foe of old now feels like his long-lost son. Kit says *Hey*, and Nutting, his throat unpracticed at speaking, can only smile and nod. Kit is assembling burgers. They look good. They smell good. This place, his restaurant, his baby, might have fallen far, fast, and hard. But no one can ever say Burger City #8 hadn't fixed a tasty burger.

Nutting's cleanest clothes aren't very clean. His white shirt is spattered with the kitchen stuff he's been wolfing on the sly, but it mostly covers an undershirt crusty with sweaty rings. The facial hair missing from Mickey has magically transferred to Nutting, a full beard on a face that has only ever been shorn pink. His beige slacks tell the worst of the tale. They are filthy with what looks like mud. Where in his office has he found mud?

The most striking thing about Bob Nutting is his lost weight. Before the Burger City Poltergeist, Nutting had stood 5'7", 230 pounds, over his target weight but on par for a 55-year-old Midwestern male. On June 1, 2017, Bob Nutting reveals himself as the first Burger City worker to suffer the ravages that will soon come for the other survivors.

Nutting's clothes dangle as if from a hanger, his shirt fluttering over his scarecrow chest to billow where his gut used to be, his belt cinched so tight that his slacks resemble a toddler's elastic diapers. He has a toddler's expression too: confused and pitiful, as if only now realizing that he's lost.

No one but Tamra has been leerier of the poltergeist than Cheri Orritt. Yet Cheri has given herself over to the evening's catharsis—Tamra has too—and clearly wants the good feelings to continue. She doesn't give Nutting's physical and emotional condition a chance to bring anyone down. She pistons her creaky knees, hobbles twenty-some feet to where he stands, and does something no other person at Burger City can imagine doing.

She wraps Bob Nutting in a big, strong, Cheri Orritt hug, disregarding his filthy clothing and sour smell. She whispers the three words he needs to hear the most.

"We've been waiting."

Cheri slings an arm around her boss's whittled shoulders and wheels him into the Grand Room. The celebrants don't hold back. They hoot. They applaud. Nutting is suddenly twice as grateful for Cheri's arm. His knees wobble. He's got no strength in his thighs. From malnourishment, but also from this unexpected explosion of joy. It hits him like atomic shockwaves, ripping tears from his eyes. His staff is cheering. *For him.*

People make room. He sits at T6. The tears fall freely now. Camera 4 shows Yesenia Ruiz handing him a Burger City–branded napkin. The clapping continues. Nutting feels brotherly slaps to his back. He realizes what the others have already figured out. Burger City #8 is finished. It might limp on a few more weeks, but that will be hospice time, a period he'll extend only to keep paying these fine folks until they find other employment. It's over. It's really over.

Which means Bob Nutting can start again. *We've been waiting,* Cheri said. *He's* been waiting too. To clean the slate, to peel the dead skin and take a second shot at being a better husband, better father, better man.

Fast-food workers plop meals on trays, but the rest is up to you. This is so foundational a tenet that Kit's and Mickey's personal delivery of four trays of burgers feels outright decadent. The table service is just the start. The tray contains plates, actual *plates* dug up from some forgotten cabinet and scrubbed clean. People push aside their drinks to make room. These are dishes fit for a proper supper, which is exactly what it is: the last one.

The staff has seen thousands of Beefyburgers, and these aren't typical Beefyburgers. The patties Kit carefully selected actually resemble Aldo Hucklebridge's intended paw shape. Atop the burgers are full, crisp lettuce leaves instead of pale-green confetti smeared in mayo. The buns are lovingly toasted and rest high and light, having never been squashed by paper-wrap.

A single salad has been prepared for resident vegetarian Amber. This is no Healthy Cowboy atrocity. It looks better than anything ever issued from a fast-food kitchen. Bright lettuce, quartered tomatoes, perfectly cubed cheese, thin coins of mushroom, a dicing of fresh avocado. Truly, anything is possible. Including ravenous hunger for what most of the staff had come to view as unappetizing junk. Cameras 2, 3, and 4 capture the wild grabbing for plates. Burgers on plates! People take pictures to document this marvel. Everyone has cameras. The Break Room Bucket is no more.

Kit sets aside his apron and squeezes in between Cheri and Amber at T4. Mickey is offered a seat at T5 but he demurs, choosing to sit alone at the T2 two-top. At 8:05, hands are wrapped around burgers just as Javi hoists his soda and calls out "Cheers to the graduates!" and Tamra beckons, "Stand up!" They do: Amber, Quin, Clem, Amy.

"Our valedictorian," Amy says, gesturing at Quin. More applause. With cameras already out, several people switch to recording video. This includes Kit. His phone is filled with secret footage, but he still has some storage left.

In Kit's video, Quin blushes. It's charming. You can tell he's not thinking about his YouTube hits. For once, he's not thinking at all. He's doing what any high-school student three days from commencement should be doing: he's soaking in sensation. Every face shows bittersweet affection, future nostalgia. When they run into one another years from now, they'll smile, won't they? They'll know they shared something once, inextricable pieces of the people they became.

Cardboard cups are no good at clinking; everyone tips them at everyone else.

Time to gorge. Even Zane, who never eats meat he can't source, digs in. Moist slorps mix with appreciative hums and good-natured jibes. No painful subject is beyond being lanced. Yesenia, of all people, pokes fun at William G. Roll and everyone delights in giving Quin shit. Javi reminds everyone how stiff Dion was in the TV9 interview. Clem and Amy do impressions of Gaetan Goodricke and Roxie Stoyle that have people choking on their meat with laughter.

The only person who doesn't eat is Kit. No one seems to notice. They are having a great time and Kit's easygoing smile hints at nothing awry. He keeps recording, panning across the feasting faces. It's as if Kit, for posterity, wishes to get everyone on video one last time. The footage has an odd orange sheen to it.

Two minutes into the dinner, Kit's recording is interrupted. A hand takes his wrist, the weight lowering his camera to his lap. The camera keeps recording: these are the final few minutes Kit Bryant ever shoots. No meat squirming across a grill. No restroom door flying open. No cooler of steaming guts. Just anonymous knees beneath a table, shifting in cute skirts, bobbing in basketball shorts, waggling in pants.

Despite her hushed tone, Cheri's voice is clear.

"Kid. Look at me. There you go. There's my kid. This was a good thing you did. I want to tell you that. You got a good heart. Always knew you did. Wish we could have done something like this for you too. I guess you graduated in the summer. Just you alone, maybe that would've been weird. Ah, still. It's a regret. One more regret. You get older, they add up. But I want to tell you. I know you know, but I want to tell you anyway. I'm proud of you, kid. Not because you graduated. Because you're a good kid. A good *man*. This whole thing, it's been tough. Toughest on you, I think. So look. I know those eyes, all right? I know those gums. I know why people who look and smell like you do wear long-sleeve shirts in the summer. I'm not saying you don't have it rough. The world's bullshit. It can bore right through your skin and drill into your bones. But there's something at your center, kid. Most of the folks at this table, who knows what's at their centers. But you—there's goddamn gold in there. Take what you did tonight, this good thing, and do one more good thing tomorrow. Then one more the day after that. What you're *on* doesn't change who you *are*. That's why I'm proud. Right now. I am proud of you right now."

The orange-tinted footage shakes. It could be Kit's knees, jerky with discomfort. It could be his whole body, shaking with emotion. We will never know. There is a rustling of fingers over the phone's mic and the video ends. For everything that happens next, we must rely on security footage and the personal accounts of flawed, unreliable, biased, broken people—the only kind of people who exist.

THE BITING ROOM

In the sixty-three days since Maxine Pinto dropped dead, Amber Smyrna has avoided the women's room as much as possible, going so far as to hold her bladder until she could burn rubber to the Kum & Go off Exit 267. But on June 1, 2017, Amber is awash in positivity. Ghosts are things of the past. All she has now is a future.

She pees. Washes her hands. So far, so good. She exits the women's room and finds Kit waiting for her in the hallway. It's 8:15: Camera 4 catches a ripple of Kit's left shoulder. Amber smiles, crosses her arms, cocks a hip against the wall. Their first sexual encounter happened right here. There's no denying they both get off on the risk of being caught. Amber tucks her chin and bats her eyelashes.

"I miss you," she says.

Kit grins. What a great grin. It distracts from the pewter skin, the sangria eyes. Amber's only thought is that maybe he's getting sick. Maybe she should avoid kissing him until after graduation. A silly thought. She knows she can't help herself.

"Come on," he says.

"Come on what?" She peaks an eyebrow lewdly. "Or who?"

Kit's grin doesn't change. Something off about it. Feels a bit like a mask. He hasn't actually said much the whole night. Yielding the spotlight to the graduates, probably. That sounds like Kit. Doesn't really *feel* like Kit, though.

He angles his head toward the BOH. "Come on."

He vanishes around the corner.

Something off, definitely. But Burger City has never felt safer. Amber arcs through the lobby. Everyone's still having fun. The Rolling Stones swear everything's a gas, gas, gas. Amber banks behind the counter and pokes her head into the kitchen. No Kit. Off-camera now, she turns right at dry goods storage. There he is, standing at the intersection of walk-in fridge, break room, janitor closet, and office. Amber licks her smiling lips and strolls forward, the swing in her hips returning.

"It's always stinky by the office, baby," she pouts.

She takes his shoulders with an underhand, through-the-armpits grip, plumps her breasts against his chest, and kicks back a leg like women on movie posters. She wrinkles her nose, though cutely, she hopes.

"It *really* smells," she says.

Amber glances left. The janitor's closet is open, which is peculiar, but it makes no impression on her next to Nutting's office door. It's ajar. This explains the force of the odor. Amber thinks she can actually see the stench, crinkling like cellophane. At last they can discover the origin. She drops her raised foot to get a better angle on the office door and pulls slightly from Kit.

He pulls her back and kisses her. His lips are cold hamburger. The corner of his mouth twitches. Amber makes up excuses. His lips are cold because he was drinking iced soda; he twitches because he's over-tired. Kit's bony arms lock across her back like metal rods. Carefully, she breaks the kiss. His teeth, weirdly enough, feel hot.

"You're in a *mood*," she teases. Again, the nose-wrinkle. "But seriously."

"It doesn't smell downstairs," Kit says.

She frowns. "Downstairs?"

Kit's grin hasn't changed.

"You want to go in the cellar?" she clarifies. She figures she can handle this. Now and then, Kit gets an idea in his head that turns her off. Making out in the Walmart parking lot, doing it in a church balcony. She's always had success talking him down without shaming him. "Baby, it's going to be all spidery and gross down there."

He reaches behind him and opens the cellar door. The hinges shriek, sharp nails down Amber's spine. It's the only door in the world capable of distracting her from Nutting's office. Not once in four years has she seen it open. At the upper corners of the frame billow the cobwebs she predicted. Everything else, pitch black.

"It's not gross," Kit says. "It's nice."

He reaches past the frame, pats for a light switch.

Amber takes hold of Kit's reaching left arm with the goal of leading it back, to her breast maybe, anything to deflect his attention. But she stops upon feeling his forearm. There's padding beneath his long-sleeve shirt, what feels like bandages. Kit feels her feel it. He tightens.

"Baby," Amber gasps. "Did you hurt yourself?"

Lust snuffed, Amber sees Kit clearer than she has all night. The big, dead grin, like his upper cheeks have been stapled there. His iron-colored teeth. Not only his lip twitching, but his chin, the corner of his right eye.

His pupils are huge. The pimples of his temples connect with more she hadn't noticed, all along his jawline.

"No," he replies.

Amber pushes up Kit's sleeve. Just as she'd thought: gauze. Frayed, loose, brown with blood. Her generous instinct isn't to suspect her boyfriend of treachery. Rather, he must be hiding his injury so she won't stress out over graduation weekend. Amber pulls his arm closer.

"What happened?"

Kit's grin might as well be painted on his face. He lets go of Amber so he can pull his sleeve back over the mess.

"Was it...an animal?" Amber asks.

"Yes. It was. Will you come—"

"Was it one of those raccoons?"

Any Burger City closer knows the nocturnal nuisances that frequent the dumpster. Kit doesn't look like he hears the question but nods anyway.

Amber glowers. "*Baby*. They could have *rabies*. You need to go to the doctor. You need to go now."

Kit's forehead succumbs to a single, small notch, the only sign that he's fighting to think beyond the meth, beyond madness. He isn't mentally equipped to improvise. He manages it, just barely.

"No, it's not—it's hard to—I'll show you. What got me is downstairs. It's—dead. We can take a picture. We can show it to the doctor."

There are many reasons for Amber to say no. Kit is clearly willing to say anything to get her down there. The lights, if they work, will be insufficient to see the stairs. There *will* be spiders, despite what Kit says. It doesn't matter if what awaits is a "good" surprise (he really does just want to take off Amber's clothes) or a "bad" surprise (there really is a dead animal to show her). The point is, his behavior isn't to be trusted.

There is only one reason for Amber says yes. We cross the most derelict of bridges for the people we love. We do it because there was a time they did the same for us, back when we were furious, depressed, impossible. These risks seem small against the long run, and that's what Amber expects from Kit: a long run. She forces a smile, shrugs, and follows him down into the black.

Kit and Amber have been noticed. Clem has been doing his funny-guy act for over an hour, but he's doing it from T4's southwestern chair, giving him a good angle into the lobby, register area, and restroom hall.

Clem's surveillance of Kit didn't begin when Clem arrived at 7:04. It began in the wee hours of May 26 when Kit bled all over Clem's front yard. Clem has gone through his final week of high school shaky about being the only one to know of the ongoing Game of Pricks. Kit nearly killed himself last time. So Clem has tried to watch him all week: before school, after school, on lunch breaks. He's tried to make sure Kit shows no new damage. But those damn long-sleeved shirts—Clem just can't tell.

He angles his body to watch Amber follow Kit into the kitchen.

Quin notices and turns in time to see Amber disappear. Quin exhales in disgust. Clem sees that his friend's carefree face has gone sullen. Tonight was supposed to be about the graduates, but to Quin, Kit is saying his academic miracles don't mean shit. Quin still can't have Amber.

Quin snatches up a napkin and wipes his fingers fussily. The way he stares toward the BOH might melt soda-dispenser chrome, kitchen-grill metal.

"I don't care if I bust in and they're naked," he says. "I hope they are. I want them to know this is not cool. It's disrespectful. You want Tamra walking back there and seeing that?"

Three security cameras show Quin rising off his chair at 8:17. A few inches off his seat is all he makes it before Clem yanks him back down by the sleeve. It's like the empty, hinging seesaw in the Puppy Pen; Quin goes down, Clem goes up. Before Quin can complain, Clem winks like it's no big deal, but it's the biggest deal possible between two friends who both know where the other is headed. Quin had far yet to go. Clem's high point might very well be right now. So let him be the protector.

"Don't screw anything up while I'm gone," Clem jokes.

Quin shrugs, and grins awkwardly, and nods. Contained in these gestures is an unspoken *thank you*. It's nice that Clem catches it before turning away. It is the last thing Quin Arthur, his best friend, will ever tell him.

The last thing on USB #2 is the May 26 footage Kit shot before arriving at Clem's house and bleeding all over his lawn. The video takes us into the cellar. There are, in fact, lights. A bare bulb with a string-pull at the top of the stairs, a second at the bottom, and a third in the middle of the room. These bulbs are filled with what look like dead houseflies and illuminate nothing but themselves. Kit's phone provides the only usable light, rippling across spiderwebs and drizzles of dust.

Available blueprints don't include Burger City's cellar, but Kit's footage depicts it as being about one-third the size of the restaurant and positioned roughly beneath the front counter, kitchen, walk-ins, and break room. The floor is buckled concrete. The walls are misshapen brick.

There is a whole lot of dirt. In the northwest corner there is a waist-high hill of it.

Black sediment blankets what looks to be leftover material from the building's 1989 construction. Rotted lumber, deteriorated brick, wilted drywall. When the camera briefly swings backward, you can see, near the foot of the stairs, the plastic remains of the old menu that used to hang above the registers.

Kit stops at what he judges to be directly beneath the kitchen spot where he'd sliced open his shoulder—the nexus of Burger City's hotspots. He tilts his camera upward. The unfinished ceiling is marred by a greasy black oval. Looks like blood but it can't be. No way it could have soaked through that many levels of flooring.

The footage goes wonky for forty seconds as Kit finds something against which to prop the camera. It points upward at an acute enough angle to capture the ceiling's black spot as well as the entirety of Kit's lanky body. He reaches into his back pocket.

He withdraws the Ginsu Yanagiba Sashimi Knife.

He rests it atop his left forearm.

With Kit's head six feet above, his heavy breathing no longer dominates the audio. The cellar's true tone emerges. It's similar to the sound of a rumbling dryer, but with a subwoofer moistness, the wobble of a baritone sax. Kit's iPhone is old and yet catches traces of what Darren Husselbee caught on his Yamaha SKRM-100 Subkick—sickening, shifting doppler waves, sonic throbs that start to resemble words.

If there is any doubt about my interpretation of the noises, it ends when Kit, eyes squeezed tight and the point of the Ginsu wiggling into the soft flesh of his forearm, begins shouting in unison with the distorted nonsense like it's a well-known radio hit.

"Gone and I'm gone and more five five five and I'm gone gone gone!"

It is chilling. I don't deny it. But there is an explanation. I spent a decade directing, shooting, and editing films, and I've seen this kind of aberration. Put simply, the sensitivity of the human ear rarely matches that of a given microphone. Kit's chanting may sound synchronous with the noise, but in reality is likely offset, with Kit repeating each sound as he hears it, like an interpreter racing along to a live speech.

The length of time Kit pulls this off is admittedly astonishing (and attributable to the meth). His screed becomes one more facet of the tornadic drone. Meanwhile, with equal control, he creeps the Ginsu down his arm, unzipping pale skin to the red muscle beneath. Blood trickles,

252 *The Ghost That Ate Us*

then spatters, until some vital tissue is breached and blood begins to spurt. It strikes the camera directly, coating the lens.

The image goes crimson, and even after Kit wipes it off later, the lens will retain an orange tint. Blood gets in the mic too, muffling the audio. Kit staggers, probably lightheaded. We see the Ginsu fall. The moment goes as still and silent as a deathbed room after a loved one's final gasp.

Kit screams.

"I'LL DO IT! I'LL DO IT! I'LL DO IT I'LL DO IT I'LL DO IT—"

Higher-pitched than possible, throat meat ripped raw, a shatter of detonating china, a hyperventilating sob, and the iPhone's mic capitulates, warbling, then cutting off, a clean decapitation, leaving nothing for the listener except regret at having heard the moment a mind was lost.

What is the nature of Kit's oath? The best clue we have comes from the final entry in *IDEAS*, written just hours after Clem helped bandage Kit's self-inflicted arm wound. Given the extent of the tragedy to come, the entry is insufficient, though it does depict the thrust of his ice-fueled psychosis.

May 27
Pos: 10
Neg: 0
Haruspex confirms it's me
Also confirmed: everyone has RSPK, that's why they feel it too
Conclusion: Smaller RSPKs interfering with primary RSPK
Solution: silence other signals

Like many survivors, Amber seems reluctant to let me go when the time comes. She dawdles with her final story—what happened in the Biting Room—until I have to lay down the law. It's late. I'm tired. Kit claims no memory of the scene, so tell me what you saw, what you heard. Tell me what the hell *happened*.

Amber absorbs my questions like withering critiques. She chews her scabby lip for a time, stands rather daintily, and disappears into the bathroom. She doesn't shut the door. I wait, but for what? The splash of sink water? The rattle of medicine bottles? I get worried. I'm halfway up when Amber's voice, clangorous against tile and porcelain, pushes me back down.

"Don't. I don't want you looking at me when I say it."

I put my recorder on the floor and use a flyswatter to push it closer to the bathroom. Amber's lugubrious sigh might last longer if not for her e-cig-weakened lungs.

"I didn't lie to the cops. I want to make that clear. I have enough to deal with without that bald-headed pig beating down my door again. When he questioned me, when he *bullied* me, he was after facts. So I gave him facts. Everything else in my head was a nightmare. I didn't trust it. Then, okay: time passes. Fuck, does it ever pass. My body shrivels up like a crone. But my mind's only gotten sharper. All those facts? The facts are what's blurry now. It's the nightmare stuff I know is true."

Dreariness folds over me like chainmail. I adjust my face mask so it covers my eyes. I tuck my head into the dark space of my knees. I can understand Amber's story later. Right now, I just want to get through it. I start counting, a child's distraction: One, two, three.

The cellar stairs (courtesy of the Cedar County Sheriff's Office).

"I can tell you about the stairs. I can tell you *all* about the stairs. They were wooden. Different patterns to the grain. Different cracks. Different splotches of blood. Kit's blood, obviously. He had those bandages, he'd been down there, maybe he'd fought an animal. I stepped off the bottom step and fell into a pool. It wasn't wet. But it was everything else. Dark and blurry, with faraway sounds, like people yelling up on the surface."

Forty-five, forty-six, forty-seven.

"The air was like warm gel. I didn't know how to move through it. But Kit had my hand and he pulled, and I could feel the air ooze. I remember thinking, did he roofie me? Is that what this is?[114] It got less gelly. Firmer. Like I was inside a body and pushing past organs. I had this thought I was inside one of the animals Burger City slaughters for food. This was my punishment for being part of it. I was going to get slaughtered with them. Some blade was going to slice open the cellar and I'd be washed out with all the guts and blood."

One hundred three, one hundred four, one hundred five.

"But organs don't have appendages. These big, hot things were sticking to me, like octopus suckers. Little things were wiggling all over. Like fingers. Or tongues. There were hard things scraping over me too, like teeth. And light things too. I thought I heard feathers fluffing, lots of feathers. Some of it—don't come over here? All right?"

One hundred thirty four, one hundred thirty five, one hundred thirty six.

"Some of it was under my clothes, against my privates. I was scared but then I heard Kit. He was so close he could whisper. He said this is what we wanted. We're going to become one, like getting married, except better. I'll be able to taste what he tastes, he said. He told me to think of William Roll, who said poltergeists center on kids going through puberty. What if it's sex-based, he said. What if all the sex we had in this restaurant, what if *we* brought it? What if it's our *baby*? And what do babies do? Babies get bigger and stronger while their parents get older and weaker. They replace us. That's just the natural way, he said."

One-hundred-ninety-eight, one-hundred-ninety-nine, two-hundred.

"I know what I'm supposed to say. That I was violated. If I don't, people will judge me. But they already do, right? It felt good. My legs

---

114 Amber downplays the chances that Kit drugged her. I think it's possible. Kit orchestrated the whole evening, sat next to Amber, and refilled Amber's drink at least once. He'd already been purchasing ice; acquiring roofies should have been easy. Amber's behavior later that night further suggests she might have ingested GMB, a depressant capable of bringing a sense of tranquility, lowering inhibitions, and, most relevant, causing dreamlike hallucinations.

were *shaking* it felt so good. I was trying to get my clothes off. Kit was trying to help and he was laughing and it sounded real, you know? Not like his fake smile. He said he'd been waiting for this. He said he'd opened a box of soda syrup and it was full of smoke. He said he'd cracked open a roll of quarters at Till 2 and worms spilled out. These were signs. He set something cold against my neck. *Good* cold. It was a knife. Even down there, packed inside all those guts, I knew it was a knife."

There was an animal in that cellar after all: Kit Bryant.

Clem at age 19 has the shape of a nose guard, short and thick, and he plows all 230 of his pounds into Kit's left side. That's the side with shoulder and arm wounds, and it magnifies the pain. Kit falls hard to the the cellar concrete, Clem sprawling on top. Amber is clocked aside. Clem yells for Amber to get out of there, run, get help.

He has no way of knowing if she does any of those things. Kit is an insect knocked to his carapace, threshing limbs, clamping jaws. Kit's fingers go for Clem's soft spots like they thirst for the blood beneath: eye sockets, the underthroat. Clem dives into it, bashing his skull against Kit's. This buys him a second. He pythons an arm around Kit's neck, muscle memory from middle-school wrestling. The coarse cement floor shreds a layer of skin from Clem's arm.

Kit's body flops like a cracking whip, the contractions of the electrically charged. Clem holds on for his life, seeing nothing, hearing nothing, praying for the end.

Clem gets his wish: Kit stops flopping, his body goes long and tense, a tortured, spread-eagle stretch. Clem feels a burst of hope. Kit's fight is gone. Clem tries to catch his breath so he can shout. Where's Amber? Where's the help? The clatter he hears behind him doesn't mean anything. Even if it did, he can't avoid what's coming.

The Ginsu sinks into Clem's shoulder. To be specific, it drives into the center of the left acromial deltoid, three inches from the spine of the scapula. The knife point audibly strikes the greater tubercle, one of the knobby protrusions at the top of the humerus. Surgeons will call the impalement "lucky," skirting both humeral and axillary arteries. It does, however, sever Clem's left axillary nerve, which will limit rotary movement and cause spates of pain for the rest of his life.

Clem doesn't know he's been stabbed. It feels more like the teeth-rattling blow of an open-field tackle. He is flung. He rolls with the Ginsu still impaled which widens a hole that will take twelve stitches to close.

Another roll knocks the knife free. Afraid of another collision, Clem rises to his knees. For a second he tries to locate Kit, then his shoulder bursts into invisible flames. He clutches at it with his right hand and notices right away that he can't feel the clutch, like he's grabbing an inanimate object. But he feels the hot blood lapping his fingers. The numbness of his left shoulder spreads up his neck and into his head. His vision swims.

Amber doesn't race into the Grand Room. It makes no sense for a girl who fears for her life to go all the way to the lobby. The back exit is closer and, unlike the front door, isn't locked. With a few sandal squeaks, she bolts down the eastern hall, collides with the push bar, and explodes outside. She never screams. Why would she? She's trying to disappear.

In the Grand Room, the back door is dimly heard beneath the Stones, who want everything painted black. A few diners cock their heads, but no one interrupts Tamra, who is being pretty hilarious telling Yesenia how to "pop her abs" with interval training and free weights. Amy and Quin joke that, as gimpy old graduates, their physiques are past being salvaged.

Three minutes pass. In retrospect, glorious minutes.

Kit ambles from the kitchen at what Camera 2 tells us is 8:24. From this distance he must look unchanged to the others, right down to the phony grin. Differences are easier to spot as he gets closer. Dirt smudges on his jeans, all over his *Mag Earwig* shirt. His shoulder-length hair is tangled. Cobweb swings from his ear. His stroll cannot hide a limp.

Quin can't help himself. "Where's Amber?"

Kit keeps coming, grin unfaltering.

"She had to go," he says.

Quin stares at Kit. Amy Mold, who is having fun with Quin and feeling that senior pang of wondering why they never hung out, looks at Kit too. She is a watchdog for fellow females and alarm bells begin ringing.

"She left?" Amy asks. "Where?"

Kit's lips part to answer, but nothing comes out.

"Baby girl's gone?" Javi adds. "Aw, I didn't get to tell her congrats."

Quin gives Kit a once-over. "You're dirty."

"What happened?" Amy presses, and people near her register her tone. This is the old Amy Mold, who never allows herself to be waved off like a fly.

Kit stops ten feet away, an odd distance. He's like a slow computer trying to think. Every eye in the joint settles on him, Kit Bryant, everyone's buddy, their big-hearted hero. The moment heavies like drying cement; their belief in him, the kind of person he is, the truth of what he said about Amber, it bends them toward the breaking point.

A word falls out of Kit's mouth: "Darcy."

It is the right word. Everyone unbends. Yes, of course: Darcy. There *is* someone missing tonight—how had they forgotten? The group murmurs in sympathy. Darcy won't be there on Sunday to watch Amber cross the stage. Darcy won't be there to buy Amber college supplies and see her off. Darcy won't be there to see Amber grow up, stretch out, figure out who she is going to be. No wonder Amber ducked out.

Not even the Stones can save the staff from sadness. They gaze at tabletops, the carnage of a finished fête. Nearly everyone consults their watch or phone. Zane exhales the one-word incantation able to unravel any social gathering: "Well." Sensing the end, Mickey stands from his two-top and brushes his khakis, probably thinking he ought to skedaddle first to save anyone the discomfort of bidding him goodbye.

Like bellows into a fire, these motions spark Kit to life.

"No, wait!" His features change at last, eyebrows leaping. "Don't go yet—we have to—dessert! What about dessert?"

Tamra puts on a shawl, Yesenia picks up her purse, Javi twirls his keyring. Kit panics and jabs a finger at the counter.

"Chillees!" His face splits into a wet, red, frantic grin. "Come on, I spent a whole night fixing that sucker. One round of Chillees? Come on. One round?"

Chillees is as canny a word as *Darcy*. Staffers glance around, trying to glean one other's thoughts. Camera 4 suggests it's Dion who gives the first why-not shrug. That's not to say the others blame him for it. What's fifteen more minutes? After all, when Burger City does close, there will be no greater loss than that of delectable Chillees.

Kit claps his hands into a joined fist and scrambles behind the counter. Per his self-appointed duty, Mickey follows to help. Everyone seems glad for the reprieve. End on a positive note, right? Not just for Darcy but for us—a fond farewell to all of us.

Someone should have noticed the item jutting from Kit's back pocket. It's perfectly evident at 8:26 from Camera 3. It's the Ginsu. If not that, someone should have noticed the red, blooming stain.

The Burger City Team Member Handbook decrees that it should take a max of seven seconds to pour a Chillee. Eleven shakes ought to take seventy-seven seconds to prepare. But Kit's repair of the Chillee Shake

Machine was really something. He and Mickey head back to the Grand Room tables with two trays of Chillees in just fifty-eight seconds.

Light clapping. Greedy, flashing eyes. Anticipatory, yum-shaped smiles. A Chillee is set before each chair, occupied or not, followed by one of the straws Mickey collected at the condiment station. Eleven pairs of hands expertly skin the straws and stab them into the creamy, mocha-colored shakes. Lips dip to suck up the cold, malty, first taste.

"Speech."

All lips unpurse. Eyes glance upward, rather guiltily, searching for the interruption's source.

It's Cheri, the only one with the starch to ignore the Chillee sitting right in front of her. Her tinted glasses hide her eyes, but there's affection in every one of her wrinkles.

"How about it, boss?" she asks. "One last word for the troops?"

Every head rotates toward Bob Nutting.

Kit stands beside Mickey at T2. Drops of sweat stream across his cold grin. Camera 2 shows his hand behind his back, toying with the Ginsu's handle. Nothing had gone right in the cellar, but he has a backup plan. He has always been full of plans.

Nutting's staff had addressed him only occasionally throughout dinner. Their boss had gone through something in his locked office, maybe a breakdown, and by silent decree they agreed to give him space. All night, Nutting had smiled, like he was re-learning how to do it. One thing seemed clear. He'd exited his cocoon vulnerable but better than before, kinder, gentler.

Cheri's request for a speech feels risky. What if Nutting can't manage it? What if he crumples, or cries, or sprints back to his office? But Cheri has known this man a long time. Nutting looks around. His eyes narrow, a thespian trying to recall a long-ago memorized passage.

He stands. Quin, who has yet to tape a single thing that night, slides out his phone and hits record. Maybe because he wants to show Clem later. Or maybe because intuition tells him that this show of courage means Nutting is going to be okay. And if Nutting is going to be okay, they all might be okay.

"Tough year." Nutting nods for a bit. He continues slowly, but slowly gains momentum. "Awful tough year. But it's a tough business. People don't think it is. Because the wages. Because we hire young people. People are dismissive. They're unkind. That's wrong of them. They depend on us. Day, night, they need something, we're here. When I was at BCU, a trainer told me, 'Bob, your little restaurant is where people will fall in love, and break up, and bring sick parents, and new babies, and laugh, and cry, and be alone with themselves. Your place will be part of their lives. They'll never forget it.' I thought that was interesting. Though mostly I just wanted a job."

Nutting chuckles. Everyone chuckles. But at a hush, and with feeling.

"I don't know what's next. For this place. For me. For any of you. But I want you to know that trainer was right. People *won't* forget this place. It's part of them. It's an even bigger part of us. You won't forget the time you spent here. Neither will I. I think I'll remember every single one of you forever. I really think I will."

He is tragically correct.

This empathetic goodwill is too much. The staff looks at one another, shy with affection and forgiveness, and raise their cardboard cups, the night's second toast. Then they drink, big, hungry slurps: communion, ceremony, ritual, a way to wash themselves of the way things were, to gird themselves for the way things might yet be. The Chillees are exquisite. Nutting has said it before and he was right: a cleaned machine really does provide a tastier product.

Six people do not drink.

Tamra Longmoor's hand slips off the cup's condensation. The shake falls to T5, a beige splat.

Amy Mold, to Tamra's left, sets down her shake to grab napkins.

Dion Skerry, behind Tamra, tables his shake to get napkins from the center of T6.

Bob Nutting still stands, his own Chillee forgotten, gazing at his happy staff.

Cheri Orritt does the same from the other end of the group, basking in the warm surprise of this piece-of-shit burger joint off this piece-of-shit exit revealing all this beauty.

Kit Bryant hasn't even poured himself a cup.

At 8:50 p.m., in the single snatched breath between the closing hum of "Paint it Black" and the banshee howl of "Gimme Shelter," two words screech through the restaurant.

"The cellar!"

Those who haven't yet felt the tightening vise of their muscles turn in their chairs, or even stand where the ferns block their view. Clemens Dumay is on the floor by Till 1, planted on his knees, right hand gripping an opposite shoulder spewing dark liquid. His clothes, arms, and face are slathered in what looks like ketchup. His body teeters yet still he cries out.

"Get out of here! Get out—"

Kit alone is not paralyzed by shock. The mask he's worn all night cracks as if struck by a hammer, revealing a pig-faced demon, a wild-eyed gargoyle of fluttering nostrils and steaming mouth. He squeals and sprints, a gray blur through Camera 2's footage.

"GET BACK DOWN THERE! GET BACK—"

Kit kicks Clem full force in the face, propelling him into the restroom hall, blood spraying like the trail of a July Fourth sparkler. Javi's innate heroism kicks in; he's up, and Mickey gets up too, and Amy, and Zane, and finally Quin, Clem's best friend, his veins no doubt sizzling with adrenaline he's never before felt.

His veins sizzle with something else too.

At 8:51, Quin presses a hand to his chest. Something's wrong. He takes his chair-back with his other hand, but can't control his muscles; the chair is upended. Seconds later, Quin upends too, clawing at his neck. Every muscle and organ of his body clenched into fists. He flops to his back, spine violently arching upward, face pulled like a maniac clown, eyes rolled white, mouth huge and slobbering, cheeks rippling back so forcefully his lips look ready to rip apart.

Others begin to gasp, and claw, and drop, the thumps of their bodies like hail pounding the Burger City roof. Quin, Javi, Mickey, Zane, Yesenia: their fate is crueler than they will ever know. Chillees, their favorite food in the world, have betrayed them.

There are a lot of nasty ways to buy it in this world, but few rival strychnine poisoning. An alkaloid produced by the Strychnos nux-vomica tree, the poison was originally used as a stimulant, most notably when it fueled Olympic runner Thomas Hicks to a Gold Medal in 1904.[115] It is most notorious for its high-profile past as a murder weapon. Jane Stanford, cofounder of Stanford University, was poisoned by strychnine, and both Alexander the Great and blues legend Robert Johnson were allegedly killed by it.

Strychnine isn't subtle. To some murderers, that's the appeal. Minutes after ingestion, the poison passes through the lumen of the small intestine, enters the bloodstream, and binds with plasma proteins, which transport the poison to spinal-cord neurons. The first effect is one that Gold

---

115   Karen Abbott, "The 1904 Olympic Marathon May Have Been the Strangest Ever," *Smithsonian Magazine*, August 7, 2012.

Medalist Hicks briefly enjoyed, an energized alertness that made Burger City's Chillee drinkers feel especially good right before the end.

Next, heartbeat and respiration quicken. Sweating becomes profuse. Muscles twitch. The victim turns blue and suffers lockjaw. Their whole face clenches in *risus sardonicus*,[116] the sort of deranged, accidental grin of someone who's wincing away from a gun to their head. Muscle contractions go wild, twisting the victim like a fish on dry land. Because back muscles are the body's strongest, the body arches drastically until only the head and heels touch the floor. Breathing is strangled. It's agony, and to make it worse, the victim's perceptions are magnified, attuning their nerve endings to their body's every rip and burn.[117] They will feel every tortuous second of respiratory death. And die they will. Strychnine has no antidote.

Germans began using strychnine as a rodenticide in the seventeenth-century,[118] and until World War II, it was one of the easiest deadly poisons to acquire in the U.S. Before being banned in 1990,[119] strychnine was great at killing animals no one gave a shit about, as evidenced by the jolly product names: Hare-Rid, Gopher-Gitter, Rat Bis-Kit, Mouse-Tox, and so on.

One such product was Kwik-Kil No. 7. Produced by Bartlesby Chemical in Omaha, Nebraska, these lethal pellets were packaged in a bird-egg-blue can. An illustration depicts a hand dispersing a pellet while an uncomfortably cute rat paws for it. Below, superlatives hype Kwik-Kil's virtues: *A tasty bait! Contains ten times the active ingredient of any other rat poison! No danger in using! Money back if it does not kill!*

Kwik-Kil No. 7 vanished from stores with the 1949 shuttering of Bartlesby Chemical. But it had been popular in the Midwest, and countless family garages were furnished with it. Businesses that relied on surefire rodent eradication stockpiled the product: pest control, groundskeepers, landscapers, superintendents, and janitors.

One of those janitors was Lyle Mozley, who worked for a shifting array of businesses throughout his adult life, before dying at age 74 in 1994. Lyle's 25-year-old daughter Desdemona inherited her dad's custodial hoard, the very piles I saw in her trailer. The products were why she kept being hired despite her attitude. Though banned, a lot of those old substances cleaned better than anything on the modern market.

116 Jenna Otter and Joseph L. D'Orazio, "Strychnine Toxicity," *NCBI*, August 3, 2019.

117 Scott Barnett, "Strychnine," Episode 12, *The Poisoncast*, podcast audio, April 30, 2017.

118 Kavita M. Babu, "Strychnine Poisoning," *UpToDate*, August 28, 2018.

119 Amber Henry and Matthew Krasowski, "Final Diagnosis—Strychnine Toxicity," *University of Pittsburgh Department of Pathology*, 2007.

When Amber pulled away from Kit's cold kiss in the BOH on June 1, her focus was Nutting's office. It should have been the open janitor's closet. Crime-scene photos show that Kit didn't even hide it. Perched atop Dez's cart was a rusty old can of Kwik-Kil No. 7. Evidence testing would find traces of it in the men's room stall, where Kit ground the strychnine into powder while wearing kitchen gloves and an apron pulled over his nose. Camera 3 footage shows Kit dumping the poison into the Chillee Shake Machine at 6:36 p.m., just after Burger City closed its doors to customers but before Cheri, Javi, and Zane were the night's first guests to arrive.

The average fatal dose of strychnine is 60 to 120 mg, often no more than a single grain. Toxicology reports released in the days following the Burger City Tragedy estimate the victims' average ingestion at four times that amount. Kit had read that strychnine tasted bitter. He figured you might taste it in a burger, but not in a sweet, creamy shake you couldn't help but gobble down real quick.

Kit misses the moment when bodies start to drop. He's hovering over Clem, gauging whether the guy needs another kick. By the time he decides no, contractions are throttling the poisoned six. Five chairs have been knocked over. Despite her petite size, Yesenia's torquing has overturned T6, pinning Dion. Quin's spams have scooted him way beneath B1. Vomit isn't considered a reliable symptom of strychnine poisoning, but it spews from between Javi's lockjawed teeth. Foamy blood sprays from the others. It comes from their tongues, some nearly bitten off.

Those who aren't poisoned can do nothing. They try to hold still the corkscrewing bodies only to be spattered with blood or puke and bucked away. Kit views the scene with what Amy Mold will later testify looks like relief. One wonders if Kit found the use of rat poison poetic, seeing how Nutting initially blamed rodents for the Lil' Beefy Anomaly. Kit must feel pride, at least. He has become, after all, a latter-day Aldo Hucklebridge. He fatted these cattle before their slaughter.

Tamra, whose Chillee spill saved three lives, doesn't participate in the futile attempts to assist the dying. We don't know what possesses her, but given her March 11 religious redesign, it's reasonable to suppose she's taken by a godly fervor. Her Evangelical beliefs and physical strength have always made her a woman of action.

The cellar! Clem had cried.

One of the many startling things Camera 3 captures on June 1 is Tamra hurdling the register counter at 8:53 p.m. It's the only path to the

BOH that doesn't require passing the knife-wielding Kit. Tamra doesn't quite clear it; her left foot leaves a sneaker print stamped in blood. She slams her shoulder into the seventy-pound BC Deluxe Select Brew coffee maker and rattles across the Chillee Shake Machine.

Kit pivots toward Tamra and unsheathes the Ginsu. It's 8:54. He's just a few yards away and springy with ice energy; Tamra is curled inward, recovering from the harsh impact. Kit will be plunging the knife into her body in two seconds tops.

From Camera 2, a surprise. Kit swings away from Tamra to address a different person, one who isn't trying to evade, but rather walking straight up to him. It is Cheri Orritt, and her final face-off with Kit Bryant is captured by all three FOH security cameras and witnessed, in frantic patches, by Amy Mold, Clem Dumay, Dion Skerry, and Bob Nutting. All of their accounts align.

The similarity of this showdown to the one with Scotty Flossen is staggering. You may recall it. At Second 14, Flossen was a psychotic killer. Cheri rendered herself blind and vulnerable by taking off her glasses, and by Second 18, Flossen was a little boy who only wanted Cheri to make all the bad things go away.

Cheri tries it again. She removes her tinted glasses and approaches the menacing young man. This time, there is no Javi to steamroll him. Behind the counter, Tamra doesn't let Cheri's courage go to waste; she staggers into the kitchen and vanishes from view. Cheri keeps going, cutting her ten-foot distance from Kit to five, to two, to nothing.

She stands defenseless before him. She wears jeans and a faded Iowa State Cyclones T-shirt. Her glasses dangle from a hand. She opens her arms. Witnesses swear Kit's livid expression melts like ice-cream, like it's his mother, Melinda, returning from her fourteen-year Alaskan exile. If only Nutting's security-cams weren't so crappy, one might feel that thing felt at performances, speeches, sports victories, graduations, college departures, births, reunions, hospitals, deaths: the reckless passage of hope and forgiveness between mother and child, both parties obliterated in absolution.

Endless smaller tragedies exist inside the Burger City Tragedy. One of them is that Kit can't bring himself to believe what Cheri said forty-eight minutes earlier, about him being golden inside, how she's proud of him no matter what. Counter-evidence is all around. Look at what he's done. He's too far into the meat grinder now. It's a harrowing prospect, but there is no path now but through.

Kit tilts forward. Cheri closes her eyes.

In a better world, he kisses her forehead and she calls him kid.

Autopsy reports will indicate that every one of the Ginsu's nine-and-a-half inches are buried into Cheri Orritt's upper left back, impaling the left ventricle and great cardiac vein of her heart and splitting open the anterior margin of her left lung. If she'd been skinny, it's possible the blade might have exited her chest and entered Kit's heart too—maybe that's what he was hoping. But Cheri is a thick woman. The tip of the blade ends in the superficial fascia of her left breast.

Cheri Orritt might have stickered the words *KILL ME NOW* on her Burger City plaque, but she didn't mean it. Her death comes not from the gradual havoc of cigarettes, booze, and cholesterol. It is instant. She slumps and Kit has to hold her with both arms to keep her from falling. Camera 2 shows us the long, tender process of Kit lowering the body of his substitute mother to the floor. He brushes her frizzy red hair from her face. He carefully folds her glasses beside her.

Kit never moves from the lobby. He remains hunched beside Cheri from 9:01 to 9:22, only leaving her side to grab handfuls of napkins to sop up her spreading blood. Kit seems determined not to let it escape. He might have spilled animal guts in this place, his own blood, and some of Clem's, but whatever he believes he's feeding inside Burger City, he doesn't want it to have a single drop of Cheri Orritt.

In the twenty-one minutes before police arrive, three things happen.

Dion Skerry untangles himself from T6 shortly after Quin, Mickey, Javi, Yesenia, and Zane begin convulsing. He doesn't have the mettle, like Tamra and Cheri, to go in Kit's direction, but that's not why he heads the other way. Meat Grief has reached its sickening climax. Swampy, sticky, moist tubes of meat fill the restaurant, floor to ceiling, squirting and hissing like billions of red snakes, pushing inside his mouth, nose, ears, urethra, anus. He's choking, he's filling, he's got to get out, but can't see anything but meat. He lurches, directionless, until he hits the Grand Room's southwest corner. He bashes a window with a chair until it breaks. He clambers through, horking up meat that isn't there, and hobbles into the night, passing out on Muscatine Road near the Cedar River.

Bob Nutting backs away from the people jerking and gasping on the floor. He looks placid on Camera 4, but in truth has been numbed by the cataclysmic turn so quickly after he'd made a life-redefining speech. The backs of his muddy knees strike the edge of B9, the Geezers' booth, and he drops onto the bench. Almost casually, he removes his phone from his pocket, dials 911, and quietly explains that people are dying at the Exit 269 Burger City off I-80. Nutting looks like he did in the police photograph taken after Ash Muckells's death, when he sat in the same booth while Detective Bank and Sheriff Weltch dealt with a different bloody wreckage.

Of everyone, Amy Mold tries hardest to administer to the dying. She has an aunt who's had epileptic seizures all her life, and she uses what she's learned, even though these poisoned paroxysms have nothing in common. She tries to turn all five sufferers to their sides, but her bandaged hand makes it hard. Plus, they spring back, punching and kicking with rigid limbs. She clears the area of dangers, the next best thing, tossing chairs and tables like a lumberjack. She attempts to loosen the tie around Mickey's crimson, bulging neck only for one of his hands to snag her hair and pull.

Eventually Amy backs away. She can no longer take being intimate with every jolt, heave, and quiver of her coworkers' deaths. She finds herself in the lobby. Kit is cradling Cheri, rocking her dead body. Clem is slumped against a wall, bleeding but breathing. Amy looks behind the counter, sees the coffee maker askew from Tamra's collision. Maybe Tamra needs help. Or maybe Amy just needs to keep moving. Either way, she goes behind a counter forever finished with commerce and through the kitchen that will only ever smell of cinder.

At 9:08, Amy turns into the BOH hall and sees the cellar door wide open. Silently she passes dry goods storage, the walk-in freezer, the walk-in fridge. She rises to her toes at the top of the cellar stairs, peering into the unfathomable dark. Amy feels on her skin an oily layer of violence, sex, glutted food. What's left of her new Christianity tears free like the cheap pages of *The Trucker's New Testament Bible*. This cellar hell proves there is no God, or that He is a coward. He's never stepped foot on *these* stairs.

Amy detects the same repugnant odor Amber noticed fifty-three minutes earlier. Nutting's office door is ajar. She ignores the cellar. She ignores the open break room. She ignores the open closet and the can of Kwik-Kil No. 7. She approaches the office. The stench is as thick as syrup, rancid in the nostrils, feculent in the throat. She gives the door a little push. It yowls its way open.

Amy Mold stares into the office.

She stares as she hears police sirens close in, cruiser doors slam, batons breaking glass. It's only when two police officers enter at 9:22 p.m., shouting for the young man in the pool of blood to drop the woman's body and put his hands behind his head, does Amy's paralysis break. She stares into what used to be Bob Nutting's office, opens her mouth, and starts screaming.

JULY-DECEMBER 2017

THE TRAPPED WOMAN

It takes an average of one to two hours to die from strychnine.[120] By 9:30 p.m., when the first ambulance arrived at Burger City, Quin, Mickey, Yesenia, Zane, and Javi had been poisoned for forty minutes. Iowa City's Mercy Hospital was twenty-seven miles away. They had a chance.

A series of challenges reduced those chances to almost nil. Though he'd had enough sense to call 911, Bob Nutting couldn't give the operator a casualty count or even say if there was an active shooter. When repeatedly asked to look, he replied, "Oh, I'd rather not," "I would just like to sit here," and "I'm doing fine in B9," the last of which rhymed and made him snort. Not expecting six people dead or dying, ambulances came in echelons, with poor Clem having to wait until 9:52 p.m.

The scene was mystifying. There had been two obvious knife attacks. There had also been obvious poisoning. Having no idea of what kind of poison, gastric pumping was used to empty victims' stomachs of Beefyburgers and Chillees. But it was too late. Strychnine was in their blood. It's likely some of the Burger City staff died en route to Mercy, though all deaths were officially declared by on-site hospital staff. The TOD (Time of Death) record is as follows:

> Quindlen Arthur: June 1, 2017, 10:41 p.m.
> Yesenia Ruiz: June 1, 2017, 10:45 p.m.
> Mickey McCormick: June 1, 2017, 11:08 p.m.
> Zane Shakespeare: June 1, 2017, 11:31 p.m.
> Javier Villareal: June 2, 2017, 2:47 a.m.

Cheri Orritt wasn't taken to Mercy. Her body was already cold. She was photographed, prodded, sampled, covered with a sheet, zipped into a bag. Her ETD (Estimated Time of Death) of 9:30 p.m. stood until security cameras solidified the actual TOD as thirty minutes earlier.

Clem's emergency surgery began at 10:40 p.m. His arms were scored with what might be animal bites and he was given tests for rabies,

120   "Strychnine Poisoning," *Wikipedia*, 2020.

toxoplasmosis, and tularemia. He was in better shape than his gore-slicked body suggested. He'd lost a quarter of his blood, but it had clotted. The real problem was the severed axillary nerve. Clem was in agony until paramedics shot him with fentanyl. Surgeons had limited options. They cleaned the wound, applied twelve stitches, and kept the kid on an IV for three days. He was discharged on June 9, with months of physical rehabilitation to follow. He didn't finish it. On December 31, 2017, Clemens Dumay left Iowa, abandoning the uncaring Greta and luckless Lysander, driving east along I-80 until he stopped for gas near Hooppole, Illinois, and decided he'd gone far enough.

The arrival of authorities to Burger City mirrored that of the Ash Muckells killing. This time, the first responders were Officers Clinton Trotter and Lesley Pool of the Cedar County Sheriff's Office. As soon as Trotter had Kit Bryant in cuffs, he called for backup, which arrived eight minutes later. At 10:10 p.m., Detective C.L. Bank arrived at the familiar scene. At 10:20, so did Sheriff Hutton Weltch.

Kit was cuffed, put in the back of a cruiser, and read Miranda rights before Detective Bank asked him if he stabbed Cheri Orritt and Clemens Dumay. "Yes," Kit replied. Asked if he poisoned the others, Kit again replied, "Yes." Kit's replies remained brief, honest, and helpful, except to questions of motive, to which he was silent and ruminative, gazing back at Burger City in a way Bank characterized to me as "sadly."

Back inside, while police tape was unspooled to safeguard bodily fluids, the two on-site survivors, Bob Nutting and Amy Mold, were escorted to the south side of the building, where they could be questioned away from Kit Bryant. Amy was debilitated by full-body tremors, yet came through like a champ, providing an invaluable list of everyone who'd been at the party, including the MIA Amber Smyrna, Dion Skerry, and Tamra Longmoor.

Bob Nutting, meanwhile, was close to getting arrested. He was probably in shock, but Detective Bank was in no mood to care. Ash Muckells had been killed here only nine months ago. What kind of nuthouse was this asshole running? Bank seethed with questions, not just about what had happened to Nutting's staff, but what in the living hell had gone on inside Nutting's office.

While Officer Trotter had been calling in backup at 9:23, Officer Pool had followed Amy Mold's screams. Pistol out, she leapt over a puddle of Clem's blood, navigated the bloody kitchen with its block of Ginsu knives—one missing—and threw open the doors of dry goods storage.

Finally, she found Amy at the precipice of Nutting's office. Pool smelled the foul odor but prioritized it for later. She shouted for Amy to turn around. Amy, screaming herself hoarse, didn't hear. Pool holstered her gun and pounced, pinning Amy's arms to her sides.

Over Amy's shoulder, Officer Pool saw the office.

Before midnight, local EMTs, 911 fire responders, and law enforcement were joined by a crime-scene leader from Iowa City, a police photographer from Tipton, a trauma specialist from Davenport, and a battalion of area evidence recorders and recovery specialists. It was a long night, and before dawn, every official on the scene had found an excuse to peek into Bob Nutting's office. What they'd heard had to be seen to be believed.

Most of the office was gone. That's the simplest way to put it. Wall-attached shelves remained in place, and the office's major objects (desk, desk chair, coat rack, standing lamp, computer, printer) were also present, though shoved along a rind of flooring that traced the room's perimeter. The rest of the floor had been destroyed. What used to be a fast-food manager's office floor was now a giant hole.

Yes, Nutting had spent two months in that office, and yes, he'd made a lot of noise. Still the amount of damage was incomprehensible. When Nutting had arrived in 2006, he'd classed up the break room and office with faux-cherrywood synthetic laminate flooring. In 2017, with indescribable patience, he'd used a pizza cutter and paring knife to peel that flooring like apple skin. Beneath was a blue foam underlayment that he tore apart with his hands; puffs of it were all over, blue snow. The next layer down, the plywood subfloor, really needed a circular saw, but Nutting made do with a hammer, bashing it to splinters. Freed from this subfloor, the lowest lumber joists were easy to wrench off and toss away.

Beneath the joists? Dirt. Soil. Mud. Clay.

Using a shovel from the janitorial closet, Bob Nutting had dug. And dug. And dug. The hole he'd made was ten feet at its deepest. The earth he'd chucked against the office's western wall sloped all the way to the ceiling.

The hole was a thing of primal force, nature's mouth trying to swallow ugly interstates, gnarly off-ramps, cheaply built restaurants with garish signage. The contours of Nutting's digging patterns exact a vortical pull, making the hole the raw embodiment of the emotional and psychological whirlpools that had taken so many lives.[121]

---

121 This isn't just flowery prose. Posting on his Facebook page on June 7, 2017, Deputy Donte Hickmott wrote, "Every cop who stared down that hole got dizzy and that's FOR REAL."

One can only stare into a pit for so long. Eventually eyes strayed to the items placed along the fringe of floor. As difficult as it was to picture pencil-pusher Bob Nutting burrowing into the earth night after night, it was equally difficult to imagine his life on the literal edge, resting and eating and sleeping on the tiniest patches of floor. Repulsive details now made it clear how he'd managed not to leave the office during operating hours.

Burger City cups lined the crust of floor. Chik-a-Chunkz poked from the top of one; from another, Spuddy Buddies; three others had straws, evidence of beverages. It was the *other* cups, stacked along the southern wall in a grocery-store pyramid, that made Officer Pool, and everyone after her, gag. Yellow and brown colors bled through the thin, waxy cups. Along with Nutting's sweat and whatever sepulchral stinks he'd plumbed from the muddy depths, this was the source of the BOH stench.

The cups were filled with two months of Nutting's piss and shit.

Detective Bank grilled Nutting about the hole. So would FBI investigators, prosecutors, reporters, filmmakers, and, eventually, me. His explanations are consistent. The Lil' Beefy Anomaly might have been an underground tremor. The Coldest Cold Spot might have been a coolant pipe on the fritz. The Men's Room Bully might have been a heating system element firing bursts of air. The strobing lights might have been faulty electrics. Since no one could find ground-level answers, he'd gone lower to find and flush the insulting channels.

It doesn't take Freud to deduce what Nutting was really doing. He *was* Burger City. The true gray matter he dug into wasn't dirt or clay, it was Bob Nutting. His family was dissolving, his job imploding. He had to dig himself out somehow.

From a cut Dion Skerry suffered on broken glass, a sheriff's deputy was able to trail him to Muscatine Road. He was found at 11:11 p.m., sitting on gravel, yawning and befuddled. A different deputy located Amber Smyrna at 11:54. Her car was still in the Burger City lot, which indicated she'd taken off on foot. Moving in the direction of her Iowa City home, Amber had hoofed it ten miles down I-80, where she'd wandered into the BP station off Exit 259. Inside, she didn't request help. She bought a sixteen-ounce bottle of Dasani water. She ripped out her nostril stud roughly enough to draw blood. Then she upended the bottle, guzzling it in one go. It doused her face, thinning the nose-blood as it dribbled from her chin.[122]

Both Dion and Amber were taken to Mercy Hospital out of an excess of caution. Amber received cursory treatment (antiseptic cleaning and oral painkillers) for roughly fifty small wounds spread over her arms, legs, and torso, what looked like bites from fine, narrow jaws. One doctor, trying to lighten the mood, said it looked like she'd been roughed up by a chihuahua.

Had Dez Mozley known this, she would have gladly flashed Amber her own Biting Room souvenirs. Dez was the only Burger City employee not present on June 1, but that didn't mean she was in the clear. It had been her can of Kwik-Kil No. 7 that had been used to kill five people. For about a week in late June 2017, the public shifted its rage from Nutting to Dez, but it didn't last. Legal experts weighed in that it wasn't illegal to own expired product, and given Dez's ignorance of the dangers, any case against her had loose footing.

As the hour hand crossed into the early hours of June 2, Tamra Longmoor remained the only missing person. Amy Mold was adamant that Tamra had gone into the cellar.

Officers had already been down there. There was blood, evidence of a struggle, but no bodies. Then Amy recalled the bloody shoe print Tamra had left on the counter beside Till 2. Specialists identified it as a Size 7 Salomon Speedcross Pro sneaker, and by midday on June 2, print analysts found dozens of Speedcross Pro prints along a five-foot stretch of the cellar's northeast corner. They took photos. I've seen them. As with so many other Burger City details, they seem designed to test skeptics.

It looks like Tamra had tried to fight her way out of the corner.

Initial on-site investigations wrapped on Saturday, June 3. The June 4 RCHS commencement ceremony was a stunned, somber event mourning the deaths of sophomore Yesenia Ruiz and valedictorian Quin Arthur. Three other graduating seniors—Amber Smyrna, Amy Mold, and Clemens Dumay—were recuperating and did not attend.

June 5 brought the first observance of the Trapped Woman, who Burger City Poltergeist believers insist is Tamra Longmoor. Today, three years after the restaurant burned, dozens per year claim to hear the high-

---

122 This was told to me by Lawrence Welly, 51, who worked the BP register that night. His own mini-ghost story is that the puddle of bloody water left by Amber, right in front of the magazine rack, reappears every now and then.

pitched, terrified moan; Trip Advisor and Yelp even offer tips on the best time of day to hear it.[123] The first report surfaced on Twitter from a classmate who visited the site to contribute a homemade wreath to a growing memorial.

Dropped off flowers to burger city, the student posted, *and there was a woman SCREAMING. Can someone go there and confirm???*

Kit was put into lockup at the Cedar County Sheriff's Office. Within forty-eight hours, he appeared before Judge Faisal Mousley. Kit's court-appointed lawyer, Lewis Kaul, made a few listless gestures, after which Kit was denied bond and processed into the Tipton Police jail. There he cooled for the rest of June, as law enforcement, prosecutors, and defenders conducted interviews with witnesses. On July 10, a grand jury hearing brought forward an indictment on six counts of murder. On July 24, Kaul issued Kit's NGBRI (Not Guilt by Reason of Insanity) plea, which launched a four-week exchange-of-information period. All parties reconvened on August 21 for Kit's competency hearing. Judge Mousley ruled in favor of the defense, and on September 1 Kit was transported to the Iowa Medical and Classification Center, a way station on his journey to Chernow.

Cameras caught the handcuffed Kit being led into the Decorah, Iowa, facility. He's pointing at a newspaper with his name spelled out in large font. He's beaming.

Kit was otherwise hidden from the public eye. This left Bob Nutting to be Iowa's whipping boy. He was clueless when it came to the press. He accepted any phone call. He approached when reporters beckoned. He answered any question, no matter how leading. He was a caricature of the rural rube and for that sin his home state hated him.

Just because Nutting bore the brunt of enmity didn't mean other survivors were thriving. The initial blaze of sympathy guttered fast. Amber, Clem, Amy, and Dion were labeled as imbeciles incapable of stepping out of the way of a slow-moving train. As details about the Iowa 80 gatherings and Game of Pricks began to leak in late August, the narrative snowballed until all four teens were generally considered culpable in the deaths, which, to make it worse, they tried to blame on the "poltergeist" they'd invented nine months earlier.

I began this book paying homage to Rachel Heinzman's "Disintegration: Ethos and Intolerance at Burger City." Let's return to it now. While

---

123 In short, dawn and dusk—the classic limnal times.

Heinzman allows space for unexplainable events, mysteries of the unknown, and all that jazz, ultimately she refuses to back down from logic. Her conclusion is that the root of both the Burger City Poltergeist and the Burger City Tragedy was "collective obsessional behavior"—aka, good old-fashioned mass hysteria.

Large-group belief in a haunted fast-food restaurant, she writes, is not so wild a concept. Consider the "dancing plagues" that caused people to boogie to their graves in the Middle Ages. The laughing epidemic that tore through Tanzania from 1962–1964. The 1967 panic among Singapore men that their penises would disappear if they ate certain kinds of pork. The 2012 case of jerking and shouting symptoms that spread among teenage girls in LeRoy, New York.

Heinzman cites Simon Wessley's groundbreaking article "Mass Hysteria: Two Syndromes?", in which the psychiatrist lays out principles for diagnosing mass hysteria, all five of which fit the Burger City bill:

> First, it is an outbreak of abnormal illness behavior that cannot be explained by physical disease. Secondly, it affects people who would not normally behave in this fashion. Thirdly, it excludes symptoms deliberately provoked in groups gathered for that purpose, as occurs in many charismatic sects. Fourthly, it excludes collective manifestations used to obtain a state of satisfaction unavailable singly, such as fads, crazes, and riots. Finally, the link between the participants must not be coincidental.[124]

Who am I to disagree with thinkers like Heinzman and Wessley? And yet, while I concur with their conclusions, I find them chilly. It is hard to have seen the grim, shriveling faces of Nutting, Amber, Amy, Clem, Dion, and Dez, and think of them as anything but haunted.

The thing Roxie Stoyle got right in her *Spectral Journeys* intro is the same thing Detective C.L. Bank got right in his conversation with me. Iowa is full of ghosts: the specters of meth and opioid deaths; the plagues of missing parents or cruel partners; the slaughter first of American Indians, second of factory-farm livestock; the dead dreams of rural decay. We know these tragedies affect individuals. But they also seep into the groundwater from which all neighbors drink. These neighbors may constitute an entire

---

124 Simon Wessley, "Mass Hysteria: Two Syndromes?", *Psychological Medicine* 17 (March 1987): 109–20.

state. Or they may make up the staff of a declining, off-ramp, off-brand, fast-food dive.

For those reading this who have mourned the Burger City dead, I urge you to think also of the Burger City living, those alleged hoaxers, those supposedly feeble-minded hysterics. They are dying too, right in front of us.

The job of ascribing final words to these survivors is too eulogic a task for me to succeed. I've spent hours with them, not days, not years. Revisiting my transcripts, however, I find some of my parting moments indicative of what each survivor has suffered and lost, as well as the direction in which their weakened bodies now point.

Bob Nutting has lost too much weight to drink like this. He stumbles after me to his front door. It leads into a carpeted stairwell rubbed nude in the center of each stair. I turn to nod farewell, the pandemic version of a handshake. Nutting has picked up Crooked Hillary. He kisses the dog's jowl and whispers reassurances regarding her status as a good girl. He's looking into her big brown eyes when he finally addresses me.

"Thanks for drinking beers with me. I didn't enjoy it. But thanks."

I apologize but he talks over it.

"Did anyone else from the restaurant go to the funerals? Nope. Just me, out there in my Men's Warehouse getup, paying respects so folks could shit all over me. But I knew those people. I spent more time with some of them than anyone else in their lives. Mickey McCormick was buried too far away for me to go, but I sent a card. You know what I wrote? Something that proves how good I knew him: *He would have hated to die in khakis.*"

I thank him for his time. Again, he's not listening.

"They weren't able to up and quit. Financially, I mean. That's what makes me throw up at three in the morning. You ever see Cheri's house? Where Clem lived? You have any idea the itty bitty size of Darcy's paycheck? They needed that shit job to stay alive. *I* needed that shit job to stay alive. The world didn't give us any choice."

I can't tell if those are Nutting's tears or moisture he picked up from Hillary.

"That's what I want you to write. Make people understand we didn't have a choice. We were trapped in a machine. You know what that machine made? Not burgers. Money. No one cared about us. Not then, not now. I hope your book does good and all that. But every one of us survivors is going to die alone."

He buries his face into Hillary's neck. His voice is muffled.

"You won't leave me, will you, Hill? You'll stay with me forever, won't you?"

Hillary coughs, and through her flab I see her ribcage expand, the tendony strain of abdominal muscles. For a second, I'm not seeing a beagle. I'm seeing cows and pigs seize up before slaughter. I'm seeing the last gasps of Darcy and Maxine. I'm seeing the final, bone-crushing convulsions of those Kit poisoned. The infections of hardship and heartbreak can be as deadly as strychnine, and there's no cure for them either.

Amy Mold walks away from me in the parking lot of OB Nelson Park. It's a beautiful dusk, sprigs of dandelion fluff soaked in sunshine, the red horizon sealing shut as children race across green grass toward summer break. Amy leans on her car door and shifts her sunglasses to the top of her head. None of nature's colors touch her. Even the colors of her scarred hand feel flat.

"I keep thinking of stuff to tell you. The ice bin—once there was something moving in the ice bin. There were ants in the soda. In March, maybe? Maybe in April? So many ants that when you poured a Diet Dr. Pepper, it was like an ant-slushee. Oh, and there was goo. Javi said it was meat gone bad, but Quin said it was ectoplasm. If I think of more stuff, you want me to call you?"

I nod vaguely, but I hope she doesn't call. Amy's voice has a hollow quality, as if these scraps of memory are mined from a pit deeper than Nutting's office. If I'm not careful, I'll fall in after her. She gives a small nod, as if suspecting what I'm thinking. Amy Mold was always Burger City's smartest.

"Sorry about the tea. The dosha stuff. It's my magic feather. Just my latest version of *The Trucker's New Testament*. It's not going to help. Nothing's going to help. While you stand by your car there? I can feel it creep back. It's like a cloud moving over the sun. I know, it sounds dumber than the tea."

I wait. The insects buzz. I'm not going to be the first to leave.

Amy Mold has been through goodbye routines before. She knocks the top of her car with her fist and smiles like it's no big deal. She salutes with her reed-thin arm and slides behind the wheel. It's difficult with the insects, and the yelling children, and the lawnmowers crawling over the buried pool, but right before she shuts the door, I hear her say a word to the shadows inside her car, which do resemble the cloud cover she predicted. It's the opposite of the breezy goodbye she just gave me, the weary voice of a 20-year-old who has learned when it's time to surrender.

"Hello."

Cedar View Village Estates dwellers halt their conversations when I exit Dez's trailer. There's a decent chance I'm a cop. Squinting eyes follow me to my rental car. I'm right beside it, beeping the lock, when I hear the rusty spring of Dez's screen door.

"Angel Boy! You come back soon, you hear me?"

With her head held horizontally, her tangled black hair drapes down, giving me a clear view of her neck. She might have outwitted warlocks with carved sigils and dispelled Iowa covens with bottles of urine, but her neck is a scrawny tube. I don't know how to respond. People are listening.

"Next month if you want to stay safe. Three months tops. We got to get more magic inside you. Because they're calling you out, Angel Boy. I can hear *their* words behind *your* words. You don't got the know-how to resist. You come back soon, we'll fix you up."

More magic inside you. What kind of magic has she given me? For a few seconds, I sweat it, thinking of her hill of toxic supplies, but I neither ate nor drank anything inside her home. The trailer park is uncomfortable, all searing-hot metal and stinking trash. I give Dez a wave, open the car door, and begin to lower myself into the seat.

"Angel Boy!"

Reluctantly, I pull myself halfway back up, braced for more lunacy.

"Be brave," she says.

Amber blocks her door with her bony, scratched-up body. It's like gravity has tipped and she's fallen hard. Her limbs are splayed and flattened, and her face is lecherous with want, the look of someone who wants one more shot of the hard stuff.

"Are you going to tell him about me?"

I ask her who she means. Her smile pulls lesioned lips.

"You know who. Kit, if you talk to Kit. Just don't tell him how I'm living, okay? I know I said you could take pictures but could you maybe not show him? I'll take care of my skin better. I'll get some shampoo. If you talk to him, tell him I'm doing fine. I'm doing *great*. And I'm—well, don't *tell* him that I'm single. But if he asks, I'm not with anyone."

To my knowledge, Amber has never used meth. Kit was her drug, a bulb of hope swelling from the point of the world's needle, and in the gloomiest of times, like right now, he still is. I have the urge to peel Amber from the door and hold her until she feels her own body again, not his. Maybe if there wasn't a global pandemic, I would.

Amber slides her body off the door and hangs her head. I repeat a farewell, undo the locks, and step onto the covered porch of the external staircase. Amber pleads in a soft tone. I hear it. I have heard it repeatedly since. I have replayed the audio, cleaned it up, toyed with filters, asked others what they think she said. The consensus is total.

"Kill him."

I stare at Amber Smyrna in disbelief. Her face is obscured behind a greasy flop of hair. I ask her to repeat herself, and when she doesn't react, I ask again. She rotates her head half an inch. I see a sparkle of eye, a glisten of lip.

"*Tell* him, I said."

The last words that pass between Kit and I are already told: *Tapes are behind the stone.* Quiet, lumbering Nuncio leads me through sets of D-wing doors, past the *HIGH ELOPEMENT RISK* sign, down the bare hallway to the elevator. Nuncio punches the down button. From here, I'm on my own: return my badge holder to check-in and get out of town.

Yesterday, Nuncio took off after hitting the button. Today, though, he sticks around and watches me with his indecipherable eyes. I check the elevator readout. Seems to be stuck on the floor below. I glance at Nuncio. He's still staring. I'm out of Chernow for good; there's no more use playing nice. I turn toward him and shrug expectantly.

"Don't you wonder how he got that way?" Nuncio asks.

This is his big reveal? I explain to him, in so many words, that how Kit Bryant "got that way" is the whole point of the project. The elevator dings. The doors purr open.

"No," Nuncio says. "How he got fat."

I'm alone in the elevator. The doors begin to close. I step forward, grab both both doors and pull them back. They retract, offended, as a buzzer whines. I look at Nuncio and state the obvious: it's the meds. Nuncio blinks heavily with a trace of a smile, as if he thinks I'm stupid but likes me anyway.

"We can't figure out how he does it. Trades for them in the caf? Steals them from the kitchen? All we know is he gets them, and eats, and eats."

Eats what, I ask, though really I ought to have guessed.

"Hamburgers." Nuncio shrugs. "Says he likes the taste in his mouth."

Dark tourists have flocked to the ruins of Burger City #8 every anniversary day since 2018. The day before I interview Amy Mold in Fairfield, I pull off at Exit 269, park along Rolf Tonks Road, and walk up to the razed site at 8:00 p.m., just before it gets dark, supposedly your best shot at hearing the Trapped Woman.

There are twenty-two people here. In the middle of nowhere, Iowa, that counts as a significant event. Half of the license plates are local, but half are not. I note plates from Ohio, Virginia, Oregon, and Louisiana. Most people are alone or in pairs, but they lightly intermingle. All have come for the same purpose, after all. Not to honor the dead, but to watch night descend over a cursed space and see if they can feel what others have felt at Gettysburg, the Lizzie Borden Bed and Breakfast, the Winchester Mystery House, and so on.

It is June 1, 2020, and 372,657 people have died from Covid-19.[125]

There has to be meaning, somewhere. Hope, somewhere.

Hanford Pendergast probably watches us through binoculars, damning these ghouls for their fetishization of other people's pain. I concur until I mingle amid the gatherers, engage in a few conversations, and turn down an ice-cream sandwich from a cooler. No one's blasting heavy-metal or taking selfies with burgers. There is light chatter and jokes, but you find that even at funerals.

An old-fashioned lemonade stand has been set up a few yards north of where Burger City's exit sign once stood. I'm thirsty, and no one sampling the wares is complaining. A sister and brother, roughly twelve and ten, operate the pop-up storefront. The stand is sturdy, leveled, painted plywood, with *LEMONADE 10¢* across the top in faux-naive hand.

I take a cup and give a dollar, keep the change, which disappoints the boy eager to show off subtraction skills. I rejoin the dark tourists standing along the edge of the ashy soil, right where the Puppy Pen used to be. Before putting the paper cup to my lips, I think of the last beverages doled out here and the people who drank it. There had been an empty chair between Javi and Tamra. I picture myself settling in. Nutting makes his speech. We all toast our cups and drink.

125 Sydney Jennings, "COVID-19 Update: Global Cases and Recoveries as of June 1, 2020," *Patient Care*, May 31, 2020.

When night falls, it falls fast. Green things go navy, then mulberry, then chocolate. Darkness swallows I-80, which fights back with orange lights on tall poles, like longship oars churning black seas. The tourists fall quiet. They put arms over shoulders, around waists. We're listening for the Trapped Woman. But we're also listening to one another, the anxious rise of our inhales against our face masks, our sighs of relief. We anticipate the lights that await us from our dashboards, hotels, and homes, and the sun that will soon emerge, all the brighter for having seen how darker days can end.

The Trapped Woman does not show herself. It gets a little chilly. The first couple heads off, shoes scrunching through dirt, and they're thoughtful when they pull from the lot, keeping their headlights off until they face the interstate. Half the crowd is gone by the time I depart. I put my empty cup in my cup holder, do my seatbelt, check behind me, and give the site one last glance.

In the dark, I can't see the ruins. I can only see people. Standing close as a family. Six of them. Maybe seven, maybe eight, maybe nine, maybe ten.

AUGUST 2021

A NEW PUPPET

Forgive me.

I beg this of you for reasons that I will make clear quickly. The least pressing reason, but one that still matters to me, is the hurried nature of this addendum: perfunctory prose, the absence of photos, the lack of footnotes. You'll have to trust me on the facts. Please trust me. I have been granted twenty-four hours to write this chapter if I wish it to be included in the published book. I would prefer this book not to be published at all. But three weeks of phone calls between legal teams have made it clear the book will not be pulled, nor will I be permitted to do major revisions.

This is because they don't believe. I understand. I used to be the same.

Our compromise permits me to paste on this final chapter, as long as I foot the bill. It is more than I can afford, but this is more important than any debt. I have even come around to agreeing that the rest of the book should remain unchanged. That way, it can stand as a testament to what a dupe I was, what a fool.

As of today, *The Ghost That Ate Us* has passed through the following steps. On February 23, 2021, I sent my finished draft to my editor, Jennifer Barnes at Raw Dog Screaming Press. On March 30, Barnes emailed me her editorial notes. I completed the first revision on April 25 and the line-edit revision on May 30. I approved the book's copyedits on June 21, and on July 12 completed notes on first-pass pages, which is when a manuscript shifts from a Word document to a something that looks like an actual book. By July 29, when I signed off on second-pass pages, all "widows" (words that break poorly at the ends of sentences) had been remarried and all photographs and captions were in place.

The book was set to be printed the week of August 30.

Four weeks before that, on August 2, 2021, I receive an email from Bob Nutting. Though I have contact info for most of my interviewees, I haven't heard from any of them since December 2020. Frankly, I'm glad. I'm impatient to get the book out of my life, out of my system. The tone I struck in the prologue wasn't entirely honest. Clemens Dumay's suicide made me loathe this project. It also made me to wonder why it took his death to make me feel that way. After all, nine other people involved in the story had already died. Ten if we count Tamra, which we might as well.

Nutting's email makes it eleven. The subject line is one I instinctively fear—*News*—and the body is simply a link to the *Tipton Conservative* website. The article is the briefest obit I have ever read:

> Desdemona Mozley, 52, of Stanwood, Iowa, passed away on July 29, 2021, at her home. Memorial details to be determined at a later date.

I am surprised by how much the death saddens me. Dez had been fearsome at her worst, off-putting at her best. But no other survivor had her fuck-you audacity, from the dramatic reveal of her scarred breasts to her alleged victories over water allergies, facial paralysis, and raccoon armies. Her trailer, the tank from which she'd taken on the world, would be repossessed, resold, or junked. New janitors across the Jonny, Iowa, area would be hired. In a few years, it will be like Dez Mozley never existed.

I send no bereavement letters. To whom would I send them? I work on other projects, each day of writing like heaving one more shovelful of dirt into the grave of *The Ghost That Ate Us*. On August 11 I receive a FedEx from Henry Holt, publisher of my most recent book. It is an unopened piece of correspondence from a reader. Physical fan mail is not unheard of, but this one makes me sit down before opening it. I know this handwriting. I've read the *IDEAS* book too many times.

Inside are four sheets of ivory-colored stationery. I'm sure the scrawled sentences will cost me my workday. That estimate, it turns out, is wildly optimistic. I will lose a lot more than that, and am still losing it, right now, typing this sentence.

> Dear Mister Kraus,
>
> I thought we were friends but I guess not!!! I might be locked away but that doesn't mean that we physcos don't get to use the <u>internet</u> which is where you are apparantly doing <u>interviews</u> about <u>our book</u> and NOT KEEPING SECRET things you know were supposed to be secret.
>
> Of course what I am talking about are the videos I told you

about <u>just between you and me</u> that you dug up and used to write our book and then GAVE TO THE FUCKING FUZZ.

And when I say dug up I mean DUG UP. Do you know what you did is illegal??? Do you know that I could tell the fucking fuzz about it in one second??? They visit me all the time now thanks to you my X-friend.

When I see you talking on the internet it makes me sick Mister Kraus. You are saying things that make me sound stupid which I am not. If I'm so stupid how did you get all the things you needed to write our stupid book??? Not <u>our</u> I should say <u>your</u> stupid book because you have BETRAYED ME.

That piece of shit your writing is going to make people feel bad about the whole thing BOO HOO HOO. No one is going to be like wow how cool was all that??? Is that your goal??? Or is your goal to make everyone feel like there better then me??????

Well I am better then you my X-friend. You still don't understand ANYTHING about ANYTHING. The internet says you talked to everyone. Wow aren't you smart!!! I'm being iroinc because <u>you</u> <u>didn't</u> <u>even</u> <u>talk</u> <u>to</u> <u>the</u> <u>most</u> <u>important</u> <u>person</u> <u>that</u> <u>started</u> <u>it</u> <u>all</u> <u>THAT'S HOW DUMB YOU ARE!!!</u>

I am very upset with you.

Kit Bryant

What looks like food grease makes the fourth page translucent. The stationery is branded, but not with Chernow's stamp. In each upper-left-hand corner is a caduceus insignia and the words *Winneshiek Medical Center.* I vaguely recall the facility from the two days I spent in Decorah interviewing Kit. Bland, beige, one-story, a couple blocks big. It's alarming to picture a criminal of Kit's notoriety housed in a facility so small.

I try to put it out of my mind. Whatever's wrong with Kit, he's in fine enough fettle to fire off this pissy missive. Kit, though, is a tick. All night I can't shake him; he's pumping me with toxic thoughts. What if he dies in that hospital and I miss the chance to add a vital postscript? What if there's something bigger I don't know? Kit underlined the penultimate sentence for a reason.

You didn't even talk to the most important person that started it all.

I wake up appalled. The little fucker is right. One major player in the Burger City affair passed right under my nose. I don't waste time. I unbox the notes I so happily boxed up months ago and find Detective C.L. Bank's direct line. He's not thrilled to hear from me again. His five-second sigh tells me he's gotten wind of my book's pre-pub publicity and is fortifying himself for one more wave of Burger City interest.

The person I ask about surprises him.

"You're back on Scotty Flossen? Don't I remember telling you there isn't crapola to say about Scotty Flossen?"

Per my March 3, 2020, transcript, Bank's exact words were, *I don't even understand why we're talking about Scotty Flossen.* Bank chews me out for a while. He doesn't want that kid having any more involvement with the Burger City sideshow. I grit through the harangue and get back on point. We might have missed something, I tell him. Scotty Flossen might have killed Ash Muckells for a reason other than the theft of some stupid switchblade.

Bank silently chews on this. I can feel when he yields to the possibility; it's like a St. Bernard rolling over. He's never wanted to believe Flossen would kill for so stupid a reason. Bank allows me to proceed with two words of warning: "All right."

I reel off everything I've got: Kit Bryant is acting like he knows why Flossen did it, and though I understand Cedar County isn't going to open a closed case on Kit's word alone, time is of the essence, partly because my book is headed to the printer, and partly because Kit's in the hospital, and who knows, it could be serious, and if Bank could give me just a few associates of Scotty Flossen, I'd share with him anything I dug up.

The St. Bernard rolls over again. Bank puts me on hold for a punishing eighteen minutes. He marks his return not with a greeting but the sharp turning of pages.

"As a detective with the Cedar County Sheriff's Office, I'm obligated to say we do not in any way condone amateur investigations." The pages stop turning. "There. I said my thing. Get a pen."

I call Bluefeather Prison's Public Information Director Gunther Overson about speaking with Scotty Flossen, but I assume my message, backed by no legal writ, will rate low alongside the usual deluge of calls. Without telling anyone, I rent a car. I'm able to zone out for three hours, all the way to the Iowa border. It's that last half hour that sickens me. This stretch of I-80 feels like a gray tongue waiting to pull me into a mouth. Vehicles are feeble platelets in dying arteries. A peeling *TRUMP 2016* billboard in a cornfield confirms this road as a wound in time, ripping back open.

Scotty Flossen had no specific home in September 2016, but Bank told me he'd spent many nights in Jonny's Jane Galveston Park. I go there. The swings creak despite there being no breeze. It takes two hours to scrounge up a human, and I'll be goddamned if it isn't Jaime of Jaime's Peaches. I read off the names on Detective Bank's list. He nods at one. Yeah, that dude used to go out with his sister's daughter.

I'm not going to print his name. No, this isn't the kind of journalism I prefer. But no one on Bank's list wanted their name public and there isn't time to sort out the legalities. Jaime says the man is at Triumph Center Ministries, a homeless shelter in Wilton. Back in the car, over I-80, past where Dion Skerry collapsed after fleeing Burger City, south down Rose Avenue, east on West 5th Street, a block off Westview Park. Twelve minutes and I'm inside.

He's there. He's actually there. He's sitting on a duct taped sofa with hands clasped. His posture doesn't change the whole time we talk. He's in some phase of getting clean where the slightest motion incites panic. It works in my favor. He doesn't dare run away. He tells me he never knew Scotty Flossen. But he knew *of* Scotty Flossen, and from what he heard, Scotty Flossen was mixed up in bad shit. My heart is battering. Bank's list of names shakes as I read them off. Three names in, the man stops me. Yeah, that's the one. Crazy bitch. Had a whole clan of crazy fucks around her.

I ask where to find her. He's sweating from the misery of not being able to move. The graveyard in Durant, he says. That was where they met. But that was years ago, and anyway, don't go looking for trouble. I go looking for trouble. A straight shot along what they call Historic U.S. 6, through all ten of Durant's blocks, ending at the cemetery on the banks of Mud Creek. It's picture-perfect, no gate, gentle hills, tall green trees, a homemade sign urging, but not shouting, *No Trespassers After Dark*. Even if it were dark, I wouldn't listen.

There's a supply shed on the south side. It's Thursday afternoon. The chances of finding the groundskeeper are slim. But I do. He's friendly until I mention the woman who used to show up here with some sort of group. His eyes razor down. He gets red in the face. They did terrible things. The kind of things you keep out of the papers. Animals. Body parts. He won't get more specific than that. I ask if he knows what happened to the woman. Damn right he does. She's buried at Plot 5 R30.

I head over there. She's dead; technically I could tell you her name. But I don't want anyone replicating my search. The second I see the grave, I know I'm on the right track, or, seen another way, the wrongest track possible. The grass on the plot is black as oil. Not dead, not burnt. Just black. The adjacent stones make it clear she was buried in a family plot. I don't think she was happy about that.

I google from my car. The woman died on April 19, 2016. She died in DeWitt (population 5,310), forty minutes northeast. I call the Clinton County Sheriff's Office in DeWitt and bluntly ask the answering deputy if she knows how this woman died. To my surprise, I receive an answer just as blunt. She was murdered. Where? In a *different* cemetery, she says: Elmwood in DeWitt. She was stabbed to death, a symbol carved onto her stomach. I ask if the symbol was a triangle with a line jutting up diagonally. The deputy clams up. Says she'll have to refer me to the sheriff. I hang up. I don't have time.

I drive north back to I-80, east to U.S. 61, off at Exit 311B into DeWitt. I'm losing the sun. I pull into a spot beside Lincoln Park in the middle of downtown and find three teens. I don't even introduce myself. I ask if there's a place where local drug addicts might congregate. One girl has the answer. Off 225th Street, after the country club, before the quarry: an abandoned mini-golf place full of benches where "the creeps" hang out. I go there, racing now, thirty-miles-per-hour over the posted twenty-five.

You want to see ghosts? Bank once asked. *Haunted houses around here are real easy to spot.*

This is one such place. It wasn't euthanized like Burger City #8. It was left to spoil. A sprawling Iowa dusk rolls like liquid over decaying mini-golf statues. A shark in attack pose has been robbed of its plastic teeth, but its glassy eyes ogle the infinite. Rusty posts have dropped a five-foot-long metal plane to the green, as if it crashed from the clouds, zero survivors.

A dinosaur with flaked green paint has dozens of beer cans crushed into its maw.

People pace like zoo animals, on and off the pirate ship, around the Aztec temple, behind the weeds fountaining from every ball cup. One of them must have known the dead woman. Her family paid to have her body buried in Durant, which likely left some of her group stranded here. I stop at a moss-coated tiki skull and call out that I'm trying to find anyone who knew her.

A man I can't see replies. "Behind the sphinx."

The sphinx of Hole 14 has been kicked in and used as a fire pit. The man sitting on the ledge beside it has the busted posture and inelastic skin of a Burger City survivor. The way he bites his cigarette and snakes a foot under the green carpet tells me he's tweaking. He shades his face with a scratched hand, but the dusk comes from the other direction. He's just ashamed.

He says he knew her, all right. He'll talk for ten bucks. I give him twenty. Instantly, tears streak from his eyes, faster than they should, as if they're missing natural coagulant. I ask him if he knew Scotty Flossen as well. He nods so hard snot falls from his nose. I hope to speak to Flossen soon, I say.

"You can't. He's in a coma. I guess a year and a half now. Heard from a lady who knows his mom. Normally I'd say pull the plug. But who knows what's waiting for him on the other side."

I'm crestfallen. I hope this guy is mistaken, but his words have the feel of truth, and days later, Gunther Overson at Bluefeather will confirm it. I sit across from the man at Hole 14. He says he knew Scotty, the woman, the junkie I talked to at Triumph Center Ministries—the whole bunch. He knew them because he was one of them. He doesn't give a shit anymore. What can they do to him that's not already done? He's dying, and plans to die right here by the sphinx.

The tall weeds quit swaying. Distant gates creak. Everyone is clearing out. Maybe they think I'm going to get them in trouble. Maybe they have heard this story before and want to avoid it. The man talks speedily, as if afraid he'll be struck down before the finish.

Let me tell you about Scotty Flossen. He was born to Liza and Stancliff Flossen of Bertram, Iowa (population 294) on June 13, 1998. He was an ordinary kid. He broke his arm falling off his bike at age 9. He won his class spelling bee at 11. He was confirmed into his local Presbyterian church at 13. He reached Life rank in Boy Scouts at 15. He graduated from RCHS alongside pal Ash Muckells at 17. At 18, he took his first hit of meth.

The tragic thing is that Scotty Flossen was ordinary. His fate wasn't unusual. It wasn't until he was 25 that his life took a strange turn. Believe it or not—I barely do—Roxie Stoyle nailed it at the start of S4 E04 of *Spectral Journeys*. You may recall it. While listing off local lore to Gaetan Goodricke, she said, *As recently as 2008, there were reports of a cemetery cult possessing people via demonic ritual.*

I know how it sounds. The disbelief you are feeling is what I felt.

Just listen, I'm begging you.

The cult, as far as I can tell, had no name. Scotty joined in 2013. There is nothing suspect in that. It's the same urge that leads the spiritually bereft to Jesus, or Scientology, or the TM programs practiced by Amy Mold. Scotty was at his lowest point in 2013. He'd been homeless for two years. He was subsisting on dumpster food. He was stealing purses from old women in broad daylight. Pocked with scabs, scratches, and needle holes, he looked, behaved, and felt like a monster.

Scotty probably saw the cult as a peer group, a means of support. Membership held at roughly eight. Their leader, the woman now beneath Plot 5 R30 in Durant Cemetery, pooled the group's money, acquired food, parceled it out. This helped Scotty. He pulled his shit together enough that he was allowed to crash at his cousin Ian's. Best of all, the woman in charge didn't scorn meth. She encouraged it, acquired it, doled it out along with the food. All she asked in return was his allegiance, his body, his blood.

In a Dark Place: The Story of a True Haunting is one of several books written, or co-written, by famed paranormal investigators Ed and Lorraine Warren. I have always considered the book to be sensationalistic trash. Now I'm not sure. In the book's introduction, page xii, the authors synopsize the backstory of the haunted house into which their subjects, the Snedeker family, have moved:

> Someone had been using the dead bodies for their own sick pleasure, and it was that person's acts of necrophilia that opened the door to possession; it was that person who made a choice—by indulging in such perverse activities— to give the forces of evil entry to that house long before the Snedekers ever moved in.

I have no evidence the Iowa cult practiced necrophilia, though the strong reactions of the Durant Cemetery caretaker suggest that it's possible. Like eons of rebellious goths before them, the cult performed rituals that made them—the forgotten, the ignored—feel important and powerful. It was probably bullshit. Their leader probably pretended to be in contact with supernatural forces, and her followers, hungry for food and drugs, just went along with it. Whatever, lady.

In 2015, something changed.

At our first meeting, Detective Bank described the flood of ice from South American cartels. This stuff was at a different level. Nick Reding's *Methland: The Death and Life of an American Small Town* quotes Dr. Sean Wells on the topic, page 229: "It'll be two decades before there are any firm findings [since] long-term effects cannot be studied in the short term." Closer to home is what Dr. Marilyn Jagodowski told me in February 2020: *The neurological damage—I don't think we've begun to appreciate it. There's loss of gray matter, shrinkage of the hippocampi. I'd know a meth addict's brain blindfolded. The surface is, like, reptilian.*

In other words, ice mutates brains in ways we don't yet appreciate. Now buckle in. What the mini-golf witness suggests to me, and what I'm suggesting to you, is that regular use of this ferociously potent psychostimulant physically altered the brains of the Iowa cemetery cult, allowing their puerile attempts at contacting a malevolent force to *actually contact a malevolent force.*

I know, I know. You think I don't type these sentences and want to go lie down in the road? But how can it be fantasy if every single element fits? Unexplained deaths litter Iowa like the trash along I-80. A few of those deaths, not enough to notice, were due to this cult. The force they'd awakened demanded to be fed. Their victims' blood drained into cemetery soil like Kit poured his own blood in the Burger City kitchen and cellar.

There is one name I will share with you—a first name. According to my mini-golf contact, one of the people killed by the cult, in early 2016, was named Bambi. Where have we heard that name before? In my hand I hold the second-pass pages of this book you're reading, which includes this passage:

> By mid-February, Darcy was calling Amber "nurse," "nice lady," or, when the delirium was worst, "Bambi." *Bambi, leave me alone,* Darcy moaned. *Bambi, please, it hurts,* Darcy sobbed. Amber felt it all. Frustration.

Humiliation. Fear. Fury. She'd never known anyone named Bambi.

Bambi might have been the last person killed at the cult leader's demand. But it was not the last person the cult killed. That happened at 8:46 a.m. on September 4, 2016, when Scotty Flossen murdered Ash Muckells at Burger City #8. The Crime, as Bob Nutting called it, was not one of passion. If Scotty had to kill to assuage the force, why not choose a victim who'd been pissing him off since graduation? He stabbed. Blood flowed. No cemetery lawn to soak into this time. Just the cardboard base of a fast-food mascot.

Now remember, the two days during which there is no record of Kit Bryant's activities: May 14–15, 2017. Previously I hypothesized this as time he spent buying a shard of ice. I was right but there was more. When I finally speak to Gunther Overson at Bluefeather, I ask him about any visitors Scotty Flossen had in summer 2017. It's easy because he only had one, on May 14.

Kit Bryant.

Overson is confused when I ask about Scotty's weight, but then lowers his voice like he's been dying to talk about it—Mr. Flossen's impossible weight gain. It has perplexed prison staff; all inmates receive the same portions. Scotty entered Bluefeather at an addict's lithe 142 pounds. When Kit visited eight months later, Scotty was twice the size. Overson lowers his voice further to divulge that Scotty doubled his size *again* before slipping into a coma in January 2020.

"He's sure dropping pounds fast now, though," Overson says.

Again, page xii, *In a Dark Place*: "Weakened and vulnerable, confused and terrified, the victim inevitably reaches a turning point and surrenders voluntarily to the forces of darkness."

Four years before I thought of doing the same, skinny Kit asked Scotty about the blood spilled at Burger City and the very real thing that had risen from it. Scotty, probably delighted to meet a new disciple, told Kit what he needed to know. There were specific people, a particular kind of meth, certain ceremonies. Five days later, Kit was high on ice, spilling a cooler of animal guts across Burger City's floor, and well on his way to spilling other blood, even fresher.

On August 13, 2021, I speed north up I-80 for two-and-half-hours, hoping a highway trooper will collar me before I get to Decorah. No such luck. I reach Winneshiek Medical Center by 10:00 a.m. and state my request to the front desk. This sets off a chain of phone calls because Kit Bryant is, after all, a prisoner. Ultimately, though, it is judged he poses no physical threat given his condition, and he is, after all, an adult capable of choosing who he allows to visit. And one final time, the one he has chosen is me.

I start recording. I don't give a fuck if it's legal.

At 10:44 a.m., I nod at the officer sitting outside the room and enter.

The average hospital bed is three feet wide. This bed is at least five feet wide, special-ordered to contain Kit Bryant. He entered Chernow at 131 pounds; by the time of our interview, he'd swelled to 355. Now his body pools over the bed, squeezing tight against the railings. A giant frock has been sewed from several hospital gowns and tied loosely around a neck the size of a basketball. It's been sixteen months since I've seen him.

Kit Bryant is 700 pounds.

His face is a thumbprint into a slab of pizza dough, his smile a tiny red gash that seems situated too high. His skin is knurled and knobby with layer upon layer of suppurating pimples. Points of pus glisten in the light. A golden crust of popped-zit sebum gives him an orange glaze.

"You came."

Speaking ruptures a pimple. White pus jets across his cheek.

Kit's voice is labored. All his words these days must be labored. No lungs can bench-press so much weight without faltering. No heart can pump so much grease without skipping beats. Kit's bodily slime is what was smeared on his letter to me. His hospital gown is soggy with it. His hair is gelled by secretions exuding from distended pores. Even the room's walls look runny with grease, through it's hard to say. An oily scrim swirls in the air.

His oxygen mask sits ignored atop one of his breasts, but rubber tubes snake out of his nostrils toward a white machine making robotic exhalations and displaying red digital numerals. The space around the bed is a jungle of tubing, cables, and wires, some clipped to an overhead panel, others trailing from gadgets, computers, monitors, bottles, and bags. Three more tubes feed into Kit's body, but folds of flesh hide their termini.

"I knew you'd come," he gasps. "You always come when called."

It feels like a mask has been peeled off. The young man I spent two days talking to at Chernow was not Kit Bryant.

My nostrils shrivel at the air-freshener burn, which can't cover the stench of rancid grease. I survey the damp bedding, the overhead rig used to turn Kit over for sponge baths, the pillar of replacement sheets. I'm at the foot of the bed. I'm afraid to go any further; it's freezing in here, probably to neutralize Kit's fever. Heat radiates from his body.

I put a hand over my nose and mouth to block the fumes, and ask the question that has sickened me all morning. What happened to Dez?

Kit's grin remains charmingly crooked.

"They should have arrested her, huh? Don't you think? For having all those chemicals?" Kit shrugs. "I thought for sure if I used her poison, they'd arrest her. She caused a ton of trouble."

I think of all the wild things Dez Mozley did. The urine, salt, and cat bells she placed to ward off warlocks, those evildoers who, as she tried to tell me, "hold meetings in cemeteries." She'd smeared her protective sigil on the walk-in freezer, beneath every one of Burger City's booths and tables. She'd been the hero all along. I pull out a wrinkled page of this book from my back pocket and read a passage out loud.

I've defeated so many lesser witches, I've ascended. Since last time you saw Dez Mozley, I became the most powerful witch in the Mississippi Valley.

Kit's blue eyes sparkle, like he's proud of me.

"Why not Dez, you're probably wondering. Why we'd come for the Burger City folks and not her. Here's the thing. It doesn't really care about blood. Think about a murder. Any murder. What's blood? It's just the first thing that happens. It gushes, you wipe it up. Poof. Gone. What keeps that death going, though? What keeps that death…alive?"

Clem, soaked in gasoline, had given me the answer.

We split up. Quit talking. It should have gotten better for us, right? Except what happened? The articles. The documentary. More talking, more talking. It keeps it alive, you get it?

I look down at myself. I could be imagining it, but it looks like the room's sticky mist is wetting my clothing, coating my skin. Mental weight is still weight; I have seen so many awful things. Footage and photos of the Burger City dead, of course. But also serial-killer series, true-crime TV, ripped-from-the-headlines movies that make heroes out of killers while the dead slip by unnoticed.

"That Starz shit was so bad, people tuned out. At least we always had Dez, you know? If she went to Casey's, she talked about it. If she went to Kum & Go, she talked about it. It wasn't much. But it helped keep it alive. You know who saved the day, though? Do you?"

Kit's nod manifests as a mere crimp of skin, but it's enough to rupture more pimples. Yellow sweat creeps over his flesh like slugs.

"You," he says.

Quin's obsession with William G. Roll's *The Poltergeist* dictated that I become obsessed as well, and yet I'd missed it, right there on page 183, when Roll notes that he "inadvertently re-created the tension and frustration which had stimulated the [psychokinetic] events in Miami." Like an asymptomatic Covid-19 carrier, the *recorder* of phenomena unwittingly became the *source* of the phenomena.

I asked hundreds of questions to the Burger City survivors in 2020. Whatever Scotty Flossen's group of meth addicts had conjured up to drool over Iowa, I'd single-handedly fed it, by talking, and talking. When I left Iowa, there'd been a dip; perhaps Dez filled that gap as usual until her death. Now, with several book-publicity interviews behind me, I'm again slicing up the flesh of the survivors, offering the force something better than the blood of Bob Nutting, Amber Smyrna, Amy Mold, and Dion Skerry.

I wipe noxious slop from my face, blink goo from my eyes, expectorate jellied gunk from my lungs. I ask Kit a question that rips me from a reporter's safe distance and snares me in the bear trap of a novel's quotation marks, right where I belong:

"Why me?"

Kit pulsates with laughter. IV stands rattle as a loaf of flesh, maybe an arm, gestures at the bedside table. I recognize *They Threw Us Away*, a novel I published since Kit and I last spoke.

"It's good. Different but good. I really did like some of your books, you know."

Days later I will pore through every photo of Kit Bryant I've kept in paper folders and hard drives. Largely they are pictures from after his arrest. In nearly every one, he's clutching a different book. He'd lied when he said he'd picked up reading only after moving to Chernow. I find a magnifying glass. None of the books had stood out to me because they'd been stripped of their dust jackets.

They are my novels.

Kit was never my number-one fan. He was studying me like I studied William G. Roll.

"Why you? Let's see. Maybe because you're so well-behaved? Scotty told me how to call you. All I needed were words, can you believe it? Words that were important to *you*."

The nonsense Darren Husselbee's Yamaha SKRM-100 Subkick picked up from the Burger City basement: *five more five more gone five gone minutes I'm five minutes gone.* The nonsense of Kit's final Game of Pricks video: *Gone and I'm gone and more five five five and I'm gone gone gone!*

Perhaps I can be forgiven for missing critical details in the texts of William G. Roll. But can I be forgiven for missing them in my own? Kit is right. These words *are* important to me. Something that impressed and, yes, flattered me during my interview with Kit was his insightful thoughts on my first novel, *The Monster Variations*. Published in 2009 by Delacorte Press, the book was a financial flop. People don't read it. They don't ask questions about it. These days, I rarely think about it.

Nevertheless, it got my foot into the door of the publishing industry. In a very real way, the career I have today, and by extension, the life I enjoy, is due to this book that no one remembers, including, apparently, myself. The first sentence of that novel, and therefore the first sentence of my career, my life, and a great deal of my self-worth, goes like this:

Five more minutes and I'm gone.

"Gonna be the star...of a Daniel Kraus book. Can you...believe it?"

Kit's delight has him panting. Mirthful tears pool in his sockets, dulling the blue irises beneath. He shakes his face like a dog shakes its wet body. Tears race in dozens of directions, carving salty streaks through oily crust. Its the liveliest motion he's made. Zits rupture like bubble wrap, releasing a dozen strings of pus. The hum and ping of hospital machinery can't hide a burst of flatulence. Sheets bunched at Kit's midsection wilt and darken. He has released diarrhea. He rolls his hips, smearing toxic shit into what must be a lake system of bedsores.

The laughs devolve into wheezing gurgles. The beeping accelerates, surely toward an alarm that will draw nurses and doctors, who will try to drag me away. But I mustn't be moved from this spot. I am part of this. I have always been part of this.

Kit Bryant is dying. I don't know if it will happen in two months, two weeks, or two minutes, but it's coming. At the very least, he'll drift into a coma like Scotty Flossen. Their lungs will billow and their hearts will pump at the bidding of advanced torture devices, keeping their bodies alive the same way factory farms keep livestock alive—as meat to be gobbled by a beast.

Kit parts thin lips. A seaweed slime flows down his neck. He finds the spit-up funny. He laughs harder, coughing, choking, forcing moist words between sprayed sludge.

"Your book's…gonna be…a hit."

My ears roar with blood. Scotty and Kit turned the agony of the Burger City staff into physical weight, and that weight will now feed the terrible thing. If my book is, in fact, a hit, if it is talked about, it will help the thing keep living until it finds a new puppet to be its mouth and stomach, to eat and grow for it, to salivate and shit.

I won't let it happen.

I swivel around; I feel the moist air billow back, like the room is filled with old, wrinkled balloons. Everything here is harmless. The tubing, devices, IV stands, medical clipboards, tables, drinking cups, it's all plastic, an abundance of safety that has paradoxically rendered me powerless. I spin and spin, while Kit beside me gobbles and spews, and then I remember this isn't Chernow. I entered this black hole with items from the real world. I jam my hands into my pockets. Recorder, phone, notebook, keys—yes, *keys*. Keys have always been important: how Kit got into Burger City, how he got Kwik-Kil No. 7 from the closet. Keys open, yes, but they also lock.

The keyring goes into my clenched fist, the sharpest of the keys jutting from between my index and middle fingers.

I plunge through the foul clouds to Kit's left. I shove aside the bedside table. The reading lamp topples; the book I wrote flops to the floor. A long plastic utility board runs the length of the wall over the hospital bed. It is where medical devices are attached and machines plugged in. It takes up a lot of room, but not all of it, not when I brush aside handfuls of cables. Like Scotty Flossen stabbed Ash Muckells, like Kit Bryant stabbed Cheri Orritt, I stab my key deep into the wall.

The whole room shakes.

Kit glares up at me, blue eyes radioactive past the pus splashed atop them. He cackles, snorts, whinnies, screeches. Snot flutters from his nose. Melted wax drains from his ears. He need only lift an arm to touch me with his earthworm fingers, at which point I will scream and run, but he can't conquer his own infirmity. He shakes and strains. His crusty lips part, releasing a swollen tongue dripping with mucus. It extends, farther and farther, trying to lick my arm, which will be worse than Amy Mold's fryer grease burning a hole into Mickey McCormick's lap.

With all my strength, I pull the key back toward me, slashing a straight line through the wall. Drywall powders onto Kit's muggy face. Some of it goes down his throat. He coughs and I feel hot slime splash my arm. I take the key with both hands and begin to rip it upward and to the left, a 45-degree angle. Kit is gibbering now like he's being slaughtered, flailing his half-ton body. Metal parts of the bed squeal, plastic parts crack. Alarms are going off now, a throbbing buzz, a dreadful flatline tone.

I pull the key downward, completing the triangle. Kit's seizuring is what shakes the wall, I know that, but the room feels alive, protesting its own butchery, a grumbling force permeating every inch of the hospital as it once did every inch of a restaurant. One last mark to make, a 45-degree slash to the upper right.

Suddenly the room is filled with people. Everywhere, all over, Quin and Mickey and Cheri and Yesenia and Zane and Javi and Darcy and Maxine and Tamra and Clem and Dez—hello again Dez, it's your sigil I'm carving, the only thing I know to do, and she and everyone else pushes my exhausted arm toward the finish. But then it's not them at all, my old, dead friends, it's people in white, it's nurses and doctors, and they don't know what I'm doing but it has to be bad because the 24-year-old beneath me is howling for air, he's howling.

The cop from the hallway wrestles me from the wall. I wail and sob and kick, but he's trained to restrain people who won't cooperate, and he drags me across the room, to the door, and I don't get a last look at Kit Bryant because his bed is obscured by frantic personnel. But I can see the shape I scratched onto the wall. Without its final line, it's a useless triangle. I scream at the cop. I feel leather, a badge, a mustache. I didn't finish it. I didn't finish.

Charges against me are being considered. I don't think they will be filed. After all, Kit Bryant didn't die. He's in a coma, technically a "persistent vegetative state," and the opinion of Winneshiek Medical Center staff is that it was inevitable, regardless of the unhinged writer who keyed the wall. From what I understand, if Caspar Bryant chooses to keep those death-machines whirring, his son's vitals might continue to register for years.

I have fifteen minutes to send in this chapter. It has been made exceedingly clear by lawyers that I won't be granted one second more. This book is being published. There is nothing I can do about it.

But there is something *you* can do. If you're one of those people who reads the last pages of books first, this curious practice has finally served you well. Do not flip back to the start and begin reading. If you are one of the unlucky majority only now finishing, all is not yet lost. Tell your friends to avoid this book. People you care about, but strangers too. Find places to post about it, to spread the word that reading it will cause more pain, more suffering.

Now burn it. Burn the book. If your copy is digital, delete it, then empty your trash.

The more that people talk about this book, the more guaranteed it will be that the poltergeist, the ghost, whatever the thing is, will return to resume its tortures. Believe me. Believe me while I still have the strength of mind to tell the truth and the dexterity to type it. It may not last much longer. Already I feel my mind begin to turn. I feel a growing satisfaction with how things are progressing. There's a certain taste in my mouth. It has been only seventeen days since I was in that room with Kit Bryant.

In that time, I have gained forty-four pounds.

The Ghost That Ate Us is a work of fiction. The photo attributions are likewise fictional. All photos are used with permission and their true credits are as follows.

Page 10: Michael Gaida (via Pixabay)
Page 16: Pete Hautman
Page 34: Michal Nevaril (via Unsplash)
Page 40: Mike Goad (via Pixabay)
Page 45: Šárka Jonášová (via Unsplash)
Page 53: Michael Rivera (licensed under under CC BY-SA 3.0).
Page 67: Jonathan Rados (via Unsplash)
Page 77: Ike louie Natividad (via Pexels)
Page 89: Daniel Castanho
Page 99: Daniel Kraus
Page 104: Daniel Kraus
Page 120: Kal Visuals (via Unsplash)
Page 128: Daniel Kraus
Page 135: Daniel Kraus
Page 145: RODNAE Productions (via Pexels)
Page 148: Rene Asmussen (via Pexels)
Page 148: Erik Mclean (via Pexels)
Page 158: DDP (via Unsplash)
Page 166: Fiona Calisti (via Unsplash)
Page 170: RODNAE Productions (via Pexels)
Page 175: Todd Cravens (via Unsplash)
Page 183: Daniel Kraus
Page 187: Omar Lopez (via Unsplash)
Page 197: Chris Bede (licensed under CC BY 2.0)
Page 200: Daniel Kraus
Page 210: Spencer Selover (via Pexels)
Page 214: Daniel Kraus
Page 223: Daniel Kraus
Page 229: Daniel Kraus
Page 242: Daniel Kraus
Page 253: Hatem Sayed (via Pixabay)

ABOUT THE AUTHOR

Daniel Kraus is a *New York Times*-bestselling author. His collaboration with legendary filmmaker George A. Romero, *The Living Dead*, was acclaimed by *The New York Times* and *The Washington Post*.

Kraus's *The Death and Life of Zebulon Finch* was named one of *Entertainment Weekly*'s Top 10 Books of the Year. With Guillermo del Toro, he co-authored *The Shape of Water*, based on the same idea the two created for the Oscar-winning film. Also with del Toro, Kraus co-authored *Trollhunters*, which was adapted into the Emmy-winning Netflix series. Kraus has won a Scribe Award, two Odyssey Awards (for both *Rotters* and *Scowler*) and has been a Library Guild selection, YALSA Best Fiction for Young Adults, Bram Stoker finalist, and more.

Kraus's work has been translated into over 20 languages. He lives with his wife in Chicago. Visit him at danielkraus.com

CPSIA information can be obtained
at www.ICGtesting.com
Printed in the USA
LVHW021906210622
721798LV00001B/1

9 781947 879553